Gage Black and the Void Dragon

Britt Asher

To Onna,
Thanks for early feedback and
for having fun with my books!

Contents

1

A Cursed Boy

"**G**age Black! Get up, you lazy wart!"

That was Gage's cue to leave. He tightened his belt around his waist and escaped the house through his bedroom window. His disgruntled guardian, Claeg, had threatened to make him clean the trash pit this morning, but Gage refused to stink like rotting garbage today—not on the most important day of the year.

Gravel crunched under his boots as he sprinted to the plaza, where the villagers were decorating for today's event. Soon, representatives from the Innaran people would arrive to test every twelve-year-old for magic. Any child who passed their test would be whisked away to study at their prestigious military academy in Runadel.

Even if Gage failed the test, he was determined to go with them. The Innaran army actively resisted the Vaskran raiders invading their kingdom, and Gage shared their resolve to see the Vaskr defeated. Ten years ago, the raiders had burned down his village, killed his family, and abandoned him in the woods to die. He couldn't let that happen to anyone else, and attending the military academy was the first step toward learning how to fight—and learning how to protect others.

But for now, he waited. Gage kicked stray rocks from the plaza and watched the other villagers work, some hanging colorful fabrics, others using thick ropes to lift huge dragon sculptures. Everyone wanted to make the place look brighter and livelier, but the decorations did little to hide the decay that permeated their village. The grass in their yards was dead, the crops in their fields had withered, and the trees in the surrounding forest stood gaunt and lifeless. Though it was midsummer, Talid Village bore the appearance of late autumn.

The cause of all this death? Gage. He killed everything around him simply by existing, or so the villagers told him. He didn't fully believe that, but even the Vaskr had thrown him out, and they were *known* for kidnapping kids.

Shouting from across the plaza distracted him from his thoughts. He turned in time to watch a rope snap off a partially lifted statue, sending the monument plummeting. Most of the villagers leaped out of the way, but the dragon's wide wingspan clipped one unfortunate man and dragged him to the ground. The sculpture crashed down on his legs with a painfully audible crunch.

Gage moved without thinking. He dove under the statue's wing and shoved his back up against it, but the thing didn't budge.

"Out of the way!" someone shouted.

A firm hand seized Gage's arm and yanked him out from under the statue. He staggered aside as several men rushed to take his place, their muscles bulging as they lifted the monument. Others quickly pulled the victim to safety. Blood soaked the man's pants in various places where the sharp edges of the sculpture had pierced him. The poor guy wailed and writhed in the dust.

Gage stepped toward him, but a familiar voice stopped him in his tracks.

"Move aside!" The village healer, Jinny, elbowed her way through the crowd. She paused only long enough to inspect the scene before falling to her knees at the injured man's side. "Someone grab my bag from the clinic! Hurry!"

While villagers ran off to fetch her supplies, Jinny withdrew a cloth from her apron and pressed it to the man's wounds. She couldn't bind the injuries until after she applied medicines, so for now, she had to focus on stopping the bleeding.

Gage prodded the glass vials in his belt, each containing a medicine he wasn't supposed to have. Jinny and Claeg had forbidden him from practicing healing, insisting he'd only hurt others. But Gage tested every concoction he mixed. He *knew* they worked. And right now, he carried one that functioned as a pain reliever and a disinfectant, the very thing this injured man needed.

"Jinny," Gage said, taking a hesitant step toward her. "I have my—"

"I don't have time for you right now." Jinny winced as blood seeped between her fingers. Turning to the crowd, she yelled, "Where is my bag?"

The man groaned in agony, his eyes rolling back. They needed to administer treatment *now* if they wanted to spare him a long, hard recovery.

Gage sighed. He knew he shouldn't irritate Jinny, and he definitely shouldn't make it more obvious that he still practiced healing, but the man needed help, and Gage could provide it. He'd deal with the consequences later.

"Remember the medicine from the botila plant?" Gage asked, pulling out the vial. "I made it. You can use it for—"

"Enough!" Jinny turned, red-hot fury flushing her cheeks. "It's hard enough to keep people alive in this village without you and your curse killing them. Stay away from my patients and away from my clinic. You are not a healer, and you never will be!"

Gage halted, her words sucking the air out of his lungs.

"Never mind the bag," she muttered. To the men gathered around, she said, "Help me get him to the clinic. Quickly!"

Two men lifted the injured man and carried him down the gravel path, a trail of blood dripping behind them.

Everyone looked at Gage with disdain as they passed. After Jinny and the men had departed, the rest of the villagers returned to their tasks, ignoring Gage entirely.

Gage clenched the vial in his fist. Frustration bubbled up inside him, but it was quickly replaced by hopelessness. Nothing he did mattered. No one wanted his help. No one wanted him around. He was only here to clean up the garbage no one else wanted to touch. The worst thing was, he couldn't even blame the villagers for rejecting him. If what they said about him was true, he'd caused them nothing but misery for the past ten years.

The forests and fields around Talid had once been lush and vibrant—until Gage came. Within weeks of his arrival, every plant around his house withered and died. The villagers moved him from one house to the next, only for the same thing to happen wherever he went, until every plant in Talid had perished.

As if that weren't enough, Gage's presence also drained Talid of its magic. A few villagers used to control water, but after he arrived, they lost their abilities. When their elementals fell ill and nearly died, the water users were forced to flee the village, never to return. No one had developed elemental abilities ever since. Sure, magic was rare outside the Innaran race, but an entire village without it? Unheard of.

Now Gage was blamed for everything. Someone got sick? Gage's fault. Someone died? Gage's fault. Someone got crushed by a dragon statue? Gage's fault, surely.

The villagers would have thrown him out years ago if not for Gage's mysterious benefactor. Someone left pouches of gold in the village once a month, along with a note asking them to care for him. He was allowed to exist, but everyone still hated him.

"What are you doing over there, leech?" Claeg's familiar voice sliced through Gage's thoughts.

Gage whirled around to find his cranky guardian storming toward him. He took an instinctive step back. It was never a good idea to be near Claeg when he was angry.

"I told you to clean the trash pit today," Claeg raged, closing the distance between them in a few quick strides. "Instead, I find you out here being useless, as usual!"

He shot his hand out like a whip, his fingers snaring Gage's wrist and yanking fiercely. Gage flinched at the jolt—and then flinched again when the vial fell from his grasp and clattered to the dirt at Claeg's feet. The old man froze, and Gage's heart stuttered.

"How many times have I told you to stop making these poisons?" Claeg snatched up the vial and then tore the others out of Gage's belt. Spinning on his heel, he marched toward the trash pit.

"Claeg, please don't!" Gage chased him, panic tightening his voice. "Those are my only vials!"

"I've had enough of you," the man ranted. "You can't do anything right, can you? Can't obey orders to save your life. If not for the gold, we'd have thrown you out ages ago, just like the Vaskr. They were the smart ones!"

"Claeg, please—"

Claeg ignored him and hurled the glass containers into the trash. Gage's eyes burned with unshed tears as he watched his only vials shatter into pieces.

"Now do as I asked and clean this pit," Claeg shouted, grabbing his arm and giving him a nasty shake, "or so help me, I'll—"

A reverberating roar silenced his tirade. A deep shadow swept over the village, followed by several more, blotting out the sunlight. Gage lifted his face as a gust of wind stirred up dead leaves and dust.

Five majestic light dragons circled the village. Brilliant white feathers gleamed across their lithe bodies and broad wings. The dazzling creatures landed gracefully in the center of the plaza and bowed their magnificent heads.

The first of the five riders dismounted from her dragon, her slender white boots touching the ground with the slightest thud. Her warm brown skin and white hair were unmistakably Innaran. She wore her hair in three long braids bound together into a single larger braid. Her layered white robes rustled as she moved, and sunlight glanced off her gold jewelry. She was the most beautiful woman Gage had ever seen.

"Greetings," she said in a melodic voice. Her eyes glimmered. "I have come to test your children for magic."

2

THE TESTING

The rest of the woman's dragon-riding companions dismounted. Three men and a woman stepped down into the dust, all handsome or beautiful in a timeless way. They wore white robes and white-and-gold breastplates. They had the same skin tone and striking hair color as the woman, but their braids were shorter and less elaborate.

"Don't move," Claeg said to Gage, squeezing his arm in warning. Then he shoved away and waltzed toward the woman with an enormous smile plastered on his face, his arms outstretched in greeting. "Welcome to Talid Village, my dear Innarans! I'm Claeg Nirgal, the mayor of this humble village. To whom do I owe the pleasure of speaking with?"

A faint smile touched the woman's lips. "I am Halayna Lightgard, second child to His Majesty, King Fraylon Lightgard of the Innaran kingdom."

"P-p-princess?" Claeg choked on his words and dropped to one knee, bowing his head.

Gasps erupted throughout the village. Everyone fell to their knees in respect—including Gage, despite Claeg's warning not to move. But he couldn't take his eyes off the beautiful woman. While everyone else bowed their heads, he made sure to peek.

She was a princess. Now her elegant braids made sense. All Innarans wore braids, but the longest were worn by nobility. The Innarans with her must have been her honor guard, men and women of magic who devoted their lives to defending the Innaran royalty.

"Forgive my rudeness, Your Grace," Claeg exclaimed, still on one knee. "Had I known the princess herself would shine her light upon us today, I would have received you with greater celebration."

"Please rise, people of Talid," Lady Halayna said gently. "We Innara exist to serve you, not the other way around. I need no special treatment."

Gage's stomach fluttered. She was pretty. He didn't give girls much consideration—mostly because all of them in Talid hated him—but seeing her smile warmed his cheeks. He had to look away. What was he thinking? She had to be twice his age, maybe more. It was hard to tell with the Innara.

Everyone rose from their bows as Lady Halayna's dark eyes swept from one end of the village to the other.

"How does your village fare, Master Claeg?" she asked. "Have the Vaskr caused you trouble as of late?"

"Not recently, Your Grace," Claeg said, dusting off the knees of his pants. "We've lost children to their attacks in the past, but they've been quiet recently. Although our scouts have found some Vaskran scum lurking in the surrounding forests. We're on our guard."

"I see." Lady Halayna furrowed her brow, the subtle shift a stark contrast to the smile it replaced. "Yes, ever since the Vaskr took the capital city from us, they have become far bolder with their incursions into our lands."

Wind rustled the surrounding trees and sent a few dead leaves swirling across the village. A lone tumbleweed followed.

Lady Halayna watched with quiet interest, her slender eyebrows knitting further together. "What happened to the plants, Master Claeg?"

Claeg coughed into his hand. "Our village is plagued by more problems than simply the Vaskr, Your Grace."

He didn't look at Gage, but everyone else did. Gage dropped his eyes to the ground and scuffed his boot. The dead plants couldn't possibly be his fault. How could someone destroy a forest simply by existing?

Lady Halayna waited for further explanation, but Claeg said nothing more. Gage was worth too much gold to risk drawing special attention to him.

"My time is short, and I have other villages to visit today," Lady Halayna finally said. "You know for what reason I have come. Master Claeg, please gather before me any child who has reached their twelfth year. I shall personally test them for magic."

The patter of footsteps came from all directions even without Claeg's summons. Six twelve-year-olds formed a line before the Innaran princess. Gage hesitated, his leg twitching to join them but his mind screaming danger. Claeg had warned him not to move and would retaliate if Gage disobeyed.

But this was his one chance to escape this terrible place, and he couldn't miss the opportunity. He hurried toward the line of kids until Claeg stepped into his path and snatched his arm.

"Where do you think you're going?"

"To be tested," Gage said.

"Tested?" Claeg snorted. "Do you think—"

"Is there a problem, Master Claeg?" Lady Halayna asked, her voice both gentle and firm.

Claeg turned slowly toward the Innaran princess. Gage followed his gaze. It took everything in him not to cry for Lady Halayna's help, to beg to be tested, to plead with her and declare his undying loyalty to her—or whatever. He needed this chance, but he couldn't risk earning more of Claeg's ire.

"No problem, Your Grace," Claeg said carefully.

"How old are you, child?" Lady Halayna asked Gage.

"T-twelve, Your Grace," he stammered, which earned his arm a vicious squeeze.

"Then you should be tested." Lady Halayna waved her hand toward the end of the line.

Gage moved to join the others, but Claeg didn't release him.

"Trust me, Your Grace," Claeg said. "You don't want this one. He's cursed. Nothing but trouble, and he can't do anything right. If you take him to fight the Vaskr, you'll lose the war."

Snickers erupted throughout the village. No one even tried to hide their sneers. Heat flared across Gage's face, and he blinked wetness from his eyes. He was used to their hatred, but not in front of the Innara.

"Nevertheless, he shall be tested," Lady Halayna said. "Those are my father's orders, and we shall not defy him. If the boy has magic, we will train him. If not, then I leave him in your care, Master Claeg."

Claeg maintained a neutral expression, but his jaw shifted as he ground his teeth. He released Gage and shoved him forward. Gage stumbled to the end of the line, struggling to keep a straight face, to not let his panic show. If he didn't have magic and wasn't allowed to leave with the Innara, he'd be in big trouble later.

"Now then," Lady Halayna said. "Let us begin."

She took a bundle of fabric from one of her guards and unraveled it to reveal a jagged, shimmering crystal. Sunlight flashed off the stone in a dazzling array of colors.

"To administer the test, we will use an Innaran crystal," she explained. "You may have seen these crystals throughout the kingdom. They are made of our magic, and we use them for various purposes. This particular crystal was created to resonate with an individual's magic." With an inviting smile, she searched the gathered villagers. "I would like to display the crystal's ability. Is anyone here capable of magic?"

Tense silence answered her. Gage's heart stuttered. He kept his eyes on the crystal, but countless pairs of eyes fell on him.

Claeg offered him a nasty glare. "No, Your Grace," he said, his words drenched in hostility. "No one here can use magic."

Gage shut his eyes and hung his head.

"No matter," Lady Halayna said, unperturbed by their unexplained animosity. "The crystal will react similarly to me."

When she placed her fingertips on the crystal, it lit up with a dazzling, colorful light that flooded the area. The villagers gasped.

"The crystal will shine when it comes into contact with ample magic in a person's body," Lady Halayna explained. "If the crystal reacts like this to your touch, you will attend Runadel Academy. We will teach you how to use your magic and how to summon an elemental."

Excited chatter ignited among the kids. Elementals. Every kid's dream. They might summon a water feline, wind avian, fire lizard, or rock beetle. The thought made Gage smile.

"Let the testing commence," Lady Halayna said. A hush fell over the village as she held the crystal out to the first kid in line. "Touch the crystal, child."

The girl reached out a trembling hand. Everyone remained silent as her fingers touched the stone. Nothing happened. Lady Halayna lingered, giving the crystal time to react, but still nothing happened. Finally, she shook her head. The girl burst into tears, hiccupping as she ran away.

Gage shivered as Lady Halayna moved to the next kid in line.

Please let me have magic.

The second kid touched the crystal. Nothing happened, and Lady Halayna shook her head. The boy fled, sobbing. Lady Halayna moved to the next, and they didn't have magic either.

Gage's stomach fluttered.

Please, please let me have magic.

Lady Halayna reached the fourth kid. Another touch, another failure. The boy cursed and ran away. The princess moved on to number five.

Heat built behind Gage's eyes. Everything rode on this one moment. His entire future. All of his hope.

Please let me have a way out of this place.

The next boy failed and ran off. Lady Halayna moved to the last child standing between her and Gage.

After the first five failures, reality settled over Gage like a sheet of ice, sending chills across his skin. He had no hope of having magic and no hope of leaving the village with the Innara. He was only special because he was cursed.

The final girl failed and ran away. Gage found himself face-to-face with Lady Halayna and the glittering rock.

"Place your hand on the crystal, child," she said.

Gage lifted his hand. The moment of truth. He would either have a future with the Innara or be doomed to live—and possibly die—under Claeg's cruel hand.

Please work! Please have magic!

Stomach clenched and fingers trembling, he touched the crystal.

Nothing happened.

His heart and stomach dropped into his boots. Lady Halayna gave him the same delay as everyone else. Then, with the slightest shake of her head, she pulled the stone away. His hand fell limp to his side.

It was over. Gage didn't have magic. He had no way out. No hope. No—

The crystal cracked in half in Lady Halayna's hands as she turned away. The sound stopped her mid-step. Another crack split the stone, followed by another, until the crystal crumbled and melted into glittering dust that flitted away on a breeze.

Everyone stared at the empty fabric. Lady Halayna lifted eyes wide with shock—and horror—to Gage. Her lips parted, but no sound came out. Not at first. Then her words pierced the oppressive silence.

"What have you done?"

3

WITH THE WORMS

Gage's heart flew into his throat. Lady Halayna stared at him with naked horror. His mind betrayed him, and he couldn't think of anything to say—couldn't think of anything at all.

What *had* he done? He hadn't done anything!

"What did you do, mongrel?" Claeg roared, grabbing his arm and twisting him around.

"Nothing!" Gage flinched from the pain. "I didn't do anything—"

"Liar!" Spittle flew from Claeg's lips. "You filthy liar! You little—" He snatched the front of Gage's shirt and raised a hand to strike him.

"Peace, Master Claeg," Lady Halayna said, stopping him. The princess slipped the empty fabric to her guard, her focus wholly on Gage. "What is your name, child?"

"G-Gage Black, Your Grace." He shook free of Claeg's grip so he could bow to the princess.

Lady Halayna's expression remained unreadable, devoid of anger but without a trace of sympathy or compassion.

"Who are your parents, Gage Black?" she asked.

"I don't have parents."

"You do not have parents?" Her brow furrowed.

"He obviously had parents at one point, Your Grace," Claeg said. "The Vaskr captured him and threw him away because he's a good-for-nothing wart who destroys everything he touches."

"Threw him away?" Lady Halayna's gaze slid from Gage to Claeg. "When?"

"About ten years ago, Your Grace. We believe it happened during the Vaskran attack on the neighboring village of Wezen," Claeg explained. "We found him outside Talid that same day." Scowling, he muttered, "If only they'd thrown him into the river instead . . ."

Gage hung his head. Maybe things would have been better for him and for everyone else if he'd drowned that day.

"Forgive us, Your Grace." Claeg took on his chiefly tone. "Please don't hold us accountable for this boy's atrocity. We never meant to harm your possessions. We would never want to hurt your cause in any way—"

"I understand, Master Claeg," Lady Halayna said. "Nevertheless, I will need some time to consider this. I should consult with my father before taking further action." Her eyes slipped to Gage in thoughtful contemplation, neither spiteful nor kind. "I will return within a few days to conclude these matters."

Gage shivered. What matters? What was there to conclude?

"Thank you for your time, dear villagers of Talid." Lady Halayna offered the slightest bow of her head. "Be on guard against the Vaskr."

She swept to her dragon in a fluttering of white robes and mounted in a dramatic flourish. Her guards did likewise. The light dragons sprang off the ground in a great rush of wind and soared out of sight.

As the beat of wings faded into the distance, deafening silence fell over the village. The weight of it crushed Gage. He was in trouble, and not just with the Innara. Claeg's furious gaze burned into him, making the hair on the back of his neck stand on end.

Run away, his mind told him. *Run. Hurry.*

Without making eye contact with anyone, Gage turned on his heel and started toward the forest.

"Oh no you don't!" Claeg snatched his arm and hauled him in the opposite direction. Toward their house. "You're not going anywhere. You've caused enough trouble for one day."

Resisting would only make things worse, but Gage dragged his feet anyway. Tears stung his eyes. He knew what was coming.

"Claeg, please don't—"

"I take you in and I raise you, give you shelter and food—"

"Claeg, please!" Panic pinched Gage's words in his throat.

"—and you insist on bringing our village to ruin!"

As Claeg pulled Gage through the village, everyone looked away and went about their business. No one cared. No one ever did. They hated Gage, every last one of them. He'd thought it impossible that he'd caused all their troubles, but he'd even destroyed the beauty of the Innara. He ruined everything he touched.

"You and your curse don't belong around normal people," Claeg said, yanking Gage around the side of the house to the cellar. "No, you belong in the dirt with the worms!"

He tore open the iron doors of the cellar to reveal a steep, narrow staircase leading underground into complete darkness. The lack of light didn't bother Gage. He'd always been able to see extraordinarily well in the dark. No, what bothered him—what pierced his chest like an arrow—was the cold, the silence, and worst of all, the solitude.

"Claeg—" Gage started, but his guardian shoved him into the hole.

"Get inside!"

Gage stumbled down the first few stairs and then scurried farther down the steps to avoid a kick in the back or an iron door to the head. He'd learned his lesson after *that* incident. Gage looked up at Claeg silhouetted by the light outside.

"Please don't," Gage whispered, chilled by the dark silence awaiting him below.

"Let's see you destroy anything while you're down there!" Claeg slammed the iron doors shut with a boom that echoed in the barren cellar, rattling flecks of dust and stone off the walls.

Last of all came the sound of an iron bar sliding into place and securing the doors from the outside, trapping Gage in darkness.

$$4$$

RUNNING AWAY

The iron doors squealed on their hinges. Late-afternoon sunlight flooded the darkness, forcing Gage to shield his face with his arm. Two days had passed—he could tell by the scant light around the edges of the doors. He always kept dried snacks and water jugs hidden in the cellar for times like this, but not nearly enough. Hunger gnawed at his stomach.

"Time to make yourself useful," Claeg said, his silhouette becoming clear as Gage's eyes adjusted to the light.

Gage trudged up the steps, keeping his head down. The warmth of the sunlight didn't reach him. Something inside him had turned to ice. He'd been locked in the cellar many times, but this time felt more serious.

"The trash pit is getting rancid." Claeg thrust a shovel and pail at Gage. "Go dig it out and bury the remains in the forest."

Gage inwardly cringed at the thought of the pit. He was the only one who ever cleaned it, meaning it hadn't been emptied for days. Every piece of village filth had been thrown inside and left to fester under the hot sun. Still, he resisted arguing. Why bother? Nothing he said would help, and sticking up for himself would only lead to worse punishments. Begrudgingly, he took the tools from Claeg.

"Get moving!" Claeg shoved him from behind, sending him staggering. "Might as well get a little more work out of you before the Innara return to deal with you." He snorted and then broke into a fit of laughter as he strolled away.

Claeg's words ricocheted in Gage's mind. Before the Innara returned to deal with him? What did the villagers expect would happen? Something bad, obviously. His stomach clenched. Choking down bile, he marched down the gravel path toward the trash pit. The farther he walked, the more reality settled over him, crushing him until he finally stopped walking.

His life was over. Nothing remained for him anywhere—not in Talid with Claeg or in Runadel with the Innara. Everyone would rather be rid of him. How had he ended up in this mess?

His eyes swept toward the trees, toward the trail that would take him to the ruined village of Wezen. His home, once upon a time. If not for the Vaskr destroying Wezen and abandoning him in the woods, he might still have a family who loved him. Now he had nothing, and he never would.

Hopelessness came over him like a dark shadow. There was no point in digging out the trash pit. No point in anything, really. Claeg would lock him in the cellar again, at least until the Innara came. They would probably imprison him—or even execute him—for what he'd done. He was doomed.

But only if he stayed in the village. If he wanted to live, he had to leave. Today. Except he had nowhere to go and no gold of his own. Even the gold left by his anonymous donor went to the villagers; Gage never saw more than a glimpse of it.

He briefly thought of seeking out his benefactor, but he stamped out the desire. Whoever it was cared about Gage enough to keep him alive but not enough to save him from this place. Whatever happened next, Gage was on his own.

Taking a slow, deep breath, he headed back to his house, happy to find that Claeg hadn't returned yet. That would make the whole process a lot easier.

A stinky old satchel would suffice as a traveling pack. He threw in his few pieces of tattered clothing and dug under his mattress, pulling out his most valuable possession: a letter from his anonymous donor. Claeg had thrown it out to be burned, but Gage had discovered it while cleaning the trash pit. The paper was of high quality and the handwriting clean and precise. Gage wasn't sure why he'd saved it, but it gave him the tiniest glimmer of hope that someone—somewhere—cared that he was alive.

He stood and looked around his small sleeping space. The house had been a place of shelter, but never a home. Not really.

Gage turned to leave, but Claeg chose that moment to march into the house, halting him in the hallway. The man grabbed some nuts and dried berries from the pantry and fetched a cup of water. Only then did he notice Gage.

"What are you doing back here?" Claeg asked.

Gage took a deep breath and held it. Then he took one step, then another, and made his way toward the door. The bag over his shoulder said enough.

"Running away, then?" Claeg asked.

Gage kept walking.

"Fine. Go. What do I care?" Claeg took a drink and then tossed some snacks into his mouth. "Maybe the village will finally thrive with you out of the picture."

Gage hesitated on the threshold. He didn't know why. A tiny part of him wanted Claeg to ask him to stay. He wanted to be wanted. But he knew that would never happen, and his mind screamed at him to take another step.

"If you leave, I won't take you back," Claeg said, his voice shifting to a slow, gleeful drawl. "You'll be on your own. No one else will want you. You have nowhere to go."

Claeg was right. Gage had nowhere to go. But anywhere else was better than here. Taking another breath, he stepped outside and closed the door behind him.

5

SHADOWS AND SPARKS

It was over. Gage couldn't go home. He walked the only road leading out of the village. Traders came and went this way, so it had to lead somewhere. But once he reached *somewhere*, what then? How would he survive on his own? People in other towns would grow to hate him as much as the people in Talid. Gage would never be able to settle down, and traveling in the winter would be brutal.

Leave it to him to make a mess of things.

The road took him beyond the withered trees into a forest still alive and thriving. Grass and weeds grew over the path, and dark shadows from the thick canopy dappled the ground. Now that the Vaskr prowled the area, fewer visitors traveled between towns, allowing nature to reclaim the roads. Chattering critters and rustling leaves filled the forest with sound.

A girl's scream halted his footsteps. The sound stopped as quickly as it started, and he questioned hearing it until muffled voices arose from his right. A pit of unease curled in Gage's belly. Though he'd never been invited to join them, he knew the village kids played in that area. His feet moved on their own, and he shoved through the thick underbrush.

When he reached a small clearing, Gage found three kids from Talid—and they weren't alone.

Four Vaskran raiders held them captive. The raiders looked like every Vaskran man Gage had ever seen—light hair, tan skin, thick frames, leather armor, and fur pelts. Earth beetles rode on the raiders' shoulders or clung to their pelts. The elementals had six sharp legs and tan rock bodies covered in spikes. A viciously curved horn stuck out of each of their heads.

Three men held the children and covered their mouths while the fourth man unraveled a coil of rope.

Gage slid a foot forward to intervene but hesitated. These kids despised him. If he swapped places with them, they'd run away and save themselves. But Gage wasn't like them, nor did he want to be. Besides, anything that interrupted the Vaskr's plans was worth doing.

Setting down his bag, he grabbed a handful of sharp rocks and hoisted himself into a tree. From there, he hurled the rocks at the raiders as hard as he could. All flew true and slammed into the men's heads. The raiders cried out in alarm and dropped their hostages so they could shield themselves with their hands.

"Get back to the village," Gage shouted at the kids, chucking his last few rocks to keep the raiders distracted. "Run!"

The kids fled into the forest, and Gage turned to make his escape. He leaped out of the tree and practically fell into the arms of another Vaskran man, this one bigger than the others and wearing more fur and armor. He shoved Gage in the chest with both hands, sending him sailing backward into the clearing. Gage crashed to the ground at the feet of the other raiders.

"Thought I heard something skulking in the trees," said the big man as he pushed into the clearing, his lips curling under his unkempt beard. An earth beetle clung to the furry pelt hanging over his trousers.

Gage bolted, but he only made it three steps before a raider snatched his shirt and dragged him back. The man hooked him under the arms and lifted him off the ground. Gage thrashed and kicked backward, but the heel of his boot struck solid rock. A glance down revealed stone forming around the man's legs in flashes of yellow magic.

"Is this one good enough, Torquil?" one man asked the big guy. "Toss him or keep him?"

Torquil—the apparent leader—rubbed his beard as he looked Gage over. Gage shot him a nasty glare.

"He's a bit scrawny," Torquil muttered, "but he'd make a nice test subject. It's always nice to have fresh blood for our experiments."

Frustration blossomed in Gage's chest, and he clenched his hands. They spoke so casually about kidnapping kids—about tearing families apart and ruining lives.

A shadow swept over them, drawing their eyes upward. Gage barely glimpsed the flash of white feathers and the draconic body passing over the trees. In a blink, it was gone.

"Innaran scum." Torquil spat on the ground and then sneered at Gage. "Don't get any ideas. They don't know you're out here. No one's coming to save you." He stepped aside so another man could bind Gage with rope.

Gage *knew* no one would help him. The Innarans were coming to execute him. What difference did it make to them if the Vaskr got him first? His frustration over the whole situation ignited into fury. He hadn't run away from Talid to become a victim of the Vaskr.

Gritting his teeth, he kicked the man tying his hands and knocked the guy restraining him off balance. Gage slipped enough to touch the ground and then leaped, snapping his head back against his captor's nose. Pain sliced through him when their heads collided.

The raider dropped him but abruptly backhanded him across the face. Gage fell to his hands and knees, his cheek now throbbing like his head. He glared up at his captor and couldn't help a smug grin when he saw the man bleeding from his nose and lips.

"Don't look at me like that, you maggot," the man snarled. Yellow light flashed in his eyes and through his outstretched fingers. Stones formed from the light and morphed into a solid axe with a razor-sharp blade. Roaring in anger, he gripped the axe in both hands and swung at Gage in a downward arc.

Gage's anger exploded. Darkness hurled out of him in all directions, lashing like ribbons in a violent wind. Pulses of energy went with it and knocked the raiders off their feet. They flew across the clearing and slammed into the trees. A wave of dirt, leaves, and twigs followed, pelting them. The man's stone axe shattered into glittering dust that flitted away and disappeared.

Gage stood at the center of it all, untouched by the forces swirling around him like shadowy clouds. Sparks twinkled in the dark-purple—almost black—mists.

"What is this?" Torquil muttered.

The other four men summoned stone axes and hammers into their hands in brilliant flashes of yellow magic. One man raced forward with a battle cry, hoisting his hammer into the air.

"Stay back," Gage shouted, bracing himself to lunge out of the way.

Another pulse swept out of him, blowing the man backward. Ribbons of night whipped across the clearing, shattering the Vaskrs' stone weapons. Gage glanced at his hands still encased by a dancing, shadowy haze. Was *he* causing this? What was happening?

Run, cried a squeaky voice in the back of his mind.

Gage staggered toward the forest, away from the baffled men. Four small stones flew over his head, and flashes of yellow light filled the area, blocking his exit. He slid to a stop as trees cracked under the weight of four earth beetles increasing in size. In their first forms, they were the size of a small cat. In their second forms? The size of a huge house. The four creatures blocked Gage's escape. The raiders must have thrown them, because earth elementals couldn't fly.

One of the beetles slammed a sharp leg against the ground. A cascade of stones tore through the earth, smashing into Gage and sending him flying. He hit the ground and rolled onto one knee—and inhaled sharply. A barrage of rocks flew at him, and he only had time to shield his face with an arm.

Energy pulsed out of him, and then something solid pushed off his chest and knocked him to the ground. A small form tore out of his body, launching into the air like an arrow and taking the darkness and twinkling sparks with it. The ball of gloom smashed through the projectile rocks, leaping off them as it destroyed them, and then dove at the nearest beetle's head. It struck and sent a wave of shadows down the creature's body. The beetle shrieked and exploded into yellow dust, reverting into its first form and falling helplessly into the underbrush. The swirling ball of shadows leaped to the next beetle, and then the next, doing the same to them.

When at last it crushed the final beetle, the ball of darkness unfurled a pair of leathery wings and glided across the clearing. The mist fizzled, revealing a creature through the murk. Gage blinked repeatedly, struggling to make sense of what he saw.

"Dragon!" shouted Torquil.

"A dragon," cried another man.

"Dragon?" Gage choked on the word. Had that thing come from him?

He'd never seen a dragon like this before. Purple scales covered its body, so dark they nearly looked black. Midnight hues of blue and purple colored its wings, belly, and the tufts of fluff over its head, down its back, and across its long tail. White spikes poked out of its spine, contrasting with its dark coloring. The creature's eyes glowed with purple light.

The men shrieked as the little dragon folded its wings, plummeted, and bashed into their heads, one after the other. It didn't fly; rather, it bounced off them like a frog leaping across lily pads until it had knocked all but one of them to the ground. Torquil remained standing, and he tore a wooden cudgel from his belt and smacked the dragon out of the air.

A jolt of pain ran through Gage's body. Agony seized his muscles and stuttered his heart—almost like he felt the creature's pain. The poor dragon hurtled across the clearing and slammed into a tree, collapsing into a pile at the base of its trunk.

Torquil summoned a stone axe and marched toward the creature. Gage moved without thinking, rising and running as fast as his legs would carry him.

"No!" He dove, caught the dragon in his arms, and rolled as the axe sliced downward.

The weapon smashed into the tree only a foot from where Gage fell with the dragon now wrapped in his arms. Slivers of wood peppered them as Torquil tore his axe out of the tree. A moss-covered log stopped Gage's roll, so he pushed himself into a sitting position, the little dragon quivering against him. The dark mist and magical lights had faded. Whatever power they'd provided earlier was gone.

"Gotta admit, kid," Torquil said, standing over Gage. "You're interesting. But I'm in the business of *work smarter, not harder*. And you're way too much work for me."

Shrugging, the man lifted his axe and swung to kill.

6

ALPHEN AND RHEMI

Sunlight gleamed off the axe as it fell. Gage only had time to turn his shoulder and shield the dragon with his body.

White flashed over Gage's head. A man fell through the forest canopy and landed a boot on Torquil's chest, sending a pulse of light through the raider and blasting him across the clearing. Torquil hit a tree so hard it cracked. The young man who'd hit him flipped in the air and landed gracefully on his feet. He glanced back at Gage, his warm brown skin and white hair unmistakably Innaran.

"You okay, kid?" the young man asked.

"Who are—" The question died on Gage's lips as the Vaskran raiders rose and armed themselves with stone weapons.

The Innaran newcomer glanced at them out of the corner of his eye. "Name's Alphen, but proper introductions will have to wait. Sit tight while I clean up the riffraff."

He lunged across the clearing, ducked under the swing of a stone axe, and punched a raider into the underbrush. When another man rushed him, he leaped, pushed off a tree, and kicked the guy sideways across the face, sending him spinning to the ground. Alphen landed in a roll that carried him to the next raider. Planting his hands on the ground, he thrust out both feet and sent that guy flying too. The next raider hesitated—which was a mistake. Alphen sprang forward, turning his quick lunge into a fierce kick that blasted the man into the bushes.

Alphen casually tucked his hands into his pockets and grinned at the last man standing—Torquil.

"That all you got?" Alphen asked. "I haven't even drawn my weapons."

"Innaran scum." Torquil spit on the ground.

"Didn't your mother teach you it's not nice to call people names?" Alphen scrunched his face in feigned offense.

Yellow flashed in Torquil's eyes. His earth beetle dropped from his fur skirt and hit the ground in a burst of yellow light, increasing in size as it shifted into its second form.

A light dragon crashed into the trees behind them, raining branches and leaves over their heads. The beetle jolted in surprise, reverted into its first form, and cowered behind Torquil's legs. Torquil ceased his magic and whipped around to find a mouth full of fangs inches from his face.

"Go ahead," Alphen said, grinning. "I dare you. Make your beetle fight. My girl, Rhemi, eats bugs for breakfast."

His dragon responded by baring her fangs in a deadly smile and licking her lips.

Torquil quivered, glaring at the dragon and then at Alphen. Unleashing a venomous shout, he charged across the clearing and raised his axe.

Alphen didn't move until Torquil was nearly on him, and then he summoned two short swords made entirely of shining white magic. Rainbow colors flamed off their edges. He chucked one sword at Torquil like someone might throw a dagger. The gleaming weapon slammed into the man's axe, shattering its blade and knocking Torquil off balance. Alphen closed the space between them, sliced his second sword clean through the handle of the man's axe, and kicked him in the gut. Torquil hit the ground with a thud, his broken axe thumping down beside him.

As his swords disappeared, Alphen glanced at the five men writhing on the ground. Rhemi plodded over and sat beside him. Like other second-form light dragons, she wasn't huge, but she still stood several feet taller than her Innaran partner.

"Wow, that was disappointing," Alphen said. He dipped his head in Torquil's direction. "I sensed his strong magic, but he was too scared of me to use it."

Rhemi snorted and squinted at him. He looked appalled.

"Scared of you?" Alphen scoffed. "Bah! Hardly. He was definitely afraid of me. Didn't you notice my dramatic entrance? It was terrifying!"

His dragon stared at him without expression before snorting and rolling her crystalline eyes. Shuffling sounds drew their attention. The Vaskran men scrambled to their feet, fetched their beetles, and fled into the forest. Rhemi rose to give chase, but Alphen flapped a dismissive hand at her.

"Let them go," he said. "I'll send some dragon knights to deal with them later. We have other business."

Reality came crashing down on Gage. He'd broken the Innaran crystal—now came his punishment. He cradled the little dragon closer to his body and gulped as Alphen approached, Rhemi plodding along after him.

The young man didn't look like most other Innarans Gage had seen. Maybe that was a good sign? He had the same skin and hair tones, but his hair was short and messy, with only a single braid hanging over his right ear. And while most other Innarans wore elaborate white robes, this guy wore a white-and-black tunic, black trousers, and a white-and-black jacket that doubled as a cloak. Still, he looked as handsome and timeless as every other Innaran, and because of that, it was hard to guess his age. Late teens, maybe?

Gage could only imagine that he wore dark clothes because he was an executioner and didn't want bloodstains on his pretty white robes.

"You're not hurt, are you?" Alphen asked.

A weird question, coming from an executioner.

"N-no, but . . ." Gage glanced at the wounded dragon in his arms. "They hurt . . ." His dragon? He wasn't sure what to call it.

"Ouch." Alphen crouched, shifting one of the dragon's legs. "Little guy took a beating, huh?"

Rhemi sniffed the smaller dragon and nudged it with her snout. The little dragon blinked blearily up at her and nuzzled its head against her nose. Rhemi yanked away, snorting.

Alphen smiled. "I think he'll be okay. Dragons are tough, even when they're young."

"He?" Gage shifted the dragon in his arms. "How do you know it's a boy?"

"Sharper ridges and bigger bones," Alphen said. "Female dragons are smaller and softer, even when they're little." He winked at Rhemi. "She was a tiny little thing when she was born, all squishy and soft and—"

Rhemi nudged Alphen with her head, knocking him off balance. He laughed.

Gage inspected the smaller dragon. He hadn't noticed the sharper edges—not that he'd know what to look for. This dragon was weird with its dark scales and midnight colors. It lay belly-up in his arms, its legs curled tightly against it. The dragon stared up at him with purple eyes. When Gage matched the creature's gaze, a strong urge to protect the little dragon overcame him, and he cradled it closer to his chest.

"Now then." Alphen patted his thighs and rose from his crouch. "We'll have to get your little friend to a wind healer. Let's go." He offered Gage a hand.

Gage frowned. "Aren't you going to execute me?"

"Execute you?" Alphen laughed. When Gage didn't laugh with him, his brow furrowed. "Oh, you're serious?" He swept his fingers through his hair. "I'm not here to execute you. I'm here to recruit you!"

7

VOID DRAGON

"Recruit me?" Gage echoed.

"You know, to study magic," Alphen said. "You are Gage Black, aren't you?" When Gage gave a tiny nod, he nodded in return. "Kinda assumed that, since you're holding a void dragon."

"Void dragon?"

Gage had heard of such things, but only in childhood fables meant to scare kids into behaving well, lest an evil dragon devour them in the night. In every legend, accursed void dragons killed people, destroyed cities, and ruined worlds. The monsters in the stories and the cuddly dragon in Gage's arms couldn't possibly be the same thing. Gage shook those thoughts from his mind; he had bigger things to worry about.

"Aren't you going to punish me for breaking your crystal?" he asked.

Alphen briefly stared at Gage before exchanging exasperated looks with Rhemi.

"You thought . . ." The man chuckled, wearing a faint smile. "Do you know *why* you broke the crystal?"

Gage shook his head.

"Your magic broke it," Alphen stated.

"I don't have . . ." Magic, Gage wanted to say, but he'd seen the dark mist and purple sparks around him during his fight against the Vaskr. And now he held a dragon in his arms.

"Don't have magic?" Alphen chuckled again. "That dragon in your arms came from your magic."

"I didn't summon him," Gage insisted.

Everyone knew people needed Innaran magic to summon elementals. Yet as he met eyes with the dragon, he knew the creature was a part of him.

"You came when I needed you," Gage whispered. The dragon nuzzled its head against his chest, its scales hard and smooth but the fluff on its head and cheeks soft and warm. Gage finally lifted his face toward the Innaran man. "You're sure I have magic?"

"Beyond a doubt." Alphen offered Gage his hand. "But first things first, let's get you to your feet. I hate talking down to people."

Gage allowed the man to pull him upright. Alphen scrunched his face, sliding his hand through the air from the top of his head down to the top of Gage's.

"I mean, I guess I still have to talk down to you," Alphen said. "You're kind of short."

Rhemi rumbled in her throat, something between a groan and a growl. Gage assumed the guy was teasing. It didn't bother him.

"My magic didn't make the crystal light up," Gage said.

"No, it didn't." Alphen laughed. "And thanks for that. Halayna was so confused!"

"Why would my magic break the crystal?"

"Because you have void magic."

That phrase again.

"The stuff from children's stories. Evil magic," Gage muttered.

"Void magic isn't evil," Alphen said. "It's just . . . not Innaran magic."

Gage's brow furrowed from increasing frustration.

"Innaran crystals react to Innaran magic," Alphen explained. "And Innaran magic creates the lesser four magic types. That's why most magic users need our help to practice magic or summon elementals." He smiled and nodded at Gage. "But void magic is completely separate from Innaran magic. They're opposites that balance each other. Innaran magic creates magic and light. Void magic destroys them. When you touched Halayna's crystal, you destroyed the magic that formed it."

The more the man spoke, the more Gage's stomach soured.

"I destroy things," he murmured. "The crops and forest dying—that really was me?"

Alphen hesitated. "I suppose unrestrained void magic could have that effect."

"And the villagers not having magic, that's my fault too?" Gage forced out the bitter words. "I destroyed any magic they might have had."

"Likely."

"I *am* cursed, just like they always said," Gage cried. "I destroyed everything, and I didn't even know I was doing it. Maybe you should execute me!" He choked out the last part with a sob.

"You're not cursed," Alphen said, gripping Gage's shoulder.

"I ruined everything in my village!"

"And now you're going to learn how to master your magic so you can save the kingdom."

Gage blinked back tears. "What?"

"The reason you confused Halayna when you broke her crystal was because void users don't exist anymore," Alphen explained. "You're likely the last one in the world."

"Probably for good reason—"

"That's where you're wrong," Alphen declared. "You have the ability to destroy magic. And we happen to be fighting a powerful enemy who uses magic against us to kidnap kids and destroy cities."

"You want me to use my magic to stop the Vaskr?" Gage asked.

"Something like that. Besides, now that we've found you, we can teach you how to control your magic. You won't destroy anything ever again—unless you want to."

"You're sure?" Gage tucked his head behind his dragon.

"Positive." Alphen smiled, and warmth radiated from his eyes.

Despite Alphen's apparent confidence, Gage hesitated. He had a chance now to learn magic and fight the Vaskr, but this wasn't how he'd wanted it to happen. Void magic was evil, and Claeg and the villagers were justified in hating him. He really had caused all their problems.

Yet when he looked into his dragon's eyes, a wave of peace crashed over him. After all this time, he finally had a friend. A little scaly one, but a friend nonetheless.

Gage lifted his head and nodded. "Okay. I'll go."

"Great!" Alphen moved to his dragon's side. "Rhemi can fly us to Talid so you can grab your things."

"Actually . . ." Gage went to the bushes and fetched his dropped bag, shaking off the twigs and leaves before slinging it over his shoulder. "Everything I need is right here. I don't want to go back."

Alphen's expression softened. "Gotcha." He dipped his head toward Rhemi. "No point in hanging around, then. Let's go."

Gage nodded and approached Rhemi, looking up at her in awe. He'd always dreamed of riding a dragon. Rhemi regarded him with calm, wise, though somewhat judgmental eyes. Gage wasn't sure how he understood all that by simply looking at her, but he did. She leaned closer and snorted over the dragon in his arms.

"Rhemi wants to know the pipsqueak's name," Alphen said, leaning against Rhemi's side with his arms folded across his chest.

It took a moment for Gage to remember that dragons could telepathically communicate with their human partners once they reached their second forms. Rhemi and Alphen could have mental conversations. A flutter of excitement stirred in Gage's belly. He might talk to his dragon someday. Then again, hadn't he already? Gage thought he'd heard a voice when his dragon had been born.

He'd worry about those things later.

"I'm supposed to name him?" Gage asked.

Alphen passed him a lopsided grin. "That's usually how it works. Names don't just fall out of the sky, you know."

Gage chewed his lower lip. Names were tough, and a dragon's name had to be awesome. His dragon was as dark as night. Perhaps he'd name him *Midnight*? At the thought, a strong sense of dislike twisted in his gut. *Night* felt like a good fit, but it needed something more. *Nightviolet*, like its coloring? That felt wrong too.

"Don't overthink it." Alphen jutted his thumb over his shoulder at his own dragon. "I named Rhemi after a chocolate bar."

Rhemi scowled at Alphen. Then she peered at Gage and nudged her head toward Alphen, as if to say, "See what I have to put up with?"

Gage smiled and returned his attention to his dragon, recalling the purple sparks and dark mists that had surrounded him. A perfect contrast of light and darkness. Not only that, but this dragon had changed Gage's life forever—for the better, he hoped. He didn't have to go back to his old, miserable life in Talid.

A weight lifted off Gage's shoulders. He'd been at the point of darkest night, but this dragon in his arms had given him a spark of hope.

"Nightspark," he said without thinking.

And it fit.

The dragon chirped and wagged his tail. Gage cuddled the creature. Nightspark. His dragon.

"Spark for short," Gage added with a smile. Spark practically purred, sinking into his arms like a contented kitten.

"I think he likes it," Alphen said.

Rhemi growled and lifted one side of her lip, showing off her fangs. She glared at Alphen, and he glared back.

"Don't be like that," he snapped at her. "You loved your name until you figured out where it came from. Too late to change it now." He flapped a hand as if to shoo her away, and then he directed his attention back to Gage. "Ever ridden a dragon?"

Gage tried to stuff down his excitement, but a smile broke onto his lips anyway. "No."

"Time to learn." Alphen gripped Rhemi's feathers and hoisted himself onto her back with practiced ease. The dragon bowed low, allowing Alphen to easily pull Gage up behind him. "Hold on!"

Rhemi crouched—Gage's only other warning. He hooked an arm around Alphen's waist, and an instant later, the light dragon launched off the ground in a rush of beating wings. Gage shrieked as the trees fell away below them, giving way to a dazzling view. Sunset colors in hues of orange and purple splashed one half of the sky, while the other half glittered with twinkling stars. Talid and the forest became an indistinguishable blur of dark colors.

Spark chirped in delight, sticking his head out and letting the wind ruffle his feathery fluff. Gage could practically *feel* the dragon's contentment stirring in his own heart, filling him with warmth. For the first time in his life, he was truly happy.

He'd been given a spark of hope in the night.

8

TWO GRUMPS IN A CLINIC

After a brief flight, a single mountain appeared on the horizon, silhouetted by the rising moon. It glittered in a dazzling array of colors, the entire thing made of Innaran crystal. Small twinkling lights appeared at the mountain's base, and a sprawling city formed out of the darkness.

"What is that?" Gage exclaimed.

"Runadel, the interim capital city of the Innaran kingdom," Alphen said.

Gage let out a stunned exhale. He hadn't realized Talid was so close to Runadel. Nor had he thought the city would be so large.

Lights shone from everywhere, illuminating pale stone walls and blue tiled roofs. Silver streetlamps with enormous crystals lined the streets. Trees, bushes, and vibrant gardens filled every open space, and flowering vines crept over houses. Enormous walls surrounded the city, with southern and eastern gates guarded by light dragons on nearby towers. Innaran knights patrolled the walls, their white robes pristine and their armor gleaming. A huge lake shimmered on Runadel's western edge, while forests surrounded it on all remaining sides save where the gravel roads departed from the city gates.

Gage's eyes followed several light dragons as they ascended from the city toward the mountain's peak. Light glittered at the top of the mountain, where a fortress had been built. He almost asked about it, but Rhemi suddenly descended and yanked his attention back toward the city below.

Even at night, people shopped at outdoor markets and socialized with laughter and chatter. Everyone moved aside as Rhemi landed, and she had little trouble finding space on the broad street. Colored flagstones formed flowers and decorative swirls beneath her feet.

Alphen hopped down and strode toward a large, elegant building with darkened windows. Gage slid off Rhemi's back and hurried after him, cradling Spark in both arms.

"Is this where I'll be training?" he asked. A sign hung over the door with a picture of a gust of green wind.

"This is the healing clinic," Alphen said. "For your pipsqueak dragon."

Gage nodded in appreciation but frowned at the dark building. "How late is it? Are they shut down for the night?"

"Nah. The healer and his elemental are two old grumps who don't like to be bothered." Alphen approached the door, formed a fist, grinned at Gage, and then pounded in the loudest, fastest, most obnoxious way possible. "Thad! Open up! It's me!"

On and on he went, pounding like a madman. Gage ducked his head, his cheeks burning, as people on the street glanced over at them. Finally, a light came on in the clinic.

Alphen paused—and then knocked harder and faster. "Thaaaaaaaaaaaad. It's meeeeeeeeeeeee. Open the dooooooooooooo—"

"Blast it all, you nuisance boy," shouted a deep voice from the other side of the door. "I can hear you!"

The door was yanked open, revealing a middle-aged man with dark, gray-peppered hair, a short beard, and tanned skin. He wore a basic shirt and trousers, a leather apron with various holsters and pockets full of medicinal supplies, and a long-sleeved jacket. His big muscles made him look more like a blacksmith than a healer.

Alphen froze with his hand still upheld to knock, and the man—Gage assumed it was Thad—glared at him.

"What do you think you're—" Thad started, but Alphen stepped aside and revealed Gage and Spark behind him. The big man stopped his tirade and pointed a thick finger at Spark. "Is that . . . ?"

"Yup," Alphen said.

Thad's critical gaze shifted from Spark to Gage before swiftly returning to Alphen. He stepped back and opened the door. "Come in."

Alphen led the way, with Gage right on his heels. Thad intimidated him. Healers were supposed to bandage wounds, not look like they'd cause them.

"Sorry to disturb you," Gage murmured.

"You're not disturbing me." Thad shot a pointed glare at Alphen. "He is."

"Rude. I haven't even done anything yet," Alphen said.

"Your existence disturbs me," Thad replied. When Alphen had the nerve to shoot him a smug grin, the older man rolled his eyes. "Wipe that look off your face, you insufferable toad. The only reason I'm not throwing you out is because I need your help healing the dragon."

"Are you a healer too?" Gage asked Alphen.

"No. Your void dragon will make it tough for Thad to heal him, since he'll destroy his magic in the process," Alphen explained. "But I can boost Thad's magic so he can heal Spark."

Gage nodded and looked around. The main room held two exam tables, four cots, various privacy curtains, and several bookshelves. Plants, vials, and canisters cluttered the counters. The floors, support beams, and furniture were made of dark wood that contrasted with the tannish-white walls. The place felt warm and inviting. Functional, but not obsessively tidy.

"How was the dragon injured?" Thad hobbled into the room with a heavy limp.

"He tried to save me from the Vaskr," Gage said, aching at the memory. Spark nudged his chin, and a wave of reassurance settled over him. An emotion from the dragon?

Thad flipped a switch near the door. Light traveled along a narrow line in the wall from the switch to the ceiling, where it brightened a dome crystal that lit the area. Gage had never seen anything like it.

"Gage is a new student," Alphen explained. "Halayna left him in the village until she figured out what to do with him and his void magic. The Vaskr attacked before I could fetch him."

"You're Gage?" Thad asked.

"Gage Black." He nodded, still frowning, as Thad flipped more switches and illuminated more dome crystals.

The older man pointed at a table as he passed. "Put the dragon down."

Gage shuffled forward and bumped into the table, his eyes stuck on the crystal lights.

"Innaran crystals," Alphen explained. "There's a crystal behind the wall, and the switch opens a pathway for the magic to travel to the ceiling."

In Talid, they'd used oil lamps and ordinary flames. Gage shook away his amazement and set Spark on the table. The little dragon whimpered and clawed at him, mewling when Gage didn't pick him back up.

"It's okay," Gage said, sensing misery, fear, and loneliness that definitely originated from Spark. "They'll make you feel better."

He smoothed both hands over the dragon's head fluff before gripping one of his front feet. Spark calmed and wrapped his claws around Gage's fingers. Some of the fearful sensations lingered, but relief and trust overshadowed them.

"Look alive, Grom," Thad said, hobbling over to the table. "I might need your help."

An exasperated groan answered from the other side of the room. Gage looked over and found what appeared to be a plump, green owl sitting on a wooden perch under a window. A dramatic crown of feathers poked out from its head, and its elaborate tail shone with a blend of vibrant greens. A sharp black beak hooked out of its face, and its bright-green eyes were shadowed by thick, pointed eyebrows, giving the creature a permanent scowl.

"Is that a wind avian?" Gage asked.

"Yes," Thad said. "His name is Gromlin."

Gage had never seen a wind avian before, but he'd always heard they were fast and sleek like sparrows. This one looked like a boulder.

"Why is he so . . ." Gage awkwardly choked down the rest of his question.

"Round?" Alphen finished.

Thad leaned both hands on the table and sent a death glare Alphen's way. Gage's face burned.

"I told you," Alphen said to Gage, "a couple grumps live here. They grump around all day and don't really move."

"I didn't ask for your commentary, boy," Thad said, adding heat to the final word. "Do your thing so I can throw you out."

Alphen smirked and touched Thad's arm, white light glowing around him and flowing into the healer. Thad placed a hand on Spark's back and sent green light into him. Spark muttered warily as he glanced between them. He scowled while Thad shifted his wings and moved his legs to search for injuries.

"A lot of bumps and scratches," Thad muttered. "Broken wing. That's no good."

"Will he be okay?" Gage asked.

"He'll be fine." Sweat glistened on Thad's brow as green lights flared from his hand.

"Don't worry," Alphen said to Gage. "Despite their grouchiness, Thad and Gromlin are the best healers in the kingdom."

Thad glowered at him from under his bushy eyebrows. "Talking pretty won't make me less likely to throw you out when we're done here."

"And despite how it sounds," Alphen murmured, "he likes me a lot—"

Thad yanked a glass vial from his apron and threw it at Alphen's face. Alphen jerked to the side so it whistled harmlessly past his head and hit the corner of an exam table before clattering to the floor.

"Hey now," Alphen exclaimed, putting on a fake look of scorn. "What if that vial had actually hit me?"

"It's a shame it didn't," Thad muttered.

"You could have taken out my eye."

"Next time I'll throw two—take out both eyes and keep it even."

When Alphen scoffed in feigned offense, Gage chewed down a smile. Even Spark was distracted by their bickering, blinking at the two men in confusion.

"There." Thad stepped back and ceased his magic. "I think that should do it."

He gave Spark a full-body shake, ruffled the fluff on his head, and nudged him in Gage's direction.

"You're okay now?" Gage asked his dragon.

Spark chirped in delight and lunged off the table straight into Gage's arms, nuzzling him fiercely. Despite his sharp edges, the dragon was strangely warm and cozy. Spark flapped his wings and wagged his tail in excitement, tossing his forelegs over Gage's shoulders in imitation of a human hug. Gage laughed and returned the gesture.

"Seems like he's fine," Alphen said, smiling.

"I'm glad." Gage gave Spark another squeeze before looking at Thad. "Thank you so much!"

Thad nodded and collected his vial off the floor, shoving it back into his apron. He looked at Spark and then at Gage with an appraising eye. "He's special, that void dragon. You take good care of him."

"I will," Gage promised.

"We should go," Alphen said. "If we're lucky, we might still catch the other kids in the dorm before they head to dinner." Walking backward, he said to Thad, "Thanks for the help."

"Thanks for leaving. Let the door hit you on the way out." Thad flicked off the lights before they'd even made it outside.

9

FLYING WITH DRAGONS

As Gage followed Alphen back down the street, Spark crawled onto his shoulder.

"We're going to fly again," Gage said. "I should probably hold you."

He pulled at the dragon, but Spark dug his claws into his shirt and wouldn't let go. After a few desperate tugs, Gage sighed and scowled. Of course he'd summon a dragon as stubborn as a cat.

"Don't worry," Alphen said. "Most dragons ride on shoulders like that. He'll be fine."

Gage wasn't so sure, but he'd rip his shirt apart if he pulled the dragon any harder. The last thing he needed was to show up in front of his fellow students with half his shirt falling off. It was bad enough he hadn't bathed properly in days.

Alphen swung onto Rhemi's back and took his usual seat. Gage used Alphen's hand as an anchor to haul himself up behind him.

"You're pretty good at this." Alphen smiled, making Gage's cheeks warm. "Let's go, Rhem!"

Rhemi launched off the ground like an arrow loosed from a bowstring. Despite having done this once before, Gage clung desperately to Alphen while Spark clung desperately to him. The little dragon's whole body flapped in the wind. A flurry of emotions from the dragon assaulted Gage, vacillating violently between terror and excitement.

"Spark's going to fall off," Gage cried over the rush of wind and beating wings.

"If he does, we'll catch him. This is good practice," Alphen shouted.

Rhemi whipped into a spiral. Gage yelped as the world spun around him in twists of light and dark. Somehow, Spark held onto him. At last, Rhemi spread her wings and soared over the city. Gage sat back and breathed deep while Spark settled on his shoulder and opened his wings, letting the wind swirl around him.

They flew toward the lone crystal mountain and a massive, walled-in property built at its base. Open walkways and covered colonnades ran between dozens of buildings of various sizes, with gardens, courtyards, and training grounds filling every space between. Guard towers stood over the stone walls as sentries in the night. Crystal lights gleamed through the windows and from shiny lampposts throughout the grounds.

"Here's our destination," Alphen said.

"That's the school?"

"Runadel Academy, technically."

"It's huge!" Gage exclaimed. "How many kids study here?"

"Not that many," Alphen replied, a grin in his voice. "The academy also functions as a training ground for knights. Since students usually graduate into our army, it makes sense for us to practice together. There are magic users of all ages and types here."

They descended toward one of the big courtyards with tiled flooring in floral designs. Gage lifted his eyes to the top of the mountain and the fortress built near its peak.

"What is that place?" Gage asked.

Alphen followed his gaze. "Runadel Castle."

"There's a castle here?"

"Ever since the Vaskr captured the capital city, Sarsier, the royal family moved here. There was already a fortress, so they repurposed it," Alphen explained. "You'll see a lot of powerful Innarans coming and going from there."

"Have you been inside?"

"Lots of times."

"What's it like? Amazing?"

"Stuffy." Alphen passed him a scowl that shifted into a devious grin. "Rhemi, freefall!"

Rhemi folded her wings and dropped like a stone. Gage would have blown away if not for his arms already hooked around Alphen. The stars and city lights whizzed around them in a blur, and Gage's stomach leaped into his throat. Spark flapped in the wind, hanging on by only his front claws. The little dragon's joy swept through Gage, and after his initial shock, Gage felt the same. The rush of wind and the world blurring around him? Perfection.

When Rhemi finally opened her wings and twirled into the courtyard at a slower pace, Gage couldn't help but feel disappointed.

"How was that?" Alphen leaped off Rhemi and grinned up at Gage. "Feeling sick?"

A huge smile broke across Gage's face. "No, that was amazing! Can we do it again?" Spark chirped in agreement as Gage slid to the ground.

"You're definitely a natural." Alphen laughed and patted Rhemi on the side. "Let's go, Rhem."

Light engulfed Rhemi, and she transformed into her first form. Despite being the same size as Spark now, she looked bigger because of her fluffy white feathers. The light dragon flew circles around Alphen before finally settling on his shoulder.

"She can fly in her first form?" Gage asked. Spark had glided a lot when first summoned, but he'd never flown.

"She learned how to fly in her second form," Alphen explained, strolling from the courtyard into a colonnaded walkway. "Now she can do it in her first form too."

"So Spark can't fly yet?"

"If he's like other dragons, not until he evolves into his second form."

Gage and Spark shared a mutual look of disappointment.

10

RUNADEL ACADEMY

Pristine marble tiles covered the walls and floors of Runadel Academy. Enormous windows framed in gold ran from floor to ceiling, and Gage imagined they let in ample sunlight during the day. For now, crystal lights illuminated the corridors in warm hues of white and gold. Decorative marble pillars and statues of dragons lined the walls.

"I'm afraid we don't have time for a tour," Alphen said apologetically. "You're coming in late, and classes start tomorrow morning. We still have a lot to do tonight, so you might not get to bed at a proper time. Sorry about that."

"It's fine. I'm used to getting by on little sleep." Gage shrugged. He regularly had nightmares, which made sleeping miserable. Restful nights were a rare treat.

Alphen's expression softened, but he didn't comment.

They headed down several corridors until they reached an area with wider halls lined with stained-glass murals.

The images depicted the creation of their world, when the Innara first flew down on their light dragons and spread magic across the dark and barren land. Their magic brought forests to life and gifted all people with the lesser-magic types. In the final murals, dark dragons spread death across the world until the Innara defeated them and wiped them from existence.

Whenever they passed others in the hall, the people—Innaran or otherwise—bowed their heads to Alphen, who responded only with curt nods.

Gage frowned at each exchange. Even Innarans with long braids showed Alphen respect. The longer the braid, the higher their status in society. It seemed odd for anyone to show Alphen honor when he wore such a short braid. Gage had heard of Innarans who did something dishonorable and had their hair cut as punishment. Had that happened to Alphen? If so, why was everyone still treating him with reverence?

"Ah, good." Alphen jogged ahead, forcing Gage to scurry after him. "We made it in time."

They passed under a large archway guarded by Innarans and found a pair of double doors at the opposite end of the hall. A din of talking and laughing arose from the next room.

"This wing houses the youngest students." Alphen strolled toward the door. "The other kids are getting ready for dinner."

He set a hand on each door and pushed them open, letting out the noise. Around thirty kids Gage's age were gathered inside the massive room. They wore tunics in colors that matched their elemental magic: yellow for earth, blue for water, green for wind, and red for fire. Some played games at tables near a fireplace, while others hung out on upper balconies lined with bookshelves. None of the kids had elementals.

Alphen whistled, and it echoed in the cavernous room. Everyone went silent.

"It's Lord Alphen," shouted a boy close to the doors.

That inspired a bunch of whispered exclamations of, "Lord Alphen!" throughout the room. One girl practically swooned over him, fluttering her eyelashes and letting out a dreamy, "Lord Alphen." Alphen didn't seem to notice or care.

The whole scene only confused Gage further. *Lord Alphen? Who exactly was this guy?*

"Welcome, Lord Alphen," said a boy in a red tunic.

"Alphen is fine," he said, loud enough for everyone to hear. "I'm glad I caught you before dinner. I'd like to introduce you to Gage Black, our newest student." He stepped aside, revealing Gage to the wide-eyed gazes of his peers.

A collective gasp followed, and the nearest students recoiled in disgust.

"What's that?" someone asked.

"What's on his shoulder?"

"A black dragon!"

"That's a void dragon," stated a boy with a mop of blond hair. He was tall, burly, and wore a green tunic.

Hushed muttering erupted throughout the room. Memories of fearful whispers and scornful stares from the people of Talid resurfaced in Gage's mind. Their hostile tones squashed his hope of a new life. This place would be more of the same.

"Hey," Alphen said sternly. When silence swept over the room, he crossed his arms, looking rather commanding. "Yes, Gage is a void user. You'll learn more about void magic in class. In the meantime, you'll treat Gage the same as any other student here."

"Void magic is evil," said a boy at the back of the group.

"We've all heard the stories," piped up a girl on the upper level.

Gage shuddered. Everyone knew the stories. And for those who didn't, the murals on the walls would tell everyone that Gage's magic was dangerous, if not outright evil. His chest ached—and Spark's ached in agreement.

"Yes, and that's exactly what they are: stories," Alphen said. "There might be some truth to them, but they don't reveal the whole picture."

"But every story about them is bad," argued the big boy with blond hair.

Alphen shifted his weight from one leg to the other and rubbed his chin. "How many of you have had bad experiences with the Vaskr?"

A large number of kids raised their hands.

"How many of you have heard bad stories about the Vaskr?" Alphen asked.

Even more children raised their hands.

"How many of you here have earth magic like the Vaskr?"

Many hands lowered, but a large number remained in the air—although they wavered. These kids wore yellow tunics, so they couldn't hide.

Alphen looked at the nearest yellow-clad student. "Are you evil? Because the stories tell us that the Vaskr do evil things."

All hands dropped, and awkward silence prevailed. Warmth blossomed inside Gage. No one had ever stood up for him before.

"But," said a girl off to the side, "the Innara destroyed the void users because they were dangerous and evil."

"So the stories go," Alphen replied without a second thought. "Void users are human, just like the rest of us. We all have the same capacity to do good or evil. We choose what we do. Gage and his dragon are no different than you. I expect you to treat them with respect, same as anyone else. Understood?"

Students muttered their agreement, and several bobbed their heads. No one seemed excited about it, though. Gage still saw the wariness in their eyes as they looked at him.

"Fine," the burly kid said, "but I don't want his bed next to mine."

Alphen glared, making the kid shrink behind another group of students.

The Innaran sighed and swept his fingers through his hair. "Gage won't be staying in the dorm with you."

More muttering erupted among the students. Gage frowned.

"Because he's dangerous?" asked the big kid.

"Because he's untrained," Alphen said. "His magic might interact with yours in strange ways."

"Because he *is* dangerous!" someone said from the middle of the room.

"All magic is dangerous," Alphen replied, now with some heat.

"Not dangerous like his," said someone hidden in the crowd.

"Oh?" Alphen leaned forward and squinted in frustration. "I guess you've never heard of young fire users burning down forests, or wind users blowing away cities, or earth users causing landslides, or water users flooding rivers. Because I hear about these things all the time. Young magic users accidentally cause all sorts of harm when they don't know how to control their magic. But I suppose none of you have had any mishaps with your magic, huh?"

Alphen arched his eyebrows. A large number of students hung their heads. Gage assumed at least some of them had negative experiences with their magic. But he couldn't imagine any of them tormenting their villages as he had.

"Uncontrolled magic is always dangerous," Alphen said. "That's why we try to find you as soon as our crystals respond to your magic. We want you to control your abilities before they run wild. You're dangerous too, just in different ways. So, as I said, I expect you to treat Gage like anyone else around here. He's one of you, and he's going to help us fight the Vaskr and make this kingdom safer for everyone."

"Okay, Lord Alphen," several kids muttered.

"Alphen is fine." He sighed and dropped his arms to his sides. "Now go have dinner and get some rest. Classes start tomorrow. Don't be late." Returning his attention to Gage, he jerked his chin toward the door. "Let's go."

Alphen led the way into the hall. Gage glanced back as footsteps followed them into the corridor. The other students shuffled after them. All of them stared at him with visible fear, and some wore disdain plainly on their faces.

His throat tightened, and he hastily looked away.

11

INNARAN WING

Alphen led Gage down several corridors to a large central keep with decorative chandeliers and fantastical sculptures of Innarans and light dragons. Enormous windows and huge murals spanned across every wall.

Despite its beauty, Gage found himself unable to appreciate it. The students' disdainful looks haunted him. Spark nuzzled against his cheek, but that only made things worse. Gage didn't want Spark to be hated. The little dragon had just been born, and it all felt so unfair.

"Alphen?" he finally said, barely above a whisper.

"Hmm?"

"What if it's true? What if I *am* evil?"

Alphen snorted. "You're not evil."

"But what if—"

"Listen." Alphen stopped and faced Gage. "You make your own choices. You decide to do good or evil. No one decides those things for you."

"But what if there's something about void magic that makes us go crazy or something?" Gage asked.

Alphen frowned and crossed his arms. "Do you want to burn down Talid?"

"What? Of course not."

"Do you want the Vaskr to terrorize the other students?"

"No!" Gage's cheeks flamed.

"And does it seem like Spark has a strong inclination toward eating people?"

Gage glanced at Spark, who hadn't shown interest in hurting anyone besides Vaskran raiders.

"No," he finally admitted.

"Then you're not evil."

"But the stories—"

Alphen sighed, taking a step closer. "Look, void magic is rare. We don't have a lot of experience with it. That means people only know about it *through* stories. And the stories we have right now aren't positive. But stories can be misleading or downright wrong. I don't think it's wise to judge all humans and elementals of a certain type based on limited knowledge. If we did, we'd risk similar stories and attitudes toward earth users, don't you think? Most stories about the Vaskr are pretty bad."

Gage wanted to argue but was forced to nod. Given the current tension with the Vaskr, the stories about them were bleak. And if those were the only stories that remained after a few hundred years, earth magic might become as hated and feared as void magic.

"I wish everyone thought the same as you," Gage whispered.

Alphen offered a sad smile. He gripped Gage's shoulder and gave a slight shake, lifting Gage's head so their eyes could meet.

"I know," Alphen said softly. "It's going to be tough for a while. That's something you'll have to accept. Do everything you can to keep your head up, and always choose to do good."

"So the other students accept me?" Gage sank under Alphen's hand. Having to impress others so they'd like him felt too heavy a burden to bear.

But Alphen shook his head. "No, so other void users after you have someone to follow. Someone better than those in our current stories." He squeezed Gage's shoulder. "The world has enough sad stories, doesn't it? Let's create some good ones. For void users, and for everyone."

A smile crept onto Gage's lips, and the weight lifted as quickly as it had settled on him. Nothing he did in Talid had ever earned him the acceptance of the villagers. The situation with the other students might end up the same, but Gage could still do good. That seemed like an easy task. He would do good for himself, for Spark, and for anyone who followed him. If others respected him for it, great. But even if they didn't, at least he'd be able to live with himself. At least he wouldn't become a cruel, cold-hearted person like Claeg.

He glanced at Spark, and the dragon offered a quick nod.

"Thanks," Gage said to Alphen. Emotion riddled the word, but it still didn't properly convey how much Alphen's kindness meant to him.

Alphen smiled, patted his shoulder, and resumed walking. Gage took a deep breath and hurried after him. They climbed a flight of stairs and passed under an archway into another broad corridor with many wooden doors surrounded by gold frames. Ivory dragon statues lined the walls.

"This is where you'll be staying," Alphen said. "Innarans live here. Our abundance of magic will keep your void magic from influencing the academy—at least until you learn to control it better. Then you'll be free to live in the dorms." He stopped in front of a door. "This one is yours." Jutting his thumb down the hall, he added, "I'm the last room on the right. If you need anything, pester me."

"I think I need to mark my door," Gage admitted, noting the nearly two dozen similar doors in the hall.

"I'll show you around for the next few days so you won't have to worry about getting lost." Alphen opened the door and stepped aside so Gage could enter.

The room was big compared to Gage's tiny room at Claeg's house. A single bed sat in the corner, complete with two fluffy pillows and a blanket.

"The door locks from the inside," Alphen said, fiddling with the handle before gesturing to a narrow alcove in the wall, where plain white tunics and trousers hung from a metal rod. "We've prepared some clothes for you, but a tailor will take your measurements after dinner. You'll have at least one uniform ready by morning." He walked over to a white metal chest at the foot of the bed. "You can store your things here." Then, with a glance toward the far side of the room, he pointed to a wooden folding screen that blocked off a small tiled area. "This is the bathing room. I've asked attendants to prepare a bath for you tonight. You'll get a haircut as well."

"Haircut?" Gage tugged on his hair. It wasn't that long.

"They won't take off much. Just enough so you aren't so scruffy." Alphen grinned. "You're looking a little wild up there."

Gage bit his tongue to keep from mentioning that Alphen's hair was longer and unrulier than his. Then again, his hair looked purposefully messy, while Gage's hair was tangled and knotted. He'd never owned a comb.

"Why don't you change into some spare clothes?" Alphen suggested. "I'll wait for you in the hall." He excused himself and shut the door behind him.

Gage glanced around the room, strangely torn about it. Living with the Innarans seemed awesome, but the room felt strangely hollow.

"What do you think, Spark?" he asked.

The little dragon unleashed a discontented gurgle, sharing Gage's sentiments. The room lacked something. And then Gage realized what was missing: a window. Not only had he often escaped through his window in Talid, but he'd always had sunlight shining over him, even indoors. This room, with its thick door and oppressive walls, closed in around him.

Spark leaped off his shoulder and landed on the bed with a soft plop. He spun in a circle at least six times before flopping down on the blanket and rolling across the bed from one end to the other. Finally, he flung up the blanket and scampered around underneath it.

"You dork." Gage chuckled, grabbed a tunic and pants out of the alcove, and changed for dinner.

12

ALWAYS THE SAME

Gage followed Alphen through a pair of massive doors made of dark wood. Chatter and laughter flooded his ears as he stepped into the academy's dining hall. A hundred different smells—sweet, spicy, salty—assaulted him at once, making his mouth water. Spark wagged his tail, and his tongue drooped out of the side of his mouth.

The cavernous room had gold-flecked marble pillars and walls with images of elementals etched into the stone. Six massive chandeliers hung from the ceiling, shimmering with strings of crystal lights in every magic color: white, blue, green, yellow, and red. Every color except one for void magic, at least. Gage tried not to be bothered by it.

Marble tables with bench seats created four long lines through the room. People seemed to gather by age or rank, but the Innarans mostly kept to themselves. Elementals in their first forms sat on the tables and ate from their own plates. Gage looked in wonder at the assorted mix of low elementals throughout the room: tan beetles with rocky bodies and spikes, blue water felines with fluffy fur and twitching tails, green wind avians with sharp beaks and hooked talons, and orange fire lizards that flickered like living flames.

"What do you think?" Alphen asked, smiling.

"It's amazing," Gage admitted. "There are so many elementals. I can't believe I get to see this."

"You don't just get to see it. You're a part of it." Alphen patted him on the back and then jutted his thumb over his shoulder toward a table full of adults. Gage assumed it belonged to teachers. "I need to let Halayna know you arrived safely." Then he pointed to the other side of the room, where a bunch of tables held enormous platters of food. "Go grab something to eat and find a place to sit."

Gage's insides shriveled, and he wrung the front of his tunic. "Does the food cost anything?"

"As long as you're training here, it's free." Alphen gave him a gentle nudge toward the serving tables. "Have at it."

Alphen headed down the aisle to the front of the room, where Gage glimpsed Lady Halayna sitting among her honor guard. Alphen stopped to speak with her without bowing or even dipping his head. In fact, he slouched and kept his hands in his pockets like he was talking to a stranger on the street. Lady Halayna didn't seem to mind, nor did her honor guard.

Spark chittered and nipped Gage's ear, distracting him. The little dragon gestured with a foreleg toward the food. As if on cue, Gage's stomach grumbled.

He shuffled to the food tables, hesitantly grabbing a silver plate. A serving lady eyed him as he approached. She wore an apron with an assortment of spoons sticking out of its pockets.

"What can I get you?" she asked.

Gage froze at the vast number of choices. Meat lathered in gravy, fish in a milky sauce, mashed potatoes, noodles in yellow cream, corn covered in spices, mixed veggies, fruits, various puddings and jellies, some kind of cake with crumbs on top and berries on the bottom, and six different pies. He'd never eaten any of these things.

"What can I have?" he asked.

"Whatever you want." The lady offered a patient smile.

"Can I try everything?"

"Sure." Raising an eyebrow, she went to work, piling a small scoop of everything onto his plate. She had to grab a second plate for the pies, which she cut into tiny slices.

Despite the small portions, both plates ended up close to overflowing. Gage grimaced as he cautiously moved down the aisles to find a place to sit. Most of the seats were taken, and people grew silent whenever he neared them.

The tension started to suffocate Gage. Word of him had apparently spread, and he clearly wasn't welcome here. He hurried to his own classmates, whom Alphen had already told to treat him kindly. He found them by singling out the big blond kid and the girl who'd swooned over Alphen, but even his peers quieted as he approached. Then they started whispering. Even though he couldn't make out what they said, it didn't matter. It was always the same.

Unfortunately, the burly blond kid sat next to the only open seat. When he saw Gage coming, he took a spoonful of meat and gravy and dumped it onto the bench beside him.

"Oh, sorry," he said. "It slipped." Even as he said the words, he cracked up and ducked his head to hide his laughter.

Gage glared. Some of the other students exchanged nervous glances, and a couple offered him apologetic looks, but no one stood up for him. Gage didn't feel like picking a fight or forcing his way into a group that didn't want him. It wasn't worth his time or energy. He'd learned that long ago in Talid.

Even though it stung, he marched over to a small table at the back of the room. Gage slid onto the bench and set down his plates. There he sat with his void dragon—the cursed kid, always alone.

13

SCALY HOARDER

Gage prodded the items on his plate until Spark slid down his arm and snatched up some of the food.

"Hey," Gage exclaimed.

Spark hoarded a bunch of meat and fruit and scurried to the other side of the table, curling around his stash with his entire body. He nibbled on a grape while eyeing Gage distrustfully.

"Don't look at me like that." Gage grinned. "You're the thief who stole it from me."

Gage laughed, shook his head, and finally gave his meal a try, first eating meat and gravy, then fish. Both launched a flavorful assault in his mouth, and everything else he'd eaten in his life now seemed bland by comparison. He tasted the veggies, fruits, and puddings. The joy of real, delicious food brought a prickle of tears to his eyes.

Footsteps distracted him, and Alphen dropped a plate onto the table across from him. The Innaran youth slumped onto the bench like a knight returning from war. The sudden clatter of his plate made Spark leap into the air and land on all fours, his back arched and his fangs bared. Rhemi took advantage of his surprise, lunged down Alphen's arm, and swiped Spark's fruit before retreating to the opposite side of the table. Spark pranced and hissed at her like an ornery cat.

"What'd you get?" Alphen asked Gage, ignoring the two dragons shooting daggers at each other with their eyes. When he saw Gage's plate, he raised an eyebrow. "Or should I ask, what didn't you get?"

Gage's cheeks warmed. "I don't know what I like, so I have to try everything." As he spoke, Spark stole a dinner roll off his plate and fled to the edge of the table. Gage sighed. "Besides, someone keeps taking my food."

"Dragons are hoarders by nature." Alphen gave Rhemi the side-eye. "Rhemi loves collecting the tin wrappers off fancy chocolates. I have an entire dresser full of them."

Rhemi fixed a cold stare on him, scampered to his plate, stole most of his fruit, and then ran away with it to the other side of the table. She scowled at him and flicked her tongue.

"It's almost like I got extra for you, Rhemi," Alphen said. "You don't need to steal it."

Nevertheless, he stabbed a piece of fruit out of her pile and stole it back. She puffed up like Spark had, her back arched and fangs bared. Then she threw herself over her food pile so he couldn't retrieve more of it. Alphen smirked and returned to his meal.

Gage smiled at the exchange, but his amusement diminished as he contemplated Alphen's presence at his table. No one else had wanted anything to do with him.

"Why are you eating with me?" Gage asked, his voice barely above a whisper.

Alphen paused with his fork in his mouth. He slowly lowered it, chewing and staring at Gage. Finally, he swallowed and leaned back with a dramatic sigh. "You hate me already, huh? It usually takes a while longer before I annoy people that much. Is it because I'm making you get a haircut—"

"What? No!" Gage exclaimed, his neck, face, and ears flaming. "I don't hate you! It's just—"

Alphen grinned. Naturally, he was teasing. That only made Gage's face hotter. He slumped in his seat and managed to look annoyed.

"The other students had guides on their first few days here," Alphen explained after taking a bite of fish. "You're odd coming in as late as you are. You still get a tour guide, but now you get me mostly to yourself. You'll be on your own once you get used to things."

Gage nodded, but he couldn't help a bit of disappointment. He liked Alphen, and it was nice having someone around who didn't hate him.

A bell rang from the front of the room, silencing the conversations throughout the hall. An Innaran guard stood on an elevated platform at the front of the room and rang a gold handbell before stepping back. Lady Halayna climbed the stairs onto the stage and stood at a podium.

Warmth stirred in Gage's belly. He'd feared Lady Halayna after the crystal incident in Talid, but now he appreciated her beyond words. That event had changed his life.

"Greetings, my dear friends," she said. Her voice conveyed wisdom and authority, carrying across the room with perfect volume, neither too loud nor too soft. "For those who have not met me, I am Halayna Lightgard, daughter of His Majesty, King Fraylon Lightgard of the Innara. I have been assigned to care for Runadel Academy for the upcoming year, and I assure you I will always keep your best interests in mind when attending to the academy's affairs. Tomorrow, a new year of study begins. You will train in history, combat, and magic. It will be challenging, and there will be many instances of failure. Do not be discouraged and do not give up. Failure cannot defeat you unless you let it. Together, let us strive toward a beautiful future of light."

Cheers and applause erupted throughout the room as Lady Halayna returned to her seat. Gage clapped, but he stilled when he noticed Alphen picking at his food and ignoring the speech. Rhemi perched on the edge of the table, watching Lady Halayna with her head low and eyes narrowed. Gage wondered about their indifferent reactions, but he didn't know Alphen well enough to ask about it.

He turned his attention to his desserts—to the last thing he hadn't tried, the crumbling cake with dark berries. He scooped up a chunk and took a bite. Sweetness and tartness hit him all at once, and he almost dropped his fork in surprise.

"Oh!" he exclaimed.

Alphen stopped stirring his food around his plate. "What?"

"This is amazing!" Gage shoved another forkful of dessert into his mouth, followed by another, and another. "What is this?"

"Blackberry cobbler." Alphen grinned. "It's pretty good."

Gage devoured another bite, and his excitement lured Spark to his plate. The nuisance dragon stole some cobbler and stuffed his cheeks like a chipmunk.

"Thief!" Gage flapped a hand at him. "This one is mine! Get your own!"

Alphen laughed as Spark stole another chunk of cobbler and darted to the far side of the table. Gage gave the dragon a hard look before shoving the rest of the cobbler into his mouth.

"This is blackberry?" Gage asked around a mouthful of food. Probably not the most respectful way to speak, but at this point, he didn't care.

"Fresh blackberry," Alphen said. "Probably mixed with lots of sugar and junk. You know, all the good stuff."

Gage cleaned his plate entirely of cobbler and even considered licking up the remaining juices. Despite eating so much, he found himself wanting more, and he eyed the leftovers on Alphen's plate. The Innaran youth continued to poke at his food, which included a nice chunk of blackberry cobbler. Gage and Alphen met eyes across the table. Gage's gaze flicked to Alphen's plate and back up again. Back down. And back up again.

"Yes?" Alphen sat back, a grin worming its way onto his lips.

Gage wagged his fork at Alphen's cobbler. "Are you gonna eat that?"

"You know you can go get more, right?" Alphen asked.

Gage hadn't known, but that didn't matter. "They'll think I'm a glutton."

Alphen's grin widened. "You *are* a glutton."

"Yeah, but I don't want them to know it."

Alphen snorted and then scraped the contents of his plate onto Gage's. Gage cheerfully ate his leftovers, including another glorious serving of blackberry cobbler.

14

THE NIGHTMARE

Gage opened his eyes and found a dead world around him. Dust cloaked the air, blown by slow but steady wind. He turned in a circle, his feet shuffling across dry, cracked ground.

Another nightmare. He had one nearly every night, and they were always the same. No matter what he did, he couldn't wake up until the dream completed its vicious cycle. So he walked, though he had no idea where he was going. Dust obscured everything, but he had to move. It was the only way out.

"Hello?" he called.

Only whistling wind answered him.

Sighing, he kicked a small rock and sent it skittering away. It clanged against something masked by the haze. Gage hurried forward and found the rock in a pile of shattered pottery. A little farther on, he found the ruins of houses, their wooden walls snapped in half and their roofs collapsed over the top of them.

He'd never found a village in this miserable dream world before.

Broken glass covered the ground. Books lay open in the street, their pages fluttering in the wind. Tables, chairs, and beds lay shattered inside demolished houses. Silverware, tools, and clothes were strewn about. It looked like the villagers had fled their homes in a hurry. Gage's stomach flipped after each house he passed.

"It's a dream," he told himself, shaking his head to rid himself of sympathy for people who didn't exist. He scrubbed his eyes, itchy from dust. "If you could wake up now, that'd be great."

He pinched his arm. It hurt, and the pain lingered, but he still didn't wake. Stupid dreams that were stupid real. Growling, he kept walking.

Gage, called a voice through the dust.

Gage had heard the voice many times before, but it used to sound like a distant echo. It was clearer now, and it sounded like a young girl, but he couldn't be sure.

"Hello?" he called. "Is someone there?"

Can . . . hear . . . the voice responded.

"Hello—"

The land rumbled, cutting him off. A nearby house wobbled and collapsed, sending up a fresh plume of dust.

So the destruction began, same as it always did.

The ground lurched and sent Gage staggering. This happened in every nightmare, but that didn't make it any less unpleasant. More and more houses collapsed from the force of the quake.

Gage sprinted out of the village to avoid the splinters shooting through the air. His toe caught on a loose cobblestone, and he cried out as he flew to the parched ground, slamming down on his arm. Pain flashed through him, but he ignored it and sat up to see the thing that truly made this a nightmare.

An ominous shadow swallowed the sky, covering the light and casting the world into darkness. It moved toward him, and a powerful gust of wind swept over the land. Gage couldn't help but think it was an exhaled breath from a giant monster.

Something crashed onto the ground, but he didn't wait to see what. He flew to his feet and ran as fast as he could. Things would only get worse from here.

"Wake up," he yelled at himself, but of course, his stupid brain didn't listen. "Wake up! Wake up!"

Cracks spread through the land like fracturing ice, and then the earth cleaved apart. Gage leaped over widening valleys and dodged erupting mountains. He ran until he couldn't breathe. He didn't know how he knew, but that thing in the sky would destroy him if he let it.

The ground tore apart in front of him, creating a vast chasm. Gage jumped and barely caught the other side.

Everything fell away into oblivion behind him as the shadow grew in the sky, drawing closer. Gage dragged himself up the ledge, but his sweat-slicked fingers slipped, leaving him hanging by one hand.

The rocks gave out under his grasp, and he cried out as he tumbled into a torrent of stone.

Gage, shouted the girl's voice, loud and clear.

Another shadow swooped across the sky, smaller and closer than the other, with a long tail and broad wings. A dragon?

Darkness swallowed Gage in the abyss. He slammed into a rock and yelped as he crashed down onto something solid.

Wrestling to free himself from a tangle of blankets, he sat up and found himself on the floor next to his bed in Runadel Academy. Even in the blackness, everything took shape before Gage's eyes as though under a dim light. His void magic likely had something to do with this bizarre ability, but for now, that didn't matter. He searched for anything amiss, but nothing seemed out of order. His boots sat on his storage trunk, his clothes hung in the alcove, and the lock was engaged on the door.

Spark screeched and thrashed under the blanket until he tore free and rolled across the floor in a confused heap. The dragon blinked several times.

Gage swept a hand through his sweat-slicked hair. The shorter style briefly caught him by surprise until he remembered his haircut. Pain echoed through his body as he moved, same as it always did, like the pain followed him from the dream into reality. He sat for a long while trying to steady his breathing.

Tossing aside his blanket, he lifted his nightshirt and fluttered it to cool himself and dry the sweat. His arm throbbed, and he absently rubbed it, which only caused more pain.

Gage drew back his shirtsleeve. A long scrape covered his arm where he'd hit the ground in his dream. He glanced at his bed and noted the corners of his bedposts. He must have struck one and injured himself while flailing in his sleep. Spark placed his forelegs over Gage's crossed legs and inspected the injury, tilting his head. Gage covered the wound with his hand and sighed.

Fantastic. Now his nightmares left him exhausted *and* wounded. Could his curse get any worse?

15

SHORTCUTS

"Gage, answer me!"

Alphen's distant voice dragged Gage from sleep. He opened his eyes to find Spark pawing at his shirt.

And then the door exploded.

Gage flew upright, sending Spark rolling to the foot of the bed. Slivers of wood rained across the room, and the door handle clattered to the floor. Alphen stood in the doorway, his eyes wide with panic. Gage stared first at the wood shattered all around his bed and then at Alphen.

"Are you okay?" Alphen exclaimed, flicking on the light switch by the door. He held a bundle of black fabric under his arm.

"Yeah?" Gage frowned, scratching his head. He shot Alphen an accusing look. "You broke my door."

"I thought you were dead!"

"I was sleeping."

"Yeah, like the dead." Alphen ran a hand through his hair and exhaled sharply. "Gage, the morning bell rang over an hour ago. How did you sleep through it?"

Gage yawned, tossing off his blanket. "I had trouble sleeping last night, that's all."

"And now you're going to be late for your first class. Get up!" Alphen flung some clothes at Gage. They fluttered to the floor. "Hurry and get dressed!"

"I can't get dressed," Gage grumbled as he grabbed the clothes. "You broke my door."

That earned him a scowl from Alphen. "Go behind the screen. I'll guard the door."

Gage shuffled across the room, dodging shards of wood, and stopped when he found the door handle in shambles at his feet.

"Seriously," he said, "what did you do to this door?"

"Gage!" Alphen threw a boot at him, forcing Gage to dodge behind the changing screen. A second boot followed.

Gage tossed his clothes over the screen as he dressed. His new uniform included a black tunic to match his void magic—although he considered Spark's colors more dark purple than black. Gage had also received black pants and a simple gray belt made of fabric. After dressing, he fetched his black boots. Spark, who'd been sitting on one of them, climbed up his arm to reach his shoulder.

"Why are we late, anyway?" Gage muttered, tugging on his boots. "I couldn't have gone anywhere without you."

A hint of red flushed Alphen's cheeks.

"Did you oversleep too?" Gage squinted at the Innaran, who had the decency to look ashamed.

"Maybe, but I had to wake *you* up after waking myself up, and therein lies the problem." Alphen tossed something wrapped in paper at him, and Gage fumbled with it briefly before securing it against his chest. "Breakfast. Now hustle!" He sprinted down the hall, Gage shortly behind him. "Rhemi, you know what to do."

The light dragon hummed in acknowledgement, sprang off his shoulder, and zipped down the hall. She vanished through an archway into the main chamber of the keep. Gage unwrapped his breakfast and found warm bread filled with scrambled eggs and cheese. Delicious. Spark nipped at his ear, reminding him to share.

"It's not safe to eat while running," Gage said while eating and running. "I'll choke."

"I'll try to save you," Alphen replied, still running.

Gage smirked and took another bite.

They reached the main keep. Gage turned toward the stairs, but Alphen caught his arm and dragged him the other way.

"Where are we going?" Gage asked.

"Shortcut."

Alphen led him down another hall full of towering windows and glittering sunlight, kicking open a pair of double doors at the end of the corridor. They swung on their hinges and slammed against the outside walls.

"What is with you and doors?" Gage asked.

Alphen ignored the question and hauled him onto a balcony overlooking a courtyard full of flowering trees. To Gage's confusion—and horror—Alphen dragged him onto the banister. Rhemi streaked over the courtyard in her second form, coming toward them.

A chunk of bread caught in Gage's throat. "Uh, Alphen—"

"Now!" Alphen leaped into open air, yanking Gage along with him.

Gage cried out in shock until Rhemi swooped underneath them. Alphen caught hold of her feathers with absolute ease while maintaining his grip on Gage in the process. Gage tightened his knees around Rhemi's sides to anchor himself and to keep his hands free for breakfast. Spark had no trouble staying on his shoulder. Rhemi hurtled past the courtyard, beyond the academy, and over the city.

"Where are we going?" Gage asked.

"Your first class is at the clinic with Thad," Alphen said.

"With Thad?" Gage frowned. "Will he be mad if I'm late?"

"Super mad." Alphen rubbed the back of his neck. "Thad is a military man. He locks his door when the bell rings. He's had students thrown out of the academy for being late too many times."

Gage nearly choked on another piece of bread.

"Don't worry," Alphen said, grinning. "The other students had to walk. We might beat them there."

Gage finished his breakfast as they zipped over the city. They passed over a bustling plaza with a glittering fountain at its center, and from there, it didn't take long for the clinic to come into view. Gage recognized it from the night before, but it was bigger than he remembered.

Unfortunately, Gage's peers were already entering through the front door.

"Oh no!" Gage pointed. "Rhemi, hurry!"

"No time," Alphen said.

He grabbed Gage, and Rhemi shrank back into her first form right out from underneath them. Gage let out another exclamation of shock and terror, which would apparently be a normal occurrence around Alphen. Right before they flattened on the ground, Alphen sent out a pulse of light that slowed their fall and allowed them to land safely, Alphen steady on his feet and Gage staggering only slightly.

A bell rang from the tower at the academy, the door to the clinic slammed shut, and a lock engaged from inside with a loud click.

"No!" Gage ran halfway to the door and stopped, his heart sinking. "We're too late."

"Don't worry. There's still the window." Alphen rushed to the window next to the door.

"What?" Gage didn't follow him this time.

"The window," Alphen said, as if that explained everything. "Hurry!" He yanked open the window, which was relatively high off the ground. Then he crouched and weaved his fingers together, creating a step for Gage to use.

"I'm not climbing in through the window," Gage stated.

"Why not? I do it all the time," Alphen said. "Come on!"

Gage stared at the Innaran in disbelief. Blowing doors apart, climbing into locked buildings through their windows—this guy was nothing but trouble. Regardless, Gage didn't want to miss his first class. When Alphen jerked his head toward the window and lifted his eyebrows as if to say, "What are you waiting for?" Gage sighed and hurried over. He stepped onto Alphen's hands so he could reach the windowsill, and then Alphen gave him a boost higher, allowing him to pull his torso inside the building.

Half the class was already staring at him, but Gage clenched his teeth and did his best not to make too much noise. And then his Innaran companion used both hands to shove him the rest of the way through the window. Gage flew onto the counter and rolled straight onto the floor, where he landed with a loud thud. The entire class stared at him now, and a handful of his classmates giggled.

To make matters worse, Alphen called in after him, "I'll pick you up for lunch," and then slammed the window shut. The Innaran youth grinned like an idiot and gave Gage a thumbs-up before disappearing from view.

Cheeks on fire, Gage pushed onto his hands and knees, pausing when he noticed Thad across the room. The big man's thick arms were folded across his chest, and a stern glare marred his face. He let out a huge sigh, rolling his eyes to the ceiling.

"Not another one," he muttered.

Another what? Gage didn't bother asking, because he was probably in enough trouble. Scrambling to his feet, he dusted himself off, coughed into his hand, and scampered to the back of the group. Thad's hostile glare followed him, so he ducked behind a taller kid.

One of the boys at the back of the class grinned at Gage and whispered, "Way to make an entrance."

16

WAR STORIES

"All right, kids," Thad muttered, folding his hands behind him and straightening his back as he paced the front of the room. "Have a seat. I don't care where, just don't break anything, and pay attention."

Everyone glanced around. Thad hadn't put much effort into making his clinic a classroom. Several large papers hung at the front of the room, including a map of the kingdom. Other than that, he'd only set up a few stools. Kids sat on them and on the edges of exam tables. Gage retreated to the counter he'd rolled across, hopping onto it and kicking his feet in the air. Only then did he notice the nearby shelves full of glass vials and droopy plants. He was lucky he hadn't shattered a bunch of stuff on the way in.

"My name is Thad Farowind," he began, his foot thumping against the tile floor as he walked. "I'll be teaching the history of our kingdom and the reasons for our current war. I was High General for His Majesty, Lord Valm

Lightgard, the late father to King Fraylon. I was also the lead healer in King Valm's honor guard. At least until this happened." He gestured to his lame leg.

"What happened?" asked a girl sitting on an exam table.

Thad spun toward her, narrowing his fierce eyes. "Do not speak unless I have designated you to speak. Raise your hand and wait to be called upon."

The girl ducked her head and raised a trembling hand.

"Yes, Mia?"

She dropped her hand, frowning. "How do you know my name?"

"I know all of your names." Thad's eyes traveled from student to student. "I make it my duty to know the names of those in my care."

Mia raised her hand again. Thad's eyebrow twitched.

"Yes, Mia?"

"What happened to your leg?" she asked.

"A Vaskran beetle bit it off."

A chorus of gasps swept the room.

"It was a rough day, as you can imagine. With ol' Gromlin's help"—Thad jerked his thumb at the avian staring at them flatly from his perch—"I was able to reattach the leg and restore some of its functions. But the damage was severe, and even with the Innarans strengthening my magic, I couldn't fully restore it. I became a liability to my men and was forced to leave the battlefield." He resumed pacing. "If you intend to join the Innarans against the Vaskr, you should prepare yourselves to see people injured and maimed. That's a part of war. If you don't think you can handle it, there's no shame in that." Thad faced the class, standing tall and proud. "Anyone want to leave now before things get tough?"

No one moved, but many students exchanged wary glances. Not Gage. He'd seen some awful things done by the Vaskr during their attacks on Talid. Injuries didn't bother him—what bothered him was not being able to help.

"No?" Thad resumed pacing. "You're braver than most. But if you ever feel like you can't face the horrors of war, then leave. An unwilling soldier is a dead soldier, and that's the last thing we want. Now then, who can tell me why we're fighting the Vaskr in the first place?" When no one spoke, Thad nodded and headed to his map. "This is a map of the Innaran kingdom around twenty years ago. You can see the elemental provinces, as well as the Innaran territory at the heart of the kingdom."

Gage inspected the map, with Nairne of the water tribe to the southwest, Pyrras of the fire tribe to the southeast, Aither of the wind tribe to the northwest, and Vaskr of the earth tribe to the northeast. In the center was the Innaran province, where they currently resided.

"Now here is our kingdom today." Thad flipped the page to reveal another map.

The map showed the territory of the Vaskr highlighted in red, except now it bled into the other territories like little red worms.

"The Vaskr have spilled into every territory, destroying cities, claiming lands, and capturing children." Thad backhanded the center of the map over a red dot in the northeastern section of the Innaran territory. "They even took Sarsier."

"How?" asked the big kid that had dumped food on the bench at dinner.

"You will not speak unless called upon," Thad stated, giving the boy a cold, hard stare. "Raise your hand."

The boy rolled his eyes and dangled his hand in the air like a dead fish.

Thad's expression darkened, and his thick eyebrows dropped. "Roll your eyes at me again, boy, and I'll pop them out of your head, throw them out on the street, and toss your body out after them."

Everyone froze and went painfully quiet, but Gage almost laughed at the absurdity of it. The big kid lowered his floppy hand and stared at Thad like a deer caught in a hunter's sights. A girl on the other side of the room shot her hand into the air.

"Yes, Serra?" Thad asked, still glaring at the blond kid.

"How did the Vaskr steal the capital if the Innara are more powerful?"

"By using a monster," Thad replied.

A few kids exchanged glances, and then several more hands shot into the air.

Thad took a deep breath and resumed pacing. "The Vaskr laid a trap for us when they took Sarsier. They started skirmishes throughout the territories and drew the Innaran forces in countless directions. They appeared out of nowhere, making them hard to track. It was during one of those sneak attacks that the Vaskr struck the capital. The Vaskran commander offered to duel the king for control of the city. For the sake of peace, King Valm accepted and won, but the Vaskr betrayed us, slayed the king, and attacked the city anyway. Most of the people in the city perished. Those who survived claim a monster attacked them, one that demolished buildings with a single breath. The capital fell in less than a day."

Silence permeated the room. The blond kid stuck his hand in the air—this time more firmly and without the eye rolling, but a partial smirk twisted his lips.

Thad glared at him. "What, Eddly?"

"Was it a void dragon?"

Gage stiffened. A wave of goose bumps rushed across his skin as half the class looked at him and his dragon.

"It wasn't a void dragon," Thad said flatly. "If you knew your history, you'd know void dragons were thought to be extinct for over two decades. And you'd know the last known void user died over a decade ago." His eyes flicked to the red dot on the map that marked the capital city now lost to the Vaskr. "No, this creature was a monster. People said it looked like a lizard, but twice the usual size. It had spikes, fangs, and claws where it shouldn't have any of those things. They also claimed black veins ran through it, pulsing with infection."

More silence followed. A stool creaked as a student leaned forward. Gage found himself leaning forward too, his heart racing at the description. Lizards typically had smooth bodies—no spikes—and small fangs and claws. And they definitely didn't have black veins pulsing through them.

"Sounds like void magic to me," Eddly muttered, turning toward Gage.

He didn't have time to make eye contact, though. Thad marched over to him. Eddly's face paled and his eyes bulged. He got to his feet like he intended to run, but Thad grabbed him by the back of his shirt and dragged him to the door, where he unceremoniously chucked him out onto the street.

"That's a demerit," Thad stated. "Earn three in my class and I'll have you thrown out of the academy. Do better next time." At that, he slammed the door and locked it.

No one moved, and Gage was sure everyone had stopped breathing. As Thad limped to the front of the room, everyone sat up straighter, pulled back their shoulders, and lifted their heads. Gage gulped. Yeah, he was never going to be late for class again.

"Anyone else have any more snarky comments for me?" Thad asked.

Silence answered him.

Thad grinned. "Good. Now, let's continue with the lesson."

17

MORTAR AND PESTLE

After class, Gage lingered on the counter until all the kids had shuffled out of Thad's clinic. A cursory glance through the window revealed no sign of Alphen. With a heavy sigh, he hopped to the floor, bowed his head, and meandered over to Thad, who had moved to the back of the room and was using a mortar and pestle to crush plants for medicines. An assortment of ingredients in jars littered the counter, including various plants, oils, and creams.

"Thad?" Gage meekly said.

"Hmm?"

"I'm sorry for being late to your class today."

"It's human to make mistakes, and I allow for them. But I hope you learn from it. Don't do it again."

"I'll do my best." Gage dipped his head in apology and started for the door, slowing when Thad threw a few familiar plants into the mortar. "You're making disinfecting salves?"

Thad paused and glanced in his direction. "You know what this is?"

"I read all the medical books our healer had in Talid." Gage rubbed his arm, his cheeks warming. "I tried making my own salves sometimes. I really liked doing it."

His eyes lingered on the pestle and mortar as Thad continued his work, though now the man watched him with a thoughtful expression.

Thad slid the instruments over to Gage. "Want to try?"

"Oh. No. I've never actually done it like this before." Gage waved at Thad's professional tools.

"I don't see why not having done it before means you can't do it now," Thad stated.

Gage squirmed. Jinny never let him touch her tools. His heart ached as he recalled her vicious last words to him. Maybe she'd been right—he wasn't meant to be a healer because of his void magic.

"But what about . . ." He poked a finger at Spark.

Thad frowned. "I don't see the connection. Don't put him in the mortar and there shouldn't be a problem." He pushed the tools closer to Gage.

Gage blinked in confusion, and then his heart warmed. A smile spread across his face as he took the mortar and pestle from Thad and crushed the plants inside. The tools felt right in his hands. It felt right to create something that would heal people. Spark jostled around on his shoulder and then leaped onto the counter, watching with interest.

"Not so hard," Thad said. "The pestle will do most of the work for you."

Gage lightened the pressure. Glancing at the ingredients spread across the counter, he found the elusive botila flower, which would give this particular disinfectant powerful numbing properties. He reached for the blossom, but Thad's hand shot out and caught his.

"What are you planning to do with that?" Thad asked.

"The petals add a numbing effect to the salve," Gage said, but his voice dwindled into a meek whisper. "Right?"

One corner of Thad's mouth lifted into a smile. "I knew that, but I'm surprised you did." He released Gage's hand and nodded. "Go ahead."

Gage tossed the crumbling red petals into the mortar and crushed everything together.

"You're a natural at this." Thad rubbed his scruffy beard.

Warmth bloomed inside Gage. This was the second time he'd heard those words since yesterday. No one had ever talked to him like that before.

"Thanks," he said. "I really like doing this."

"Want to make a few others?" Thad showed Gage a piece of paper listing several medicines and quantities.

"Sure." Gage finished his current concoction and dumped it into an empty jar. He'd add cream to finish the ointment later. Taking the list, he inspected the five different medicines.

"Will you have any trouble with these?" Thad asked.

"I don't think so. I know what they are."

"Ingredients are up here." Thad opened a cupboard above the counter to reveal containers of various sizes. Raising an eyebrow, he added, "If you don't mind, I'm going to finish a few other tasks around the clinic."

Gage's heart stuttered in surprise, but he said, "I can handle it."

Thad nodded and left him to his work. Stunned, Gage watched him go. Thad trusted him, and not with something trivial, but with medicines that impacted people's lives. Then again, most of these medicines were hard to mess up. Still, no one had ever trusted Gage as long as he'd been alive. He blinked away the sting in his eyes and resumed his duties. After rinsing the mortar and pestle in a nearby washbasin, he began mixing the next salve.

Spark watched him work. *Happy?* Gage could practically hear the dragon pressing the word into his mind. He smiled. Yes, he was happy.

Thad moved the stools out of the main room of the clinic, gathered a basket of dirty linens, and carried them into a back room, never once looking back. Gage watched him over a half wall. Thad dumped the laundry into buckets of soapy water and then grabbed a basket of clean, wet laundry and headed outside. Through a window, Gage glimpsed him hanging garments on a line to dry.

Gage focused on creating the different medicines, crushing ingredients, adding creams and oils, and mixing everything together in tins and jars. When Thad finally returned, Gage had finished the list.

"Well done," Thad said. Something mischievous twinkled in his dark eyes. "Want a challenge?"

Gage smiled. "Sure!"

Thad scratched his beard before heading to a far cupboard and pulling out a wooden recipe box. Taking out a card, he handed it to Gage.

"Do you know this one?" he asked. When Gage shook his head, he continued. "Most of the ingredients are fairly common. I have them in my back storage area."

Gage read the list. He recognized every ingredient except one, which he pointed at. "I don't know this plant."

"It's a type of fern. It grows on a long white stem and has twelve white leaves with violet tips."

That sounded like a fern that grew in the forest near Talid, but something felt wrong about the whole situation. Thad had mentioned a challenge. Was this some sort of test? Gage wasn't sure what to make of it, but he wanted to figure it out on his own. Spark lunged onto his shoulder as he headed into the back room.

Shelves lined the walls, storing linens and rows upon rows of medicinal supplies. Gage found a rack of plants—both alive and dead—and several more cupboards of ingredients. He found the white plant hanging upside down to dry and reached to pluck a leaf. Then he stopped. This was identical to the plant in Talid, but something felt wrong. The santhem plant only had eight leaves.

Test? Spark impressed the word upon him.

"Test," Gage whispered, and then he frowned.

That little voice in his mind wasn't his own. Was Spark speaking to him? No. Elementals didn't gain their voices until they evolved into their second form. Spark shared his feelings, and Gage must have imagined words to go with them.

Shaking those thoughts away, Gage focused on puzzling out Thad's challenge. His eyes traveled the rack and landed on a white plant he'd missed in the back. It sat in a little pot of dirt and looked nearly identical to the fern from Talid, except it had twelve leaves. He plucked a few of the leaves, grabbed the rest of the necessary supplies, and returned to Thad.

"It's almost identical to the santhem fern," Gage said, holding up one of the leaves.

"Good eye." Thad patted him on the shoulder. "You *are* a natural at this. I know many healers my age who still can't tell the difference between those plants."

Brimming with pride, Gage unloaded his supplies onto the counter and went to work following his new instructions.

"Be careful with this one," Thad said. "If you mix it wrong, the tonic becomes lethal."

Gage dropped the pestle onto the counter with a loud clatter and looked at Thad in horror.

"Don't worry." Thad's eyes twinkled. "If you mix it wrong, I'll know. It goes from a pleasant-smelling green drink to a putrid brown sludge. But I don't think we'll have that problem."

He patted Gage's shoulder and went into the back. Gage watched him over the half wall, expecting Thad to check on his work. He didn't. Thad got up to his elbows in soap suds, scrubbing the laundry and ignoring Gage completely.

"He really trusts me," Gage whispered to Spark, who chirped and wagged his tail.

Gage smiled while he worked, and his happiness grew when the tonic remained perfectly green as he mixed it. He was pouring the finished product—still perfectly green—into a jar when a side door to the clinic opened. He glanced at the newcomer and then fumbled several times while trying to put the lid on the jar. Where he'd expected to see Alphen, he found a beautiful girl instead.

"Hey, Dad," she said, her focus on the door as she closed it behind her. She'd entered the kitchen and dining area of the building, which was connected to the clinic by an open doorway and another half wall. She carried a large brown package in one arm. "Rhoda's stall was open, so I grabbed some lunch for—" Her eyes finally found Gage, and she froze in the middle of the dining room, a bewildered look claiming her face. "You're not my dad."

18

THE HEALER'S DAUGHTER

Gage's mouth and tongue refused to work, and his cheeks burned as he stared at her. She was pretty. Like, Innaran pretty. She was older than him, but probably not by much. Her dark, red-purple hair tumbled over her shoulders in loose waves, framing her pale face and highlighting her turquoise eyes. She wore elegant clothes, including a purple jacket with a hood.

As Gage stared at her like a cotton-headed goat, Thad returned from the back, drying his hands on a towel.

"Welcome home, Nihsa," he said, tossing the towel on the counter. "I see you've met Gage."

"I know I asked you to hire some extra help around here, but he's a little young, isn't he?" Nihsa set the package on the dining table.

A twinge of disappointment cut through Gage, snapping him out of his stupor. She thought of him as a kid.

"He's a new student at the academy," Thad explained. "He hung around after class, so I put him to work. Don't let his age deceive you. He made some difficult medicines better than men my own age. He's a natural."

Gage's already warm cheeks burned hotter. He hastily returned to his work, spinning the lid on and tossing his instruments into the washbasin. He rinsed his hands and dried them on Thad's towel.

"You must be special, Gage," Nihsa said. "My dad doesn't give out compliments easily. Or ever, really."

"Oh, please." Thad snorted and headed into the dining room, pulling dishes out of the cupboards.

"Seriously, Dad. The last person you complimented was . . ." Nihsa furrowed her brow. Then she scowled at the floor. And shifted her weight.

Thad paused, his eyebrows furrowing to match hers.

She crossed her arms. "Hold on now. I'm still thinking."

Thad growled and rolled his eyes, setting out plates and silverware.

"He gives out compliments like gold." Nihsa winked at Gage. "Never."

"Oh, get off it," Thad muttered, unraveling the package Nihsa had brought and pulling out small containers of food. "I just don't lie. Honesty matters."

Nihsa flashed a smirk before extending her hand to Gage for a firm shake. "It's nice to meet you, Gage. I'm Nihsa. Thanks for helping my dad."

"No problem," Gage said. "I really like doing this sort of thing. It's been fun."

"And who is this?" Nihsa wagged a finger at Spark on Gage's shoulder.

"My void dragon, Nightspark. But I call him Spark," Gage said, forcing himself to answer despite the anxiety curling in his stomach.

"You're the void user Alphen brought back last night?" Her eyes widened.

"You know Alphen?" Gage asked. His comment made Nihsa's warm smile diminish. Not entirely, but a little.

"Of course I know him." A little too quickly, she added, "From the academy."

"Are you a student?"

Her smile strengthened. "Kind of. I'm a knight recruit."

"A knight recruit!" Gage's jaw dropped. As far as he knew, most people didn't become recruits until they were seventeen or older. "How old are you?"

"Sixteen. I'm young for a recruit, but I got an early start." Nihsa turned toward her father dishing food onto plates. "Because we were always around the Innara, I was exposed to a lot of their magic. I ended up summoning Mishu when I was younger than most students."

She pointed at an elemental Gage hadn't noticed. A water feline sat next to an empty food dish on a counter near the door. The elemental looked somewhat like a regular cat with extremely fluffy ears. Its sleek, dark fur shimmered in hues of blue, as did its sharp eyes. It stared at Nihsa, its tail twitching, and occasionally shot lethal glares at Thad as he pulled out more food.

"Your magic must be really strong," Gage said.

"Not strong enough. Yet, anyway," Nihsa replied. "I have to get better if I want to become one of King Fraylon's honor guard."

"You're going to join the king's honor guard?"

"Not if I can help it," Thad muttered, yanking out a chair at the table.

Nihsa squinted at him and opened her mouth to reply, but Mishu hissed and smacked its food bowl with a paw, sending it skittering across the counter.

"Pipe down, Mishu." Nihsa let out a sharp exhale and gave Gage a despondent look. "Don't mind her. She's a bear when she doesn't eat."

"Then it's a good thing it's time for lunch." Thad dumped some food into Mishu's bowl before taking a seat at the table. "Come sit, you two."

Nihsa headed to her seat, but Gage froze, staring at the three places at the table. Thad had already loaded the plates with food, including meat, veggies, rice, and strange fried logs. Everything smelled delicious, but he couldn't move. Not even when Nihsa sat and she and Thad looked at him expectantly, waiting for him to join them.

"Oh, uh . . . I probably shouldn't," he said, tugging on his tunic and then twisting his belt. "Alphen should be here soon to pick me up."

"He made you wait this long. Now he can wait for you." Thad gestured toward the chair next to him. "Sit."

"But . . ." Gage squirmed. He didn't want to be a bother.

"You won't get anything from the dining hall as delicious as ol' Rhoda's cooking," Thad said.

"Besides, you helped my dad today," Nihsa added. "Lunch is the least we can offer."

Gage opened his mouth to protest but shut it without saying anything. He didn't know how to handle situations like this, but the most appropriate response was probably to accept their offer. With a slight nod, he joined them at the table. Warmth rushed through him, fluttering in his chest. Before eating dinner with Alphen last night, he'd never shared a meal with anyone like this—like a family.

None of the food on his plate looked familiar, but it smelled delicious. Spark seemed to agree. He slowly slid down Gage's arm, trying to be stealthy, and then lunged onto the table, making the silverware clatter. The dragon snatched the two fried logs from Gage's plate, leapt to the floor, and vanished behind the leg of an exam table. Gage sighed.

"Dragons," Thad muttered, placing two more logs onto Gage's plate. "Can't have you miss out on these. Rhoda's pork rolls are the best."

"Thanks." Gage mimicked Thad by dipping the pork roll into an orange sauce and taking a bite. The combination of sweet and salty was absolute perfection.

"What do you think of Runadel and the academy so far?" Nihsa asked between bites.

"I really like it." Gage tried a scoop of meat, veggies, and rice. Also delicious. "I love seeing all the elementals."

"Have you made any new friends?"

Gage offered a noncommittal shrug.

"What's wrong?" Nihsa asked.

Gage stirred the food on his plate. "The other students don't trust me. Because of my void magic."

"That's ridiculous." Nihsa scowled.

Gage shrugged again. When he'd imagined having magic, it looked a lot different than this. He'd hoped to escape Talid and find a place where people didn't consider him cursed, but nothing had changed.

"They refused to sit with me at dinner," he said. "Only Alphen ate with me last night."

"People fear the old stories," Thad said. "You'll just have to prove them wrong."

Gage poked at his veggies.

"I'm sure it'll just take time for them to warm up to you," Nihsa said, managing a weak smile.

"Not like I'll spend much time with them outside of class," Gage muttered.

"You'll see them plenty in the dorms."

"I'm not staying in the dorms."

"Why not?"

"Because of my magic. It's . . ." Gage recalled the reason he'd been separated from everyone in the first place. He flew out of his chair, bumping the table and clattering the dishes. "My magic is dangerous. I should go."

Nihsa and Thad stared at him.

"My magic destroys magic," Gage said. "I'm probably hurting your magic just by being here."

"That's what the crystals are for," Thad replied.

He waved toward a crystal in a wooden frame on the wall. It looked similar to the rock Gage had broken in Talid, but smoother. Gage noticed similar crystals in frames throughout the room. They blended in so well he hadn't noticed them.

"The Innarans keep crystals around their cities to strengthen everyone's magic," Thad explained. "You might destroy some of our magic, but these crystals should repair the damage easily enough."

"But you needed Alphen's help healing Spark last night," Gage said.

"Because I was healing the dragon directly. His body destroyed the magic I put into him, so the boy had to add his magic to overpower him. The same would be true if I tried to heal you," Thad said. "But that's different than simply having void magic in the area. You're not doing anything negative to us just by being here. Nothing an Innaran crystal can't resolve."

"Those crystals are at the academy too?" Gage frowned. He shouldn't need to stay away from the other students, then.

"Yes, but Nihsa and I have stronger magic than your peers," Thad explained. "Your influence won't impact us the same as inexperienced magic users."

That made sense, although Gage wasn't sure how much they understood about void magic. Nevertheless, he slipped back into his seat and took a few more bites of his meal.

"They have you in the Innaran wing, I imagine?" Nihsa asked. When Gage nodded, she scrunched her brow. "There aren't many students your age there."

Gage shrugged. "Alphen is nearby."

"Even worse," Nihsa muttered. Whipping her napkin next to her plate, she stood, slapped her hands onto the table, and looked fiercely at her father. "He should stay here with us."

19

SUNLIT HOME

"What?" Gage and Thad said in unison.

"Think about it, Dad. It's perfect." Nihsa's face lit up. "You've been looking for help around here—"

"No, *you've* been looking for help around here."

"You *need* help around here," she continued, ignoring the withering look he gave her. "And Gage said it himself—he loves this sort of thing. He could live here and work for you in his spare time, and then he won't have to stay in the Innaran wing. You know the other students will treat him worse if they think he's getting special treatment."

"And living here wouldn't be special treatment?" Thad asked.

"Not if they know he's working." Nihsa paced in the dining room, gesturing with her hands as she spoke. "Most students with family in Runadel live and do chores at home. It's perfectly normal."

"I don't want to be a bother," Gage murmured.

"You wouldn't be. My dad really does need help around here." She crossed her arms and shot Thad a pointed look. "He's not as young as he thinks he is—"

"Hey, now." Thad wiped his mouth and tossed his napkin onto his empty plate.

"His old injury makes it hard for him to take care of everything, and I'm too busy at the academy to help like I used to. This could actually work great," Nihsa said.

Gage glanced at Thad, who offered a nod and a slight shrug.

Nihsa's eyes lit up, and she snapped her fingers. "He can stay in Alphen's old room." She marched through the kitchen and down a hall toward the back of the building. "Gage, come see."

Alphen's room? Gage frowned, but he didn't have time to ask about it. Instead, he hurried after Nihsa. Spark followed with scurrying little footsteps. Thad came last, plodding along with far less enthusiasm. They reached a large sitting area and another hall with various wooden doors. Nihsa opened one to reveal a bedroom on the other side.

The room held a snug bed with a colorful blanket and fluffy pillows, a wooden wardrobe, dresser, and bookshelf, and an enormous window that let in huge sunbeams. Gage warmed at the sight of the window. Spark scrambled onto the bed and stretched himself out in the sunlight, and it took everything in Gage not to join him.

"No one is using it now," Nihsa said, lifting her eyebrows at the room and then at Thad, who leaned in the doorway with his arms crossed.

"Alphen used to live here?" Gage asked.

"More often than not," Thad said.

"You know this is a good idea," Nihsa told Thad, and then added to Gage, "Welcome home." With that, she flipped her hair over her shoulder and tromped out of the room like she'd won an argument, her footsteps receding down the hall.

Gage searched the room. If Alphen had lived here, little remained of him. A few trinkets sat on the dresser, as did a very dead houseplant in old, crusty dirt.

Spark curled into a ball in his patch of sunlight and closed his eyes, and Gage sensed absolute peace from the dragon. He prodded the nearby dresser and glanced at Thad, who remained in the doorway, watching him with dark, knowing eyes.

"I'm fine with it," Thad said, "but don't let her bully you into a decision."

Gage looked around again. Thad's clinic felt like *home*, like the place Gage had wanted his entire life. A bedroom with a window. A table where he could eat with a family. A clinic where he could heal. Of course he wanted it. Still, he couldn't ask Thad to do this for him. He barely knew these people. His heart sank at the realization, and his shoulders sank with it.

"Lad, I really could use help around here," Thad said. He threw in a shrug. "I'm old and lame, after all."

Gage swallowed hard. His heart screamed to stay, but his mind told him to run.

Stay, Spark said, or felt, or whatever. The little creature opened an eye to peer at Gage before yawning and curling up again. Comfort and peace came from Spark—or were those Gage's feelings?

"Honesty is important," Thad said softly. "What do you want to do, lad?"

When Gage met his eyes and found only welcoming acceptance, he said, "I want to stay."

Thad grinned under his scruffy beard. "Then the room is yours. Welcome home."

He limped down the hall toward the clinic, leaving Gage alone with Spark in the room. In *his* room. Gage's heart fluttered. Home. He'd never used that word to describe his house in Talid, but here with Thad, Nihsa, and Spark, in this little room with its sunny window, the word fit. Bubbling with happiness, Gage marched to the bed.

"Move over, you cow," he said to the dragon.

He shoved Spark to the other side of the bed, earning an overdramatic flail from the void dragon. Gage flopped into the sun, appreciating the bounce of the bed and the fluff of the pillows. Spark scowled, flicked his tongue, and then sprawled out beside him.

20

WINDOW PROBLEMS

From his comfy position on the bed, Gage peered at the trinkets on the dresser. Next to two metal bookends stood a small wooden carving of a dragon—except the dragon was short, fat, and covered in spikes. Frowning, Gage slid to his feet and grabbed the carving, inspecting it. He'd never seen anything like it.

Curious, he brought it into the main clinic to ask about it. Spark scrambled after him, catching his pant leg and climbing up his clothes to reach his shoulder. Thad carried laundry in from outside and put clean gowns and sheets into a storage cabinet. Nihsa mashed the leftover food together and dumped it into a dish on the counter behind Gromlin's perch.

"Looks like Alphen is late, as usual," she said to Gage. "I'm going to do dishes, and then we can head back to the academy together."

"Okay. Thanks." Gage couldn't help the joyous flutter in his belly.

She carried the dishes into the back room, where she dunked them into a washbasin and scrubbed them, blowing aside wisps of hair that fell into her face. Thad returned to gather up the packaging from their lunch.

"Do you know what this is?" Gage held out the sculpture before Thad got carried away with his task.

Thad wiped his hands on his apron and took the item. "Something the boy sculpted with his magic."

"The boy?" Gage asked.

"Alphen," Nihsa said from the other room.

So Alphen really had stayed in that bedroom. Gage considered asking why, but Thad sank into a chair at the table and unleashed a long sigh. He turned the sculpture over in his hands.

"What's it supposed to be?" Gage asked.

"Something he used to dream about. The boy had terrible nightmares," Thad muttered.

Gage straightened. Nightmares? Alphen had them too?

"Rather than bothering us," Thad continued, "he stayed in his room and created these things. He had a basket full of them, but he took them with him when he left." He set the sculpture on the table and shifted it from side to side. "I found this one behind a dresser while I was cleaning." Sadness—and maybe longing—shadowed Thad's eyes.

"Alphen really used to live here?" Gage asked.

"For nearly a decade."

"Why?"

Thad's dark eyes never left the sculpture. "He was a frail kid. Often fell ill with high fevers, shaking chills, terrible pain. It was awful. There's nothing worse than seeing a child so near to death."

"What was wrong with him?"

Thad shrugged. "I'm not positive. Best I could tell, his magic became imbalanced and caused a reaction in his body. I used to give him a potion made of Innaran Sunbursts. It's a flower that provides magic when ingested. It helped him some, but not a lot."

"He doesn't seem sickly now."

"About a year ago, everything changed. *He* changed. Didn't get sick anymore, and he gathered his things and moved out." Thad tapped the sculpture on the table and sighed. "I suppose I ought to get rid of this."

Sadness lingered in his eyes, some kind of hurt Gage didn't understand. But Thad didn't say more, and Gage didn't want to pry.

"Can I keep it?" Gage asked. "I think it's pretty neat."

Thad glanced at the sculpture before passing it to Gage. "Not much I can do with it. It's yours."

Gage smiled at the spiky dragon. Alphen had turned his nightmares into a creative endeavor. Maybe Gage could do the same rather than being miserable every night.

Nihsa returned to the room, drying her hands on a towel. "Ready to go, Gage?"

"Sure. Let me put this back." He wagged the sculpture in the air and hustled to his bedroom, where he set the wooden critter on the dresser.

Knocking echoed down the hallway as he returned to the main clinic. Nihsa opened the front door, revealing Alphen on the other side.

The Innaran youth offered a casual smile. "Hey, Nihsa. I'm here for—"

She slammed the door in his face. Gage stared in disbelief as she marched in the other direction.

"We'll go out in a minute," she said curtly, fiery hostility in her eyes.

"He's here for me." Gage laughed awkwardly and opened the door, finding a perplexed Alphen on the other side. "Hey, Alphen."

"Hey—"

Thad nudged Gage aside, locked eyes with Alphen, and slammed the door in his face, same as Nihsa. Then he casually limped away. Tension thickened the air, but Gage laughed anyway. Awkwardly, because he didn't know whether to be nervous or amused. Clearly he was missing something.

Nihsa and Thad occupied themselves with other things, Nihsa tidying up the placemats on the table and Thad moving supplies from the counter to the cupboard. One of the clinic windows opened with a resounding crack. Alphen climbed inside, rolled off the counter onto his feet, and shut the window behind him. Mishu hissed from nearby, as he'd practically rolled over her empty food dish. Thad stopped to stare at him before casting his eyes to the ceiling.

"I think something is wrong with your door." Alphen straightened his clothes.

"The window is the problem," Thad muttered. "I knew I should have nailed it shut."

Gage chewed his lip, trying not to laugh. He settled on being amused despite the tension.

"We should head back to the academy," Alphen said to Gage, ignoring the hostility blanketing the room. "Your next class starts soon."

"Gage is going back with me." Nihsa marched between Alphen and Gage as she made for the door. She flipped her hair and almost smacked Alphen in the face, though he deftly dodged. She looked at Gage, replacing her harsh scowl with a warm smile. "Mishu can take us. You don't need a light dragon to get around the city."

Alphen scoffed. "Please. Nothing beats flying with a dragon. He's sticking with me. Right, Gage?" He looked at Gage expectantly. So did Nihsa.

Gage choked on a breath, feeling caught in the middle of a fight he knew nothing about. Nihsa lifted her eyebrows at him in suggestion and sashayed out the door, pausing only long enough for Mishu to scamper out ahead of her. Alphen stared at her. So did Gage.

"No offense," Gage whispered, leaning closer to Alphen, "but I'm going with the pretty girl." At that, he headed for the door.

"Traitor," Alphen muttered.

Gage shrugged and offered an apologetic smile. He hurried after Nihsa, but a surprised yelp and the shuffling of feet drew his attention behind him.

"Out." Thad marched Alphen outside, gave him a not-so-gentle shove onto the street, and then slammed the door and locked it behind him.

Alphen dusted off his clothes and scowled.

Something had definitely happened between Alphen, Nihsa, and Thad. Their strange behavior made Gage more than a little curious, but he'd worry about that later, when he knew them better.

He hurried down the street to join Nihsa, who stood next to Mishu now in her second form. Gage took in the full view of the fluffy housecat turned lethal hunter. Mishu appeared as a lynx—save her long tail. Her fur rippled like ocean waves, and her eyes twinkled like sunlight on water.

Nihsa gripped Mishu's fur and swung onto her back. She offered Gage a hand. "Hop on."

Gage allowed her to pull him onto the feline's back. He swung a leg over the creature and immediately wobbled.

"What do I hold?" Gage asked.

"Her fur," she replied, flashing a smile over her shoulder. "Mishu is tough and doesn't mind. You can hold onto me, too, if that's easier."

Gage's face burned at the idea of putting his arms around her waist, so he gripped handfuls of Mishu's fur instead. He yelped as the water feline sprang onto the roof of a nearby building. After another leap, he was forced to wrap both arms around Nihsa to keep from flying away. Mishu jumped from roof to roof with ease.

"Is this safe for the buildings?" Gage cried, expecting the houses to crumble under Mishu's weight.

"Every building in Runadel is built with dragons in mind. They can handle it," Nihsa said.

As Mishu bounded across the city, a familiar white dragon swooped around them. Alphen shot them a smug grin and a two-fingered salute before Rhemi darted away with him toward the academy. Mishu hissed, her fur fluffing across her back.

"That man." Nihsa growled and leaned forward, her brow furrowed in concentration. "Hold on, Gage. Mishu, you know what to do. Let's leave those two in the dust!"

Mishu lunged from house to house, barely letting her paws touch down between jumps. Nihsa had no trouble hanging on, but Gage shrieked and clung to Nihsa for dear life as they flew across the city to the academy.

21

MAGIC LESSONS

Alphen and Rhemi won the race to the academy, greeting them with smug grins in the main courtyard. Nihsa held the heels of her hands together in front of her and clapped in a quick motion—which Gage assumed was a rude gesture—before dragging Gage to his next class. She kindly informed him that she would move his belongings to the clinic and pick him up later so they could walk home together.

Home. The word filled Gage with warm flutters. Brimming with happiness, he pushed through the double doors into his next classroom.

The class took place in a spacious room with a dozen long tables facing the front, with four or five stools clustered at each table. Most of the stools were occupied, but Gage found an empty seat in back—next to Eddly, naturally. Gage snuck up on him and snatched the stool aside before the burly kid could do anything to it. Eddly scowled as Gage moved it to the other end of the table.

Lady Halayna entered through a door at the front of the room right as the academy bell rang. She wore less jewelry than the night before but looked no less royal.

"Hello, everyone." She folded her hands in front of her, offering a warm smile. "For those who missed dinner last night, allow me to introduce myself. I am Halayna Lightgard, and I will be teaching this class. Together, we will learn about elementals and their magic, and you will strive to summon your own elemental by the time the year ends."

The inevitable wave of eyes swept in Gage's direction, but he ignored them. Spark slithered down his arm and sat on the table, narrowing his eyes at the students.

"I would like to begin with a brief history of magic." Lady Halayna stepped over to a large illustration on the wall, which showed the Innarans riding down on light dragons and gifting magic to the world. "All magic is Innaran magic, which is considered the high magic of our world. It gave birth to the four lesser magics, known as low magic."

Eddly raised his hand. Apparently, he'd learned his lesson after dealing with Thad.

"Yes, child?" Lady Halayna asked.

"Void magic isn't Innaran magic," he said, shooting Gage a disgusted look.

Gage passed the bulky boy a sideways glare but otherwise didn't bother responding. He wasn't worth his time.

Lady Halayna offered Eddly a patient smile. "You are correct. Void magic is separate from Innaran magic and the lesser magic types." She dipped her head toward Gage. "I forgot we have a void user in our presence after all these years. Most void users vanished centuries ago."

"Yeah, because the Innara had to kill them all," Eddly muttered, only loud enough for Gage to hear.

Gage ground his teeth but refused to reply. Spark hissed at Eddly until Gage poked the dragon in the side. If Lady Halayna heard Eddly's snide remark, she ignored it.

"Our studies will need to adapt to this change," she said. "Allow me to correct myself. Innaran and void magics have existed in conflict with each other since the dawn of time. One gives, the other takes. One creates, the other destroys. Both are immensely powerful." She gestured toward the illustration of the Innarans creating their world. "As far as the history of this world is concerned, void users have little influence here. I hope our young void user will understand why we tailor our classes toward the Innaran and low magics that exist in abundance throughout our world."

Gage nodded. It didn't make sense to study void magic in class if he was the only void user at the academy—and in the world.

"In our ancient past," Lady Halayna said while looking at the illustration behind her, "the Innarans came to this world and spread their light across the land. Life flourished, and humanity received the gift of the four types of low magic:

fire, water, wind, and earth. Each of you underwent a test when you arrived at the academy to determine your magic type. You will use that knowledge to aid in summoning your elementals."

A girl's hand flew up.

"Yes, child?"

"Can we summon our elementals now?" The girl practically bounced in her seat.

Several students squirmed in anticipation.

Lady Halayna let out a tinkling laugh. "You will summon within this year, I should hope. But the timing will depend on your inherent magical strength." She moved to an illustration of the four elementals in their first forms. "Your elementals are a part of you, and they await the opportune moment to be born from your magic. You will only be able to summon them when your magic greatly increases. Innarans usually develop enough magical strength to summon their dragons around the age of ten. Users of low magic typically increase in magical strength around the age of twelve, which is why we test children at that age. However, your magic alone will not be enough to summon your elementals. Thus we Innarans must expose you to our magic."

"Gage summoned a dragon without Innaran magic," a girl commented. Again, a wave of eyes slithered in Gage's direction.

Did he hear a hint of jealousy in her voice? He curled an arm around Spark and tugged the dragon closer.

"Like Innarans," Lady Halayna said, "void users are able to summon their own dragons."

"So Gage has more magic than us?" asked a boy.

Gage ducked his head, his cheeks burning. Eddly snorted and rolled his eyes.

"Yes, he does," Lady Halayna said quietly, which only made Gage shrivel up further. "Gage will grow powerful, but so will the rest of you with enough time and study. Focus on improving your own abilities, and do not envy that which does not belong to you."

The other students shifted in their seats, re-centering themselves toward the front of the classroom. Gage sank anyway, a shroud of discouragement smothering his heart. The other kids were jealous. No wonder they hated him. Even if he proved he wasn't evil, they'd probably still dislike him.

"I am giving each of you an Innaran crystal to aid in your studies. The crystal is yours to keep, and you should carry it at all times." Lady Halayna lifted a wooden box off a table and walked it down the aisle. She handed a grape-sized crystal to each student. "For the remainder of this class, you will hold this crystal and attempt to reach its magic with your mind. I will walk around and aid you individually as you practice." She gave Eddly a crystal but stopped at Gage. "I cannot give you a crystal, for obvious reasons."

Gage's face burned as Eddly and the rest of the class stared at him—again. They hadn't witnessed what he'd done to the crystal in Talid, but since everyone knew about him, he assumed rumors had preceded his arrival. Lady Halayna returned the box to its table and fetched a book off one of several bookshelves against the wall. She laid it before Gage.

"For this lesson," she said, "I want you to read about elementals in greater detail. In this, you will be ahead of your peers, but it also places you at a disadvantage. They will learn how to control Innaran magic with great accuracy. Unfortunately, I cannot teach you to control your magic in the same way."

"It's okay," Gage said. "Thank you."

Lady Halayna made her way through the class, talking to each student, holding their hands, and guiding them with her magic. White lights flashed throughout the room as the students touched the stones, and the light increased tenfold whenever Lady Halayna joined her magic with theirs.

Gage watched enviously as each student held Lady Halayna's hand. Eddly rolled his crystal on the table and wiggled his eyebrows at Gage like the obnoxious blob he was. Gage considered grabbing his crystal and breaking it with his void magic, but that would only get him in trouble. And Eddly probably wouldn't even care.

Instead, Gage opened the book, and he and his void dragon peered at the pages. Colored illustrations showed light dragons and the four low elementals. The early chapters spoke of summoning, repeating what Lady Halayna had said, while the later chapters spoke of first and second forms, things Gage already knew about.

While interesting, the book didn't teach him anything about void dragons or his own magic. He numbly flipped through several more sections, halting at some additional illustrations of light dragons—only these were bigger, sleeker, and far more majestic.

Light dragons had a third evolution. Impossible. Gage had never heard of such a thing. He skimmed the text. A third evolution hadn't been recorded in written history, but legends suggested that the first Innarans in the world had third-form light dragons. Their overwhelming strength allowed them to shape the world and gift magic to everyone.

Gage glanced at Lady Halayna. Maybe some Innarans had third-form dragons in secret. But no. If they had access to that kind of power, they'd have already won the war against the Vaskr.

Spark scrutinized the evolved light dragons before looking up at Gage.

If you could evolve twice, that'd be awesome, Gage said in his mind, hoping his dragon could hear him.

Spark wagged his tail like he *had* heard him—and then chewed on the corner of the book, gnawing off little scraps of paper and leather. Gage sighed.

22

AN INNARAN PRINCE

"I will see you later this week for a class on defensive magic," Lady Halayna said to dismiss them after the bell rang. "Take care until then."

Gage moved his stool back to its original position at the table, ignoring Eddly's scowl.

"Gage," Lady Halayna called. "If you would stay a moment, I would speak with you."

Several kids looked at him in envy as they exited, and Eddly slammed his stool against the table before storming out. Gage resisted an eye roll. The soft rustle of Lady Halayna's robes drew his attention back toward her. The princess shuffled down the aisle to meet him, but when Alphen entered the room, she halted.

"One moment, please," she said to Gage, and then she gestured for Alphen to join her.

Alphen lingered near the door, furrowing his brow. Finally, he sighed and headed over to her. They whispered so Gage couldn't hear what they were saying, but he made his way around the room and pushed in all the stools while watching them out of the corner of his eye. Spark stared at them from his shoulder.

Lady Halayna remained calm throughout their conversation, but Alphen crossed his arms and shifted his weight from leg to leg like he was ready to bolt. Lady Halayna maintained a respectful demeanor, but Alphen's face twisted into a dark scowl. And then the princess glanced at Gage, which only darkened Alphen's expression.

Gage's heart skipped a beat. Were they talking about him?

Alphen said something heatedly, loud enough for Gage to hear the tone but not the words. Lady Halayna nodded, and Alphen spun on his heel and marched toward the exit.

"I'll wait for you in the hall," he whispered to Gage as he passed.

Lady Halayna watched Alphen depart before joining Gage near a back table. "Thank you for staying, Gage. I wanted to apologize."

"For what?" he asked.

"I know so little about void magic, and I fear I am an insufficient teacher for you."

"It's okay. I know my magic is unique. That's not your fault. Besides, I like learning about all types of magic."

A genuine smile spread across Lady Halayna's face. "You are wise for your age."

Gage's cheeks burned, and his heart melted at her praise. She was so pretty.

"Nevertheless," she said, "I will arrange for you to have special lessons with someone who can aid you better than I."

"Will I get to stay in this class?"

"Of course." Her eyes glowed with warmth. "This class will still teach you about magic, even if not your own."

"Good." Gage grinned. Because he absolutely wanted to stay in class with the pretty princess. Even if Eddly was there.

"I admit this is not the only reason I pulled you aside." Lady Halayna lightly took his arm and pulled him deeper into the classroom, away from the doors. Gage tried not to pay too much attention to her fingers over his sleeve, but her warmth was distracting. "I see you are growing attached to my brother."

Gage frowned in confusion. He knew King Fraylon had sons, but he could only recall the one who led the fight against the Vaskr.

"Your brother at war?"

"No, dear child. Alphen."

Gage continued to stare at her. "Alphen . . . is your brother?"

"He did not tell you." She exhaled slowly. "I cannot say I am surprised. Alphen does not get along well with our family. But yes, he is the youngest child of our father, Fraylon."

"Alphen is an Innaran prince?" Gage couldn't think clearly enough to ask anything else.

"Yes." Lady Halayna's lips twitched into a tiny smile.

Gage wobbled. He'd been discovered by an Innaran princess and rescued by an Innaran prince. And he'd been spending time with that prince like a friend, riding his dragon and sitting with him at dinner. Had he been rude? Behaved poorly? Then Gage's mind went back to Alphen shoving him through a window. And climbing through said window shortly thereafter. His confusion intensified.

"Are you sure he's a prince?" he asked.

Her smile brightened. "My brother does not behave like a prince, does he?"

"Not at all." Gage laughed.

"Gage, I must caution you about becoming close with Alphen," Lady Halayna said, now with a harsh edge to her otherwise soft voice. "He straddles the line between duty and anarchy. He is rebellious by nature against my father, this academy, and the Innaran kingdom. I fear he will lead you astray."

"I don't understand."

Once again, the princess placed her hand on his arm. "You are in a unique position, one in which you will be unfairly judged by those around you. As the sole void user, you have a responsibility to represent yourself, your dragon, and your magic well. Alphen may cause you to tarnish your name." She gripped his arm, her slender eyebrows furrowing. "Learn what you can from him, but do not allow him close to you. Do not trust him as you would others in this academy. He will only cause you grief in the end."

She let her hand fall away from his arm, and Gage felt a chill in the absence of her touch. She searched his eyes, gave a stern nod, and then exited through the door at the front of the class. She left him with a strange storm raging in his chest.

Alphen, dangerous? Gage couldn't believe that. He'd been a little weird, and maybe a bit of a rule breaker, but that didn't seem terribly rebellious. Alphen had been the first person to show him kindness and had stood up for him when others ridiculed his magic and his dragon. Even Lady Halayna hadn't done that.

When Gage met Spark's gaze, the dragon only shrugged. Gage sighed, not sure what to make of the conversation. Shuffling toward the exit, he slowed when noisy bickering reached his ears. He stepped into the hall to find Alphen and Nihsa exchanging heated words. Mishu and Rhemi sat on the floor, both scowling at their human partners.

"You can't just insert yourself into any situation you please," Alphen said to Nihsa.

"Oh, you're one to lecture me on propriety." Nihsa snorted, setting her hands on her hips. "You climb through people's windows to bypass locked doors."

"I wouldn't have to climb through windows if people would just let me in, now would I?"

"That's called breaking into someone's home."

"Not always. Today, I broke into the clinic." Alphen lifted his nose at her. "It's technically a public facility. What if I'd been dying?"

"Then you would have died on the doorstep and my dad would have dealt with your body. Good riddance."

Alphen clasped a fistful of fabric over his chest. "Ouch, Nihsa. That hurts my heart."

"You don't have a heart."

"Are you two dating?" Gage asked.

Alphen and Nihsa scowled at him in perfect harmony. Gage almost laughed, but he coughed into his fist instead and looked away. The elementals at his feet tittered over his comment, so at least someone was amused.

"Oh, pipe down over there, you miserable potatoes," Alphen snapped, which only made them cackle harder.

"Don't insult them," Nihsa snapped back. "Besides, Gage asked a valid question. Why don't you answer him?"

Alphen's eyebrow twitched. "Because it's irrelevant. As of right now—"

"We *were* dating," Nihsa said over him. "In fact, we were betrothed. Until this swine of a man lost his mind and broke up with me for no reason."

"Uh, correction. You broke up with me." Alphen stuck up a finger like he was making a grand point. "I seem to recall you slamming a door in my face—"

"Yeah, after you turned into a raging lunatic." Nihsa slapped his hand down. "And for the record, my father slammed that door in your face. I was too busy crying because of everything you'd said and done."

"Uh, guys?" Gage's heart skipped several unpleasant beats. He'd been joking about them dating. Mostly. He definitely hadn't planned on unleashing all these dirty secrets.

Alphen and Nihsa looked at him, their eyes widening as they realized he was still there. Alphen sighed and swept a hand through his hair. Nihsa huffed and crossed her arms, but the red heat in her cheeks faded, as did the vengeful fire in her eyes.

"So no, we're not dating," Nihsa said to Gage. "We were. Alphen messed it up by being a jerk." Flinging her hair over her shoulder, she shot Alphen one last glare. "It was his loss. I dodged an arrow by not getting stuck with this pig-headed boar for the rest of my life. *Good riddance.*"

"Good riddance, indeed." Alphen snorted and rolled his eyes.

The two glowered at each other, but Gage noticed something lurking in their eyes. Grief, and maybe a hint of longing, though he couldn't be sure. He chewed back the desire to ask for more details about what happened between them. He'd save that for when he knew them better.

Alphen and Nihsa turned on him at the same time and said, "Let's go, Gage." Then they glared at each other again.

"What do you mean, 'Let's go'? He's coming with me," Alphen said.

"Why do you think I'm here?" Nihsa grinned smugly. "I came to pick Gage up so I could walk him home. Starting now, he's living at the clinic with us."

"What?" Alphen looked at Gage in shock.

Gage ducked his head and avoided eye contact.

"I just had his things moved to the clinic," Nihsa said. "My dad filed the paperwork with the academy to take on Gage's guardianship."

"Why?" Alphen asked.

"Because of the awful circumstances you put him in." Nihsa poked Alphen's chest. "The Innaran wing? Really? The whole point of the academy is to grow alongside your peers."

"He doesn't have any peers at the clinic," Alphen stated.

"No, but he'll associate with a lot of people at the clinic, including magic users from the academy. It'll be much better for him than being stuck with stuffy old Innarans."

"I'm in that wing."

Nihsa deadpan stared at him. "All the more reason he needs to get out of there."

Alphen sighed and faced Gage. Hurt lingered behind his eyes. "Are you okay with this?"

Gage withered and died a little on the inside. "I don't dislike living at the academy," he said, although he did dislike eating alone, being treated like an outcast, and not having a window. "But I really like helping at the clinic. I'm good at that sort of stuff."

Alphen frowned.

"Let's go, Gage. We can help my dad with a few things before dinner." Nihsa strolled down the hall, Mishu falling in step behind her.

Alphen crossed his arms and watched her go. Looked her over from top to bottom. Once again, Gage caught a flash of longing behind his eyes, but it was there and gone so fast he didn't know what to make of it.

"Traitor," Alphen muttered to Gage, though without animosity.

Gage sputtered, unable to think of a response. His cheeks burned.

Alphen feigned a pout. "Let's go, Rhemi. I can see when I'm not wanted."

"Clearly not," Nihsa shouted from farther down the hall, "or you wouldn't show up at my house so often."

Alphen put the heels of his hands together and clapped in a quick, fluid motion—the same gesture Nihsa had done earlier. She choked out an exasperated sound and mimicked the motion right back at him.

Alphen cast her and Gage a bitter scowl and then turned to walk away. Gage thought he glimpsed something more on his face—something decidedly *not* bitter. A twinkle in his eye, maybe, or the briefest twitch of a smile. But before he could get a better look, Alphen disappeared around a corner. Rhemi zoomed after him.

What was that about? Alphen had seemed genuinely hurt by Gage staying at the clinic but appeared rather pleased at the end.

But more important than anything else—what did that weird clapping gesture mean?

23

KICK YOUR TEACHER

Gage had another nightmare that night, slept in late, and woke up to Thad dragging him out of bed by his ear. He'd slept through the morning bells again. Nihsa shoved a fruit muffin at him and rushed him out the door. They arrived at an outdoor area of the academy filled with various training grounds.

"I need you to do me a favor, Gage," Nihsa said as she marched down the walkway of colonnades.

"Okay?"

"Torment the teacher in your next class."

"Huh?"

"Beat him up and torture him. Be as annoying as possible," she stated. "You have my permission to throw him on the ground and kick him."

Gage frowned. "Do you hate everyone in this academy?"

"Only some people." She grinned, patted him on the back, and shoved him the rest of the way down the corridor. "Good luck!"

Nihsa departed, and Gage headed to his classroom—a huge training ground with no ceiling. Weapon and armor racks lined the stone walls. Most of the other students were already there, looking around in confusion because they had nowhere to sit. The final bell rang to announce the start of class.

The students milled about until another pair of footsteps drew their attention to the door. Gage expected their teacher to enter, but Alphen arrived instead with a stool tucked under his arm. He casually strolled to the back wall, set down his stool, and perched on its edge.

"Um, Lord Alphen?" a girl said.

"Alphen is fine." He leaned the stool back on two legs.

"Who is our teacher?" asked a boy.

Alphen looked around and then dropped the stool onto all four legs. His eyebrows arched under his hair. Rising, he strode toward the front of the room.

"I guess that's me, huh?" he muttered.

Everyone gawped.

"You?" Gage exclaimed. "You're our teacher?"

Alphen snorted. "I know. I'm surprised too."

"How old are you?" Gage asked.

"Seventeen."

"You're not old enough to be a teacher," a girl said.

"Teacher is putting it loosely. I'm here to beat on you until you learn how to stop me." He grinned, an evil gleam in his eyes. "Welcome to close-combat training. I'm going to teach you how to stay alive." He plucked two wooden practice swords off a rack and meandered among the gathered students. "Let's start with a little preview, shall we? I need a volunteer."

He twirled a sword with a single hand, flipping it in the air, around his wrist, and back into his grasp with expert ease. Several students visibly paled, and a handful stepped away from him. Which didn't matter anyway, because Alphen's eyes locked on Gage.

"Gage, how about you?" He had the audacity to grin.

Gage's stomach sank to the floor. He stared in wide-eyed horror as Rhemi fled from Alphen's shoulder to the nearest weapon rack. Gage took her desperate escape as a bad sign and gulped down the lump in his throat.

"Um, no thanks," he said.

"Way to take one for the team, kid." Alphen tossed Gage one of the wooden swords.

Several students snickered.

Gage scowled, leaned closer, and whispered, "Are you punishing me for yesterday?"

"What?" Alphen dropped his jaw in shock. "Of course not!"

Rhemi nodded violently in the background.

Gage scowled at her and then at Alphen. "You're a terrible grown-up," he muttered.

"Being an adult is overrated, so I take that as a compliment." Alphen poked Spark with his training sword. "Sparky, you might want to get out of the way."

"Don't leave me," Gage whispered to the void dragon.

Spark didn't even look back as he lunged off Gage's shoulder and glided over to join Rhemi. When Gage shot him an accusing glare, the dragon gave a tiny shrug without an ounce of remorse.

"Traitor," Gage grumbled.

"Okay, Gage. You get three free hits on me." Alphen held out his arms. "I'll defend, but I won't attack. Do whatever you want. You win the game if you can strike me."

Gage tested the weight of the training sword. Heavy, but not too bad. He scrutinized Alphen's unthreatening pose, which didn't fool him in the slightest. He'd seen him fight in Talid.

"You have magic," Gage pointed out.

"I won't use any." Alphen gestured with his fingers for Gage to approach. "Come at me, kid."

The other students hurried to the fringes of the training ground, out of the way. Gage sighed at the miserable situation but decided to play along. Alphen wouldn't hurt him. Probably. He circled the Innaran man, looking him over for potential weaknesses. Alphen had a loose grip on his sword, which Gage copied. Alphen practically slouched, making him seem like an easy target, but Gage knew better.

Still, he took the bait and lunged, swinging at him. Alphen barely moved his arm to lift his blade and deflect the attack. Their swords cracked together. Gage staggered backward, his arm tingling from the jarring deflection. The students oohed and aahed, and Alphen watched Gage with a slight smile.

Gage circled Alphen and rotated his shoulders to keep them loose. If he wanted to hit the guy, he'd have to trick him. He dove and swung from the right, but Alphen pivoted and deflected with the slightest flick of his wrist. Gage pushed on their connected swords to shove Alphen off balance—which didn't work—and slid his blade down toward Alphen's legs. When the prince jerked his sword to intercept, Gage shifted his attack upward. Alphen took a casual step back and struck Gage's sword aside with a quick, clean swipe of his blade.

Gage had failed his three attempts.

Alphen rammed his shoulder against Gage's chest to destabilize him. Knocking Gage's training sword upward and then immediately downward, he tore the weapon out of Gage's hand by sheer force. Then he hooked Gage's legs with one of his own and yanked them out from underneath him. Gage slammed onto his back in the dust, his sword clattering down beside him.

Alphen finished by poking the tip of his blade against Gage's chest. "You're dead," he said with a smile.

The other students laughed, but Gage stared in amazement at Alphen standing over him. He'd disarmed Gage without even nicking Gage's fingers. Alphen offered him a hand and pulled him to his feet, his expression growing serious.

"This is exactly the scenario I want to help you prevent," he said to the class. He patted Gage on the shoulder and ambled around the ring of students, looking them each in the eye. "If the Vaskr attack this academy tomorrow, I want you equipped to defend and escape with your lives."

"Escape?" Eddly snorted. "That sounds cowardly."

Gage rolled his eyes. That kid and his huge mouth. His running commentary in every class was getting ridiculous.

Alphen faced the boy. "Eddly, right?"

"Yes." Eddly lifted his nose in a hoity-toity manner. Since Alphen was taller, it wasn't effective.

"Do you want to die, Eddly?" Alphen asked.

Eddly hesitated—and wilted. He shook his head.

"The Vaskr kill each other for sport in their coliseums," Alphen stated. "They're constantly competing with each other and using brute strength to gain and hold power in their society. Given the opportunity, they'll use their weapons and magic to crush you."

Eddly quivered. "To face them would be brave."

"To face them would be stupid and would mean certain death." Alphen gave Eddly a fierce look that made the boy cringe before resuming his march around the circle of students. "To fight foolishly means to throw your lives away, and your lives are too valuable for that. If one of the Vaskr picks a fight with you, run. Don't engage. Have I made myself clear?"

Students muttered throughout the room and bobbed their heads in agreement. Eddly hesitated, scowling at Alphen instead.

"Have I made myself clear, Eddly?" Alphen asked.

Eddly frowned but finally nodded.

"Save the heroics for when you're older." Alphen continued his circle until he made his way back to Gage. "Right now, your enemies are bigger and stronger than you—and they have far better control over their magic. You're at a disadvantage, but I'll teach you some tactics to keep you alive. Everyone, pair up and grab a practice sword."

Gage grabbed his training sword off the ground while the rest of the class scrambled to pair up. Unfortunately, they paired up in perfect numbers without him.

"You're with me, then," Alphen said to Gage. "Good. I can use you to show them how it's done."

"You just want to beat me up some more," Gage muttered.

"What?" Alphen put on a pathetically exaggerated look of surprise. "Noooooooooo."

In the background, Rhemi nodded intensely. Gage squinted at her and then at Alphen.

Alphen spent the remainder of class discussing and displaying proper sword techniques. He walked around and individually corrected everyone's postures. For most people, he twisted and turned them by hand. For a few others—particularly Eddly—he whacked them with his training sword to straighten them up.

After teaching basic poses and maneuvers using Gage as his example, Alphen said, "Bigger and stronger opponents might have the upper hand over you, but that doesn't mean you don't have advantages of your own." He paced the room with his sword slung over one shoulder. "Gage had the right idea earlier, eyeing me up. You want to find your enemy's weaknesses. And trust me—they have them. The bigger ones, like the Vaskr? They use huge, clunky weapons and depend on brute strength to defeat their opponents. That makes them slower. Use your small size as an asset against them. Move fast. Get close and move behind them. If you're experienced enough, you might land some sneak attacks. The bigger those brutes are, the harder they fall." He paused at the center of the room, twirling his sword before leaning on it like a cane, both hands over the pommel. "But only if you're experienced enough. Because in the meantime, if the Vaskr attack, you're going to do what?"

"Run away," said the class with great fervor.

"Good job." Alphen grinned. "Now get out of my class."

24

CROWNS AND TIARAS

After class, Alphen led Gage around the academy for a detailed tour, showing him gardens, research rooms, and the two-story library with bookshelves from floor to ceiling. Gage planned to raid the library for medical books later, but the gardens fascinated him the most. He'd seen glowing white flowers that he wanted to test for medicinal purposes. Alphen revealed they were Innaran Sunbursts, the magical flower Thad had mentioned. They only grew in places where many Innarans lived.

Their tour moved from the academy to the city. Alphen led Gage down flagstone streets past huge shops and houses with extravagant gardens. They passed dozens of market stalls covered with colorful canopies and displays. Alphen bought Gage something called a chocolate-covered banana. It was the best thing he'd ever eaten, but Spark swiped most of it and practically swallowed the thing whole.

People filled the streets of Runadel. Gage had expected large numbers of Innarans, but the endless swarm of low-magic users amazed him. For most of his life, no one in Talid had elementals, and few elementals passed through the village besides the light dragons that visited annually and the earth beetles that attacked with the Vaskr. Now he saw them everywhere: water felines trotting along the ground, earth beetles riding on heads, fire lizards wrapped around arms, and wind avians perched on shoulders.

In the central plaza, humans with lizards juggled spheres of fire, and people with felines made water dance in the fountain to the tune of a flute. Wind avians hurled water and fire into the sky, creating brilliant explosions. Meanwhile, people with beetles created sculptures of visitors, selling the finished products as souvenirs.

A lot of vendors in the plaza sold products specifically for elementals, including leashes, clothes, and various types of headgear. Gage hadn't seen any elementals wearing stuff like that, but he suddenly had a strong urge to get Spark a hat.

They finally made their way to a restaurant for lunch. Alphen bought their meals, and they sat on an outdoor patio to eat. Their food consisted of breadsticks, mixed fruit, and meat and noodles in white sauce. Spark fled under the table with some fruit but immediately reemerged, crawling up Gage's leg like a rabid squirrel, filling his claws with noodles, and ripping them off the plate. Back under the table he went.

"You don't have to steal it, Spark." Gage sighed and searched for sauce stains on his dark clothes.

Alphen grinned and twirled some noodles on his fork. He paused with the food at his lips when Rhemi's foreleg popped out from under the table, her claws scratching the air in the fork's general direction. Alphen held the fork within her reach. She hooked the noodles with her claws and disappeared under the table once again.

"Dragons." Alphen shook his head and twirled more noodles.

"Thanks for showing me around, Alphen," Gage said. "And for lunch."

"No problem."

They ate in companionable silence. Gage occasionally peeked at Alphen between bites. Alphen, the Innaran prince with a single short braid. The prince who demanded people call him by name, without honorifics. The prince who shoved students through windows—and sometimes climbed through them himself.

"Are you really a prince?" Gage asked.

Alphen stopped with his fork an inch from his mouth. A noodle came loose and dangled over his plate. He shoved the food into his mouth and stared at Gage while he chewed. Finally, he swallowed. And squinted a little.

"My father is the king," he said. "So yeah, I guess that makes me a prince."

"Do you ever have to wear a crown?"

"Thankfully, no."

Gage leaned closer, glancing around before whispering, "How about a tiara?"

Alphen grabbed a cluster of grapes and threw fruit at Gage's head. Gage dodged and laughed. At least Alphen was smiling now. That made it easier to ask his next question.

"You don't like being a prince, do you?"

Alphen bobbed his head from side to side, stirring his noodles. Rhemi's leg popped over the edge of the table. He stabbed some fruit and let her pry it off the prongs of the fork.

"It's not that I don't like it," he finally said. "But my siblings are a lot older than me, and I'll probably never sit on the throne. I'm personally okay with that. I don't really like the king's politics, anyway." He took a bite of noodles.

"How old is your sister?" Gage blurted out. When Alphen froze, fork in his mouth, Gage coughed to clear his throat. "Uh, how old are your siblings?"

Alphen leaned back. "Calvex is thirty-four. Halayna is thirty-two."

"She's old!" Gage exclaimed, slumping in his chair with a groan.

"Why do you care how old she is?" A slightly evil grin reached Alphen's lips.

"Because she's nice," Gage muttered. He stabbed a breadstick with his fork as heat spread across his cheeks. "And she's pretty."

"She's my sister."

"Don't worry. You're pretty too."

Alphen snorted and threw a breadstick at Gage's face. Gage dodged, and the breadstick bounced off his chair and tumbled toward the ground. Spark lunged to catch it, rolling with it and diving back into hiding under the table.

"We should get going," Alphen said, still smiling. He rose and tossed his napkin onto the table. "Your next class is one you can't be late for. Your teacher would kill me." Dipping his head down the street, he added, "You take the lead."

Gage rose and warily glanced toward the academy. "Why?"

"I'm not going to be your guide forever. I want you to be able to find your own way around."

Gage nodded. He probably should learn the way. He didn't want to hold someone's hand his entire time in the academy. Although if it were Nihsa's or Lady Halayna's hand . . . Gage sighed. He was hopeless. He pushed his chair in and headed down the street, pausing when Alphen didn't follow. Glancing over his shoulder, he caught Alphen slipping a gold coin under his plate for the server. Gage immediately looked away, hiding a smile.

"Who is my next teacher?" he asked when Alphen joined him. Spark and Rhemi toddled along behind them with their heads held high.

Alphen grinned. "Nihsa."

"Wha—" Gage threw his hands into the air. "Why are all the teachers so young?"

"Age doesn't matter if you have the smarts and the skills," Alphen said. "Most people grow wiser as they age because they've lived a long life. They make mistakes and learn from them. But the really smart people learn from the experiences of others. They pay attention."

"Like you?" Gage asked.

Alphen grinned rather evilly. "Dear, sweet, innocent Gage. I've got you fooled, huh?"

Gage rolled his eyes.

25

NIHSA SHOWS OFF

Gage got turned around multiple times in the city. When they finally made it to the academy, he led them to the library three times from three different directions. Alphen didn't mind and didn't offer any guidance. When they finally arrived at the main keep, Alphen led Gage to the training grounds.

Along the way, they passed several Innarans in full armor rushing down the corridor. Alphen stepped aside and watched them go with mild interest.

"What's going on?" Gage asked. He'd never seen Innarans in full armor before.

Alphen narrowed his eyes. "Not sure."

A single clang of the academy bell reminded Gage he needed to move. He left Alphen to wonder about the Innarans and sprinted down the hallway to his next class. The last thing he wanted was to get on Nihsa's bad side. He lived with her now, and she could make him extremely miserable. Thankfully, he slammed through the double doors into the classroom as the final bell rang.

The other students glanced at him as he arrived. As did Nihsa, and her eyebrow twitched like she wanted to scold him, but he wasn't technically late.

"All right, everyone," she said. "Find somewhere to sit."

Gage walked through the wooden room, which had only three walls and held various weapon racks. One side of the room opened into an archery range with tall stone walls and no ceiling. Several targets lined the range at varying heights and distances. Most of the kids sat on the room's edge, their feet resting in the grass below. Gage joined them. Nihsa grabbed a bow off the wall and fastened a quiver of arrows onto her belt. She stepped off the platform and onto the grass so she could face them.

"I'm Nihsa Farowind, and I'm going to teach you ranged combat techniques. We'll cover archery and ranged magic in this class. By the time you're finished here, you'll be closer to doing this."

With speed and precision, she yanked one arrow after another out of her quiver, drew them back on the bowstring, and let them fly. She hit five targets across the field, all in a matter of seconds, each a perfect bull's-eye. Jaws dropped, including Gage's. Nihsa slung the bow over her shoulder.

"We'll also work on this," she said.

She summoned water into her hands, forming a magical bow and arrow. She drew the bowstring and launched arrows across the field, once again striking every target with perfect accuracy. Jaws continued to dangle.

"And hopefully, you'll get one step closer to this," she said with a smile.

Nihsa held her palm outward, and water swirled against her hand. A flash of blue on the other side of the room made the students jump. Mishu strolled out of the shadows, blue light flaring from her eyes and rippling off her fur. The feline sprinted and leaped to the wall, running along it as if on flat ground. A trail of water swirled behind her, and her body grew larger until she reached her second form. By then, a vortex of water spun around Nihsa, and Mishu leaped into it and merged their magic together, creating a great torrent.

Reaching into the churning waters, Nihsa formed a massive bow and arrow from her magic and aimed them straight upward. When she launched her arrow, two dozen additional arrows appeared out of the whirlpool and hissed into the air. The magical projectiles exploded across the sky like shimmering blue clouds, and then dozens upon dozens of water arrows fell and battered the archery range.

When the last of them had fallen, Nihsa curled her fingers around her magic. Every last trace of water evaporated. Mishu, in her first form, sat in the grass beside Nihsa and licked her front paw, her tail flicking back and forth.

Everyone stared. Mouths still hung open.

Gage came to his senses before anyone else. "Are you showing off?" he asked, snapping the rest of the students out of their stupor.

Nihsa smiled, a devious twinkle in her eyes. "Maybe a little." Pacing in front of them, she said, "Since most of you don't have access to your magic yet, we'll spend more time on archery in the beginning. I know you're all at different skill levels right now, so let's do some testing to get a feel for where you're at."

For the rest of the class, Nihsa gave a lesson on basic archery. Dread sat like a rock in Gage's belly. He'd tried hunting with a bow and arrows on several occasions, but he'd never been able to hit anything. Ever. When the time came for them to show off their skills, Gage almost got sick all over the floor. A cold sweat broke out across his skin and dampened his hands. Spark sent feelings of encouragement his way, but it didn't help.

Most of the kids before Gage performed poorly, which made him feel a bit better. Most of their arrows landed near the targets, but only a few kids managed to hit them. Eddly was one of them, and he made sure to hoot and holler the entire time, until a girl finally snapped at him, "Be quiet, Eddly."

When Gage took his turn, his hands shook as he pulled the bowstring. He narrowed his eyes on the targets—big, bright, and obvious. He let the arrow fly with a nice thrum of the bowstring. Watched it whistle through the air. And then it vanished in the grass waaaaaaaaaay beyond the targets. He sighed and dropped his arms to his sides.

"Geez, Voidy," Eddly said. "What were you trying to hit? I think the Vaskran lands are somewhere over there. Were you aiming for them?"

Several kids snickered, but at least it sounded good-natured. Gage glared at Eddly anyway. *Be quiet, Eddly*, he muttered in his head. Squeaky laughter followed in his mind, and Spark's tail wagged.

26

VASKRAN ATTACK

G age stumbled into class the next day, covering a yawn with his fist. He'd had another nightmare. Thankfully, his class today started later than usual, so Thad didn't have to drag him out of bed. And because it was supposed to be more intensive than other classes, it was the only class of the day. Gage trudged down the covered colonnade into yet another training field—this one circular, surrounded by stone walls, and filled with weapons and armor. Spark rode on his shoulder, as usual.

More kids trickled in, and Lady Halayna entered last of all, sealing the double doors with a loud clang. Everyone straightened at her arrival.

"Welcome to your defensive magic class, children." Lady Halayna smiled and folded her hands in front of her, prim and proper in her pretty robes. "Normally, we would spend the first day discussing basic magic techniques. However, we have a special event today that I believe will aid in your studies. Several towns were attacked by the Vaskr last night, including one near the academy. Small skirmishes continue even now, so we will fly to the battlefield to witness the fighting. It will serve as an excellent example of magic."

Gage shifted uncomfortably at the idea of going to a battlefield—to a place where the Vaskr were tormenting innocent people. The students around him seemed to share his concern, glancing at each other in alarm. Even Spark emitted a slight growl.

"Is that safe?" Eddly asked.

"You will be perfectly protected by our defensive magic." Lady Halayna spoke with such certainty that most of the students relaxed. "My brother, Calvex, is there. Perhaps you will be lucky enough to meet him."

"How will we get there?" asked a girl. "None of us have elementals to ride."

"A troop of knights is heading to the location now," Lady Halayna said. "We will ride with them on their light dragons."

At the mention of riding dragons, the students' wariness dissolved, replaced by laughter and excited chatter. Lady Halayna called to someone on the wall above them, and light dragons swooped onto the field. They wore dazzling armor, as did their knights. A knife of discomfort twisted in Gage's gut. It seemed unwise for students in tunics to visit a battlefield where knights needed full armor.

But no one else shared his concerns, and the students happily climbed onto the dragons. As the first round of dragons took flight, another landed to gather additional students. Gage climbed onto one behind a dragon knight and a girl, and they took off into the bright sky.

A plume of smoke billowed into the air on the other side of the forest. Gage's stomach dropped. Were the Vaskr really that close to Runadel? Alphen had mentioned preparing his class for a Vaskran attack, but Gage hadn't realized how likely that scenario was.

The dragons carried them northeast to a town built over rolling hills. Lush trees flourished between the brick-and-plaster buildings. Where the hills finally flattened, vast farmlands began. It would have been pretty if not for the smoke. Gage had seen what the Vaskr did to villages. They'd burned Wezen to the ground and destroyed countless buildings in Talid over the years.

Spark rumbled something between a groan and a growl, sharing Gage's unease.

As they drew closer, Gage could make out some of the Innaran army on the near side of the town. The army consisted of almost twenty Innaran dragon knights and several dozen low-magic knights. The town stood between them and the Vaskr.

On the far side of town, light dragons and wind avians swooped through the air and harried a large group of earth beetles on the ground. Allied earth beetles, water felines, and fire lizards assaulted and pushed the enemy beetles away from the town. Wind stirred up flames that ate through the farmlands, pushing their foes farther away but destroying the townspeople's livelihood in the process.

Gage's mount spiraled toward the ground, away from the town and the fighting. The students who had already landed watched in amazement as rocks, water, fire, and wind flew about the battlefield. Each attack created massive explosions that sent up more clouds of smoke, covering the sky in a thin gray blanket. Light dragons dropped magical spears that blasted the beetles and punched massive craters into the ground. The beetles and their human riders fell back, pummeled by the relentless attacks.

The class huddled behind Lady Halayna, who stood beside her dragon. Even at a distance, the ground rumbled from the attacks. Elemental shrieks and human screams filled the air.

"Close your eyes and focus on the movement of magic," Lady Halayna said over the terrible sounds. "You will feel the strength moving through you and around you."

She and many of the students closed their eyes, but Gage couldn't bring himself to do it. Instead, he watched the light dragons pierce through the Vaskran army, tearing down their beetles and crushing the lingering humans. His chest ached at the thought of the people hurting and dying over there.

One of the nearest earth beetles unleashed a scream and reared on its hind legs. Rocks tore up underneath it and shot out in waves of spikes across the land, smashing through the town walls and slicing through the Innaran army—heading straight for the students. Gage and the other kids cried out. Even the knights around them cringed away from the earth magic knifing toward them.

Only thirty feet away, the spikes shattered to dust against a magical light barrier. The formerly invisible barrier glittered on contact before fading out of sight.

Lady Halayna released a slow exhale and then smiled at the students. "As you can see, we are perfectly safe."

Gage scratched his arm. They hadn't seemed perfectly safe a moment ago.

"Now you will bear witness to something incredible," Lady Halayna said, lifting her face toward the smoke-smeared sky.

A magnificent light dragon in sleek armor swooped overhead. A man rode upon its back, his armor far more extravagant than the gear worn by his allies, and he wielded a majestic sword with a gleaming white blade.

"Behold, my brother, Prince Calvex, the current High General of the Innaran army," Lady Halayna said. "Watch and witness the true might of an Innaran."

Lord Calvex and his dragon soared over the army, light radiating from their bodies. The light brightened around his sword and created an impossibly long, magical blade. It reached so high it pierced the smoke smothering the sky. Lord Calvex swung his sword, cutting down earth beetles and carving jagged chasms through the land. Again and again he swung the blade, until nothing but dust remained in his wake.

The students oohed and aahed at the strength of the prince, but every scream of an earth beetle or human sent a ripple of cold up Gage's back.

"You are witnessing what we call a surge," Lady Halayna explained as the light around Lord Calvex and his dragon intensified. "Using a surge, experienced magic users are able to increase their magical prowess for short periods of time."

Lord Calvex cut through the rest of the army and destroyed every last earth beetle opposing him before the glow around him faded. The light around his sword dissolved into a glittering stream, and then he sheathed the metal blade that remained. Cheers erupted from the Innaran army.

"The battle is over," Lady Halayna said. "We are victorious."

27

ROYAL BICKERING

The students joined in the cheering, but Gage couldn't muster more than a smile. His eyes lingered on the ruined town. Cheering felt wrong when the people who lived there had lost everything.

"Are you out of your mind, Halayna?" exclaimed a familiar voice.

Rhemi descended, and Alphen leaped off her back and marched toward his sister with his jaw and fists clenched. Rhemi shrank and flew to his shoulder, ruffling her feathers. Lady Halayna wore her usual passive expression, but her eyebrows furrowed slightly.

"Alphen," she said mutely.

"You brought your class to a battlefield?" Alphen's voice bordered on yelling as he stalked over to her.

"Of course. What better way to learn war and magic than by example?"

"They're kids. They don't have magic they can use to defend themselves. You could have gotten them killed."

Lady Halayna's eyes darkened. "I know my business better than you, Alphen. The children were perfectly safe behind our defenses."

"Mistakes happen," Alphen snapped. "Defenses can fall."

"Not ours."

"Ours fall too!" Alphen pointed at the town. "We lost Delevar! People died!"

The surrounding knights and students shifted uncomfortably. Gage glanced at the ruined town and ached for the people inside.

"We have control again," Lady Halayna stated, her words clipped.

"Yeah, after the Vaskr got away with a bunch of kids," Alphen yelled.

More awkward shuffling from the audience followed. Lady Halayna straightened. Anger smoldered in her eyes despite her mask of calm.

"You brought a bunch of kids here and practically dangled them in front of the Vaskr," Alphen continued. "Do you want them to attack Runadel?"

"That is enough," Lady Halayna said.

Alphen opened his mouth, but a new voice spoke over him. "Enough, Alphen!"

A familiar dragon in full armor landed at a slight distance, with several dragons in lesser armor clustered around it. Knights dismounted and approached the crowd, one man ahead of them all. He removed his helmet and carried it under his arm. Lord Calvex was unmistakable with his elegant armor and the royal sword on his hip. His honor guard fell in step behind him.

The eldest Innaran prince held his head high and walked with a strong, steady gait. He was taller than Alphen, with a broader build. He wore his white hair in a massive braid tied in a knot at the back of his head. How he fit it into his helmet, Gage had no idea. The man wore a regal white tunic, white trousers, and white boots, all with golden trim. A gold circlet shimmered on his brow.

"Brother," Lady Halayna said, tipping her head in respect.

The students and knights bowed toward Lord Calvex. Gage did too, but he peeked at the siblings as he did. Alphen didn't bow. Instead, he scowled at his elder brother.

"How dare you question Halayna in front of the troops and her students," Lord Calvex said to Alphen, his dark eyes narrowed. "Know your place."

Alphen's eyebrow twitched. "This is my place—standing between these kids and foolish decisions."

If the royal siblings cared about their squabble being public, they didn't show it. Lord Calvex stepped closer to

Alphen until he stood inches from him and looked down at him. Alphen held his ground.

"Foolish decisions?" Lord Calvex echoed. "What do you know of foolish decisions? You know nothing more than the gossip you hear while safe in your classroom. Halayna is our brightest tactician. She knows more about war than you could ever dream of knowing. It is her right to make these decisions regarding her students. Now still your loose tongue before you further embarrass yourself with your nonsensical babble."

Alphen didn't respond, but he didn't give ground to his brother, either. Not even when Lord Calvex stepped closer, so that their noses practically touched.

"Father will hear about your behavior here." Lord Calvex lowered his voice. "And about this unauthorized excursion."

"I'm sure he will," Alphen replied, sounding just as hostile.

The two glared at each other in a battle of wills.

"Why are you here, Alphen?" Lady Halayna asked.

Alphen scowled at Lord Calvex a moment longer before turning aside, putting distance between them. He glowered at Lady Halayna instead. "I saw a bunch of fully armored dragons leaving the academy with students and figured something idiotic must be happening. And I was right." He shoved past Lord Calvex and headed toward the town.

"Where are you going?" Lord Calvex snapped.

"To help the people." Alphen didn't look back as he stormed into the crowd of knights.

Lord Calvex watched him go and then turned toward the class, his harsh demeanor wilting. "I apologize that you had to witness such a spectacle."

"It is no matter." Lady Halayna flapped her hand and smiled at the students. "I have arranged for us to eat lunch here so you can mingle with the knights."

As she spoke, several low-magic knights arrived with baskets on their arms. Most wore colored tunics that matched their elements. They handed out small biscuits made with nuts and dried fruit.

"Our lunch today consists of ration bars, the same sort eaten by our troops. Let this be another example of the realities of war," Lady Halayna explained, showing her biscuit. "As you eat, speak to the knights gathered here. They are happy to answer your questions."

The students dispersed, most surrounding Lord Calvex and Lady Halayna. Only a few students broke away to speak with other nearby knights. Laughter and chatter devoured all traces of the tension that had befallen them while the royal siblings argued.

Gage nibbled on his ration bar, handing small chunks to Spark as he searched the crowd. His eyes wandered to the town with plumes of smoke still rising to the sky. How many people had died in Delevar? How many were injured and suffering? How many children were taken?

Something more important weighed on Gage than an opportunity to speak with the knights. Shoving the rest of his ration bar into a fold of his belt, he snuck through the crowd and weaved his way toward the town to see if he could help somehow.

28

MEDICINE THIEF

Gage had hoped to catch up with Alphen on his way into town, but he didn't find him among the increasing number of knights regrouping in the area. Beyond the knights lay the town with its crumbling houses and crushed waterways. His chest ached for the people who had lost everything in one cruel act of violence. The Vaskr needed to be stopped so this wouldn't happen again. Heat burned behind his eyes, and grief prickled his nose. He sniffed and blinked away the sensations.

It hurt? Spark asked in a squeaky voice.

Gage gripped his tunic over his chest. "It hurts."

Then he glanced at the void dragon. Elementals couldn't communicate with their humans until they reached their second form. Gage had to be imagining things. Spark could impress emotions on him. These ones must be stronger than most.

Or so he told himself as he marched forward, because he couldn't think about that right now.

Gage passed a heap of rubble that used to be a house. A family sobbed near its remains. Farther down the flagstone street, fire ate through another home. Everywhere he looked, Gage saw only destroyed homes and ruined lives. Wails and sobs carried on the stale air.

These people had lost everything.

A desperate cry hastened his steps toward a central plaza. People gathered around an old woman with white hair and wrinkly skin who sat against a flattened house. A middle-aged woman in a healer's apron removed a shard of wood from the old woman's forearm before wrapping fabric bandages around the gash. The injured woman groaned and wailed the entire time. A variety of medicine vials dangled, unused, out of the healer's apron. Gage was certain he saw disinfecting and numbing salves among the healer's collection. They'd ease the woman's suffering and clean her injuries. A dirty wound could lead to a lost limb—or worse.

"Why didn't you disinfect the wound? Or use a numbing medicine?" Gage asked, wringing his hands.

"Because we don't have any," the healer said without looking up.

"You have some in your apron."

The healer glared at him from under a heap of brown curls. "Let me clarify: we don't have enough. We're running low on supplies, and replenishments aren't due until tonight. What we have now is reserved for the army, to keep them on their feet in case the Vaskr return."

"The knights can fly to Runadel and get supplies from the clinic there," Gage said. "Or the healer in Runadel could come here. He has healing magic."

"Magic healers aren't inexhaustible resources." The healer continued wrapping the wound. "Anyone with grave injuries will be flown to Runadel for care. The rest of us have what we have, and we don't have time to make trips to and from Runadel for resources."

It sounded like the healer didn't want to bother with extra work. Thad had commented on the lack of good healers, and now Gage understood why. This healer even unwrapped her bandages to adjust the padding underneath, restarting the bleeding. He cringed at the whole scenario.

Yes, the knights fighting the Vaskr were important, but they'd want civilians cared for too.

Gritting his teeth, Gage snatched the two vials from the healer's apron. She turned to grab them back, bumping into him in the process and knocking them both off balance. She tottered out of her crouch and landed on her backside. Gage hastily took her place, kneeling in front of the old lady and removing the bandages from her arm.

"Hey! Stop that!" the healer yelled, and two Innaran knights came running. "Who do you think you are?"

"I'm here with Lady Halayna," Gage stated.

His words had the desired effect; the knights slowed their approach. Even the healer didn't dare grab the vials away from him now. Still, he'd spoken a half-truth, and he didn't want to lie.

"I'm one of her students," he admitted.

He opened the disinfectant and used the bandage to spread the salve over the injury. The potent medicine would sting but would also kill off anything dangerous and promote faster healing. The old lady winced, but he hastily followed the salve with numbing medicine. He chastised himself for not washing his hands first, but the disinfectant should deal with any harmful substances on his fingers. Finally, he bunched up the bandages and placed them as a new covering over the wound.

"That's much better," the old woman said with a weary smile. "Thank you, deary." She patted his hand.

Gage blushed. She offered genuine gratitude, unlike the people in Talid who'd scorned his attempts to help them. He glanced back at the gathered people. No one appeared bothered by him now—except the healer. She scowled but didn't stop him.

"Think you can finish bandaging this?" Gage offered the leftover bandages to the healer.

She tore the fabric out of his hand and took his place as he moved aside. Another pained cry arose from deeper in the town, drawing Gage's attention. It seemed he had work to do. Rising, he sprinted down the street toward the source of the sound.

"Hey," the healer shouted. "You can't take those!"

"I'll bring them back later." He shoved the two vials into his belt. If she wasn't going to use them, then he would.

29

SOME WILL NOTICE

Gage only made it a few steps before he remembered the blood on his hands from helping the old lady. He glanced around for somewhere to wash, but ash filled the river weaving through town, and the visible wells had collapsed.

"Is there anywhere I can wash my hands?" he called out to the people nearby.

Most ignored him, but one of the healer's assistants brought him a towel and a clay jug. Gage recognized the large container. Both Thad and Jinny kept disinfecting solutions in them for washing hands between patients. The liquid burned like fire in an open wound, but it worked.

"Thanks!" Gage held out his hands and let the young man pour liquid over him, and then he dried his hands on the towel. "Can you come with me?"

He didn't wait for an answer, because someone wailed behind him. Gage hustled to the next injured person, and after a brief delay, the healer's assistant followed.

Gage went through the town and helped every wounded person he found by applying medicines and directing the injured to the healer for bandages. The young man cleaned his hands between each patient. Gage was just finishing with a cut on someone's arm when a loud crash erupted down a nearby street, followed by shouts of terror.

He dashed around a corner and found Rhemi standing over a collapsed house, her front claws curled under one of the toppled walls. Alphen crouched underneath it so that the wall rested across his back and head. He pushed off the ground and wedged the wall upward so Rhemi could get a better grip on it. As Rhemi peeled the wall aside, Alphen grabbed another section of wall and lifted it. Men from the town rushed to help him while a crowd gathered on the street.

A man cried out from the debris, buried alive by his own home.

Gage's heart stuttered, and he dove into the ruins, shoving his weight under the wall and lifting with the other men. Spark squawked and tumbled off his shoulder, forced to cling to his chest to keep from getting squished.

"Someone grab him," Alphen shouted as they lifted the wall off the poor man.

Several people hurried forward and dragged the old man out of the ruins. The victim howled in agony as they moved him onto the street.

"He's clear," someone shouted.

Gage and the others lowered the wall. Rhemi waited for everyone to clear out before dropping the second wall, and then she reverted to her first form and flew to Alphen's shoulder.

"Oh, Daddy," cried a woman. Tears poured down her cheeks.

Gage dropped to his knees beside the man, inspecting the damage. Both of his legs were bent at odd angles, and a gash ran across his thigh. It didn't appear to be deep.

"The blood," the daughter whimpered, hiding her mouth behind her hands.

"Mostly surface wounds. Don't worry." Gage managed a smile and then returned his attention to the old man. "Your legs are broken. How are you holding up?"

"After having a house fall on me?" The old man let out a bark of laughter, deep wrinkles creasing his face. "Not too shabby." His laughter turned into a groan.

"Oh, Daddy, now isn't the time for jokes." The young woman laughed despite her tears.

"Cleaner, please," Gage called to the young man, who rinsed and dried his hands. Gage scooped up a glob of numbing salve and held it to the injured man's lips. "Eat this. It'll numb the pain for when your legs are set and splinted."

The man accepted the glob and cringed. "That's awful. Death might be better."

People in the crowd laughed.

"Sorry, no dying today. You'll have to deal with the taste." Gage patched up the thigh injury as best he could. While he worked, he called out to the crowd, "There's a healer about three streets up and to the left. Please bring her here. I can't deal with the broken legs on my own."

In truth, he couldn't deal with them at all. He had no experience with broken bones, and he made a mental note to ask Thad for guidance as soon as possible. But Gage did what he knew how to do and applied salves to the scratches on the man's face and arms.

"Where did you get those medicines?" Alphen asked, watching over Gage's shoulder.

Gage shot the prince an awkward glance. "I may have stolen them."

Alphen arched an eyebrow, visibly wrestling against a grin. "That's not usually recommended."

Gage shrugged. He'd deal with the consequences later. For right now, he was helping the people in Delevar, and that's what mattered most.

The healer finally arrived, pushing past the crowd. She locked eyes with Gage, and her face contorted into a furious scowl.

"His legs are broken and need to be splinted," Gage said, ignoring her hostility. "I've never done it before, but I can help."

"You've done enough," the healer snapped, kneeling next to the old man. "I certainly don't need help from a child. Especially one with a void dragon sitting on his shoulder." She yanked bandages out of her apron and covered the wounds Gage had treated.

Gage stepped back, a dull ache forming in his chest. Comments like those still cut through him like barbed arrows. It was Talid all over again. He couldn't help people if everyone hated and feared him. His thoughts spiraled until Alphen patted him on the back and led him away from the group. Gage allowed the healer's assistant to rinse and dry his hands one last time before sending the young man to help the healer set the patient's legs.

"Wait!" The old man's daughter jogged over to them, tears streaking her face. She grabbed Gage's shoulders. "Thank you for helping my dad."

She pulled him into a fierce embrace. Gage stiffened at the gesture, and before he could think to reciprocate, she drew back. Her hands remained on his upper arms, clasping tightly.

"Thank you," she said, and she kissed his cheek.

After releasing Gage, she gripped Alphen's arm, gave a fierce shake, and returned to her father's side. Gage stood, paralyzed.

Alphen patted him on the back again. "Some people will notice the good you do."

Gage nodded, and the crushing weight lifted off his lungs.

Alphen ushered Gage away from the crowds. "You should probably head back before you get in trouble."

Gage shook his head. "There are more people to help. I'll leave when I'm done."

A warm smile reached Alphen's lips. "Let's go, then." He slapped Gage's back and marched down the street.

Gage followed.

30

STOLEN CHILDREN

The rest of the day passed in a blur. Gage and Alphen searched the remainder of the town for people to assist. With Rhemi's help, Alphen spent most of his time digging through rubble and rescuing buried people, and by the end of the day, he looked like a disaster. Sweat and ash smeared his skin, his clothes were torn, and little cuts covered his hands. His fingers had started to bleed. Gage would need to heal him too.

Gage's tasks were easy compared to Alphen's, but they wore on him anyway. They'd found fifteen more people with moderate injuries, and he'd used every ounce of medicine he'd stolen. Guilt prodded his conscience. The knights probably needed the medicines too, but Gage couldn't turn a blind eye to the people in front of him.

By the time Gage and Alphen returned to the town's entrance, late-afternoon sunlight bathed everything in murky red light. Knights built campfires and set up tents on the outskirts of town, and a few dragon knights patrolled the camp's perimeter.

To Gage's surprise, Lady Halayna remained with the troops, right where he'd left her. Most of the students hung around, chatting with the knights. A dragon here or there would take off with a few students to return to Runadel, but only when the kids wanted to leave. Lord Calvex stood next to Lady Halayna, his arms crossed, his face in a rigid frown. The curly-haired healer from town stood before the two Innaran royals, ranting and gesturing wildly with her arms. Her cheeks were bright red with rage. Gage could think of only one reason she'd be complaining to them.

"Oh, great," he muttered.

"What?" Alphen asked.

"I took the medicine from her."

Alphen's gaze swept to the healer. After a moment of consideration, he bumped Gage's side and opened his hand behind them, using their bodies to shield the gesture.

"Give them to me," he said.

Gage looked up at him in surprise. He didn't want Alphen to get in trouble, but he passed the vials to him anyway. The healer glimpsed them out of the corner of her eye, turning toward them as Alphen put proper distance between himself and Gage.

"That's him, Lady Halayna." The healer pointed at Gage. "That's the boy who accosted me and stole my medicine!"

Alphen tossed the vials to the healer, who juggled them between her hands before securing them against her chest. She blinked in bewilderment.

"I believe those belong to you," Alphen said lightly. "I wanted Gage to use them to help people around town, but I didn't realize he accosted you for them."

Gage's cheeks flamed. "I didn't accost anyone. We bumped into each other and she fell over."

Alphen stared at him and raised his eyebrows in suggestion. Gage frowned at Alphen and then at Rhemi when she raised her eyebrows too. Which was a weird expression to see on a dragon. Spark fluttered his wings and nipped Gage's ear.

Sorry! Spark shouted in his head, making Gage jump.

"Sorry!" he exclaimed—in the healer's general direction—and then coughed to clear his throat. "I'm sorry I bumped into you and took the vials." He threw in a bow.

"I apologize too. I didn't mean any harm." Alphen bowed, and the healer relaxed.

"I will take care of things from here," Lady Halayna said to the healer. "Thank you for bringing your concerns to me."

"Thank you, Lady Halayna." The healer bowed deeply to her and Lord Calvex, slightly to Alphen, and then scowled at Gage as she walked away.

Gage bowed toward Alphen's older siblings. "I'm sorry for any trouble I caused, Lady Halayna."

"Apology accepted," she said. "I feel the greater blame rests on the shoulders of the older boy in your company." Her gentle expression turned into a stern frown at Alphen.

"I won't apologize for helping people," Alphen stated.

Lady Halayna sighed. "If only you would use this fierce resolve to aid Calvex and me." She rubbed her brow as if to ward off an ache.

Alphen ignored her and turned toward Lord Calvex instead. "Now that we got the scolding out of the way, I need to borrow ten of your dragon knights."

Lord Calvex folded his arms. "Whatever for?"

"I'm going after the captives taken by the Vaskr."

A wave of mutters swept through the surrounding crowd.

"You will do no such thing," Lord Calvex said.

"Why not?" Alphen gestured toward the east. "They likely haven't traveled far. We need to strike now before they rejoin their main forces."

"And if they have already rejoined their army?"

"Then I'll sneak in and rescue the kids."

Lord Calvex inspected Alphen with unrestrained disdain. "No."

"But—"

"My answer is no," Lord Calvex said. "I do not have the resources to chase after the Vaskr every time they steal something from us."

"They stole children," Alphen snapped, clenching his fists.

"Yes, and that fills me with grief. But we cannot risk losing ten dragon knights to save a few lives. We are vastly outnumbered as it is."

"A few children's lives."

Lord Calvex stepped toward Alphen. Same as before, Alphen held his ground.

"This is war, Alphen," Lord Calvex said. "Civilian losses are inevitable. We must protect our inferior numbers, or more children will be taken in the future. Forward thinking—this is something you lack."

"Fine." Alphen glared daggers at his brother before turning toward town, but Lord Calvex caught his arm.

"You are not to pursue them," said the elder prince. "Go back to the classroom where you belong, as Father has ordered. If you even think of trying anything foolish, Father will hear of it."

Alphen tore his arm out of Lord Calvex's grip. The two men glared at each other.

Lady Halayna sighed and folded her hands in front of her. "It would be a great help to me if you returned to the academy, Alphen. I had hoped to stay here on the battlefield awhile longer." She gestured toward Gage and a red-clad girl lingering nearby. "These two need a ride back to the academy. If you would, please."

Alphen shot a poisonous glare at Lady Halayna. His elder siblings were forcing him to behave. He couldn't sneak off to the Vaskr if he was hauling kids in the opposite direction. But Gage found he didn't agree with the elder royals. If they had a chance to rescue prisoners and disrupt the Vaskr's plans, they should do it.

"Fine," Alphen said, marching toward an open area.

Rhemi flew from his shoulder and shifted into her second form. Alphen climbed onto her back and yanked the red-clad girl behind him. Gage joined them. Alphen shot his siblings one last scowl—full of fiery defiance—before Rhemi launched into the sky and veered toward Runadel.

31

LATE-NIGHT ESCAPADE

Darkness had fallen by the time they returned to the academy. Rhemi landed in a courtyard near the training grounds, and Alphen helped the girl dismount as Gage slid to the ground.

"You two should head to the dining hall and grab dinner," Alphen said. "Get some rest tonight."

He followed the walkway leading to the training ground where he held class. Rhemi shrank and swooped to his shoulder.

The girl turned the opposite way, pausing when Gage lingered. "Aren't you coming?"

Gage watched Alphen and Rhemi leave and whispered, "Not right now."

The girl frowned but exited the courtyard without further question. Gage waited until Alphen's footsteps receded before pursuing the prince. Alphen hadn't brought them to the courtyard near the dining hall. He was obviously planning something, and Gage was determined to figure out what. He hurried along the colonnade, using the pillars to stay out of sight.

What do? Spark impressed upon Gage's mind in a squeaky child's voice. *Suspect?*

Gage slowed, leaning against a pillar. Spark tilted his head. The dragon definitely spoke to him, which shouldn't be possible. Not yet, anyway. Gage resisted the urge to question this now, because Alphen's footsteps had faded. He'd deal with Spark later.

Alphen had entered his outdoor classroom. Tearing through a rack of supplies, he shoved things into his belt.

"I returned to the classroom like you wanted, Calvex," he muttered. "Happy now?"

He cringed as he moved something aside on the rack, glancing at his hands still bloodied from digging through debris. He rinsed them with a jug of water kept on site for drinks during sparring sessions.

Gage leaned into the open doorway to get a better view, only for Rhemi to suddenly look in his direction. He threw himself backward, out of sight. Either she had fantastic hearing or she'd sensed him somehow. Scurrying down the hallway, he ducked into the shadows behind a decorative pillar. For a moment, he heard nothing, and then Alphen resumed slamming things around. Gage let out a breath, having expected Rhemi to send Alphen after him. He waited a few beats before stalking back to the doorway.

Without a doubt, Alphen planned on going after the kids—and Gage intended to go with him. Only, he had little to offer that might persuade Alphen to let him tag along. He could barely fight and definitely couldn't use magic, and neither could his dragon. There was only one thing he could do that might make a difference.

"Let's go, Rhemi," Alphen said. Magical energy hummed as the light dragon shifted into her second form.

Now or never.

Gage took a breath and ran out to join them. "Take me with you!"

Alphen jumped. "Gage?"

Rhemi didn't look surprised at all. Gage ran past Alphen and grabbed handfuls of her soft feathers to ensure she didn't fly away without him.

"You're going after the Vaskr to rescue the kids, right?" Gage asked. "Take me with you."

Alphen furrowed his brow. "No. It's too dangerous, and I'm already in enough trouble as it is. I'm not dragging you into this."

He gripped Rhemi as if to pull himself onto her back, but Gage grabbed him and yanked him down. Gage maintained his grip despite the startled—and somewhat frustrated—expression on Alphen's face.

"It's dark out," Gage stated.

"Yeah, I noticed." Alphen reached for Rhemi, but Gage pulled him back down again.

"I can see in the dark," Gage blurted out.

Alphen froze. "What?" he asked, his tone more confused now than annoyed.

"You'll have a hard time tracking the Vaskr in the dark. But I can see, so I can find any trails they left behind."

Alphen rubbed his forehead. "Is this a part of your void magic?"

Gage shrugged. He'd been able to see in the dark for as long as he could remember, just like he'd been cursing things for as long as he could remember. But the origin of the ability didn't matter, only that he had it.

"I can help you find the Vaskr before they escape," he insisted. "Please take me with you."

Alphen shook his head, but more like he was arguing with himself rather than deciding against taking Gage along.

Gage stepped closer, steeling his resolve. "The Vaskr stole kids from Talid when I was growing up. They would have taken me, too, if you and Spark hadn't intervened." Gage gripped Alphen's tunic, and his next words came out pleadingly. "I want to help."

Alphen's shoulders sank. "You might get in trouble."

"I don't care. This is the right thing to do."

Alphen searched his eyes. Looking for doubt or weakness? Gage wasn't sure, but he set his jaw and furrowed his brow, trying to look as resolute as possible. It wasn't hard, as he didn't feel an ounce of hesitation.

"Fine," Alphen said. When Gage smiled, he hastily added, "But you stay with Rhemi unless I say otherwise."

"Deal." Gage turned toward Rhemi, but Alphen shuffled him to the side.

"Sit in front this time," he said. "You're Rhemi's eyes."

A nervous flutter stirred in Gage's belly, but he nodded and climbed onto Rhemi's back near the base of her neck, where Alphen usually sat. Alphen hopped up behind him a moment before Rhemi sprang off the ground and took to the sky full of glittering stars.

32

TURNING OFF THE LIGHTS

Under Gage's guidance, Rhemi followed the river to Delevar before swerving toward the flatlands. The stars did little to brighten the scenery, and the moon had yet to rise. Even though Gage could see in the dim light, his task proved more daunting than he'd expected. His night vision didn't help him see things far away.

Thankfully, Rhemi flew low enough for Gage to make out disturbances in the plants below. The Vaskr hadn't been discreet. Huge fields had been crushed in a line heading northeast from Delevar toward the Vaskran homeland. After a while, the trail veered slightly south, revealed by footprints in the mud by the river.

"There," Alphen said after a long while. He pointed toward orange flecks of light on the horizon. "Looks like they didn't make it back to the main army. Good."

A military encampment formed out of the darkness. Each of the several dozen tents appeared capable of holding

213

at least three burly Vaskran men. Wooden torches stuck out of the ground, their flames flickering in the night like dancing stars. A trail of crushed weeds circled the camp—a place where sentries patrolled, no doubt.

"Land over there, Rhemi," Gage said, pointing toward a patch of sparse trees. "Guards don't patrol that area."

Rhemi veered into the trees. As Gage and Alphen hopped to the ground, she shrank into her first form and zipped toward the camp.

"Where's she going?" Gage asked.

"To scout." Alphen tapped a finger on his temple. "I can see through her eyes. She'll help us find the captives."

"You see through her eyes? All the time?"

"Now that would be disorienting, wouldn't it?" Alphen leaned against a tree, crossing his arms. "I can only see through her eyes when I want to and she allows it. It uses my magic, so we don't do it often."

Alphen closed his eyes. Gage let him focus and turned to inspect the camp. Despite the torches, darkness and shadows ruled the area. Creeping around would be pretty easy. A twinkling light drew his attention to the far edge of camp, where a patrolling guard with a long, scraggly beard walked with an axe in one hand and a torch in the other. He followed the ring in the grass Gage had seen from the sky.

"Found them," Alphen muttered, his eyes still closed. "The kids are at the center of the camp, monitored by several guards. Rhemi peeked inside and confirmed they're okay, but they're shackled to posts in the ground. That makes things a little tougher."

"Can we move in the shadows to reach them?" Gage asked.

"Maybe." Alphen's brow furrowed. "Yeah, it looks like it." Finally, he opened his eyes and settled a stern look on Gage. "But I can do the rest. You need to wait here."

Gage crossed his arms and scowled. "I can see in the dark. I got us here, and I can move us through the shadows to reach the kids. I'll make this rescue a lot faster, safer, and easier."

Alphen stared at him, his rigid posture suggesting he'd already made up his mind. He was good at battling wills with his older siblings, so Gage would likely lose this fight. Instead, he chose a different approach.

"I can do this," he said softly. "Please let me help."

Alphen dropped his rigid pose and sighed, looking off to the side. He swept his fingers through his hair. "Finc, but if I tell you to do something, do it. If I tell you to hide, hide. If I tell you to run, run. Even if I'm about to be captured or killed—if I tell you to go, swear to me you'll go."

Gage would have agreed if not for Alphen's final demand. He couldn't abandon him. Whatever happened, they'd face it together. Still, he nodded. He'd at least *try* to follow Alphen's orders.

Alphen scrutinized him but finally crept toward camp. "Let's go. Stay close."

Alphen led the way with slightly hunched but quick strides. Gage followed in a similar posture. The patrolling guard had moved out of sight, so they were able to sneak unhindered into a dark alley between two tents. Rhemi soared over them and landed on one of the tent posts.

Alphen grabbed Gage's wrist. "She'll lead the way, but don't let me trip on anything."

Gage swallowed the lump in his throat and ignored the knot forming in his belly. If he messed this up, everyone could end up dead. No pressure. Rhemi leaped off her perch and flew above the tents, leading them toward the center of camp. Gage pulled Alphen around barrels, crates, and heaps of weapons and armor as he pursued her.

Rhemi suddenly dove out of sight, halting Gage in his tracks. When he opened his mouth to question her disappearance, Alphen wrapped an arm around him and yanked him backward.

"Quiet," he whispered into Gage's ear. Gage froze, his heart stuttering.

Directly ahead of them, a guard marched out from between two tents. He held a torch aloft and inspected the area.

"Imagine darkness covering the torch," Alphen whispered.

"What?" Gage barely squeaked out the word.

The Vaskran man turned in their direction, lifting the light toward them.

"Imagine darkness covering the light, and imagine pushing your magic out," Alphen insisted.

The torchlight drew closer as the raider stepped toward them. Gage did as Alphen said and envisioned darkness covering the flames the same way dark mist had covered Spark at his summoning. Nothing happened. Gage willed his magic to cover the light, pleaded with it—imagined grabbing it and shoving it out of his body. Something stirred in his chest. Something warm and strong.

Shadows and a brief burst of purple sparks snuffed out every nearby flame. Darkness fell over the camp. The guard shook his torch.

"What happened?" shouted a man elsewhere in the camp.

"Gust of wind must have taken out the lights," called another, more irritable than the first. "Hurry and get them lit."

"There's no wind," muttered the man near Gage and Alphen. He licked his finger, stuck it in the air, and shook his head. Growling, he fumbled his way back between the tents, disappearing from view.

Gage exhaled. He hadn't realized he wasn't breathing. Alphen kept a firm grip on him until the raider's heavy footsteps faded. Gage sank with a shuddering sigh. Rhemi fluttered back into view and landed on a tent pole.

"Did I do that?" Gage whispered.

"Sure did. But we'll have to work on your focus. It looks suspicious when every light goes out." Alphen smiled and nudged Gage forward. "Keep going."

Tension tightened Gage's muscles as he followed Rhemi. They'd been so close to getting caught. But excitement overwhelmed his panic. He'd used magic!

Rhemi finally led them into a circular area with lots of torches and a single spacious tent. She perched on a pole and fluttered her wings. Gage and Alphen crouched in the shadows as a guard marched through the area.

"That's it," Alphen whispered. "We'll wait for the guard to leave, and then we'll sneak under the tent. It doesn't look too taut."

As they waited, Rhemi watched the area with sharp eyes. Gage assumed she was relaying information about the guards to Alphen. He glanced at Spark. The void dragon glared at the tent with his head ducked low and his wings tight against his body.

You okay? Gage asked Spark in his mind. When the void dragon nodded fiercely, Gage felt a surge of determination in his chest.

We save littles, the dragon replied.

Realization finally crashed over Gage. Spark could speak. Impossible.

"Now," Alphen whispered. He tugged Gage to the tent and lifted the material upward. Gage worked his way inside. Alphen joined him a moment later.

33

NEFARIOUS REASONS

Fifteen kids huddled together in the tent, and they cried out when Gage and Alphen arrived.

"Shh," Alphen whispered. "We're here to help."

Several kids slapped their hands over their mouths.

"It's one of the Innara," a child murmured.

"Lord Innara," a few others said.

"Shh," Alphen reiterated. "Call me Alphen, please and thank you."

He crouched next to the nearest kid, inspecting the shackles around their wrists. Pulling two metal rods out of his boot, he stuck them into the lock and wrestled with it. Gage wasn't sure what surprised him most: the fact that Alphen had lockpicks or that he knew how to use them.

"Is everyone here?" Alphen asked as he worked. "Were any kids taken elsewhere?"

"We're all here," replied an older boy.

"You came to save us?" asked a girl.

"Sure did." Alphen smiled, still tinkering with the shackles.

Gage inspected the captives. The youngest had to be about five years old, while the oldest had to be close to his own age. He hadn't expected so many kids.

"Alphen," he whispered, swallowing a lump of tension in his throat, "I don't think I can sneak everyone out of here." Getting himself and Alphen through the camp had been hard enough, and they'd almost been caught.

"Rhemi can't fly them all at once, either. One problem at a time, though." Alphen flinched as he worked on the lock.

Only then did Gage notice Alphen's trembling fingers. Fresh blood smudged onto the metal from the cuts on his fingertips. The prince gritted his teeth and cursed to himself as he worked.

"Can I help?" Gage asked.

Alphen paused and looked at his own bloodied hands in resignation. "Hard to pick a lock when your fingers are peeling off." He wiped the lockpicks on his tunic and passed them to Gage. "Shouldn't be too hard."

"Walk me through it." Gage took Alphen's place by the child. His stomach twisted into a knot, but he took the lock and set his jaw.

"Tension wrench and hook," Alphen said, indicating the tools he'd provided.

He explained how to turn the wrench like a key while using the hook to move pins inside the lock. It took Gage forever to find the pins, but when he hit one, it gave a quiet click. When he finally hit every pin, the wrench turned. Gage stared in surprise as the shackles fell away.

"Seems like you're a natural at a lot of things." Alphen patted his back. "Next thing you know, you'll be a master thief."

"Just what I've always wanted," Gage muttered, shooting Alphen a dubious look before moving on to the next lock. "Why do you even have lockpicks?"

"Nefarious reasons." Alphen grinned.

Gage rolled his eyes and focused on his work. He struggled with the first few locks, but the others got easier. Each lock had six pins, and he started to get a feel for the space between each pin. One of the younger kids stared at him in awe.

"Are you a dragon knight?" the boy asked.

Gage froze, looking first at the boy and then at Spark.

"In training. Yes, he is," Alphen said, patting Gage's shoulder.

"Your dragon is black," said an older boy.

Gage ignored the nervous churn of his stomach. "He's a void dragon."

"What's his name?" a girl asked.

"Nightspark. But I call him Spark."

"He's cute," said another girl.

Warmth stirred in Gage's chest. He couldn't tell if the feeling originated from him or his dragon. He finally picked the last lock, dropped the shackles to the ground, and offered the lockpicks to Alphen.

"Keep them," Alphen said. "I have another set at the academy."

Gage frowned. One lockpick set was weird enough, but he had more? What exactly did he do in his free time? But none of that mattered now. They needed to get those kids back to their families. Gage tucked the tools into his boot, same as Alphen had done.

"Okay, everyone," Alphen said with a smile, "we're going to sneak out of here. You'll need to stay quiet, even if it gets scary, okay? And you need to do exactly as we say."

Heads bobbed throughout the tent.

"Everyone, hold hands," Alphen continued. To Gage, he said, "You take the lead, I'll take the rear. Rhemi will guide us like she did before, and if things get bad, she'll create a distraction."

Gage nodded, his mouth suddenly parched. A cold sweat broke out on his skin, and he took slow, deep breaths to ease his racing heart. A lot of lives weighed on his shoulders. But he refused to leave these kids with the Vaskr even a moment longer. He took one kid's hand while the rest formed a chain behind them.

I is help, Spark said, hopping off Gage's shoulder to the ground and sticking his head under the tent flap. *Wait.* The tip of his tail flicked. *Wait. Wait little.*

A light moved across the side of the tent. The silhouette of a beefy guard passed across the wall, and then the light faded. No one moved.

Is good, Spark said, scurrying up Gage's arm and onto his shoulder.

"All clear," Alphen confirmed. "Let's go."

Gage hurried under the tent and held up the material so kids could crawl underneath after him. Alphen grabbed it from the inside so Gage could lead the kids out of the area. Rhemi led them into the shadows, retracing their earlier route. Gage moved the kids at a steady pace until Rhemi dove out of sight. He froze and threw out his arms to shield the kids from whatever lay before them.

A guard rounded a nearby tent, holding a torch high and bathing the area in light. Gage's throat tightened as the man's gaze swept toward them. And then moved right over them as he held his torch in a different direction. Finally, he turned and walked another way. Gage stared in confusion. The guy had looked right at them, and the torchlight had shone over them—at least a little. He had to have seen them.

"Keep going," Alphen called in a muted voice.

Gage barely heard him over the pounding of his heart in his ears. He could hardly breathe. The poor kid holding his hand was dealing with a sweaty mess right now. Gage moved swiftly through the shadows, desperate to be out of this place.

On and on they went, until at last, they reached the end of the camp. Only the guards patrolling outside stood in their way now.

"Run," Alphen shouted, his voice slicing through the silence. "We've been spotted!"

A bellowing horn followed. So did a lot of angry shouts from raiders throughout the camp.

"Run," Alphen yelled again.

Gage ran, dragging a chain of children with him.

34

DESTROYING MAGIC

"Run!" Gage shouted at the kids, breaking his grip so they could run freely. He waved them ahead of him onto the field. "Go!"

Guards closed in, brightening the area with torchlight. Rhemi swooped overhead, shifted into her second form, and landed hard in front of the kids.

"Rhemi, grab some kids and go!" Alphen remained at the back of the line, ushering the kids forward and ensuring no one got left behind.

Gage hoisted two older kids onto her back. Rhemi leaped from the ground, snatched up four younger kids in her claws, and took off at a rapid pace.

"Keep running," Gage hollered at the remaining kids.

Only distance could save them from the Vaskr now, at least until Rhemi returned to grab more of them. He'd seen Alphen fight, but the prince couldn't take on an army alone.

Once the children had passed, Gage faced the encampment, where Alphen stood silhouetted against the torchlight. Yellow magic flared throughout the camp. Over ten earth beetles shifted into their monstrous second forms, charging through camp, flattening tents, and dropping torches along the way. Several reared and slammed their front legs into the earth, sending stone spikes rippling across the field in Alphen's direction.

The prince threw up his hand against the spikes. A barrier of light ignited from his palm, and the rocks exploded into dust against it. An army of nearly a hundred men rallied against them, armed with axes and spears. Gage counted over two dozen beetles now. The thunder of enemy footsteps rattled the ground.

"Time for your next lesson in void magic," Alphen called to Gage. "Look for the threads of magic connecting the Vaskr to their elementals."

"How?" Sweat beaded on Gage's brow.

"Focus on what you want to see. Imagine it into existence. It's always there, you just need to find it."

Gage recalled what Lady Halayna had said when she told the class to close their eyes and concentrate. So, he closed his eyes.

No! Open! Easy! Spark nipped at Gage's ear. *I helps!*

Gage opened his eyes. His vision blurred and then abruptly cleared, though now everything had a strange ethereal glow. Strings of light glittered around every living thing—most white, some thick and pulsing, others thin and faint. The brightest pulsed around humans, binding them to their elementals. Tangles of white threads with flaring yellow edges gleamed from inside the Vaskran raiders and their beetles.

"I see them," Gage exclaimed.

"Good," Alphen said. "Now destroy them."

Gage opened his mouth to question the command, but Spark shoved a memory into his mind that silenced him. He recalled Spark's summoning through the dragon's eyes—how he'd seen the threads of magic around their enemies and torn them apart, erasing their magic with his own.

If I does, Spark said, *Master better.*

Translation? If Spark could do that, Gage could do much more.

"Okay," Gage whispered.

"On the count of three," Alphen called over the shouts of the Vaskr, the thunder of footsteps, and the clatter of weapons and armor. "One . . . two . . . three! Now, Gage!"

Gage threw up his hand—he wasn't sure why—and imagined ripping the threads apart. Dark mist swallowed the light of the threads and severed them, and the beetles reverted into their first forms in flashes of gold, falling harmlessly out of sight.

"Did I do that?" The words caught in Gage's throat.

Did! Spark exclaimed. *Master strong!* The little dragon shrieked and wagged his tail, his whole body moving with it.

"Focus," Alphen hollered.

The Vaskr summoned more beetles and raced forward, shouting in anger. Gage and Alphen fell back as Rhemi returned to gather up the last of the kids. They only had to hold off their enemies a little longer. Gage lifted his hand again—it helped him focus—and severed the threads connecting the humans and beetles. More of their foes fell, but exhaustion smothered him in return for his effort. A fog settled over his mind, his muscles ached, and sweat plastered his clothes to his skin.

With their beetles defeated, the raiders instead sent spears of stone through the earth toward Alphen and Gage.

"Focus on their magical attacks," Alphen shouted, lifting both hands toward their oncoming foes. "Destroy them, Gage!"

The stones shredding through the earth shone with white-and-gold light. Gage tore through them, as well as the arrows of rock hurtling through the air after them. He demolished every trace of yellow-tinged magic he could find.

Finally, the raiders gave up on using magic, lifting their axes and charging forward instead. Gage swiped his sleeve across his face to clear his eyes of sweat and dust. He couldn't fight an army with his magic. Not yet, at least. Alphen realized that, too, and fell back to stand beside him.

"You okay?" Alphen asked, sweeping his fingers through his sweat-soaked hair as he watched the approaching army.

"Never better." Gage fought to catch his breath but managed a smile.

A huge Vaskran man sprinted ahead of the others, an axe gripped in one hand and a torch held high in the other. Firelight cast his face in red light and angry shadows, giving him a feral look. He wore heavier pelts and thicker armor than the rest.

"Innaran scum," he roared in a painfully familiar voice.

Gage's stomach dropped as the voice and face registered. Torquil, the leader of the men who'd attacked him in Talid.

"You!" Torquil roared when he saw Gage, lifting his axe and throwing himself forward in a wild dash. His army raced behind him.

Alphen wrapped an arm around Gage and smirked at the oncoming army. Saluting, he leaped off the ground with a boost of magic, hauling Gage into the air with him. Torquil swung his axe, missing them by inches. Rhemi swooped, caught them on her back, and carried them away into the stars.

Torquil's voice bellowed after them as they fled.

35

MORNING HOPE

Pink spread across the eastern horizon as Gage and the others returned to Delevar. Rhemi flew steadily throughout the night, carrying one batch of kids after another across vast distances until at last they reached the ruined town.

Several people stood watch around Delevar. They shouted and blew horns when they saw figures approaching, but their panic transformed into confusion when they spotted Rhemi. When they recognized their children, confusion shifted to joy. Parents and grandparents ran and scooped up their loved ones, tears flowing from their eyes.

Gage choked on his emotion, overwhelmed by the scene.

We helps? Spark asked, wagging his tail.

"We helped," Gage whispered, and a smile stretched across his face.

After their joyous reunions, the townspeople invited Gage, Alphen, and their dragons inside. Tents had replaced destroyed homes and shops. The people had nothing, but they still offered gold as a reward for returning their children. Alphen declined the coins, but he and Gage accepted a simple meal of jerky and water to replenish their strength.

As they ate, many people asked Gage about his dragon. The rescued children happily informed the adults that he was a void dragon. No one feared them, especially when many people recalled Gage aiding them with medicines. To them, Spark was yet another elemental belonging to a dragon knight. For the first time in his life, Gage felt fully accepted. Some of the broken pieces inside him mended.

"We better head back," Alphen said to Gage after they ate, patting him on the shoulder. "If we hurry, you might still make it to your next class."

Gage shot him a sour look that made everyone laugh. Right then, his bed held far more appeal than class.

"Before you go, the children put something together for you," said a woman.

A gaggle of kids ran to them with flower crowns in their hands. A little girl missing her two front teeth approached Alphen, dancing on her bare toes.

"For the Lord Innaran." She held up a crown made of green weeds and yellow flowers.

"Alphen is fine." He smiled and dropped to one knee, bowing his head like a king being crowned.

She giggled at his grand gesture and plopped the crown on his head. "King Lord Innaran!"

"Alphen, please," he insisted, standing.

"King Lord Alphen," she replied with great cheer, which made him shake his head and chuckle.

"For you," said another girl, running to Gage. She held up a crown of purple and blue flowers.

"For me?" Gage lifted his eyebrows.

"Of course." She giggled. Like the other girl, she danced on her toes.

His face burned as he bowed his head so she could crown him.

"And for Sparky," said a third girl.

She reached out to place a tiny crown of blue flowers on the void dragon, but Spark dodged her attempts.

Foods? he asked.

No. Hat, Gage thought at him.

Hat? Spark tilted his head.

The girl managed to thrust the crown upon him, plopping it on his head. Spark froze, his eyes wide and unblinking, like he had no idea what was happening. Gage smirked, and the surrounding girls giggled.

"For Miss Rhemi," said another girl, rushing over with a crown of red and white flowers.

Alphen leaned forward, and Rhemi bowed her head and allowed herself to be crowned. Then she stood tall on Alphen's shoulder.

"Worn like a true queen, Rhem," Alphen teased.

Rhemi puffed up her chest and lifted her head higher, making everyone laugh—until a girl shrieked.

"Oh no! Sparky, no!" she exclaimed.

All eyes swept to the void dragon. Spark had half the crown in his mouth, chewing away. He halted when their attention turned to him, and then he chewed a little more. And swallowed a chunk of his crown.

"I guess he's still hungry," Gage muttered awkwardly.

Everyone laughed, even the girls who'd created the crowns.

After many thanks and goodbyes, Alphen shared a few last words with the mayor of Delevar, promising to send more Innarans to guard the region. He also gave the mayor a pouch of jingling coins.

"No, I can't accept this, Lord Alphen," the mayor said.

Alphen grabbed the elderly man's hand, set the pouch on it, and closed his fingers over it. "Alphen is fine. And please. I wish I could do more for Delevar."

"You've done enough already." The mayor smiled under his white mustache. "You brought back our children. They are far more important than silver or gold."

"Then use this to take care of them," Alphen insisted.

The old man's face scrunched, and his eyes gleamed. "Thank you."

Alphen smiled and headed toward the edge of town, where Rhemi shifted into her second form. Gage watched the mayor look at the pouch with tears running down his wrinkled cheeks. Turning, he hurried to join Alphen.

"Good job last night," Alphen said, slapping Gage on the back. "You make a pretty good sidekick."

"Sidekick?" Gage scowled. "I did most of the work."

"Dream on, kid."

Alphen pinched him in the side, but Gage whacked his hand away and retaliated by jabbing his fingers into Alphen's stomach.

Alphen dodged with a snort of laughter and leaped onto Rhemi. He offered Gage a hand. "How are you feeling? Tired?"

"I'm okay." Gage accepted the help, wobbling from exhaustion. He smiled anyway. "Actually, I feel pretty good."

Rhemi took to the sky, circling the town as she ascended.

"I want to do more of this," Gage said quietly.

"Staying up all night in life-and-death situations?" Alphen raised an eyebrow.

"Doing good," Gage said. The town looked different now, without all the smoke and flames. Bathed in morning sunlight, it looked hopeful somehow. "I want to help people. Like this."

Alphen glanced at him and then settled down and looked ahead. Gage glimpsed a small smile on his face.

"You're a good kid, Gage," Alphen said softly. "Don't lose that, okay?"

Gage smiled again. Then he leaned forward, rested his forehead on Alphen's back, and closed his eyes for some rest.

36

A Stinging Reprimand

Rhemi landed on the street next to Thad's clinic, forcing a few bemused civilians to move out of her way. Gage slid off her back and wavered on his feet, leaning against her for balance. His strength had finally betrayed him, and he desperately needed his bed. Spark draped over his shoulder like a wet rag, barely conscious. Gage tottered toward the clinic, pausing when Alphen followed.

"You don't have to come with me," Gage said.

Alphen shrugged. "I want to make sure you reach the door okay."

Gage glanced at the space between him and the door—about ten steps. He didn't bother pointing that out and walked the rest of the way to the clinic. He gulped as he turned the handle. It clicked open.

"It's not locked," he whispered to Alphen, a sense of dread overtaking him.

"Of course not. He's probably been waiting for you." Alphen lifted an eyebrow. "Did you think he set a trap for you or something?"

Gage blushed, because that's exactly what he'd thought. He'd planned on climbing in through the window. Holding his breath, he shoved the door open and stepped into the main clinic. Thad was mixing medicines at a nearby counter, but he stopped when Gage entered. His face darkened with anger.

"Where in the blazes have you been, boy?" he asked, throwing down a towel he'd used to wipe his hands. "We've been up all night worrying about you. Nihsa just took a team scouting for you. What sort of hairbrained, nonsensical thinking could possibly lead you to—"

Alphen chose that moment to step into view.

Thad froze. His thick eyebrows dropped, fury burning in his eyes. "Oh. You," he muttered. "The knights reported that you'd run off again and taken Gage with you, but I didn't think you were dumb enough to do that."

"It wasn't Alphen's fault. I made him take me," Gage said.

Alphen rolled his eyes. "You didn't make me do anything."

"Doesn't matter. Alphen is older, and he should know better," Thad snapped, marching over to Alphen. "What were you thinking, boy? Bringing an untrained student on a ridiculous excursion like this, and for what? To play the hero? Is this a game to you?"

Rather than getting defiant like he had with Lord Calvex and Lady Halayna, Alphen shrank back from Thad, lowering his head and shoulders.

"You put an innocent boy at risk," Thad continued. "And to make matters worse, you—"

"We saved the kids," Gage blurted out.

Thad and Alphen both frowned.

"We saved all of them," Gage said, pulling back his shoulders. "And the Vaskr destroyed their own camp while trying to stop us. We hit them where it hurts, and that's a good thing. We did the right thing." Then he threw in a smirk, shrugging and dipping his head toward Alphen. "I did most of the heavy lifting, but Alphen helped a little. I guess."

Alphen snorted and crossed his arms. A tiny smile cracked his lips. Thad shot Gage a withering look, but Gage refused to wither. Finally, the older man huffed and glared at Alphen. Some of the tension melted out of him.

"It was still foolish," Thad muttered.

Alphen rubbed his forehead. "Noted. Now are you finished yelling at me? I'll find Nihsa's team and send them back."

"Fine. Go away." Thad waved a dismissive hand before returning to his work at the counter.

Alphen reached for the door handle, giving Gage a glimpse of the gashes on his fingers.

"Wait!" Gage grabbed Alphen. "Thad, please heal Alphen's hands."

"My hands?" Alphen looked at them and raised his eyebrows in genuine surprise. "Oh, right." He turned his palms outward.

Thad took one look at the wounds and let out an annoyed sigh. He snatched a towel off the counter and threw it down for no apparent reason. "What in the blazes did you do now, boy?"

"I tried to hop onto an earth beetle so I could ride it heroically into the sunset—"

Gage smacked Alphen in the stomach with the back of his hand. "Knock it off," he grumbled. To Thad, he explained, "Houses collapsed on people in Delevar. Alphen hurt his hands digging through the debris to save them."

Thad arched an eyebrow.

Alphen groaned. "Gage, you're really messing with my reputation."

"Yeah. I'm making you look good."

"I know. Stop it."

Alphen scowled, and Gage responded with an eye roll.

Thad cast his eyes to the ceiling with a dramatic sigh. "Fine." He gestured toward the back room, where they kept a washbasin and cleaning supplies. "Wash up. I'll heal you."

Sighing, Alphen trudged toward the back.

"And use disinfectant," Thad ordered.

A groan escaped Alphen as he veered around a corner. Audible splashes followed.

Thad looked Gage over from top to bottom. And then sniffed. "You stink."

Gage slumped.

"Go wash up and change clothes," Thad said, giving Gage a firm pat on the back. "If you're lucky, you can catch an hour or two of sleep before your next class."

He didn't smile, but his eyes gleamed, and Gage couldn't tell if he was joking or not. Gage dragged his feet into the back, where he found Alphen dumping disinfectant onto his hands. When the liquid made contact, Alphen gritted his teeth and growled. Gage cringed on his behalf.

"It burns," Alphen muttered.

"Toughen up," Gage said, chewing down a smile. "You're fine."

"This is your fault, you know."

Gage grinned. "I know. I did it on purpose."

Alphen flicked leftover disinfectant at Gage before storming into the main clinic. Spark leaped into the washbasin and splashed around in the water while Gage peeled off his dirty clothes and gave himself a quick rinse.

Alphen yelped from the other room. "I already used disinfectant!"

Gage grabbed a spare nightshirt from the linen closet and slipped it over his head. Spark leaped to his shoulder, and together they returned to the main room.

Thad had applied disinfecting salve to Alphen's hands, and now he lifted his eyebrows in mock surprise. "Oh, did you? So sorry." He didn't sound sorry at all.

Gage smiled as he headed toward the bedrooms.

"Can't you use that numbing medicine or something?" Alphen asked Thad.

"We don't have any."

Gage glanced at a shelf as he passed, noting seven full vials of numbing salve.

37

ORELIA

O nce again, Gage found himself marching in a wasteland of dust. Another nightmare. Why couldn't he have fun, exciting dreams? What was wrong with his brain?

Gage, called the girl's voice, distant like an echo. *Gage!*

"Who are you?" he shouted. Then he rolled his eyes at himself for asking an imaginary girl for her name.

My . . . is Orelia. I . . . the girl replied, but her voice faded.

Orelia. Gage didn't know anyone by that name. Weird.

He rubbed his forehead and continued through the dust until a blurred shadow swept over him, stopping him in his tracks. Something nearby unleashed a menacing roar that froze him to his bones, and his heart managed several stutters.

Master, cried a familiar voice in his mind.

"Spark?"

Another shadow swooped overhead, and Gage looked up in time to glimpse something in the murk. Something huge, jagged, and covered in spikes, with the broad wings and long tail of a dragon. The creature released another roar that vibrated through Gage's body.

Spark screeched, and Gage felt the dragon's terror cut through him like a blade of ice.

Master! the dragon cried.

"Spark!" Gage bolted in the direction of the dragon's shrieks and found himself following the shadow of the massive creature above him.

Spark formed out of the dusty haze, scampering and tripping over his tiny legs in his desperation to reach Gage. A shadow fell over them, followed by a string of booming roars. A monstrous creature dipped out of the sky toward Spark, its jaws open wide and full of razor-sharp fangs.

"Spark!" Gage shouted, and his void dragon looked up.

Master! Spark shrank toward the ground. *Magic! Save!*

Gage threw up his hand against what appeared to be a massive, spiky dragon. He pushed out his void magic and struck the creature the same way he'd attacked the earth beetles in the Vaskran camp. An explosion of darkness surrounded the dragon in a tangle of pulsing, writhing threads. The creature jolted in the air like it'd been hit by a massive arrow, and it smashed to the ground with its huge wings crumpled beneath it. Gage dove and snatched Spark into his arms, rolling and then leaping aside to avoid the creature's tail as it slammed down.

Master! Spark shuddered in Gage's arms.

The ground rumbled as the monstrous dragon rose. Gage took in the full form of the creature and froze in fear. Its eyes were completely black, throbbing with the same black veins that webbed across its body. Its form reminded Gage of a light dragon plucked of its feathers. Skin lay draped over its muscles and bones. Lean and sinewy, the dragon appeared starved. Hundreds of black spikes jutted from its flesh.

"What is that thing?" Gage gasped for breath.

Run, Spark whispered in his mind.

The mangled dragon bellowed, its hot breath curling over Gage and making his skin crawl.

Gage, run! screamed the girl's voice, crisp and clear.

Gage jolted at her warning and sprang sideways to dodge the bite of the gnarled dragon. With Spark held fast in his arms, he ran. The beast's footsteps thundered behind him, but he zigzagged in an attempt to lose it in the murk. The dust would hopefully mask his scent.

He'd never seen things like this in his dreams. Never a monster, never Spark. Everything was horribly wrong.

Another shadow passed over him, followed by the ominous thump-thump of leathery wings.

Up! Spark cried.

Gage ducked under the claws of a second gnarled dragon swooping over his head. It failed to catch him but landed in front of him, blocking his escape. Gage tripped over his own feet to keep from running right into its mouth and instead sprawled into the dust before it. He shielded Spark but scraped his forearm in the process. Rolling back to his feet, he lunged to evade the dragon's snapping fangs. He'd only taken two steps in the other direction when the first dragon landed behind him. The two monstrosities prowled in a circle around him.

When one of the dragons pounced, Gage held out his hand and obliterated the magic surrounding it. It shrieked and toppled, writhing in misery. Gage ran toward it so he could use its body to block the other dragon while he escaped, lunging onto its head and up over its shoulder.

Only to find a third gnarled dragon diving straight toward him.

"No!" Gage cried.

He dove for the ground, but the third dragon soared past him and smashed into the second dragon—which had been dangerously close to devouring Gage from behind. The new dragon snapped its fangs around the other's neck, gave it a fierce shake, and flung it across the wasteland.

The dragon Gage had felled with his magic now clawed its way to its feet. The new dragon tackled it to the dust, and the two wrestled, tearing with their claws while aiming fangs at each other's throats. The new dragon finally caught its opponent's tail in its mouth and whirled it around like a slingshot, releasing it and letting it fly. Then it positioned itself between Gage and the other dragons.

Although gaunt and sickly like the others, this dragon had fewer black veins and spikes, and it still looked like a light dragon. A poof of white feathers glittered from the tip of its tail, and its feathered wings sparkled. The dragon glanced at Gage with golden eyes.

Gage, run, cried the all-too-familiar voice of the girl.

The other two dragons lunged at Gage, but the third intercepted them. Gage did the only logical thing he could think to do: he ran. Dust choked his lungs, but so did panic. The girl's voice came from the dragon!

A monstrous form in the sky eclipsed the light. Gage's stomach clenched, and he tightened his grip on Spark still trembling in his arms. A violent crash sounded in the distance, followed by an earthquake.

"No, no, no," he cried. "Not now!"

Another crash sounded, followed by a quake that tore the ground asunder. Shelves of rock cleaved upward while others sank into black chasms. The crashing rocks and fighting dragons created a deafening roar of violent sounds. Spark added a terrified shriek as Gage tripped and staggered. The earth opened into a black abyss beneath them.

Gage, please, cried the girl, sounding faint now. A sob choked her voice. *Please hurry!*

Desperately clutching his dragon, Gage fell into darkness, the dusty sky and ominous shadow fading away. He screamed, but he couldn't hear himself. Nor could he hear the crumbling rocks or raging dragons. He heard only the muted voice of the girl.

Please save us.

38

JUST A DREAM

Gage jolted awake, screaming as he flew upright in bed. He gasped for air that wouldn't come. His eyes flicked around the room, and hazy confusion shifted to clarity. He was in his room at Thad's clinic. His frantic movement had sent Spark tumbling to the edge of the bed, where the dragon huddled and shivered with his wings close to his body.

"Gage," Thad shouted from the hallway, his uneven footsteps thudding in haste toward the room. The door whipped open, revealing the older man with his sleeves rolled up like he'd been washing laundry. "Are you okay? What's wrong?"

Words escaped Gage. He couldn't breathe well enough to answer. He looked out the window at Runadel. Outside, normal people walked around doing normal-people things. Late-afternoon sunlight streaked through the glass and covered Gage with its warmth. No darkness, no dust, no earthquakes, no creepy dragons trying to eat him, and no monstrous things devouring the sky.

"Dream," he finally muttered. "It was just a dream."

"Are you sure? That was a lot of yelling for a dream," Thad said.

"Yeah." Gage wiped sweat off his forehead with the back of his hand.

Spark stared at him, still curled into a tight ball. Had Gage given the dragon his nightmares the same way Rhemi gave Alphen her vision?

Thad lingered in the doorway.

Gage forced a smile. "I'm okay. I promise. It was just a nightmare. I get them sometimes." All the time, actually. "I'll be all right."

Thad hesitated, his brow furrowed in concern. "You sure?"

"Yeah. I'll be out in a bit."

Thad nodded and exited the room, clicking the door shut behind him. His footsteps receded down the hall.

Gage looked out the window as he took several slow, steadying breaths. That had been quite the nightmare. The worst he'd ever experienced. Everything had seemed so real, and it was the first time he'd seen creatures like that or heard the girl so clearly. She'd called herself Orelia.

Please save us.

A shiver ran through him. Save who, and from what? He shook his head and laughed awkwardly. It was just a dream.

An awful, miserable dream. Scrubbing his forehead with both hands, he threw off his blanket and slid out of bed.

"Sorry for giving you my nightmares," he said, ruffling Spark's head fluff.

Gage grabbed fresh clothes out of a drawer and peeled off his sweat-slicked shirt. As he pulled on a fresh tunic, pain seared through his arm. He jerked in surprise and bumped the corner of the dresser, toppling everything on it, including the dead plant and Alphen's dragon sculpture. He righted the plant and grabbed the dragon to do likewise—and then stopped. Turning the sculpture over in his hand, he inspected its feral expression and numerous spikes. It was the same type of dragon from his dream. Smaller and chubbier, maybe, but undeniably similar.

He'd dreamed of the creatures because he'd seen the sculpture. That made sense.

Master, no dream, Spark whimpered. He remained huddled, trembling. *It real.*

Gage's arm continued to burn. He set aside the sculpture and pulled up his sleeve. A nasty scrape ran along his forearm in the same location he'd been injured in his dream.

39

SHUT UP, EDDLY

A few straggler students trickled into the academy training ground for a second class with Alphen—this one covering magical combat. Gage stifled a yawn and stretched. Again. For the billionth time. He still hadn't fully recovered from his overnight escapade in the Vaskran camp with Alphen two nights before. Thankfully, his only class yesterday had been with Thad, and it turned out to be a class about first aid and survival techniques. Thad had let him sleep through it since Gage already knew basic first aid.

Gage had needed the rest, especially after his nightmare, but also because of what he planned to do after class today. He intended to confront Alphen about *his* nightmares and the dragon sculpture. Gage needed answers. But more than that, he needed Alphen to tell him that he was crazy and that Spark was wrong. Because dreams couldn't be real.

While students lazily chatted with each other, Eddly had the nerve to waltz over to Gage with a grin plastered on his face. Gage glared at him. He was *not* in the mood for this guy.

"You skipped class yesterday, Voidy." Eddly wiggled his eyebrows. "Looks like you're not such a great student after all."

Gage's eye twitched. "Yet only one of us has been thrown out of a class, and it wasn't me. Weird, huh?"

Eddly's smile withered. He scowled, rolled his eyes, and walked away.

The academy bell clanged from the bell tower. The chatter ceased, and eyes swept the grounds.

"Where is Lord Alphen?" asked a girl.

No one answered. Students resumed whispering to each other. As time stretched on and Alphen didn't arrive, worry squirmed like worms in Gage's stomach. Every moment that passed doubled his concern.

"If he's not here in five minutes, I'm outta here," Eddly said.

"No one would miss you," Gage muttered.

Eddly whipped his head around, but judging by his bemused expression, he hadn't heard Gage's exact words.

"Why don't we practice magic with Lady Halayna's crystals? That's the point of this class, after all," a girl said, and she pulled out her magical stone. Several students around her did likewise.

Eddly tossed his own back and forth between his hands, grinning smugly at Gage. "Too bad you don't have a crystal, Voidy."

Gage gave him a cold, hard stare. "Because I don't need one. I can already use magic." He grinned and sidled closer to Eddly, reaching for his crystal. "But here, let me see yours—"

"Back off!" Eddly hid his crystal behind him and scampered across the room.

Gage laughed, and a few other students snickered. The double doors slammed open, causing everyone to whirl toward the entrance. Alphen staggered into the room and flashed a smile—a weak, pathetic, fake one. His eyes sank into his face, heat flushed his cheeks, and he shivered from head to toe.

"Sorry I'm late," he said, his voice raspy and faint. "I've been a little under the weather."

Rhemi flew in behind him and landed on a nearby weapon rack, chattering angrily and scowling at Alphen. He ignored her as he stumbled across the room.

"Are you okay?" a girl asked.

"I'm fine," Alphen said, but a boy had to grab him to keep him from tipping over. "Or maybe not. To be determined." He hobbled to his usual stool, never once straightening his legs, and then sat with his back to the wall. "Welcome to another magic class. Today, I want you to focus on sensing your magic. You'll need to master this skill before anything else. Some people find it easier to close their eyes, but it's not necessary. Just know there's magic inside you and look for it."

"Should we use our crystals?" A girl held hers up.

"Yeah, go for it. That should brighten your magic and make it easier for you to see."

The rest of the students pulled out their crystals.

"Your magic should look like a sphere of threads inside you," Alphen explained, his voice growing weaker. "Most of it should be knotted, but you'll see some strings waving around. Your magic should be bright and steady, and when you touch it with your mind, it should feel invigorating and warm. You won't see anyone else's magic, so don't bother looking. Only Innarans and void users can see others' magic."

"Of course he got that ability too," Eddly grumbled.

"Shut up, Eddly," someone muttered before Gage even had a chance to think it.

Gage snorted.

"If Innarans can see magic in everything, why do they need to test us with crystals?" a boy asked.

"Good question." Alphen leaned his head on the wall. "Most living things have magic in them. When you guys are young, it's hard for Innarans to differentiate between the magic of life and actual magical aptitude. We don't bother trying. Creates too many false positives and disappointed kids later on. The crystals are better suited to finding magic users early."

"Unless Voidy breaks them," Eddly murmured.

Almost instantaneously, a boy whispered, "Shut up, Eddly!"

"Go ahead and get started. I'll give you some time." Alphen crossed his arms and closed his eyes.

The others clutched their crystals and scrunched their faces in concentration.

Gage focused on the magic around him the same way he'd done in the Vaskran camp. Once again, the world shifted into a brighter version of itself. Inside every kid shone an orb of white light edged with blue, red, green, or yellow depending on the student's magic type. Some of their magical threads unraveled and fluttered around them, breaking away and fading into the brightness.

Next, Gage turned his attention to Alphen, whose shriveled ball of magic pulsed erratically inside him. His threads coiled inward before violently exploding outward. Gage had never seen an Innaran's magic, but he assumed that wasn't normal.

Thad had said that Alphen used to get ill as a child because of a magic imbalance. Maybe it wasn't a coincidence that Alphen was ill while his magic looked like that.

Gage glanced at his own magic. A steady sphere of purple light shone inside him, with threads fluttering around him like ribbons on a breeze. They wormed through the air, whipped around the shining threads of his fellow students, and snuffed them out of existence. He gasped and yanked an errant thread back into himself, but six more popped out and obliterated the magical threads of his classmates.

Can you stop my magic from destroying theirs? Gage asked Spark.

No do, Spark replied, shaking his head.

Gage's heart sank. Trying to restrain his magic only made things worse, so he finally gave up. This was what had destroyed the life and magic around Talid, the thing that had labeled him cursed for his entire life. This was the thing he needed to control.

Loud clattering startled him from his thoughts. Alphen had staggered to the nearest wall, toppling his stool in the process. A group of kids raced to his side, but he waved them away.

"I'm fine," he said, but then he flinched and rubbed his forehead. "Actually, maybe not. I should rest. You're dismissed. Go practice your magic on your own."

Most of the kids hesitated, but when he flapped a hand at them, they shuffled out of the room. Gage lingered. Rhemi had flown to a rack closer to Alphen and now hissed and spit at him, ruffling her feathers in anger. He ignored her.

"Did something happen?" Gage asked when the other students had gone.

Alphen shot him a pathetic grin. "Bad breakfast." He hobbled like an old man toward the exit. A shudder swept through him, nearly taking him off his feet. Rhemi went back to squawking at him.

"I think you should see Thad," Gage said, hurrying after Alphen.

"Bah. This is nothing. A little sleep will fix me right up."

"You look and sound terrible, Alphen. And you can barely walk. You need help."

Alphen scowled. "Great. You've lived with Thad for less than a week and you already sound like him. Don't worry. I'll be fine. I'm heading right to bed. I promise." After offering Gage a two-fingered salute, he exited.

Gage glanced at Spark, who glanced at Rhemi. She leaped off her perch, chasing her human partner. Gage followed, determined to at least see Alphen safely to bed. A thud from the hallway hastened his steps into the corridor, where he found Alphen collapsed and shuddering on the floor. Rhemi screeched and landed beside him.

"Alphen!" Gage ran to him and put a hand on his shoulder. Overwhelming heat seared his palm through Alphen's clothes. A fearful chill swept through Gage as he wrapped Alphen's arm across his shoulders, pulling his weight off the floor. "Hang on, Alphen. I'm bringing you to Thad."

40

How About I Stab You?

"Thad!" Gage shoved through the clinic door, dragging Alphen with him. "Alphen needs help!"

Thad rounded a corner from the back room, hastening toward them as soon as he saw Alphen's sorry state. "What did you do now?" he asked with comical accusation.

Alphen blinked blearily without offering a snarky reply. His head bobbed.

"Get him to the table," Thad commanded, turning serious. He wrapped an arm around Alphen's back and eased most of his weight off Gage. "What happened?"

"He collapsed after class." Gage helped Thad seat Alphen on the edge of the exam table and then rolled his shoulders to loosen his muscles. "His magic is out of sorts. I saw it."

"Don't go telling my secrets," Alphen grumbled.

"Would you rather I guess what's wrong with you?" Thad crossed his thick arms. "Maybe poke you with a few needles while I figure it out?"

Alphen managed a glare.

"It's been a while since I stabbed you with anything," Thad added. "What do you say?"

"I think I'm good for now, thanks."

"Too bad." Thad scrunched his face in mock disappointment as he drew a thermometer out of his apron. He shoved it into Alphen's mouth before turning to Gage. "Go into the back and grab a vial of glowing liquid out of the storage cabinet."

"Glowing liquid?" Gage asked.

"Made from an Innaran Sunburst."

Gage nodded and hustled into the back, opening the cabinet. Light radiated from the top shelf. Shoving a few items aside, he grabbed a vial filled with a bright, twinkling liquid. He'd never seen anything like it. Returning to the main room, he found Thad checking the thermometer.

The healer let out a low whistle. "That's quite the fever."

"Can he drink it like this?" Gage asked, holding up the vial.

Alphen suddenly covered his mouth with both hands and rushed into the back room. Buckets and basins clattered, followed by awful retching sounds that sent shivers up Gage's spine.

Thad smiled and patted Gage on the back. "You'll get used to that after you've worked here awhile."

"Will this help?" Gage wagged the vial.

"It's not a perfect fix, but it'll help stabilize him." Thad headed toward the back. "Mix the full vial with equal parts base elixir and a dose each of frizian and merifal."

Gage rushed to the counter while Thad helped Alphen. Frizian would lower the fever, while merifal was a potent sedative. Thad apparently planned on holding Alphen hostage for a while. Gage mixed the ingredients together and dumped them into a small cup. He was just finishing when Thad hauled Alphen back into the main room toward a cot by the wall.

"Sit," Thad said.

Alphen plopped onto the edge of the cot. Only Thad's grip kept him from falling over. Gage handed him the cup, but Alphen's hand trembled, splashing the liquid around. Thad finally took it and helped him drink.

Alphen cringed and stuck out his tongue when he finished. "That's disgusting."

"Only the best for you." Gage tossed the cup into their bin of supplies that needed washing.

"Now lie down and rest," Thad said, pulling aside the blanket.

Alphen eased onto the cot. Once he settled his head on the pillow, his body deflated, his eyelids fluttered, and a shiver swept through him. He took the blanket and curled into it, trembling. Thad watched him with genuine concern.

"Will he be all right?" Gage asked.

"Should be. He's always come around before." Thad swept a hand down his face. "It's been a long time since he's fallen this ill."

Worry wormed inside Gage. He swallowed hard and wrapped his arms around himself. "Is this my fault?"

Thad's eyebrows pinched together. "Your fault? Why?"

"Because of my void magic. I spent an entire night with him rescuing those kids, and I leaned on him when we flew back. Maybe my magic—"

"No, no," Thad said, shaking his head. "Innaran magic is everywhere in this kingdom, and Alphen happens to be a particularly strong magic user. There's no way your void magic overpowered him."

"But—"

"Remember," Thad interjected, "he used to get sick as a child too. We certainly didn't have void users running around causing these issues back then. You're not to blame." He patted Gage on the back, grabbed some supplies off the counter, and carried them into the back room.

His words made sense when Gage thought about it logically. Alphen's magic had allowed Thad to heal Spark, meaning he could overpower void magic. Still, Gage couldn't shake the thought that this was somehow his fault. After a lifetime of killing fields, destroying magic, and being hated because of his curse, the last thing he needed was to be the reason his first real friend lay deathly ill.

41

MISSED OPPORTUNITY

"I grabbed lunch for us on my way home," Nihsa called into the clinic after spying Gage and Thad mixing medicines at the counter. She let Mishu inside before kicking the door shut and carting her packages to the kitchen table.

"Perfect timing." Thad capped a vial of medicine and set it aside. He used a towel to wipe his fingers.

Gage finished mixing his own concoction and poured it into a vial. Thad had spent the remainder of the morning teaching him how to mix new medicines. He'd forgotten about lunch until the delicious smells from the packages made his stomach rumble.

Nihsa noticed Alphen asleep on the cot as she set down the bundles, and her cheerful expression darkened into a scowl. "What's he doing here?"

"Sick like the old days." Thad set the table and unwrapped lunch.

Nihsa maintained her glare at Alphen. "Did you stab him with some needles?"

"Unfortunately not."

"Too bad. Missed opportunity, Dad."

Gage grinned as he finished his work and wiped his hands. He glanced at Alphen curled in a tight ball under his blanket. His boots now sat beside the cot. Earlier, Gage had come out of the back room to find Thad removing the boots, presumably to make Alphen more comfortable. When Thad noticed him, he huffed and muttered something about not wanting his cot to get dirty, and then he went on to straighten the blanket over Alphen, basically tucking him in. It had taken everything in Gage not to laugh.

"Come eat, lad," Thad said.

He and Nihsa filled their plates with shredded beef, carrots, and potatoes lathered in gravy. Nihsa was pulling out dinner rolls when Mishu yowled dramatically from beside her food dish on the counter. Nihsa sighed and brought her food. Gage glanced around for Spark, who had gone to lounge in a windowsill but had since disappeared.

"I guess this means you have the afternoon free," Nihsa said to Gage. "We should go shopping."

"Why would I be free? I have another class."

"Alphen is your teacher this afternoon for individual studies."

"Oh." Gage frowned. Lady Halayna had picked Alphen to teach him void magic?

"So you both have the afternoon free? Fantastic." Thad clapped his hands as he slipped into his chair. "I have some tasks for you to do around the clinic."

"Dad." Nihsa flopped into her seat.

"Now hear me out." Thad wagged his fork at them. "If you help me for a few hours, I'll give you both some silver to spend this afternoon."

"You don't have to pay me," Gage said, devouring a forkful of beef, carrot, and potato. Rich, salty flavor exploded across his tongue. He scooped up more, only for a familiar dark foreleg to spring up from under the table, swipe the food off his fork, and disappear again. Gage huffed. "You don't have to steal it, Spark!"

Thad ignored their antics and looked meaningfully at Gage. "I don't have to pay you, but I want to. I make a good living here; it doesn't hurt me any." When Gage opened his mouth to protest, Thad added, "Besides, you've been more useful to me in a few days than people I'd hired for months. You've earned something extra."

"Then I accept." Gage smiled.

After finishing lunch, Gage and Nihsa helped around the clinic for a few hours, doing dishes and laundry, cleaning every corner of the building, and mixing various medicines. Despite all the banging around they did, Alphen never once stirred. The sedatives would likely keep him knocked out until much later, if not through the whole night. Once their work was complete, Thad gave them a list of supplies to purchase and gifted them each a pouch of jingling coins.

They set out into the city, Spark riding on Gage's shoulder and Mishu trotting along behind them with her tail straight up in the air. They passed various stores and market stalls until Gage saw a shop beyond the main plaza that sold the plants and herbs on Thad's shopping list.

"Should we stop here?" he asked.

"Not yet. Let's head to the other side of the city first and work our way back."

"Is there anything specific you're looking for today?"

"A new jacket and boots."

A devious grin formed on Gage's lips. "Trying to impress someone?"

Nihsa pinched the back of his arm, making him laugh. "Not like that, you little imp. King Fraylon is coming to the academy tonight."

"He is?"

"Yes. He'll give a speech during dinner. We're eating at the dining hall tonight."

Gage followed her determined march through the city, watching as several wind avians twirled through the air with colorful ribbons in their talons.

"So," he started, "you're buying a fancy new outfit to impress an old guy?"

She aimed to pinch him again, but he dodged her fingers, only to earn a playful shove instead.

"To impress a king, thank you very much." Her cheeks turned pink. "King Fraylon deserves the best. My family owes him a lot."

"Why's that?"

"When my dad was injured, King Fraylon gave him the clinic here in Runadel so he had a place to live and work after leaving the army. He also let me begin my training early so I could become a knight recruit at a younger age."

"He sounds like a good person," Gage said.

"He's one of the best. He's everything a king should be and more. You'll like him." Tilting her head to the side, Nihsa asked, "What about you? Is there anything you're shopping for today?"

"Not really. But I'd love a chocolate-covered banana."

Nihsa chewed down a smile. "Big spender, aren't you?" She pointed down the street. "The chocolate-covered snacks should be down there. Why don't you grab one?" She jutted her thumb in the opposite direction, toward a two-story building with a dress on its sign. "I'm heading there and might be a while. Come find me in a bit? Unless you want to try on pretty clothes too?"

"Yeah, thanks, I'll pass." Gage smirked and headed the opposite way.

He located the snack-selling vendor in the same place he'd found it with Alphen. He bought a few different chocolate-covered snacks for him and Spark, including strawberries, blueberries, and something called pineapple.

Then he bought two chocolate-covered bananas, one each for him and Spark.

After eating his snacks, he went after Nihsa. He hadn't gone far when he found her eyeing tables set out by a street vendor. Rings, bracelets, and necklaces glittered on display. The merchant flitted about to ensure no one stole his goods.

"Buying something pretty for King Fraylon?" Gage teased.

"No, I'm actually looking for . . ." Nihsa stopped, and her cheeks flushed with color.

Gage rotated his hand in a circle, gesturing for her to continue. The flush of her cheeks deepened, and she wrapped her arms around herself.

"You can't tell my dad," she said.

"Okay?"

"I'm looking for the ring Alphen gave me when he proposed."

"He gave you a ring?"

"Of course." Nihsa scrunched her face. "And promptly took it back when we broke up. A week later, he told me with absolute glee that he'd sold it to a traveling merchant."

Gage shifted uncomfortably, scratching his arm. "That doesn't sound like Alphen."

"No." Nihsa stared at the jewelry, the light sparkling in her eyes. "It wasn't like him at all. He became a totally different person, and he only went back to normal when we stopped spending time together."

"Then why do you want the ring?"

"It's stupid, I know," she whispered. "But that ring was the best thing I've ever owned. Alphen sculpted it with his magic, adding a white gemstone to represent him and an aqua gemstone to represent me. Then he twisted the white metal into a beautiful design." Her fingers traced a nearby ring with twirls in the metal. Tears filled her eyes. "It meant the world to me."

Gage looked at the jewelry because he couldn't stand seeing people cry. More and more, Alphen confused him. He pretended to be a jerk, but he wasn't. At least not since Gage had known him. Apparently, he'd been soft and sensitive with Nihsa before going crazy and breaking her heart. And now he was obviously still infatuated with her while pretending not to be. None of it made sense. Half of Alphen's personality seemed to be an act.

Which made Gage wonder—was the Alphen he knew real or fake?

"So you look at these shops all the time?" Gage asked to distract himself from his thoughts. He wasn't sure what he'd do if he found out Alphen was lying to him.

"I know it's pointless," Nihsa said. "The ring is probably long gone."

"Maybe he didn't sell it?"

"Oh, I'm sure he did." Nihsa blinked away the tears thickening in her eyes. "You didn't see him back then. He was ruthless." Sighing, she added, "I just wish he hadn't thrown away something so important to me."

Gage got the feeling she meant more than just her ring. She obviously still cared about Alphen.

He put a hand on her back. "I'm sorry."

Nihsa laughed awkwardly and shook her head. "I'm sorry, Gage. I don't know why I'm rambling like this. I've only known you for a few days, but you already feel like my little brother."

"I always wanted siblings," Gage admitted, smiling.

Nihsa smiled, too, and pulled him into a tight hug. Gage returned the gesture. She sniffled a few times, and when she finally let him go, she'd composed herself.

"You know," he said, "if I'm the little brother, that means I have to be annoying sometimes. It's part of the job."

Nihsa snorted and leaned to the side with one hand on her hip. "Hang around Alphen long enough and you'll be plenty annoying in no time, don't worry."

42

TIDINGS OF WAR

Excited chatter filled the dining hall as students, recruits, knights, and teachers ate dinner while awaiting King Fraylon's arrival. The sounds blurred into a loud droning. Every seat at every table had been filled. Gage sat with Nihsa and Thad at the teachers' table. The other students glared at him in envy, but he didn't mind. Not much, anyway.

Mishu sat politely on the table next to Nihsa, daintily eating her food like a princess. Spark remained under the table and swiped food off Gage's plate despite having his own food dish. By dragon logic, stolen food tasted better. Gromlin had refused to come, so Thad tasked him with keeping an eye on Alphen.

An Innaran knight stepped onto the front stage and rang a handbell. The room silenced.

"Now presenting His Majesty, King Fraylon Lightgard of the Innara," the man said before descending the steps and joining a line of knights against the wall.

Everyone rose from their seats and either bowed or dropped to one knee. Gage mimicked Thad and Nihsa, bowing, but he lifted his face so he could peek at the king.

Twinkling gold curtains parted at the front of the room, and King Fraylon stepped out in splendor and majesty. He appeared older than his children—as expected—but still looked impossibly handsome and ageless, as Innarans always did. While not as powerfully built as Lord Calvex, he wasn't as lithe as Alphen, either. Much like his children, he had warm brown skin, dark eyes, and white hair, which fell to his waist. The top half was tied into small braids and twirled into an elegant design. The lower half was bound into a single braid interwoven with golden threads. A gold crown sat atop his head, and he wore elegant armor and robes in many layers. His light dragon perched on his shoulder with regal grace, holding its head high.

The king approached the podium, looking over the crowd. "Thank you for the welcome, but please be seated, my friends," he said in a deep voice, both powerful and gentle.

Everyone returned to their seats, but their attention remained wholly on King Fraylon. Even Spark perched on the table to watch.

"First of all, I want to thank you for coming tonight," said the king. "I consider it an honor to be worthy of your time. Regardless of your position, I thank you for your efforts here at the academy. Runadel and the Innaran kingdom would be a lesser place without you. You have my sincerest gratitude."

Gage warmed at the man's genuine words. Yet as smiles spread across the room, King Fraylon's face fell. He gripped the sides of the podium and closed his eyes.

"Those who know me know I am a man of few words, so allow me to be brief." He scanned the room, taking in every face. "We are losing the war."

Shocked silence swept over the crowd, followed by hushed whispers. The volume increased as people spoke over each other in panicked voices.

King Fraylon lifted a hand from the podium, quieting his audience. "I do not mean to alarm you, but I will not deceive you. The water and fire tribes have already fallen, and the Vaskr now seek to overtake the wind tribe in order to surround us. They breach our defenses and harry our forces deeper inside Innaran territory every day. The endless skirmishes have vastly decreased our numbers, while the Vaskran forces grow with each passing day."

The king took a deep breath and searched the crowd, meeting people's gazes. "My friends, I must tell you the truth about why the Vaskr took Sarsier from us. Two reasons you know, a third reason you do not." He gripped the sides of the podium. "First, they attacked to decimate the number of Innarans. Many of my people resided in the capital city. Most perished in the attack. By defeating us there, the Vaskr drastically decreased our numbers and our ability to fight back. Second, they stole Sarsier to obtain our largest stores of magical crystals, the very items we spread across the land to share our magic with you. Fewer people today have magic as a result."

He continued, "But the Vaskr took Sarsier for a third and far more important reason. It is for this reason that the Innarans fought for the capital and ultimately lost their lives, including my own father and brother. Sarsier Castle holds within its walls a crystal of unimaginable power. By this crystal, the ancient Innarans gifted magic to this world. The Vaskr attacked Sarsier to steal this crystal from us, and now they use it to increase their numbers and magical prowess."

King Fraylon's hands slipped from the podium. "If we want any hope of defeating our foes, we must retake the capital and reclaim this crystal. Without it, we will perish. And so, it is with a heavy heart that I come to you now. I am pulling all active forces from Runadel immediately. We will launch a coordinated assault to retake the capital by year's end."

Everyone started talking at once. Gage didn't understand the commotion. Active forces were meant for battle, weren't they?

"I understand your concerns, my friends," King Fraylon said, speaking over them and drawing them back into nervous silence. "Rest assured, I have no intention of leaving Runadel and our students unguarded. The children here are our most valuable assets. The knight recruits will remain to defend and teach them, as will any retired senior knights. My own daughter will remain to keep watch over this city." He nodded firmly. "I will give no more ground or precious lives to the Vaskr."

His words were probably meant to inspire confidence, but he received no cheers or applause.

"When do we leave?" someone asked.

"Tomorrow morning," said the king.

Some people shuffled on their benches and muttered to one another while others sat and stared in silence. Most of the people Gage had seen at the academy would leave, including most of the Innarans. Some might never return. The thought chilled him to the bone.

"War does not wait for a convenient time or place," King Fraylon said somberly. "It is cruel and relentless. It will snuff out everything we hold dear unless we overcome it. Surrender is not an option. I will not give this beautiful land to the Vaskr who seek to subjugate us. I will not allow you or your children to be abused and enslaved. And so, tomorrow at dawn, we rise and fight."

Only muted cheers and applause answered him, mostly from the older members of the gathering. Gage sat in silence.

Alphen had suggested that the Vaskr might attack the academy. That once-incomprehensible scenario now seemed like an inevitability. The Vaskr had already gotten close to Runadel during their attack on Delevar. How close would they get if Lord Calvex and his forces weren't lurking nearby? How long would Runadel stand if all the powerful fighters left for Sarsier?

Gage's stomach twisted into a knot, and he shoved away his plate. He'd suddenly lost his appetite.

43

A King's Warning

Dessert followed dinner. No one left the dining hall after King Fraylon's speech, and Gage quickly learned why. The king stepped off the stage and made his way down the aisles, greeting everyone individually. He shook hands, kissed cheeks, and hugged people. He didn't linger long, but he didn't skip anyone. Everyone seemed to love him—some bowed or knelt before him, and others wept in his presence.

Gage watched with interest and pretended not to notice Spark stealing the rest of his food. The dragon didn't even bother taking it under the table anymore. He simply moved aside, devoured it, and returned for more.

At long last, King Fraylon reached their table. Everyone rose. Gage wiped sweat off his hands onto his pants as his heart thudded in his chest. He was about to shake hands with one of the most important people in the world.

"Nihsa," King Fraylon said with cheer when he reached her. He kissed her cheek, gave her a quick hug, and stepped back to look her over. "You remain as smart, capable, and beautiful as ever."

Nihsa practically melted into a puddle. "Thank you so much, Your Majesty."

"How are your studies?"

"Successful, for the most part. But I believe I can do better."

His eyes twinkled. "Curious. When Master Warren reported the latest testing results, he said you are among the best and brightest in your class."

Nihsa's cheeks flushed. "He speaks too highly of me."

"Ever the modest one, dear girl. Brains, brawn, beauty, and humility. My son was a fool to let you go."

"I know. I tell him that as often as I can."

King Fraylon grinned and dipped his head. When he turned to move down the line, Nihsa's hand flew out and caught his sleeve.

"I wish you would let me go with you, sir," she said quietly, snatching her hand away.

The twinkle in King Fraylon's eyes diminished. "I appreciate the sentiment, Nihsa, but I have no desire to see young people sacrificed on the battlefield." His gaze swept across the students and recruits in the room. "I hope to end the war swiftly so you never have to see a real battle."

Tears glistened in Nihsa's eyes. "Thank you, sir."

He touched her shoulder and moved down the line.

"Thad!" He clasped the man's forearm in a fierce grip, pulled him into a hug, and thumped him on the back. When they parted, he asked, "How is the leg?"

"Still attached," Thad said gruffly, though he smiled.

King Fraylon barked a laugh. "I am pleased to hear it. I continue receiving excellent reports about your clinic. And I hear you found yourself a new assistant."

Thad stepped aside, revealing Gage. "Gage Black, sir. One of the new students at the academy. He has a knack for healing."

"Is that so?" King Fraylon smiled at Gage.

Gage's cheeks warmed. "I practiced medicine before coming to the academy. I'm excited to learn more."

"Thad could use the help," said the king.

He patted Thad on the shoulder and then shook Gage's hand. The shake was quick but firm.

"You are the new void user, correct?" King Fraylon asked.

Spark chose that moment to leap up Gage's back and perch on his shoulder, staring at King Fraylon with much interest. The king returned the scrutiny, though he smiled.

"Void user, indeed," he said lightly.

"Thank you for letting me attend the academy." Gage fidgeted with the edges of his tunic. "I wasn't sure what would happen after I broke the crystal."

"I apologize for the delay in retrieving you." Lord Fraylon chuckled. "My daughter was quite surprised that day."

"I'll bet." Gage recalled the horrified faces of the Innarans when he'd shattered their rock with a single touch.

King Fraylon looked Gage over and forced a smile. His eyes lacked their usual sparkle. "Actually, I was hoping to meet you here tonight. I wanted to have a word with you. Would you take a walk with me around the east garden?" He gestured toward the exit.

Gage stared, stricken, and then glanced at Thad and Nihsa. Thad tilted his head, and Nihsa nodded adamantly, all but shooing him away with her hands. But Gage didn't move. No one else had been pulled aside by the king.

"I have no ill intentions, I assure you," King Fraylon said with a mild laugh. "I will not keep you long."

"Okay." Gage nodded and waited for the king to lead the way.

King Fraylon placed a hand on his back and ushered him forward, keeping Gage alongside him. They headed toward a set of double doors on the east side of the hall. Two guards followed. As Gage passed his peers, most stared at him with wide eyes and gaping mouths, but a few scrunched their faces in jealous anger. Great. Another reason for them to hate him. Most people didn't get invited on an evening stroll with the king.

Their walk took them down several marble hallways and through a massive archway into a garden. Two guards waited at the garden's entrance and confirmed the grounds were empty. King Fraylon dismissed them with a wave of his hand before leading Gage down the stone walkway. Innaran Sunbursts lined the path, glittering in the darkness.

"I had hoped I would not need to have this conversation with you," King Fraylon said, slowing his walk. "No man with honor wants to place this sort of responsibility on a child's shoulders, yet here I am." He stopped, and Gage followed his lead. "Gage, your magic is special. The Vaskr have grown too powerful, and your ability to destroy magic may be the only thing capable of stopping them."

"Can't you outsmart them?" Gage asked.

"To make small gains, yes. But for every city we reclaim, we lose ten others. The Vaskr appear out of nowhere and constantly blindside us." King Fraylon rubbed his brow, now seeming more like an ordinary man than a majestic king. "I do not wish to see children in battle, but there may come a time when we ask for your aid. Your magic may well be our last hope against total annihilation."

Gage's breath hitched in his throat. No pressure. None at all. "Alphen told me my magic might be needed," he said. "I'm willing to help."

"Word of your bravery precedes you." King Fraylon resumed walking. "I heard about your recent misadventure with my son in the Vaskran camp."

Gage didn't move. "It wasn't Alphen's fault I was there. I wanted to go."

"Nevertheless, he should not have taken you." King Fraylon stopped again. "It was irresponsible on his part.

Had you been injured—or worse—it would have been unforgiveable."

"I would have gone with or without him," Gage stated, and he meant it. "Alphen just made it safer and easier."

King Fraylon arched his eyebrows. Gage lifted his chin and straightened his back, and Spark mimicked his posture on his shoulder.

"The Vaskr need to be stopped," Gage continued. "They're the reason I was orphaned, and they attacked the village where I grew up. I have lots of reasons to fight them, with or without Alphen."

"Your dedication is admirable. I only hope it does not turn into recklessness that costs you your life." King Fraylon frowned. Quietly, he said, "Child, be careful around Alphen."

"What?" Gage blinked in surprise.

"You spend a great deal of time with my son, and I fear he will get inside your head. He is not to be trusted."

"He's my teacher."

"In combat and magic, yes. But he should be nothing more."

A spark of fire ignited in Gage's belly. "He's not a bad person."

"So he would have you believe. If you are not cautious, you will become another Nihsa." King Fraylon resumed his walk, watching the flowers rustle on a breeze. "Alphen has a one-track mind. When he wants something, he seeks it relentlessly, and he will do whatever it takes to obtain it. He will befriend you, and when he has no further use for you, he will betray and discard you."

Gage followed the king. He no longer wanted to walk alongside him. Anger prickled in his belly. He'd seen Alphen do countless kind acts—things no one noticed, things he hadn't done to deceive anyone.

"What would he want from me?" Gage asked, unable to stop the clipped nature of his words.

"That remains to be seen," the king said softly. "Perhaps he views you as a tool for war. Or perhaps something else. I cannot fathom what goes on in the boy's mind. I have tried to break him of his rebellious nature, but my attempts only make matters worse." Turning swiftly, he faced Gage with a fierce frown. "Gage, he will betray you. It is not a matter of if, but when. Do not let your guard down around him."

"Lady Halayna said the same thing," Gage said.

"For good reason." King Fraylon placed a hand on Gage's shoulder, giving a gentle squeeze. His eyes and voice were soft as he said, "Do not let Alphen destroy you."

After squeezing Gage's shoulder once more, the Innaran king retreated down the path, returning to the building and leaving Gage and Spark alone with his words.

44

Benefit of the Doubt

Gage followed Thad and Nihsa into the clinic. When they turned on the lights, Gromlin made a low sputtering sound, ruffled his feathers, and squinted in annoyance. It was the most movement Gage had seen from the wind elemental.

"Oh, pipe down, you churlish old cod." Thad tossed his fancy jacket over the back of a chair. "I asked if you wanted to go, and you refused."

Gage smiled as he meandered toward his room. Gromlin was basically just Thad in elemental form. The two suited each other perfectly. He hoped he and Spark would share a similar connection someday. Or maybe they already did.

Spark stared intently across the room, drawing Gage's gaze in that direction. Rhemi stared back at him from where she lay across Alphen's chest. Alphen blinked at them with bleary eyes.

"You're awake!" Gage hurried to his bedside. "How are you feeling?"

Alphen blinked again, his eyelids heavy. He couldn't even muster a reply. His coloring remained poor and his eyes sunken.

"Feeling that well, eh?" Thad set a hand on Alphen's forehead and tsked. "I'll make another dose of medicine." He limped into the back storage area to collect supplies.

"Your father visited the academy tonight." Nihsa smiled, her hands on her hips.

Alphen propped himself up on an elbow, wincing. "Why?"

"To give a speech and gather troops. And to talk to us in person." Her grin widened. "As usual, he assured me you were a fool to let me go."

"He spoke to everyone?" Alphen's gaze flicked toward Gage.

"Yes, even Gage. Especially to Gage." Nihsa crossed her arms and frowned. "He took him on a private stroll through the garden."

Alphen flew upright, sending Rhemi tumbling into his lap. She sat up and scowled.

"What did he talk to you about?" Alphen asked.

"Yeah, what *did* he talk to you about?" Nihsa turned to Gage.

"Mind your business," Thad muttered, returning with several medicine vials in hand. He glowered at Alphen as he passed. "Lie down, boy."

Alphen didn't move. "What did Fraylon say to you?" he asked again.

"He told me that my magic might be important in fighting the Vaskr," Gage said, squirming under the scrutiny.

Alphen gave him a hard look before flinging aside his blanket and standing. He leaned against the wall to pull on his boots and staggered toward the door. Rhemi hissed at him and begrudgingly flew to his shoulder, chittering in annoyance.

"Where do you think you're going?" Thad snapped from the counter where he was mixing medicine. "Get back in bed. Now!"

"Where are you going?" Gage asked.

"To talk to the king." Alphen stormed out, slamming the door behind him. The walls rattled, and vials and tins clinked together in the cabinets.

"Stubborn as a donkey's uncle, that boy." Thad slammed down the vial he'd been pouring, huffing in irritation. Worry and anger warred in his eyes.

"What was that about?" Nihsa grumbled.

Gage wondered the same thing, though he had an idea. Did Alphen know King Fraylon had spoken ill of him? Was that what made him upset? Regardless, Gage didn't fully trust what King Fraylon or Lady Halayna had said. Of everyone Gage had met at the academy, Alphen was one of his favorites. He was fun to be around and genuinely kind. The thought that Alphen might be manipulating him made Gage ache.

He'd keep their warnings in mind, but he'd give his friend the benefit of the doubt. For now, at least.

45

SUMMONING STORIES

Half the semester passed without further attacks from the Vaskr. The vibrant greens of summer had given way to the fiery reds and golds of autumn.

Gage stared out the window, the steady stream of Lady Halayna's instruction lulling him to sleep. A fog had settled over his mind after reading books for most of class. Thus was the difficulty of being so advanced that he never needed to pay attention.

He excelled at most classes besides archery. Even now, his stomach twisted into knots thinking of Nihsa's upcoming test. She'd hinted about it for several weeks, and now it was upon them. No one knew what sort of challenge she'd planned for them, but they were never easy.

Gage had made the mistake of mentioning his anxiety to Alphen, about how he hated performing in front of others and how he'd look like a fool. The idiot prince had tried to make him feel better by inviting himself to watch the test—as if a larger audience would help. The last thing Gage wanted was for Alphen to see him fail.

At least Gage did well in Lady Halayna's classes. Though not uncommon for their age, none of the other students had summoned their elementals. Lady Halayna still spent most of their classes adding her magic to theirs, guiding and directing them while sharing words of encouragement.

Gage had stopped paying attention and instead focused on books from the library. He'd read most of the medical books, which helped with his work in the clinic. He'd also studied books on magical battle techniques and how to form magical weapons—a skill he'd practiced with Alphen but hadn't yet mastered. Now he returned to one of his favorite subjects: dragons and their third evolution.

You want I evolve? Spark asked, tilting his head as he peered at the images on the page. His language abilities had improved a lot in the past few months.

I like you the way you are. Gage ruffled Spark's head fluff and gave his body a fierce pet. *Evolve when you want. I won't make you.*

Warm, fluttery feelings flowed into him from Spark—a pleasant sensation immediately obliterated by Eddly slamming his crystal onto his table and cursing.

"This isn't working," he yelled, and then he waved a finger toward Gage. "How did he summon that stupid dragon without even trying while the rest of us are having this much trouble? It's not fair!"

"Enough, child," Lady Halayna said. "I will not have you take that tone in my classroom."

"Sorry." Eddly slumped and flicked the crystal on the table.

"How *did* you summon your dragon, Gage?" asked a girl toward the front of the room.

"Yeah, how?" A boy spun in his chair to face Gage.

Gage's cheeks burned at the attention, made even worse by Lady Halayna smiling at him.

"I am curious as well," she said. "Gage, would you be kind enough to come to the front and tell everyone how you summoned your dragon? It might be useful for them to hear."

When a handful of students uttered their agreement, Lady Halayna gestured for him to join her at the front. A nervous lump in his throat threatened to strangle Gage as he rose from his seat. Most of the kids looked at him with curious anticipation, but a few—like Eddly—scowled in jealous irritation.

He shuffled to the front, tugging on the edge of his tunic. "Um . . ."

"How did you summon him?" Lady Halayna pressed. "Were you using magic? Were you meditating to discover the magic within yourself?"

Gage frowned, thinking back to the moment Spark had entered his life. It seemed a long time ago now. "I was about to die."

Most of the class sat up in their seats. Even Eddly.

"It was after the magic testing," he went on. "I'd just broken the crystal and didn't even realize I had magic. After the Innara left, the Vaskr attacked my village."

Stools scraped as people scooted forward. Their attentiveness made the words flow easier from Gage's tongue.

"I got cornered by the Vaskr. One of their beetles launched an attack at me, and then . . ." He glanced at the void dragon on his shoulder. "Spark leaped out of my chest, attacked the Vaskr, and destroyed their magic. He was hit in the process, and they were about to kill him. That's when Alphen showed up and rescued us both." Gage nodded at Lady Halayna and then gazed at the mesmerized faces of his peers. "I didn't summon Spark. He summoned himself."

Silence filled the room until Lady Halayna hummed and tapped a finger on her lips. "I have heard legends of elementals summoned by their own will, usually at a time of great peril for their humans. Elementals born in this way tend to have abnormally strong bonds with their humans, resulting in exceptionally powerful magic for both."

Eddly sighed. "So we need to pick a fight with the Vaskr and hope our elementals show up and save us?"

"Absolutely not." Lady Halayna offered a patient smile. "I would rather we continue practicing as we are. Most elementals today are summoned with safer techniques, such as using crystals to infuse bodies with magic and compelling the elementals to come forth. While our elementals may have less overall magical strength, ten mid-level magic users are far more effective than ten dead ones."

"Not if the Vaskr keep increasing their numbers," Eddly muttered.

"You may return to your seat, Gage," Lady Halayna said. "Thank you for sharing."

Gage nodded and sat at his table.

A girl across the aisle leaned over to whisper, "I'm glad Spark was born. I think he's neat."

Gage's cheeks warmed. "Thanks. I think so too."

Spark lifted his head and puffed out his chest.

"Now then," Lady Halayna said, "let us—"

The door to the classroom swung open, and an Innaran guard hastened inside. "Sorry for the interruption, Your Grace, but it is urgent."

Ignoring the bewildered looks of the students, he whispered into Lady Halayna's ear. She listened at first with stoic disinterest, but then a muted gasp parted her lips. Her gaze swept across the room.

"You are dismissed for the day," she said to the class. "Your homework is to continue practicing with your crystals."

"Freedom!" Eddly grabbed his bag, slid his notepad into it, and darted out the door.

The other students moved a bit slower, several watching with interest as the guard and Lady Halayna exchanged quiet words. Gage tried unsuccessfully to read their lips, and even after his peers had trickled out, he stuck around and shuffled his books on the table. That is, until Lady Halayna noticed him.

"Class dismissed," she firmly stated.

Gage shoved his books into his bag, slung it over his shoulder, and headed out the door.

46

THE CHALLENGE

"All right, who's ready for a challenge?" Nihsa asked the students gathered in the wooden room that opened into the archery range. She rubbed her hands together, beaming with excitement. A silver whistle dangled from a rope around her neck.

"Not me," a boy murmured.

A wave of snickers passed through the group.

Nihsa smirked. "Fantastic. Sounds like you're ready." She fetched a training bow off a rack and stepped to the edge of the room, facing the targets across the range. A quiver of arrows swayed on her hip as she walked. "We've spent most of our time this semester practicing how to do this." Twirling an arrow, she effortlessly launched it and struck a distant bull's-eye.

Everyone gawped.

"Yeah, we can't do that," Gage muttered, inciting another round of snickers.

"Archery is incredibly useful," Nihsa said, "but when you add a touch of magic, it becomes much more powerful."

She marched across the field and moved eight portable targets into a row in front of the stationary targets at the end. Returning to the students, she launched another arrow at the line, but it hit and bounced off the first target with a dull thud.

"A regular arrow won't pierce these targets. But add a touch of magic . . ." She twirled another arrow and drew it on the bowstring.

A blue aura swirled over the arrow, and when she released it, an explosion of light erupted behind it, sending it hissing forward in a streak of blue. It tore through all eight portable targets and slammed into the final target with a deafening crack.

Everyone ran across the field. Nihsa's arrow had not only hit the bull's-eye of the farthest target but had blown a hole through it and hit the stone wall behind it. Jaws dropped, and all eyes fixed on Nihsa.

"I just performed what we call a surge," she explained. "Surges involve unleashing short but powerful bursts of magic from our bodies to impact the world around us. All magic users surge when they first summon their elementals, or when their elementals evolve, but with enough practice, they can learn to surge whenever they want. Surges can be used for a variety of things, including launching powerful attacks or leaping through the air with small bursts of magic."

Nihsa walked down the field and shoved the torn targets out of the way. "Surges are powerful but dangerous. If you unleash too much magic at once, you could collapse—or worse, overextend yourself and die. And surges can only be used on something you're physically touching, like an object you're holding or the air directly around you. Attempting to surge something without direct contact will cause your magic to scatter and may kill you. Use this skill sparingly, and only after significant study. Thus the purpose of our challenge today."

Grinning, she strolled to the side of the field where someone had built a haphazard stand against the external stone walls of the academy. Four slender wooden legs supported a wooden platform that sat level with the wall's walkway. A rickety staircase led to the top. Nihsa took the stairs in a few short strides, though the platform creaked and wobbled under her steps. Gage and the others stepped out onto the grass for a better view.

"Our regular targets are too close for what we're doing." Nihsa gestured beyond the academy wall. "For today, we've set up three large targets in the surrounding forest."

Despite the wall blocking their view, several students craned their necks as if to see over it. Gage felt his own chin lifting but snapped it back down and blushed at his own silliness.

"Don't worry. The targets are hard to miss," Nihsa said. "You're going to take turns surging an arrow to hit one. Or try to, at least. Three recruits volunteered to stand below the targets. If your arrow so much as grazes one of the targets, they'll toot a whistle." Nihsa blew her whistle in a few short bursts. "If you hit a bull's-eye, you'll hear a long, low whistle." She blew for a few seconds. "Any questions?"

"Are we being graded?" a girl asked.

"No."

Everyone sighed in relief, Gage included. He could barely hit a target with a regular arrow, even up close. He was far better at close-combat training. He'd pick a sword over a bow any day.

"Today is just for fun. You'll be tested on this at the end of the year." Nihsa trotted down the stairs and rejoined them in the grass. "This is my way of gauging where your magical skills stand right now."

Gage scrunched his face. She'd use this test to determine who was miserable and needed extra attention. He technically already received extra lessons from her during their free time, and he still barely hit the targets.

"Everyone, line up," she said, handing the bow to the student closest to her—the first unfortunate victim. She gestured toward a pail of arrows by the stairs. "Have at it!"

While the first student climbed onto the platform, everyone else formed a line. Gage hung back so he could be last, but he still ended up in the middle. Worse yet, Eddly stood behind him. Gage wiped his sweaty palms on his pants and took deep breaths to slow the rapid flutter of his heart. He barely noticed the first few students taking their turns until whistles peeped beyond the walls. A girl screeched and jumped for joy, jostling the platform before scurrying down the steps.

"Good job!" Nihsa gave her a high five and passed the bow to the next person.

Gage smiled. At least someone had succeeded. He watched the girl scurry over to another girl inside the building, hugging her and jumping for joy. Only then did he notice Alphen leaning casually against the wall with his arms crossed. The prince grinned at the girls and then at Gage. Gage forced a smile and looked away, inwardly groaning. He'd hoped Alphen had forgotten about the test. Now he'd fail in front of him too. Fantastic.

Someone else hit a target, earning more whistle peeps and inspiring more squeals.

"Look, Voidy," Eddly said. Gage glowered at him, but the bulky boy continued, "Remember how you tried to shoot an arrow all the way to the Vaskr during our first skill test?" Pretending his finger was an arrow, he sailed it over his closed fist—which Gage assumed represented the target. Then he hooked his thumb toward their current targets. "The wind tribe is this way, okay? Don't shoot an arrow at my people."

Gage deadpan glared at Eddly. "Don't worry. You're not over there, so why would I bother?"

A few students snickered. To Gage's surprise, even Eddly grinned, though he threw in an eye roll.

On and on the tests went. Only a few students hit the targets, and none the bull's-eye. Gage found the magical displays impressive. Blue, red, yellow, and green lights ignited around the students as they launched their arrows. Gage focused on the explosions of magic when they surged, enthralled until he noticed his own magic attacking and destroying theirs.

But he didn't have time to worry about that now, because his turn had arrived.

He took the bow, grabbed an arrow from the bucket, and began the soul-sucking march up the stairs. His heart thundered in his ears, and his head got muddled. Stepping onto the platform, Gage saw the three jumbo targets looming above the forest. They appeared small, but only because of their distance. A steady breeze ruffled his hair. His hand trembled as he placed the arrow on the bowstring.

Is okay. I can do, Spark said without an ounce of concern.

"You can?"

Yes. Look, see.

Gage frowned and took aim. His vision fuzzed, and then everything zoomed closer until he could see the fine weave of the target's fabric. Spark had enhanced his vision to that of a lethal predator. Gage could also feel the wind, could sense how it moved and how it would impact objects it touched. He shifted his aim to accommodate.

"You can see and feel all these things?" Gage asked.

I is dragon. Is good hunter, we are. Spark lifted his head in pride.

"You don't hunt."

Do not need. I good steal instead.

Gage laughed but didn't argue. He summoned his magic, and darkness swirled around him, glittering with purple sparks. Gritting his teeth and concentrating on the target using his high-powered vision, he loosed the arrow with a violent shove of his magic. The arrow exploded from the bowstring, hissed through the air like a dark shooting star, and slammed into the center of a target.

"We hit the bull's-eye," Gage choked out.

That not eye of bull. Bull is boy cow.

Gage ignored his dragon, listening for the whistle. A low, steady shriek sounded from the trees. Gage yelled in delight and flung the bow down onto the platform, dragging Spark into a hug and prancing around with him on the wobbly stand. Cheers and applause arose from everyone below.

"We did it! We hit the bull's-eye!" Gage held Spark at arm's length and gave the little dragon a shake. Spark narrowed his eyes on the target, still not understanding, but Gage didn't care. "Spark, we did it!"

The drone of the whistle suddenly cut off, followed by a muffled shout—and then silence. Gage stopped and looked out at the trees. The celebration died away, as did the songs of the birds and insects in the forest. Eerie silence fell over the land.

A chill shuddered up Gage's spine. He leaned down to grab the bow off the platform when he heard the distinct hiss of an arrow, right before one slammed into the platform two inches from his hand.

47

ASSAULT ON THE ACADEMY

Gage jerked away from the arrow, tottering on the edge of the platform. Cries of alarm arose behind him as he reclaimed his balance. He glimpsed Rhemi perched on the parapet of the wall and followed her steely gaze toward the forest. Twinkling lights lifted out of the canopy of leaves. His stomach plummeted. Those weren't lights—they were arrows heading straight at him.

"Get off the platform, Gage!" Alphen yelled over a cacophony of shouts and pounding footsteps.

Gage pivoted to jump, but Alphen had already reached the platform and kicked out one of its legs. The whole thing crumbled in a barrage of wood. Alphen snatched Gage out of the air and pushed him behind him, extending a hand and casting a barrier of light over the range. Dozens of arrows pattered against the barrier, tinkling like rocks on glass. Alphen shoved Gage and the other students toward the academy doors.

"Get inside," he commanded. "Now!"

Several boulders soared over the wall and shattered against Alphen's barrier. The explosive blasts sent most of the students screaming and bolting toward the building.

"Get into the dining hall," Alphen told them. "That area is shielded by magic. Hurry!"

Gage let the others go ahead of him before following. As he exited the archery range, he saw Alphen running for Rhemi and Nihsa leaping onto Mishu.

"Take the north wall," Alphen called to Nihsa as he took flight. "I'll cover the south."

"On it." Nihsa leaped away with Mishu.

Gage's stomach clenched in fear for his friends, but he trusted they could look after themselves. He followed his peers through the maze of colonnades and hallways toward the central keep that housed the dining hall. They kept a brisk pace until a massive explosion rocked the marble floors under their feet. Several students staggered with startled cries.

"What was that?" a boy squeaked.

A heartbeat later, a high-pitched shriek rattled the walls.

Gage's throat tightened at the familiar sound. "Earth beetles. The Vaskr are inside the academy. Run!" He shoved the nearest students and got the whole group running again.

Several more explosions shook the academy, but no one faltered this time—until the Vaskr stormed into the hallway, shouting curses and blocking their path. The students slid to a stop, but Gage shoved past them, running as fast as he could. A Vaskran man raced toward them with an axe lifted above his head. Gage shoved his dark magic over the crystals in the corridor, snuffing out the lights. The raider tripped on his own feet, and Gage bolted straight at him.

Alphen had taught them to use their size and speed against their enemies, and that's exactly what Gage intended to do. He slid across the tiles and took the huge man's legs right out from under him, sending him to the ground with a loud thud. Gage gave the guy a few solid kicks to his iron-helmeted head until the man's eyes rolled back and he sprawled unconscious on the floor. When Gage uncovered the lights, he found his peers staring at him in awe.

Screams from the opposite end of the hallway distracted everyone—as did more Vaskran shouting and cursing. Gage pushed through the group to intercept their attacks, but an explosion of blue light filled the hallway, followed by a deluge of water that slammed into the Vaskran men. Gage found a girl at the back of the group with blue lights glittering around her. A water feline sat in a puddle at her feet, licking its front paw. Water slicked the floor of the entire hallway. Every trace of the raiders had been washed away by a surge of magic.

"Did I do that?" The girl stared at the elemental near her feet.

"Everyone, keep moving," Gage shouted, nudging the girl.

She snatched up her elemental and hurried down the hall. They'd only made it to the next corridor when another string of blasts erupted around them. Boulders smashed through one of the walls, raining stone debris over their heads. Vaskran raiders poured in through the newly formed holes. Gage ran to intercept with his magic, but lights ignited all around him in hues of green, yellow, red, and blue. Flames burst down the hallway, followed by gales of wind, spears of stone, and another deluge of water.

Gage stared in shock. Over half the students had elementals at their feet or in their arms, magical light surging around them. Six Vaskran men lay at the end of the hall, unmoving. Eddly stumbled toward them, clasping an eagle-shaped wind avian like he wasn't sure what to do with it.

"I didn't even try," he muttered as he looked in horror at the fallen men.

"Don't worry about it," Gage said, and then he shouted to the group, "Grab your elementals and let's go!"

The kids collected their new companions and raced down the hallway with Gage leading the way. He slid around a corner, fully aware of the enraged shouts of the Vaskr echoing behind them, drawing closer. Many of the kids had already summoned their elementals and wasted their surges, and Gage could only do so much on his own.

They rounded one last corner, the path to the dining hall clear save for one Innaran guard standing at the doors. As the students charged into view, the guard jumped to attention.

"The Vaskr are behind us," Gage shouted.

"Hurry!" The man shoved open the doors.

Gage stepped aside and let the other students run ahead of him. Flashes of yellow light filled the hall behind them, followed by an onslaught of boulders and rock daggers hurtling toward the students. Gage stuck out his hand and tore apart the magic, darkness and purple sparks swirling around him and his void dragon as stone attacks fell to dust over their heads. Unfortunately, the Vaskran men kept charging with very real axes in their hands.

"Get inside," the Innaran commanded.

Gage dashed into the dining hall as the raiders hurled another barrage of stones. The Innaran guard dove inside and yanked the doors shut, slamming a huge metal bar across them before pressing his palm against the wood. A magical barrier flashed over the entire wall from floor to ceiling, muting any sounds from the other side.

48

ENOUGH IS ENOUGH

Several hours had passed since the attack on Runadel began. The guards patrolled the entrances to the dining hall, though all four doors had been sealed by iron bars and powerful magic. The kitchen staff fetched snacks for everyone, but time dragged. Gage and the other students sat in relative silence.

The quiet grated on Gage's nerves. He worried for Alphen, Nihsa, and Thad—and for everyone in the city who hadn't had time to grab weapons or seek shelter. A lot of terrible things could have happened. Spark slept on the table in Gage's folded arms, and he tugged the dragon closer.

Someone knocked on the main doors. Three short knocks, followed by a string of rapid ones, two slower ones, and one last knock after a long delay. The Innaran guards hustled to the doors and lifted the bar. The magic disengaged and the doors groaned open, revealing Lady Halayna with her honor guard. Grime soiled their clothing and armor, and their faces were tight with tension.

Lady Halayna stepped into the room. With a hollow voice, she said, "The battle is over. We are victorious."

The students shifted in their seats.

"Status update?" asked a recruit.

Lady Halayna took a deep, intentional breath. "We suffered significant losses."

"How did the Vaskr get close to the city without us noticing?" asked another recruit.

"A trap." Lady Halayna walked slowly down the aisle. "The wind tribe has fallen to the Vaskr. We are now surrounded. The Vaskr lured us to the defense of several western towns and then attacked out of nowhere. We became aware of it too late."

Momentary silence fell over the room.

"What now?" asked another recruit.

"I have sent word to Calvex and my father. We will wait for them to—"

A knight stormed through the doors in a great clatter of armor. He wore a green tunic and had an avian perched on his shoulder.

"Forgive me, Your Grace." He bowed to Lady Halayna. "Is Gage Black present?"

Gage perked up. Everyone looked at him, sending a rush of heat to his cheeks.

"That's me." He pushed off the table and rose from the bench.

"Sir Farowind requests your presence," the knight said. "It's urgent."

Gage choked down cotton, his mouth dry as dust. At least Thad had survived, but why the urgency? Had Nihsa or Alphen been injured?

"What does he want?" Gage asked, but the words came out squeaky. No one mocked him for it.

"Help with healing." The knight gestured out the door.

Gage swallowed a lump in his throat and glanced at Lady Halayna. She nodded. He hated to leave and miss her explanation of what was going on, but surely Thad would fill him in later.

After lifting a bleary-eyed Spark onto his shoulder, Gage followed the knight through the academy. Some of the walls had collapsed, leaving heaps of stone and shattered crystals on the floor. Much of the debris had already been swept aside to create walkways. Muted voices and banging sounds echoed throughout the academy. Cleanup and repairs, no doubt.

Gage sucked in a breath when he stepped outside the gates. The towering buildings beyond the academy now lay in heaps on the ground. Smoke puffed from the charred ruins of homes and businesses, filling the air with ash. Shattered glass glinted on the street. Knights, civilians, and elementals worked together to clean up the debris.

The knight led Gage to the plaza, where countless people came and went in haste. A long line of people lay on the ground, some badly wounded, many not moving. More people were brought on stretchers and added to the line. Gage searched for familiar faces, letting out a breath of relief when he found Thad. The older man sat on his knees next to one of the injured, both hands placed over a large wound in the person's abdomen. Green light shimmered through him and into his patient's body. Gromlin sat on Thad's shoulder, the portly bird as round and unruffled as ever, but his eyes and feathers radiated green light.

Further relief washed over Gage as he found Alphen and several Innarans taking turns touching Thad and fueling him with their magic. Alphen currently took his turn, his hand on Thad's shoulder. He and Thad were covered in sweat and ash, their clothes filthy and tattered.

"It's Gage," called a familiar voice.

Gage couldn't help but smile when Nihsa rushed down the opposite street carrying bandages in one arm and a jug of water in the other. She nodded at him as she hurried to Thad's side.

"What do you want me to do?" Gage crouched by Thad. Spark wrapped his tail around Gage's neck for stability.

"Heal people," Thad said, his words breathless and clipped. "If any injuries are urgent, send them to me. If they're non-urgent, treat them until I get to them later."

Gage glanced at the long line of mortally injured people awaiting Thad's care.

"My bag is over there." Thad jerked his head to the right, toward a heap of cleaning supplies gathered against a pile of rubble. "Use whatever you want. You know what to do."

Gage located the bag and searched inside, finding an abundance of medicines and bandages. He slung the leather satchel over his shoulder and around his chest, allowing it to fall at his hip.

"You four," Thad called to some recruits from the wind tribe. "Go with him. Do whatever he says as if you're answering to me." When the young men hesitated, he barked, "Stop loitering! At least disinfect his hands between patients!"

"Sir!" The four recruits scrambled to grab jars of water and disinfectant.

Gage spent the rest of the afternoon and early evening checking injuries, distributing medicines, covering wounds, and sending people to Thad for urgent treatments. He started on one side of the city, and when he finally stopped to catch his breath, he'd reached the other side.

The city lay in ruin. So many families wandered aimlessly, picking up the pieces of their broken lives. A deep ache bloomed in Gage's chest at the vacant looks in their eyes and the misery on their faces.

The village where he'd been born had probably looked much like this when the Vaskr destroyed it—homes crushed under boulders and ominous smoke clouds devouring the sky. Talid had come close to a similar fate on several occasions. How many villages, towns, and cities had fallen to the Vaskr? How many people had lost their homes and loved ones?

White-hot anger smothered Gage's grief. The Vaskr needed to be stopped. Which meant he needed to become powerful enough to stop them. If King Fraylon and the Innara wanted Gage to be a weapon against the Vaskr, so be it. He wouldn't let the Vaskr do this to anyone else, ever again.

49

ORDERS TO MARCH

A week had passed since the attack. They'd managed to remove most of the debris from the city. Now everyone focused on putting their lives back together.

Gage prodded his dinner, barely aware of the muted conversations around him in the dining hall. Lady Halayna intended to give a speech soon. Though everyone was interested in hearing a report about the war, no one was excited. Last they'd heard, they were losing.

Spark stole off Gage's plate without even trying to be sneaky. He grabbed slices of meat, dinner rolls, and various vegetables before escaping under the table. The other elementals at the table stared at Spark in confusion, eating from their own dishes like *normal* elementals. Dragons were weird.

For the first time, Gage sat with his fellow students. He'd intended to join Thad and Nihsa, but the other kids had invited him over. Apparently, they appreciated how he'd saved them during their flight from the Vaskr. No one thought ill of his magic or dragon now.

Finally, a knight marched onto the stage and rang a handbell. "Presenting Her Majesty, Princess Halayna Lightgard."

Everyone rose as Lady Halayna climbed the stairs and stepped to the podium, her white hair and gold jewelry gleaming in the bright lights. Gage noticed Alphen standing against the eastern wall. He hadn't been eating with them, and Gage hadn't seen him enter. In fact, he hadn't seen him since the attack.

"Thank you for coming tonight," Lady Halayna said as everyone returned to their seats. "I wish we could meet under better circumstances. We suffered many losses during the attack and would have suffered many more if not for the quick thinking of our knights, recruits, and students. But the battle is not over. I sent word to my father and elder brother. Calvex made haste to return with my father's instructions. He shall speak with you on our father's behalf."

She dipped her head and stepped aside in a rustling of fabric. Lord Calvex climbed the stairs, his hair, robes, and armor immaculate in the light. Everyone rose in respect, but he gestured for them to be seated.

"My father's tidings are dire," he said. "The Vaskr now have us surrounded. It is only a matter of time before they annihilate us. It is for this reason my father has ordered that all able bodies and magic users are to join him in one last campaign against our foes. We will march to reclaim the capital and seize the crystal, and then we will use the crystal's magic to restore order across the land." He displayed an unopened letter with a wax seal. "My father has summoned fighters from across the land to converge on the capital for a final assault this very month. No one is exempt; all are commanded to march—retired and senior knights, knights, recruits, and students."

The room erupted with noise, and many people rose from their seats in indignation. It took Gage a moment to understand their frustration. Students would march to the capital. He and his peers would march to war after only a few short months of study.

"Students?" Alphen's voice echoed through the room, silencing the noise.

Lord Calvex shot his younger brother a warning look. "Yes. Students."

"You can't take the students." Alphen straightened. "They're kids. Half of them haven't even summoned their elementals yet. You expect them to fight the Vaskr?"

"They attend this academy for the purpose of joining our army," Lord Calvex said, his tone demanding Alphen's silence.

Naturally, Alphen didn't get the hint. "No, they attend this academy to gain control of their magic so they don't accidentally destroy everything around them. They're given a choice to join the army when they're older and properly trained. Right now, it's suicide."

"This is an order," Lord Calvex said.

"It's a stupid order—"

"Enough," Lord Calvex demanded. The vicious tone silenced Alphen and sent everyone else back to their seats. "Not another word out of you, or I will have you dragged from the academy and tried for treason."

Alphen quieted, but he pulled back his shoulders and curled his hands into fists at his sides. Pivoting, he shoved through the eastern doors and slammed them behind him. Gage watched him go before looking to Thad and Nihsa. Nihsa frowned, staring at her hands in her lap. She had to be torn between her desire to protect the students and her desire to march with King Fraylon. Thad sat back with his big arms folded over his chest, his face red with anger. He would come out of retirement and fight without question, but he was surely furious about Nihsa, the recruits, and the students being sent to war.

"Missives from the king regarding your orders will be delivered to you and your families as you leave tonight," Lord Calvex said to the students. "We march in three days."

At that, he headed down the stairs and departed with his honor guard through the eastern doors. Everyone sat in silence. Kitchen staff removed dinner plates and brought out desserts, but no one paid any mind to the cream puffs, cakes, and pudding. Even Spark climbed onto the table and watched Gage in concern, ignoring the treats entirely. The other students squirmed in their seats.

A girl hugged her puffball avian, burrowing her face in its feathers. "I don't want to go to war. I just summoned her. I don't want to lose her."

"Me neither." Another girl cradled her earth beetle like a baby.

"This is what we signed up for. Fighting the Vaskr," said a boy, his flame lizard draped over his shoulder.

"I signed up to learn magic so I could become a knight as an adult," muttered a girl, stabbing a cream puff and flicking it into her pudding. "Not this."

No one argued, and everyone toyed with their desserts instead of eating them.

Spark waddled to the edge of the table and stood on his hind legs. *Master scared?*

Gage considered the question, surprised to feel relief at finally being able to march against the Vaskr—and anger toward them for having caused so much harm in the first place.

For myself? Not really, he answered. He glanced at his fellow students. *I'm afraid for them, though. And for you.*

I not scared. Is dragon. We big strong. Good fight. Spark nodded fiercely, scuttled over to the plate, snatched a cream puff, and dove under the table.

50

A Little Dumb

Gage snuggled under his blanket, with Spark sprawled across his torso. Classes had been cancelled for the next two days prior to their departure. So Gage lounged in bed and reread the king's letter for the twentieth time.

Dear student,

If you are reading this letter, you have been called to fight against the Vaskr. Do not fear. We are strong and capable, and it is an honor to defend this land. You will be a part of reclaiming what has been taken from us and restoring peace to the Innaran kingdom.

Your family has received a missive containing three gold coins. Use them to purchase supplies. A list has been included for you.

At month's end, you will join me at the capital. I look forward to fighting with you at my side.

The letter wasn't signed by the king but was instead stamped with his dragon seal. King Fraylon probably never touched the letters, using scribes to write and stamp them. Bitterness stabbed through Gage's chest like thorns. The king had basically sentenced them to death, and he couldn't even be bothered to write his own letters.

Gage shook those thoughts from his mind. The letters were impersonal because King Fraylon had more to worry about than writing dozens of messages for everyone at the academy. The man had an army to lead, a kingdom to protect, and a war to win. He clearly cared about them since he'd sent them gold to be outfitted for war. Thad had received Gage's family letter and had already given him the coins.

Clattering arose from the kitchen. The smell of bacon oozed under the door. Spark flew upright, his wings shivering and his nostrils flaring. He bit the front of Gage's nightshirt and tugged, attempting to drag him upright.

Time eat, yes? asked the void dragon.

"I guess." Gage set aside his letter and rolled out of bed.

He dressed for the day in his standard black tunic and pants. As he tied his belt, Spark climbed his leg like a savage kitten and draped his body over his shoulder, wagging his whole backside. In the kitchen, Thad cooked at the stove while Nihsa set the table. Both paused when Gage entered. Thad resumed his work, but Nihsa let her stare linger.

"How are you holding up, Gage?" she asked, slowly setting down a fork.

Gage shrugged, slipping into his usual seat. "I'm fine."

He leaned back so Thad could serve him fried eggs and bacon. The food barely touched his plate before Spark flung himself over it, snatched every slice of bacon available, and vanished with them under the table. Gage scowled in the dragon's general direction. Thad gave him more bacon, filled Mishu's food dish, and then took his seat. Gromlin sputtered at having to wait for his meal, but he preferred everything mashed together, so the delay was his own fault.

"Are you nervous?" Nihsa slipped into her chair.

"Not really," Gage said. When Nihsa and Thad exchanged dubious glances, he added, "I mean, I'm not excited about going to war. But this is why I joined the academy. It's just sooner than I expected. Everyone keeps talking about how my magic might help, and I'm ready to try. The Vaskr need to be stopped."

"You're brave," Nihsa said.

"And maybe a little dumb?" Gage asked.

"Maybe a little." She scrunched her face and then smiled.

Thad chuckled, Gage smiled back, and they started eating. More than most things, Gage would miss eating together as a family. He hoped he'd be able to stay close to Thad and Nihsa while marching to the capital—and close to Alphen too—but it wouldn't be the same.

"How about we go shopping after breakfast?" Nihsa said.

"Shopping?" Gage frowned.

"You have to buy supplies, don't you? I can show you where to buy new clothes."

"I can wear what I have." He plucked at his black tunic.

"Not to war," Nihsa said. "You need something sturdier and warmer. We have a clothier here in Runadel that creates the best gear. Thankfully, they survived the attack. I'll take you there."

"Thanks!"

Once they finished breakfast, Thad and Nihsa cleaned up the leftovers and dishes. Gage lingered with his plate, swirling a chunk of bacon in the egg yolk before popping it into his mouth. Yet another thing he'd miss—Thad's cooking. Military rations would never measure up.

A knock on the door distracted Nihsa. She set the dirty dishes on the counter and opened the door, revealing Alphen on the other side.

"Hey," he said with a lazy smile.

Nihsa slammed the door in his face and locked it. Thad tossed his dishes onto the nearest counter, grabbed the window with both hands, slammed it shut, and held it. A smile tugged at Gage's lips.

A window on the other side of the room creaked open. Alphen hoisted himself inside and flopped onto the counter like soggy bread, knocking down an assortment of vials and tools in the process. He rolled straight off the counter—taking everything with him—and dropped onto the floor. Vials skittered in all directions, clanging against cabinets and table legs. Rhemi hopped onto the windowsill and chittered in disdain at her master. Gage chewed down a laugh, especially when Thad threw his head back and rolled his eyes to the ceiling.

"For cryin' out loud, boy!" he exclaimed.

"Not my fault." Alphen stood and dusted himself off, lifting his nose with an air of dignity. "If your door would stop slamming in my face, your counters would be fine."

"What are you doing here?" Nihsa crossed her arms.

"I'm taking Gage shopping," Alphen said, grinning.

"You are?" Gage asked.

"You need new clothes, right?" Alphen shrugged.

"Too bad for you," Nihsa said, smirking. "*I'm* taking Gage shopping."

Alphen stared dully at her before frowning at Gage. "You can't let a girl pick out your clothes. She's going to make you look cute. You don't want to look cute."

"Don't act like I have poor fashion sense." Nihsa backhanded Alphen's shoulder. "Look at me. I'm stylish."

Gage took in her sleek outfit, fancy belts, and purple jacket. She was stunning. Alphen looked her over too. And kept looking—until Thad cleared his throat and slammed a vial onto the counter.

"Yeah," Alphen said, also clearing his throat, "but I don't think Gage is going for drop-dead gorgeous."

Nihsa blushed and looked away even though Alphen's full attention was on Gage now. Thad's eyebrow twitched as he cleared the remainder of the dishes.

"He's going to want clothes that accentuate his roguish good looks," Alphen continued, his hands on his hips and a smug grin on his face. "And who better to help him than someone roguishly handsome like me?"

Nihsa rolled her eyes but didn't argue.

At that point, Gage blushed for both of them. "You two need to hurry up and kiss or something," he muttered.

"What?" Nihsa's face snapped in his direction.

"Nothing." Gage took his dishes to Thad in the back. When he returned, he picked up the things Alphen had knocked onto the floor.

"Whatever. Gage is going with me." Nihsa scowled at Alphen. "Now take your roguishly good looks and shove them right back out the window where they belong."

With a lazy shrug, Alphen marched to the window and began the laborious process of hauling himself onto the counter, knocking several more things onto the floor. Rhemi screeched and hopped aside on the windowsill like an ornery bird.

"Oh, blast it, boy! Knock it off and use the front door," Thad yelled, coming around the corner and chucking a balled-up towel at Alphen's head.

Alphen returned to his feet. "Can't say I didn't try." Grinning at Gage, he jerked his thumb toward the door. "Let's go!"

"No, he's going with me," Nihsa snapped. "You can't just—"

"Mom, Dad, stop fighting," Gage grumbled, rolling his eyes.

They stopped and looked at him. Rather, Alphen looked, Nihsa glared. Their unified reaction gave Gage a brilliant idea. A grin stretched across his face.

"Why don't we go together?" he asked.

"Sure," Alphen said, while Nihsa and Thad said, "No."

"Terrible ideas. Terrible children." Thad stormed into the back and tossed dishes around in the washbasin, muttering loudly while he cleaned them.

Nihsa glared miserably at Gage. "What did I ever do to you? Do you hate me?"

"What better way to find the perfect outfit?" Gage asked. "I'll get insight from a guy with roguish good looks and the approval of a drop-dead gorgeous lady. Definitely seems like it'll lead to the best possible outcome."

"Agreed! Let's go." Alphen flung open the door and strolled into the sunlight. Rhemi growled and flitted out the window after him.

"I hate you right now," Nihsa grumbled at Gage as she headed out the door.

Gage smirked, scooped up Spark, and hurried after his friends.

51

ROGUISHLY HANDSOME

Gage browsed jackets on a rack at the clothier, but nothing stood out. He used to wear whatever people threw away in Talid, so style and colors didn't matter much to him.

But they clearly mattered to Alphen and Nihsa. The two bustled around the shop, flitting from rack to rack, pulling out clothes and assembling outfits. They sometimes bumped into each other and threw tantrums like children. Nihsa moved an entire rack into Alphen's path at one point, trapping him in a corner while she scampered to the boots. The shop owner did his best to ignore them.

They seem to be having fun, Gage commented to Spark, who perched on a rack near the dressing rooms.

They no fighting? Spark squinted at them and cocked his head to the side.

Not fighting. This is their way of falling in love, I think.

Oh. Spark tilted his head the other direction. *This is their mating?*

Gage choked on a laugh and burrowed his face in some jackets when Nihsa walked by. Thankfully, she was too distracted to notice him.

Something like that, he replied to the dragon, chewing back his laughter.

"I think I'm ready." Nihsa spun toward Gage with both hands hidden behind her back. "I have the perfect outfit for you."

"I have an even perfecter outfit for you." Alphen stomped out from between two racks, his hands also hidden behind his back. When Nihsa stared at him in expectation, he dipped his head. "I'm a gentleman. Ladies first."

Nihsa glared at him before pulling the clothes out from behind her back, a shirt and jacket in one hand and pants and boots in the other.

"What do you think?" she asked with a bubbly smile.

She'd selected a long, bright-green jacket with blue accents and matching boots. The undershirt was dark gray, and the pants were simple and dark. Gage rubbed the materials between his fingers. Solid and warm but flexible.

"They're not bad, I guess." Alphen scrutinized the clothes.

"You guess?" Nihsa scowled. "What's wrong with them?"

Alphen scrunched his lips to the side. "They're a little bright, aren't they?"

"Of course they're bright. He's been stuck wearing black this entire time. It's about time he wore some color."

"Black is sort of his thing. It's literally his name. And he has void magic. Which is—you guessed it—dark. He can't be an awesome nighttime assassin in bright, sparkly colors."

"Then it's a good thing he's not trying to be an assassin, you goathead," Nihsa snapped. "And he doesn't have to wear colors that match his magic. That only applies to academy uniforms." Turning her attention to Gage, she asked, "What do you think?"

Gage scratched his cheek. "It's not bad."

"You don't like it?" Nihsa pouted.

"I like parts of it," he said, but that only made her pout harder. He winced. "It's a little too bright for me. I don't like to stand out." When her moping continued, he tugged at the jacket and plastered a smile on his face. "But the style is really nice!"

"Fine." Nihsa flung the outfit onto a nearby table and crossed her arms, glaring pointedly at Alphen. "What do you have?"

Alphen revealed a dark-gray jacket with silver trim and matching boots, and a black shirt and trousers. Although quite dark, it was impressively stylish. Almost princely. Maybe a little too princely. It reminded Gage of what Alphen wore.

"Check it out." Alphen wagged the items in the air. "Perfect for nighttime assassins!"

Nihsa rolled her eyes. "He's not an assassin!"

"Well, now he can be, because he has this awesome outfit." Alphen grinned at Gage. "What do you think?"

Gage pinched the jacket. The material was soft and solid. "It's not bad."

"Ha! He doesn't like yours, either." Nihsa stabbed her finger into Alphen's shoulder.

"It's not bad," Gage said again, heat rushing across his face. "I like parts of both. But, um, this one is a little dark."

Alphen stared at him in disbelief. "It suits your name, Gage. And your magic."

Gage stared back. And threw in a little shrug.

"He hates it. Give up and go away." Nihsa nudged Alphen aside and marched to the nearest rack. "Don't worry, Gage. I'll find another one for you."

"You already tried bright colors. What next? Pink and purple frills?" Alphen flung his outfit onto the table beside Nihsa's discarded clothing, storming after her.

Gage watched as the two scurried around the store, hurling casual insults at each other as they worked. He shook his head and viewed the discarded clothes. His friends had obviously given the outfits some thought—they'd wanted them to suit him. And he did like parts of each outfit. The jacket and boots Alphen had chosen had a nice style that might actually pair well with Nihsa's functional shirt and pants. He dragged those four pieces off the table and slipped behind the dressing screen.

After changing, he inspected himself in the mirror. The clothes were a bit big, but that could be remedied. They felt warm, flexible, and durable. His friends had made excellent choices, and putting their heads together had produced the best possible outcome. With a smile, Gage returned to the main room.

Spark wagged his tail and showed off an awkward toothy grin. *Good look!*

"Thanks," Gage said.

Nihsa and Alphen both had jackets in their hands, bickering about who'd chosen the best one.

"Guys?" Gage said, but they kept fighting. "Guys!"

They stopped and glanced at him. And then glanced again when they realized he'd changed. They put the jackets back in their proper places while staring at Gage. Nihsa's bewildered expression cracked, and a huge smile lit her face.

"You're so cute!" she exclaimed.

Gage's cheeks burned, and he swung right back around into the dressing room. "Cute is not what I'm going for."

"No, no, no! You're not cute! You're not cute!" She dove and grabbed his arm. "I'm sorry. That's not what I meant."

Gage ran both hands down his face and willed the heat to fade.

Alphen looked him over with a critical eye, rubbing his chin. "Not bad, but it's missing something."

He marched to the accessories and dug around in a bin before returning with a layered brown belt and matching gloves. He tossed the gloves onto the table so he could add the belt—which looked like several belts combined—to Gage's outfit. Once he attached it, he patted one of several pouches on it.

"For the lockpicks," he said.

"What does he need lockpicks for?" Nihsa snapped.

Alphen shot her a deadpan look. "For picking locks."

Nihsa threw her hands up. To Gage, she said, "You need to stop spending time with this man. He's a horrible influence."

Gage grinned as he put on the gloves. Meanwhile, Alphen tweaked the white collar of Gage's jacket and fluffed his hair, straightening it in some places and ruffling it elsewhere. Then he stepped back, his face scrunched in thought.

"You look so . . ." Alphen took a deep breath before thrusting his hands forward and pinching Gage's cheeks. "ADORABLE!!"

"Leave me alone!" Gage flailed and whacked Alphen away.

Alphen stepped back. His grin melted into a warm, genuine smile—one that he normally kept hidden under smug masks and obnoxious teasing.

"You look roguishly handsome," Alphen said, offering a nod of approval.

Gage's cheeks warmed, but he smiled too.

"Not cute at all," Nihsa concluded while looking at Gage like he was a teddy bear. There were worse ways to be looked at by a girl, so he'd take what he could get.

Gage officially had his outfit. Well, almost. With a determined nod, he went to the front counter to ask about having the garments tailored.

52

GENERAL SELECTIONS

"Attention!" Lord Calvex's voice boomed, silencing most of the chatter from the crowd gathered on the outskirts of Runadel. When some voices continued, he shouted, "When I call for your attention, soldiers, you shut your mouths and listen!"

Eerie silence washed over the crowd, broken only by the birds and insects in the nearby autumn forest. Nearly three hundred people had answered the king's summons, and everyone was separated by rank: students, recruits, knights, and senior knights. Lord Calvex stood on a temporary wooden stage with several retired and senior knights in line behind him. Thad was among them, looking odd in armor rather than his healer's apron.

"The men and women standing before you are elite knights," Lord Calvex said. "They are the generals who will train and lead you as we march to the capital to meet with my father. I have given them permission to build their units as they see fit. Anyone not selected to join a general's team will fight on the frontlines alongside my father and me."

Gage's brow furrowed, and the students around him exchanged nervous glances.

"If a general selects you," Lord Calvex continued, "feel honored. No questions, no complaints. If you show weakness, you have no place within this army or within the walls of Runadel Academy. Now, on to selections. We march at high noon."

Thumping a fist to his breastplate, he spun with a great flourish of his cape and stepped down from the stage, vanishing into one of several large tents pitched for the gathering.

Sweat beaded on Gage's brow. Lord Calvex had placed their lives in the hands of those generals. If someone didn't choose them, they'd be thrown onto the frontlines to be butchered by the Vaskr. None of the students knew how to fight well enough to survive that—or to make them worth choosing.

His peers clearly felt the same, shuffling around and wiping sweat off their faces with their hands, sleeves, or handkerchiefs. Some students squeezed their elementals in their arms, practically strangling the poor creatures.

The generals meandered through the crowd. Most approached the senior knights first. But not Thad. He limped straight to the students, his jaw set with fierce determination. Hope fluttered in Gage's chest.

"All you wind kids, you're with me," Thad commanded, giving the students only a passing glance as he jerked his thumb over his shoulder. "Let's see if I can make some of you into viable healers." Then he marched toward the knights.

Gage's heart sank. Of course Thad wouldn't pick him. He'd want a team that specialized in healing magic—even if the students didn't have that ability yet. Still, it felt like a rejection, and it stung.

Thad paused and glanced at Gage out of the corner of his eye. His thick eyebrows pinched together. "What are you doing, just standing there?"

"Me?" Gage pointed at himself.

"Yes, you." Thad threw in a dramatic eye roll. "I'm not letting my most competent healer go to waste. Now get a move on."

The older man continued his determined hobble through the crowd, now tailed by a handful of wind students practically squealing about being chosen so quickly. Gage had to bite back his own relieved smile as he scrambled to walk alongside Thad.

"Nihsa, you're with me," Thad called when he reached the recruits.

"Yes, sir!" She hustled out of the crowd to join his ranks.

"Congratulations," he said. "I'm promoting you to knight. Your first order is to select a handful of recruits to join our numbers. Grab the strongest wind users first—I'll see about developing their healing magic. We'll also need powerful fighters to get us across the battlefield in one piece. Hard to heal anyone when you're dead."

"Yes, sir. How many do you want?"

"At least one for each student. We'll need to pair them up so the students have someone to ride with."

"Yes, sir." Nihsa bounded into the crowd, lifting her head with pride.

Gage let his eyes drift beyond her to the edge of the field, where Alphen stood alone, his arms crossed and a scowl on his face. His eyes occasionally flicked to the side, and Gage followed his gaze to the students not yet chosen by generals.

"What is Alphen doing over there by himself?" Gage asked Thad.

"Disobeying orders, as usual."

"Where is he supposed to be? With the recruits?"

Thad raised an eyebrow. "He's not ranked."

"He's not?"

"No, but if you want to get technical, he'd rank with the senior knights, where he's supposed to be now."

"Senior knights?" Gage exclaimed. "But he's seventeen!"

"And he's very powerful for a seventeen-year-old," Thad said.

Nihsa returned with a handful of recruits. "I selected the best and brightest, sir."

"Then let's move on to the knights." Thad headed through the crowd, his team following like lost puppies.

Gage searched the remaining knights and senior knights, most of whom were low-magic users. The Innarans had separated into their own units, with only one or two Innarans on the non-Innaran teams. In fact, Thad's team was the only one without an Innaran.

Meaning no one would be there to control Gage's magic.

"Um, Thad?" Gage tripped on his own feet.

"What?"

"I think we need to bring an Innaran with us."

"Why?"

"Because if we don't, I'll destroy the entire team."

53

DISOBEDIENT MAN-CHILD

T had halted.

Gage fidgeted with his jacket while trying to discern the man's scrunched face. "I need someone to keep my magic in check, or I'll destroy everyone else's magic and keep them from getting stronger. No one will develop healing abilities with me around."

Thad crossed his arms and sighed. "I suppose that makes sense. And it doesn't hurt to have an Innaran with us. They can pump magic into the kids and boost their strength. Let's see . . ." His eyes roved the crowd of Innarans.

Gage took a deep breath. "I think we should bring Alphen."

"No."

"Hear me out—"

"My answer is no," Thad said sternly. "I don't need that disobedient man-child causing a rebellion within my team." He limped toward the knights.

Gage exchanged glances with Nihsa before they hurried after him. She hadn't said a word against Alphen. That gave Gage hope.

"He won't disobey orders," Gage insisted.

"It's in his nature to disobey orders," Thad said. "Did you forget the part where I said he's supposed to be over there?" He stabbed a finger toward the senior knights. "Rebellion is what he knows best."

"Alphen disobeys orders to help people," Gage said.

Thad stopped, but he crossed his arms and scowled. The rest of their team stopped behind them.

"You want a strong team of healers, right?" Gage asked. "You want a team that can help people. Alphen will follow orders as long as that's what we're doing. He only takes risks to protect people. Plus, he knows how to control my magic. And he understands void magic—he can make me stronger." When Thad maintained his scowl, Gage added, "You wanted someone powerful to help us move around the battlefield, right? Who better than an Innaran at the level of senior knight?"

Thad's mustache twitched. So did his eye. He shifted his jaw as he considered Gage's argument. Then he shot Nihsa a questioning look.

"He's not wrong," she said, shrugging.

Thad glanced back and forth between them before letting out a sigh mingled with a groan, sweeping his hands down his face. "Oh, fine." To the rest of the team, he said, "The lot of you, stay here and wait." To Nihsa, he said, "Grab some knights to join our ranks. I'll be back." His sharp glare hit Gage next. "You. With me."

Gage gulped as he followed Thad through the crowd. Alphen remained by himself, glowering at his elder siblings as they exited their tents. But then his attention returned to the students who still hadn't been chosen. When he finally noticed Thad and Gage approaching, he dropped his arms and his frown, genuine confusion washing over his face.

"Fall in line, boy," Thad snapped. "You're with me." Pivoting, he hobbled back the way he'd come.

"Wha . . .?" Alphen's eyes flicked back to the students before returning to Thad. "No."

Thad turned only enough to make eye contact with him. "Pardon?"

Alphen shrank back briefly before forcing himself to straighten. "I said no."

"I heard you." Thad took slow steps toward Alphen, thumping his lame leg extra hard with each step. "But I wanted to give you a chance to fix your answer. You don't get to tell me no. I outrank you."

Alphen frowned. "I'm a prince."

"Not right now." Thad poked Alphen in the chest. "Right now, you're an unranked nuisance, and we're currently at war. That means I outrank you. Now fall in line behind me and let's go. You're on my team."

Alphen's cheeks darkened. "No, I'm not. I'm staying right here."

Gage watched, absolutely flummoxed. He'd never seen Alphen flustered—nor had he seen Thad this angry. The wind healer turned a harsh glare on Gage, making him jump. Spark was so startled by the sudden hostile attention he nearly tipped backward off Gage's shoulder. The dragon clawed desperately to keep upright.

"See?" Again, Thad stabbed his finger into Alphen's chest. "Rebellion. I don't have time for this." He turned to hobble away.

"Wait!" Gage caught Thad's arm to keep him from leaving. Turning back to Alphen, he asked, "Why won't you come with us? I need your help."

Alphen's shoulders sank, and his eyes flicked to the side. Gage followed his subtle gaze back to the students. To the students still not recruited by generals. To the students destined to fight on the frontlines.

Realization dawned on Gage, and he almost laughed and wept at the same time. Alphen must have been planning on forming his own team with any students not selected by generals. Was he allowed to do that? Gage wasn't sure, but he had no doubt about Alphen's intentions.

"Please, Alphen?" Gage pleaded. "Isn't there anything we can do to convince you?"

He raised his eyebrows and jerked his head toward the students. If Alphen admitted his intentions, Thad would recognize that he was rebelling to help people, not to cause needless trouble.

"Please?" Gage begged.

Alphen let out a long sigh and met Thad's gaze. "I'll join your unit if you recruit the rest of the students."

Thad blinked twice and said, "No." With that, he turned to leave.

"What?" Gage grabbed Thad's arm a second time. "Why not?"

"I don't need a herd of children following me around when I also have Alphen on my team," Thad muttered. "Believe me, he's more than enough child to manage."

Gage clung to him and dug in his heels, but Thad's attention had landed on the students, and now he willingly stopped. Most of the kids looked around for someone to choose them, their eyes wide with fear. Some wept, but they did their best to hide their tears. Thad took a deep breath and let out a long, slow exhale. His face softened, though he crossed his arms.

"Fine," he said.

Gage's heart leaped in his chest, and a smile broke onto his face.

"What?" Alphen asked.

"I said fine," Thad snapped. He marched up to Alphen and poked him—again—in the chest. "But so help me, boy, if you so much as question me—"

"I won't, sir," Alphen said. "You have my word."

Thad scrutinized him. Alphen must have meant business. Gage had never heard him call anyone *sir* before.

"Now fall in line and obey orders," Thad stated.

"Yes, sir." Alphen stepped behind him and waited to follow.

Thad hobbled over to the students and barked, "The rest of you kids, you're with me. Let's go. Don't make me regret this."

Dozens of students jumped in surprise, tripping over themselves to scramble after him. Gage smiled. When they reconvened with Nihsa, who had a group of knights with her, she frowned at the line of children tailing her father.

"Grab more knights," Thad called to her. "We're taking the students."

"We are?" Nihsa stopped at a slight distance.

"Yeah. Apparently that one"—Thad jerked his thumb toward Alphen—"won't join us unless we bring a herd of kids along. I'm guessing he wants to have people around who are more immature than he is so I pay less attention to his bad behavior."

Nihsa frowned. Alphen frowned. Overall, there was a lot of confusion. Nihsa's gaze slid from Alphen to the students, and realization dawned in her eyes. Without another word, she marched off to collect more knights.

Gage smiled again. Alphen wasn't the only one who cared about the students, and if he'd been honest about his intentions, things would have gone a lot faster. But that thought swept away Gage's smile. What was the point of all these games Alphen played? All the rebelling, all the pretending to be a careless idiot when he was actually selfless and kind? None of it made sense.

Not for the first time, Gage had a strong sense that Alphen was hiding something, but for the life of him, he couldn't figure out what.

54

PRACTICE DRILLS

The newly formed army set out at high noon, as Lord Calvex commanded. The students rode with knights and recruits on their second-form elementals, both in the sky and across the land. Despite the size of their army and the different elemental types, they moved in harmony. Gage and Spark rode with Alphen on Rhemi, soaring over vibrant red-and-yellow forests, golden fields, and glittering blue lakes.

Lord Calvex and Lady Halayna flew with their Innaran teams toward the front of the army while the defensive teams, like Thad's, hung at the back. They headed north until sunset, when Innaran messengers told everyone to land for the night. The units kept mostly to themselves in their own little camps, with their own tents, firepits, and meals. Elementals remained in their second forms and patrolled their surroundings while the humans hunkered down for the night.

Thad's camp had several large tents, split between men and women, and a smaller tent for the general. Thad refused the luxury of having a tent to himself and joined the other men. He reserved the single tent for Gage, to keep him apart from the other students. Gage had balked at being singled out and separated until Alphen offered to stay with him. The tent was big enough for both of them, and Gage was glad to not be alone. Nihsa took charge of one of the women's tents, and the girls' laughter could be heard late into the night. Thad had to yell at them to go to sleep.

After breakfast, they spent time training while waiting for Lord Calvex's orders to move. Alphen dragged Gage away from the others to a grassy plain that Rhemi had crushed down for them.

"Today, we're going to work on getting control of your magic." Alphen pulled a handful of small magic crystals from a case on his belt.

"I can't touch those," Gage said flatly, setting his hand on the pommel of his new sword. He'd received it right before leaving Runadel, but he still hadn't adjusted to its constant weight on his hip.

"I didn't ask you to touch them." Alphen rolled the crystals between his palms and then held them out. "Okay, touch one."

Gage scowled. "I'll break it."

"Not if you don't break it."

Gage rolled his eyes and snatched a crystal off Alphen's palm. His fingers barely connected before the crystal melted into dust.

"See?" He dropped his arms to his sides.

Alphen smiled and set five crystals onto the ground, arranging four in a circle around one in the center. "Breaking the crystals that easily is a good sign. It means your magic is strong. We just need to work on your control." He nudged the crystal in the ring with his boot. "I want you to focus on destroying every crystal except this one. With your mind."

"How?"

"The same way you destroyed magic in the Vaskran camp," Alphen said. "Find the threads and rip them apart."

Gage slowly rotated the hilt of his sword. He focused on the magic. Brightness stained everything, and glowing threads weaved into existence around him. The crystals' threads glared so brightly he couldn't differentiate them. When he imagined shredding the threads around the outside crystals, all five shattered. He slumped in defeat.

Alphen set out another batch of crystals. "Try again."

"I'll break them all," Gage muttered.

"So? I'll make more."

"You made these?" When Alphen nodded, Gage asked, "Is that hard to do?"

"It takes a chunk of magic out of me, but it isn't hard. I can make a few each day." Alphen crossed his arms, smiling.

"I made a bunch for training you. I expect you to break them while you practice, so don't worry about it. Try again."

Gage took a calming breath, squinted at the crystals he intended to break, and pushed out his magic. The ring of crystals shattered in a slow wave—and then the center crystal went with them.

He threw his hands up. "I can't do this!"

"It's called training for a reason, Gage." Alphen patted his shoulder. "You wouldn't need to train if you could do everything perfectly on your first try." Digging in his belt, he pulled out more crystals. "Let's—"

"Boy!" Thad's voice drew their attention. He limped toward them, focused on Alphen. "I need you for a minute."

Alphen pocketed the crystals and followed Thad to where the students and recruits stood in several lines. Gage followed out of curiosity. Nihsa stood nearby, her hands folded behind her back.

"I need you to give the trainees some magic," Thad told Alphen. "We're doing practice drills."

"All of them at once?" Alphen scanned the group of nearly fifty people. Everyone stared at him expectantly.

"It's not helpful if you hold their hands one at a time, now is it?" Thad asked.

"Can you give them magic all at once?" Gage had only ever seen Innarans touching people to share their magic.

"Yeah, but it's not easy, and it's wasteful," Alphen said. "Magic tends to go everywhere, getting lost in the space between people. Direct contact is way more effective. Doing this will take a lot out of me."

"Oh, quit griping," Thad muttered, rolling his eyes to the sky. "You can take a nap later."

Alphen smirked and lifted a hand toward the group—an action Gage found technically unnecessary but useful for focus. White light sprang up around him, encasing his body in a soft glow. Gage focused on the magic while shielding his eyes against the blinding brightness. Strings of light spun around Alphen and then shot outward in all directions. They hit everyone around them, surging through the people and increasing their brightness tenfold. One of the strings struck Gage and washed over him like warm water. It filled him briefly with feelings of hope and peace before fizzling out, crushed by his void magic.

Sweat glistened on Alphen's forehead. Gage felt bad for him, constantly giving others magic at his own expense.

"All right, Nihsa," Thad said. "You're up."

"We're going to spend the rest of the morning running through drills," Nihsa said to the group. "These lessons are about control—the sooner you have it, the better off you'll be." Holding out her hand, she summoned water into a perfect rope within her grasp. "First, you'll create a rope of magic. Your goal is to make it into a tangible thing you can hold."

Several older trainees formed ropes out of their magic, filling the area with red, blue, yellow, and green lights. A few younger trainees tried to mimic them, but they could only summon balls of elemental magic.

"Once you learn how to create a rope, you'll learn to move it like this," Nihsa said.

She demonstrated a variety of maneuvers with her rope, flicking it in waves, twirling it in the air, and lashing it like a whip. Finally, she drew it back into her hand and closed her fist around it. Nothing remained, not even a drop.

"I can't do that," Eddly muttered, still fumbling with a tiny ball of wind magic.

"You can, in time. Everything takes practice. Focus on forming ropes first," Nihsa said. "The knights and recruits will help you, and so will I. You've got this! We'll be the best unit in no time!"

She smiled as she mingled with the kids, giving them directions. Several knights and recruits joined her, each giving individual attention to students and teaching them how to control their magic.

"Do you want me to practice with them?" Gage asked Thad.

The older man's expression sank. "You'd better not. Your magic might interact with theirs, and I need them at their best. Besides, your magic might have dire consequences if it goes awry. I can heal a body but not damaged magic." He set a comforting hand on Gage's shoulder. "Sorry, lad. We'll focus some lessons on you later."

"Okay," Gage said, struggling to hide the disappointment in his voice.

Thad patted his back, gave his shoulder a shake, and then hobbled into the group of trainees to give pointers. While Nihsa and the knights gave gentle instruction, Thad barked commands and made several kids fling their magical spheres in random directions. Gage should have laughed, but the sting of being an outsider—again—sucked the joy out of him.

"Thad, do you need me for anything else?" Alphen asked.

"Not right now."

Alphen slung an arm around Gage's shoulders, dragging him away from the group. "How about we get some more training in?"

"I'll just break more of your crystals," Gage muttered.

"I have something else in mind."

"Such as?"

Alphen grinned, but it was an evil one. "Something fun. Don't worry about it."

Naturally, Gage worried about it.

55

GETTING CONTROL

Alphen led Gage to an open area at the edge of camp. Rhemi and Spark wrestled nearby—rather, Gage assumed they were wrestling. Spark latched onto Rhemi with his legs and shook himself as hard as he could. Rhemi, in her second form, merely swiped at him and sent him rolling. He scurried back over and latched on again, only for her to bat him away once more. As soon as the dragons noticed their approach, Spark perched on Rhemi's head, and they watched with interest.

"What are we going to do?" Gage asked.

"Battle training," Alphen said.

Gage drew his steel sword an inch from its scabbard before shoving it back in. "We don't have any practice swords."

"Not that kind of battle training. In fact, toss that aside. It'll get in the way." Alphen unbuckled his double swords and threw them near the dragons.

Gage removed his and tossed it aside. Alphen held out his hand, and a surge of white light swept outward and formed a massive dome around them. The magic ran through Gage and warmed him from head to toe.

"What sort of battle training are you planning?" Gage asked.

"The fun kind." Alphen summoned two swords of blazing white magic into his hands.

Gage's throat constricted. "Alphen, you know I can't do that."

"That's why it's called training." Alphen smirked. "You really struggle with that word, don't you?"

Heat spread across Gage's cheeks. "I'm just going to fail again."

"You can't fail in training," Alphen muttered, rolling his eyes. "TRAINING. T-R-A—"

"You know what I mean. I can barely make a sword. I definitely can't fight with it." When Alphen opened his smug mouth, the word *training* on his lips, Gage hastily added, "And you heard what Thad said. My magic is dangerous."

"I've already created a barrier around the area. You can fling your magic around as much as you want. It won't reach anyone else."

"It'll reach you."

"That's why I put barriers around us too."

"You can do that?" Gage asked.

"Can and did." Alphen flipped one sword into the air and caught it, then did the same with the second. "Everything will be fine. Contrary to popular belief, I know what I'm doing."

"Promise?"

"I promise." Alphen smiled—one of his warm, genuine smiles that put Gage at ease.

Gage had wanted to practice, hadn't he? Inhaling slowly and holding his breath, he summoned magic into his hand, forming a sword. Or trying to, at least. The dark energy stretched into the length of a short sword but rippled like flames.

"Nice," Alphen said, inching closer. "Now take a few swings at me."

Gage instinctively backed away. "A few swings? It's barely a sword!"

He waved his magical blade for emphasis, and it fell apart at the slightest movement. Calling it a sword was like calling Spark the deadliest dragon on the planet.

"It doesn't have to be perfect," Alphen told him.

"It's just a wobbly blob!"

"Come at me with that wobbly blob, then. Let's do this!" Alphen grinned and lunged at Gage with one sword swinging.

Gage yelped and swung his sad excuse for a blade to fend off Alphen's strike. Their magical swords clashed with a reverberating hum, and Gage's dark sword exploded on contact.

"Let's run through our usual sword routine," Alphen said, pressing his blade against Gage's roiling magic.

"I can't," Gage muttered, glaring at his sword and willing it back together. Alphen's blade sliced through it like butter.

"Sure you can. We've practiced hundreds of times."

"I mean, I can't with this thing." Gage jumped backward, putting space between them, then wagged his pathetic sword at Alphen.

Alphen smirked. "That just means I get to hit you a lot, I guess."

He closed the gap between them, forcing Gage to retaliate against his slow, steady swings. Somehow, Gage's blade held against the barrage of hits. Even though Alphen wasn't moving fast, he struck with enough force to numb Gage's arms. They did their routine twice, slowly, before Alphen grinned.

"Faster," he said. It was a command, not a request.

Alphen picked up speed, and Gage barely had time to react before Alphen's white sword struck his arm, sending a burst of energizing warmth through him. Alphen didn't gloat and simply struck again.

"Alphen, I can't—" Gage swung and missed, earning him another blow from Alphen's shining weapon.

Alphen pressed him. Swing. Thrust. Parry. He didn't slow.

"Stop thinking about your sword," Alphen told him. "Focus on the fight. Focus on the routine. Just know that you have a sword in your hands and keep swinging."

Gage took a steadying breath and shifted his focus from his pathetic sword to the routine. Every movement familiar and calculated. Every step precise. They'd done this hundreds of times, and it was second nature to Gage now, like breathing. He slipped into the routine, getting faster and landing fiercer blows.

To his surprise, the magic forming his blade grew steadier and stronger.

"Good," Alphen said. "Faster!"

He increased their pace while repeating the same practice drills again and again. They swept across the field in their familiar dance.

"Now you've got it!" Alphen grinned. Sweat plastered his hair to his forehead.

Gage was probably just as sweaty, but he didn't mind. The water users provided excellent showers every night. Besides, nothing beat a great swordfight. The stress melted out of Gage's muscles.

"Ready for more fun?" Alphen shoved off Gage and stepped back. "No more drills. Let's go freestyle. Come at me with everything you've got." He twirled both swords, white streaks and sparks trailing the blades.

Alphen swung with expert precision. Gage deflected one but was struck by the other. He fell back into defensive maneuvers, deflecting and parrying most of the attacks. They sparred constantly, and he probably knew the prince's moves better than anyone, but that didn't make the fight any less brutal. Alphen was bigger, stronger, and faster.

Instead of trying to win with brute force, Gage searched for an opening. He managed to knock Alphen off balance with a quick stab and then a thrust. Alphen deflected with one blade while swinging the other. Gage couldn't move fast enough to defend and haphazardly shoved his magic out to block the attack. Darkness swelled over his arm like a shield. Alphen's blade shattered it, but it gave Gage the chance to jump backward to avoid further blows.

"Well done!" Alphen exclaimed. "Now you're getting it!" He slammed into Gage again, forcing him to summon more magical shields.

"I can try anything?" Gage asked as Alphen pummeled him.

"Anything," Alphen replied, grinning from ear to ear.

Gage found himself grinning too. He smacked Alphen's sword aside and formed a dagger in his other hand, aiming for the prince's side. Alphen pivoted and transformed his second sword into a shield, which the dagger struck, shattering on contact. Gage pressed forward anyway and kicked Alphen in the stomach—not hard, but enough to make him stagger. Then he slashed from the side.

Alphen turned his stumble into a spin and flicked his sword upward, knocking Gage's blade aside. He kicked

Gage in the stomach to destabilize him and sliced through him with another burst of warmth from his white sword. Gage slashed at Alphen's arm in the process, but the prince deflected with another shield. Alphen thrust for his gut, but Gage formed his own shield and pushed his magic into it, slamming it against Alphen's blade. The prince's sword exploded on contact.

"Someone's getting feisty!" Alphen laughed and reformed his sword.

"I'm learning from the best." Gage grinned.

Alphen jumped backward and slashed a hand through the air. A barrage of light arrows launched at Gage. Several hit before he could block them, and then he dropped dark arrows on Alphen from above. The prince sliced through them with his sword, dodged to the side, dropped to a knee, and slammed his palm to the dirt. Light spears exploded from the ground below Gage, who dodged all but a few as he hurled balls of darkness over Alphen's head. Alphen held up a light shield to block the bursts.

A sense of satisfaction overwhelmed Gage. He had Alphen more and more on the defensive. Meanwhile, Gage was getting hit less and less. He could practically feel Alphen's magic tingling in the air before it struck, allowing him to shield or dodge. If this had been a real battle, he'd have died at the start. But this was training, and he was learning.

Finally, Alphen closed the gap between them, locking their blades and pinning them face-to-face.

"We should wrap this up," Alphen said. "You have one minute to hit me, or I'm putting you in the dirt."

Gage gritted his teeth. Alphen wouldn't put him on the ground without a fight. He assaulted the prince with magical swords, shields, and an onslaught of arrows from the sky. Alphen parried and deflected with perfectly timed slashes and swings. He hammered Gage backward with several precise blows, and as Gage lost ground, he realized Alphen had been holding back. Strangely, that didn't bother him, but it made him strike that much harder and faster. Alphen dodged every attack. Maybe he could feel Gage's magic the same way Gage felt his.

"Time's up," Alphen said.

He moved so fast Gage almost missed it. The prince knocked Gage's sword upward and rammed him with his shoulder and a burst of magic that sent Gage flying. Gage crashed into the dirt with a startled cry, rolling several feet before stopping in a cloud of dust. He pushed onto his elbows, wincing and sputtering dirt out of his mouth. The blow hadn't hurt him, only knocked the wind out of him.

Cheers erupted from all around. Sometime during the fight, an audience had gathered, including trainees, knights, and even some generals from surrounding units. Thad and Nihsa stood among them, clapping and cheering like the rest. Gage flushed at the attention.

"Well done, Gage." Alphen offered him a hand.

"I failed again. I lost." Gage accepted a tug out of the dirt.

"Did you?" Alphen flipped something out of his belt and into the air.

Gage instinctively caught the glittering object, bobbling it a few times before clasping it to his chest.

"Sometimes it's not about winning or losing," Alphen said. "Sometimes it's about getting control."

Gage looked at the object on his palm: one of Alphen's crystals. Whole. Not falling apart. He lifted his face and stared at Alphen in disbelief.

Alphen flashed that warm, genuine smile. "I'd say you did just fine today." He patted Gage's shoulder and headed toward the dragons.

Gage ignored the cheers around him and stared at the glittering crystal in his hand. His heart fluttered when it didn't so much as crack. Joy and warmth welled up inside him, overwhelming him with pride. He lifted his face and watched Alphen grab his swords and join Rhemi, thankful the prince didn't look back. Gage couldn't resist the tears stinging his eyes.

"Thank you, Alphen," he whispered, squeezing the crystal and drawing it to his chest.

56

BESIEGED

Three weeks passed. Autumn gave way to winter. The trees surrendered their fiery colors, and snow blanketed the world in white. Lord Calvex's army had nearly reached the capital—and then disaster struck.

The army had only recently taken flight when an Innaran knight darted past, shouting, "By Lord Calvex's orders, land immediately. I repeat, land immediately. By Lord Calvex's orders—"

Off he went, flying out of range, still shouting. Gage and Alphen exchanged concerned frowns.

"Land?" Alphen echoed. "We barely took off for the day."

Nevertheless, they and the rest of the airborne units descended toward the snowy field below. Alphen guided Rhemi to the front of their unit, where Thad spoke with Nihsa and a second Innaran messenger. Once Rhemi landed, Gage and Alphen dismounted and trudged through ankle-deep snow to join them. Rhemi shrank and flew to Alphen's shoulder.

"Did something happen?" Thad asked the messenger.

"There's a skirmish up ahead," said the knight. "The Vaskran army is besieging a nearby town."

"And we're going to aid them?" Alphen asked.

The messenger's brow furrowed. "No, Lord Alphen. Lord Calvex has asked all units to divert to the east and then resume a course north to the capital."

"What?" Gage and Alphen asked at the same time.

"Why aren't we helping them?" Alphen added.

"Lord Calvex believes it is in our kingdom's best interest to reach the capital immediately," the messenger said, though he adjusted the collar of his tunic as Alphen's glower intensified. In a pitiful voice, he added, "Thus the High General's orders."

"The kids in that town will be captured," Alphen snapped.

"I am only the messenger, Lord Alphen." The man bowed and placed a fist on his breastplate.

"What is Calvex thinking?" Alphen asked. "He—"

"That's enough, boy," Thad stated, his words clipped. He nodded to the knight. "Thank you for the message. You're dismissed."

The messenger bowed again, returned to his light dragon, and departed.

The news knotted Gage's insides. Images of burning houses in Talid came to mind, followed by the ruins of Delevar and Runadel.

"We're just going to let the Vaskr do what they want?" Alphen aimed his hostility at Thad.

"Those are our orders." Thad shot him a stern look and then focused on the others around them. "Prepare to move. We're heading east."

The surrounding knights and trainees hurried to their elementals, but Nihsa lingered, a worry line between her eyebrows. Alphen and Gage didn't move, either.

"We can't abandon the town," Alphen said.

Thad let out an exasperated sigh, like a father dealing with a nuisance child. "I understand how you feel—"

"I don't think you do or you wouldn't speak so casually about letting the Vaskr massacre a town and kidnap kids." Alphen's hands curled into fists.

Thad's expression hardened. "This isn't a casual matter for me. You know that. I'm a general. It's my duty to think of the greater good of the kingdom. And as prince of this kingdom, it's your duty as well." Thad took one step closer to Alphen, but the prince didn't lose an ounce of tension—or defiance—in his tight features. "I'm a healer, boy. I don't take pleasure in death. But in war, you can't save everyone. Certain people must make choices to save the most lives. One hundred people matter more than one."

Alphen's cheeks flushed with anger. "Tell that to the mothers and fathers who lose a child to the Vaskr. Or to the orphan—tell them that a hundred people matter more than their mom or dad." He swallowed hard, visibly shaking. "That one person matters to someone, and I won't ignore them."

He turned away, but Thad gripped his arm.

"Don't even think about it," said the older man. "Whatever you're planning, I command you to stand down. You will continue on to the capital with us. We'll reclaim the crystal and use it to retake the kingdom, saving more lives than you would by fighting the Vaskr for a single town. Focus, Alphen!"

Thad and Alphen waged war with their eyes. Neither budged. Gage saw the same defiance in Alphen that he saw when the prince opposed Lady Halayna and Lord Calvex. But Thad sounded more like a father than a general, and Gage had never heard him call Alphen by name before. Worry was buried under his harsh tones.

"Then send me alone," Alphen said. "The rest of you can focus on saving the kingdom. I'll save the town."

Thad released him and rolled his eyes. "If their army is large enough to divert Lord Calvex, you won't stand a chance on your own. They'll simply kill you along with everyone else."

"You don't know that. And at least it would give them a chance."

Thad looked Alphen straight in the eye and lowered his voice. "My answer is no, Alphen. We need you here. Alive. A heroic death doesn't help the kingdom. Stop thinking with your heart like a naïve child and use your head for a change."

Alphen recoiled like he'd been slapped. Thad's eyes widened briefly before the scowl returned to his face.

Gage couldn't breathe. He agreed with Alphen. Did that make him a naïve child too?

Alphen glared at Thad, turned on his heel, and marched away, shoving past a few lingering knights.

"Alphen," Thad shouted, but the prince ignored him. He growled and swept both hands down his face and then one hand through his hair. "That boy is going to be the death of me."

Thad looked at Nihsa as if searching for moral support, but she kicked snow into little piles in front of her and paid an unnatural amount of attention to her boots. Thad sighed, his shoulders sinking. He'd never before looked so defeated, not even when dealing with the horrific aftermath of Runadel's attack. Finally, he turned toward Gage.

"Go after him," he said quietly.

"What?" Gage choked out the word.

"I want you to follow him. He's used to having you around, and he won't question it." Thad folded his arms, but the tension left his body. "If he's planning anything stupid, talk him out of it. And if he leaves on his own, warn me at once."

Ice flooded Gage's veins. Thad wanted him to spy on Alphen—to betray him—when Alphen only wanted to help people. Even worse, Gage agreed with Alphen. His insides writhed until he felt like he was being torn to pieces.

"I'm trying to keep him alive, lad," Thad said with a strange sort of tenderness.

Gage knew that. He was worried about Alphen too. But the whole situation felt wrong. Nevertheless, he offered a quick nod and hurried after Alphen, his heart tearing apart the entire time.

57

I Go Where You Go

Gage hustled through a flurry of activity. Everyone prepared to take flight, and most of the units ahead of them had already returned to the sky. Only a few remained, with Thad's team bringing up the rear. If he didn't find Alphen soon, the prince might escape using the chaos as cover. Thankfully, the prince's fluffy white dragon was easy to spot.

Gage pressed toward them, his heart aching the entire time. As he repeated Thad's words in his head, he found more and more that he disagreed with them. Not about the role of generals and kings—he understood all that—but someone had to stick up for individual people while generals and kings fought their wars. But to stand with Alphen and to defy Thad and Lord Calvex meant . . . what? Treason? Punishment?

What do you think I should do, Spark? Gage asked the dragon on his shoulder as he approached Alphen—who was stuffing supplies into a travel bag he hadn't carried before. Not at all suspicious.

Vaskr hurt Master. Many time, Spark replied with a hiss. *Must stop, I thinks.*

The words encouraged and terrified Gage. Because realistically, what could he and Alphen do against an army on their own?

"Alphen," he called, stopping at a slight distance.

Alphen paused his work but didn't look back. He resumed stuffing his bag with rations and waterskins he must have stolen from the supply carts.

Gage said the first thing that came to mind. "I go where you go."

Alphen slowed. "I'm not going anywhere."

"Then why are you packing supplies?"

Alphen stopped. Rhemi rumbled in her throat and rammed him with her head, turning him around to face Gage.

Alphen kept his eyes on the ground. "I can't take you with me."

"Why not?"

"For starters, Thad and Nihsa would kill me. They care about you."

"They care about you too."

Alphen's lips lifted into a weary smile. Gage got the impression that Alphen didn't believe him.

"Besides," the prince said, "I'm not going to get you thrown out of the academy."

"I think you missed the part where I said, 'I go where you go.' As in, I'm making the choice, not you." Gage crossed his arms and braced his feet apart.

"I'm older, remember?" Alphen's tired smile lingered as he returned to stuffing his pack.

Gage recalled how everyone had used that excuse to blame Alphen for Gage's presence in Delevar. But Gage wasn't getting pushed along by Alphen's whims. He wanted to do the right thing, and he firmly believed this to be it.

Inhaling deeply, Gage dashed and flung himself onto Rhemi's back. She squawked in surprise and thrashed her wings, knocking Alphen aside in the process. Gage clung desperately to her feathers, but she didn't attempt to buck him off. Spark squealed at the whole debacle and lunged onto Rhemi's head.

"Hey!" Alphen shouted. "Get off!"

"I go where you go," Gage stated. "And no one is to blame for it except me. This is my choice."

"Gage, knock it off," Alphen said heatedly. "Get down."

Gage wrapped his arms around Rhemi and held fast. "Make me."

Alphen opened and closed his mouth repeatedly before shaking his head and letting out a pathetic, exasperated sound. He directed a scowl at Rhemi, but she lifted her head in a snooty manner. He was probably telling her to throw Gage off or something.

"Rhemi," Alphen snapped.

Rhemi snorted, laid down her head, and sprawled on the ground. Whatever Alphen had ordered her to do, she was obviously doing the exact opposite. Gage remained safely perched on her back, and Rhemi practically purred. Spark mimicked the sound as he sent feelings of smugness from Rhemi to Gage.

"She's not going to throw me off. She agrees with me," Gage said. "You're not alone, Alphen. Stop acting like you are."

The frustration dissolved from Alphen's face, replaced by . . . agony? Gage couldn't quite read the emotions raging behind his eyes.

"This isn't a game," Alphen said.

"I know that." Gage sat straight, though he kept both hands full of Rhemi's feathers, just in case. "Alphen, I agree with you. Kings and generals have to worry about the entire kingdom, but *someone* has to care about the needs of individual people. Every person matters."

Gage met Alphen's eyes, but his friend looked away. Alphen toyed with the edges of his brown cloak—fidgeting the same way Gage did when he was anxious.

Someone shouted from the front of their unit, and people throughout the area took flight. It was now or never.

"Please let me help you," Gage said. Resolutely, he added, "I go where you go."

Alphen ran both hands down his face. "You're stubborn."

"I learned from you."

"Fine, but you stay with Rhemi, got it?" Alphen tossed the travel pack onto Rhemi's back before mounting the dragon.

Rhemi stood and lifted her head, forcing Spark to frog-hop off Alphen's head and onto Gage's shoulder.

"Stay on her back and use your magic from a distance," Alphen ordered. "You're not ready for direct combat with the Vaskr. Understood?"

Gage nodded. He didn't plan on throwing his life away.

"All right," Alphen said. "Let's go see what we're up against."

Rhemi chirped in agreement and burst out of the snow, ascending with the rest of their unit. As the army veered east, Rhemi fell back and set her course due north. No one stopped them.

58

WILDLAND TRAP

Endless white wasteland stretched ahead of them, making Gage wonder if they'd been led astray by Lord Calvex's messenger. The situation grew worse when it started snowing, whiteness blotting out everything in the distance. Rhemi flew slower than usual, and Gage pulled Spark inside his jacket and hunkered down with his head against Alphen's back. He lamented not having a nice cloak and hood like the prince.

"Down there," Alphen said, drawing his attention to the ground.

Gage glimpsed footprints through the fresh snow. Some human, some earth beetle. Structures formed out of the white haze ahead, revealing a town with a backdrop of thick pine trees. As Rhemi flew closer, Gage noticed broken windows in the nearest buildings, as well as a house collapsed under a boulder. Other than that, the place seemed fine. No sign of a Vaskran army besieging it.

"Did we get lost?" Gage asked.

"I don't think we flew far enough for that." Alphen patted Rhemi, and she glided to the ground and landed on a gravel path buried under the snow.

Gage and Alphen hopped down. A chill swept up Gage's spine, and numbness tingled through his legs. He staggered and grabbed Alphen's arm for support and then touched his frozen ears and cheeks. Alphen looked him over, a frown forming creases between his eyebrows. He shook Gage off his arm so he could remove his cloak.

"We should have gotten you better winter attire," Alphen said, offering him the cloak. "I hadn't thought about how bad it gets this far north. I'm lucky I take my cloak everywhere."

"You'll be cold without it," Gage pointed out.

"I can use my magic to stay warm."

"You don't use fire magic."

"No, but do you remember my magic hitting you? It was warm, wasn't it?"

Gage couldn't deny it, but Alphen wasn't wearing many layers, and it would likely take a lot of magic to keep warm. When Gage still hesitated to take the cloak, Alphen rolled his eyes and flung the garment around him. And threw the hood over his head, burying him underneath it. And straightened the thing out like a nitpicky mom.

"Man, you're stubborn," Alphen muttered after finishing his ministrations.

Gage peeked out of the hood and pulled the cloak tightly around his body, reveling in its warmth. He'd need to get something like it. Spark purred, burrowed under the fabric over Gage's shoulder.

Alphen turned toward the town as people appeared out of the snowfall. Three men wearing thick fur hats and jackets marched out to meet them. One of the men held a large umbrella over himself and the others, fending off the massive snowflakes pouring from the sky. An older man with a hunched back led the way. His eyes widened when they found Alphen.

"Lord Innara," the man exclaimed, offering a slight bow. The other two men followed his lead.

"Please," Alphen said, flicking his hand dismissively to end their bows. "We received word of a Vaskran attack in the area. Was this information correct?"

"The Vaskr were here nary a few hours ago," said the old man, "but they left as soon as we gave them what they wanted."

"Kids?" Gage's stomach twisted.

The old man laughed. "Of course not. They wanted weapons, food, and blankets."

"Supplies for war," Alphen said.

"Yes, I suppose."

Alphen folded his arms. "Which way did they go?"

"East," said the young man with the umbrella.

"East? You're sure?"

"Yes. We were confused too." The older man shifted his jaw so his mustache wriggled like a caterpillar on his face. "They came from the west. They have several strongholds that way."

"What's to the east?" Gage asked.

"Lakes and forests, mostly. Wildlands," said the middle-aged man. "It's nice in the summer but nasty this time of year. Lots of blizzards. Not much to see."

Gage's stomach kept twisting. Why would the Vaskr gather supplies and head that direction if nothing of value existed there? Not unless . . . Gage snatched Alphen's sleeve and shook it. Alphen's face had already fallen, as if his thoughts had gone the same direction.

"Be on your guard," Alphen told the men. "The Vaskr might return if they have bases in the area."

"Thank you kindly for your concern, Lord Innara," said the old man. He and his company bowed.

Gage practically dragged Alphen away from the men, who were heading back into town.

"It's a trap," he whispered, unable to catch his breath. "They're luring us away to destroy us so we can't join King Fraylon at the capital."

Alphen rubbed his brow and gave a slight nod. "Let's hurry."

They hopped onto Rhemi's back, but Alphen caught Gage's arm in a fierce grip.

"Hold onto Spark," he said. "And hold onto me."

Gage's heart fluttered with anxiety as he secured Spark in one arm, wrapping the other around Alphen's waist.

Alphen gripped them tightly and leaned forward. "Rhemi, you know what to do."

Rhemi burst off the ground in a shower of snow, shooting straight upward. They rose higher and higher—higher than Gage had ever flown before. White light swirled around them, shielding them from the snow and cold as the white world and dark forests shrank beneath them. Gage's ears popped, and the whir of wind and movement around him sent a ringing echo through his head. His breaths came out as white puffs, shorter and harder than before. His head went fuzzy.

"I can't breathe," he murmured.

"Hang on," Alphen said, tightening his grip on Gage as they hurtled upward.

Higher and higher they went, until they pierced a foggy haze of clouds. A burst of magic swept out from Alphen with a violent whoosh, one that Gage felt as a surge of warmth through his chilled limbs. The clouds shattered and gave way to glaring sunbeams. Yet Rhemi flew higher still, and the world seemed to bend. The mountains curved on the horizon, distant and small. The forests and fields blurred together.

"Alphen," Gage said, panic pinching the word.

"Hold tight. Just a little longer." Alphen's eyes scanned the world below.

Rhemi rumbled in her throat and leveled out in the air. Gage fought for every breath that reached his lungs.

Alphen's eyes narrowed on something far below. "Found them. Rhemi, dive!"

Rhemi folded her wings and plummeted. Gage cried out and clung to Alphen and Spark. Thankfully, Alphen held fast to him. Gage barely moved, but that didn't stop his heart and stomach from flying into his throat. Little by little, he caught his breath. The land sprang back up around them—mountains with their white-capped peaks and forests with their snow-covered pines.

Once they'd reached a comfortable height, Rhemi spread her wings and flew in a steady line. The glow of magic around them fizzled, taking the warmth with it. The sunshine did little to negate the chill, and a harsh wind battered them.

"It's a trap," Alphen snapped, scowling toward the east. "The Vaskr are approaching Calvex's army from the north and south to cut us off."

"You saw them?" Gage asked, but then he recalled how Spark had sharpened his vision during the archery test. Rhemi could probably do likewise.

"Yes. Rhemi, to the south!"

Rhemi swung southward, frantically beating her wings.

"Why south?" Gage asked.

"Because Calvex should be able to fend off the Vaskr attacking him from the north," Alphen said. "But the raiders striking us from the south? They'll hit our weakest point. Our kids are back there."

A sinking feeling settled in Gage's gut. The most powerful knights marched with Lord Calvex and Lady Halayna. The trainees and recruits marched in the back with units meant to swoop in and flee, not engage in battle. Now a Vaskran army was headed straight for them.

59

BUYING TIME

Rhemi soared across snowy plains, rolling white hills, and forests filled with pine trees. Her sides heaved from exertion—Gage could feel it under his knees. Increasing clouds dispensed sparse snowflakes as they swooped over a line of trees and discovered their army marching across an endless plain of drifted snow.

Magic erupted from the northern end of the plain, flooding the horizon with white and yellow lights. An onslaught of beetles struck their frontline forces. Dragons speared their enemies with light, followed by low elementals blasting their foes with waves, landslides, tornadoes, and flames. Enormous Vaskran men charged through the elements, and weapons clashed in showers of sparks, metal ringing against metal.

A second Vaskran army marched toward them from the south, too far to be seen except from so high.

"We're too late," Gage exclaimed.

"Not yet. Rhemi!" Alphen called.

Rhemi darted toward the Vaskran army approaching their rear, closing the distance in a few fierce wingbeats.

"Rhemi, take Gage back to the others and warn them." Alphen swung a leg over her back.

Gage snatched Alphen's sleeve before he could jump. "What are you going to do?"

"Delay them." Alphen pulled free, leaped to the ground twenty feet below, and used magic to pad his fall.

"I'm coming with you," Gage shouted.

Despite not knowing how to soften his landing, he leaped. Rhemi dove and caught him inside a cage she made with her claws.

"Rhemi, no!" he cried.

The light dragon ignored him and hurtled toward their allies, leaving Alphen and the Vaskran army behind. Alphen summoned dual light swords and faced hundreds of Vaskran warriors and their vicious beetles.

"Rhemi, put me down!" Gage tore at her claws. "We can't leave him!"

Hums erupted from Rhemi's throat.

Spark peeked his head out of Gage's hood. *Alphen is strong,* he said with clarity that didn't match his usual speech—sharing Rhemi's words with Gage, no doubt. *He will be okay. He wants you to be safe.*

"*He* needs to be safe!" Gage cried.

She paid him no mind and flew to their army. The students remained at the back, sheltered from the fighting to the north but ignorant of the danger approaching from the south. The knights had left them on their own. Gage stared at his peers in horror as he and Rhemi flew past.

"Rhemi, tell the rest of the army what's going on," Gage called, "but leave me here with the students."

Rhemi muttered her annoyance, but she flipped around and swooped low, dropping Gage next to his peers, who cried out at their sudden appearance. The light dragon shot away, roaring her message to the masses. Gage focused his attention on the southern horizon. For now, all he could see was barren wasteland.

"Where have you been?" a girl asked.

"It doesn't matter. The Vaskr are coming!"

"We know," Eddly said, staggering over with a cloak billowing around him. "Our forces are already fighting them."

"Not them." Gage pointed south. "The Vaskr are coming from behind. They have us surrounded."

As if on cue, a sphere of light ignited on the horizon and rushed across the plain, blasting snow into the students' faces. Gage shielded himself with an arm but flinched as he peered over his sleeve. The entire horizon heaved upward in sprays of water before crashing back down. An ominous crackling sound followed, and fractures spread across the ground under their feet.

"Ice," Gage said, stunned. "We're on water."

He lifted his face southward. The Vaskran army marched toward them, unhindered.

"Alphen," Gage breathed, but he shook aside his fear for his friend. Everyone was in danger now—the students, the army, and the fate of their kingdom. He whirled toward his peers and shouted, "Run! Get to the rest of the army! Now!" He drew his sword and ran into the space between his allies and foes.

"What are you going to do?" a girl asked.

"I'm buying you time."

The army's approach rumbled through the ice under his feet, but their numbers had decreased considerably. Alphen had done something to halve their army, but at what cost?

The crunch of footsteps on snow distracted him. Several students joined him in standing against their foes. He knew them from class, though they weren't friends. Emery, a girl with straight brown hair and a water feline draped over her shoulder. Finn, a boy with blond hair, spectacles, and an earth beetle that rode on his head. Breslin, a girl with twin brown braids and a fire lizard wrapped around her upper arm like a snake. To Gage's surprise, Eddly joined the line, his wind avian perched on his shoulder.

"What are you doing?" Gage asked.

"We're here to help." Eddly pulled his steel axe off his belt.

"Tell us what to do," added Emery, wielding a bow and drawing an arrow from the quiver on her hip. Finn drew a steel sword and Breslin a slim sword.

Gage opened his mouth to protest but quickly slammed it shut. How could he tell them to flee and save themselves when he refused to do likewise? They wanted to protect the others at any cost, same as him. He wouldn't stand in the way of that. Taking a deep breath, he drew back his shoulders and stood tall.

"Let's put the Vaskr under the ice," he told them.

Using his dark magic, Gage formed lines across the ground to show them what to destroy. They'd break the ice and plunge the whole army underwater. When the other four nodded, he withdrew his magic to hide their plan. He summoned a ball of darkness in one hand and gripped his sword with the other while his companions summoned their own magic.

The ice shuddered and groaned as the Vaskr approached. Most of the men were on foot, but others rode their beetles. They came fast, and they came angry.

"Get ready. On my word," Gage said to his peers.

The Vaskr unleashed a great battle cry, and their beetles screeched like metal on glass.

"Wait for it," Gage said. "Wait."

The bulk of the approaching army entered the space he'd marked with magic.

"Now!" he yelled.

All five of them dropped spears of magic onto the ice, shattering it so that huge fissures spread in all directions. The lake split apart under their feet, forcing Gage and his companions to lunge for safety. But it was worth it. The Vaskran men screamed over the sounds of crashing ice as they and their beetles went under.

"Run," Gage shouted to Eddly and the others.

They fled toward safety, but more of the ice tore apart. The entire surface of the lake came undone. Right when Gage hopped to a section that hadn't yet crumbled, several Vaskran men soared over his head, flung by their beetles right before the creatures went underwater. Two men hit the ground and launched boulders at Gage, but he tore their magic apart with his own. Another Vaskran warrior dove at him from behind, forcing him to dodge an axe strike and take down a barrage of stone daggers with void magic. As he deflected attacks, he noticed miserably that his peers were caught in their own battles.

A loud thud drew his attention to an assailant who landed nearby, and he had to duck under an axe swing as he scrambled and slid across the ice. The ice likely saved him, because his opponent slipped too. When Gage locked eyes with the man, they both stopped. Terror paralyzed Gage's heart.

"You again," Torquil snarled, reclaiming his balance and grinning his ugly, rotten smile. "You're mine now, vermin."

The big man swung his massive axe again and again. Gage blocked the blows with shields of dark magic, but when his strength waned, he used his steel sword instead. Torquil's axe hit his blade with such force that it sent tremors up Gage's arm. His hands numbed, and Torquil's next hit knocked the sword straight out of his grasp. It flew across the ice and went underwater.

Gage created one last magical barrier between him and Torquil and turned to flee, only to find another Vaskran man waiting behind him, the butt of his axe thrusting against the side of Gage's head. Excruciating pain flared through his skull, and white flashed across his vision.

Darkness followed.

60

THE VASKRAN PRISONS

Master, wake up!

Gage woke to something nudging his jaw. The slight motion sent a pulse of pain through his head, resulting in a wave of nausea. He groaned and forced his eyes open. Even that sent agonizing pain lancing through his brain.

Spark stared at him with his front feet on Gage's face. *You is okay?*

Another wave of nausea kept Gage from answering. He turned his head to eye his surroundings. A rough stone floor chilled him from below, softened only by damp, musty hay. A line of bars blocked him from a hallway of dirt and uneven stone.

Groaning, he sat up, sending Spark tumbling into his lap. He grabbed his throbbing head. "What happened?"

"Gage," Breslin said from behind him, "are you okay?"

Gage turned to find four familiar faces. Eddly, Emery, Finn, and Breslin sat against a rough wall held together by stone slabs and wooden planks. Their elementals slept in their arms.

"I think so," Gage answered. "Where are we?"

"A dungeon," Finn said.

"What?" Gage blinked the glaze off his eyes until he could clearly see the rusted iron bars sealing them in. "What happened?"

"The Vaskr surrounded and captured us," Emery replied.

Gage noted that none of his peers made eye contact with him, and he couldn't find a light in the dim room. He silently thanked his void magic for his ability to see in the dark.

"Is everyone okay?" he asked.

"We're fine," Finn said. "For now, anyway."

"Everyone else escaped," Breslin added. "We took care of most of the Vaskr, so they ended up retreating. Innaran reinforcements were on their way by the time the Vaskr brought us to shore."

"The Innara just missed us," Finn said. "The Vaskr burrowed underground and escaped with us."

"Was Alphen with the Innarans?" Gage asked.

"I didn't see him, but we were kind of far away." Breslin shrugged.

Gage pushed aside his increasing concern for his friend, dragging himself to his feet. Spark scurried up his shirt and onto his shoulder. Gage gave the bars a mild shake. They rattled but held.

"Have you tried using your magic to escape?" he asked the others.

"We don't have magic anymore," Eddly replied.

"What?"

"The Vaskr made us drink some kind of black liquid," Emery explained. "When we did, our elementals fell asleep, and we haven't had magic since."

Gage stared at them in confusion. He could still see in the dark, and his magic didn't feel any weaker. "I didn't drink anything, did I?"

"Yeah, they forced you to swallow some when you were unconscious," Finn said. "Your dragon fell asleep like the rest."

Gage furrowed his brow at Spark, who flashed a mouthful of fangs in a devious grin.

I was pretend, he said, wagging his tail.

What was the black liquid?

Is void magic.

Gage's frown only deepened. Void magic couldn't be ingested, could it? Then again, the Innaran Sunburst could be consumed. Maybe something similar existed for void magic. The Sunburst liquid affected people temporarily. Hopefully, the Vaskr's black liquid would work the same way.

His eyes swept over the shoddy prison, landing on a padlock and chains near the ceiling by the door. Thankfully, the Vaskr had only taken his sword belt, so he still had his lockpicks in the hidden compartment of his main belt.

"How far are we from our army?" Gage asked.

"It felt like we traveled for a long time," Breslin said.

"Their tunnels go everywhere," added Emery.

"This must be how they're taking over the kingdom so easily," Finn said heatedly. "They travel underground and sneak up on us."

That made sense. By traveling underground, the Vaskr bypassed scouts and struck without notice. It was honestly brilliant. Which was why Gage and the others needed to escape. They had to warn the army about this.

"Which way did we come from?" Gage glanced left and right. Neither looked more promising than the other.

"Right, I think," Breslin said.

From that way. Spark nudged his head toward the right.

Can we get out that way?

Think can do. But big danger. A shudder swept through Spark.

Big danger?

"What are we—"

"Hold on," Gage interrupted Eddly. "I'm talking with Spark."

"Huh?" All four of his peers frowned.

Right. Gage wasn't supposed to be able to mentally communicate with Spark yet. He ignored their confusion for now.

What's over there, Spark? he asked.

Is not sure, but big scary. Did not see.

An elemental?

Spark nodded, hesitated, and then shook his head. His little dragon eyebrows furrowed.

What is it? Gage pressed.

Spark tilted his head to the side. *Big magic. Big, scary magic.*

What's that way? Gage dipped his head to the left.

I look see. Spark slid down Gage's cloak, hit the floor with a light plop, and scampered out of the cell. His claws clacked on the floor as he went, echoing in the tunnels.

"Spark is checking things out for us," Gage told the other kids.

"You shouldn't be able to talk to your dragon yet," Finn said slowly.

"I know. But I can."

"Your magic is weird, Voidy," Eddly said.

"I know."

Spark scurried back to the cell, and Gage lifted him onto his shoulder.

"What did you see, Spark?"

Stinky Vaskr is close. No safe go that way.

Gage returned his attention to the right. It had to lead to a way out. Even if the Vaskr covered their exits, Gage and the others might be able to break through any weakened ground with their magic. Gage still had access to his.

Can we safely get around the dangerous thing? Gage asked Spark.

Spark only blinked, but feelings of unease churned in Gage's belly.

"I don't think we have much choice," Gage stated, nodding with determination. "Time for us to get out of here. Eddly, I need your help reaching the lock on the door so I can pick it."

"How can you even see the lock?" Breslin asked.

"I can see in the dark."

His peers barely reacted to the statement.

"Of course you can." Eddly rolled his eyes and slid up the wall. "What do you want me to do?"

Gage grabbed Eddly's arm and led him to the bars. "Get on your hands and knees. I'm going to stand on your back."

"What?" Eddly shook his hand off. "I'm not doing that!"

"Do you want to escape?"

Eddly glared in Gage's general vicinity and sighed. "Fine, but you better not be making this stuff up, Voidy, or you're in trouble."

He dropped to his hands and knees, keeping his back straight like a table. Gage nudged Eddly against the bars and pulled himself up to stand on his back.

Gage picked the lock with practiced ease and sighed in relief when it disengaged. "Got it!"

He stepped down and gently laid the chains in the hay. The door creaked open, and Gage moved it slowly so they didn't draw any attention. The others rose to their feet.

"I can guide you through the dark, but you'll need to hold hands and stay close," Gage said.

Gage helped them link up and then led his chain of companions slowly down the right tunnel. No one spoke. Gage heard nothing but their footfalls. The path curved several times, and they climbed several hills.

"How did the Vaskr see down here?" he finally asked.

"Innaran crystals," Finn said.

"Do you guys have yours?"

"Yeah, but our magic doesn't work on them right now," Emery said. "We tried."

Gage nodded. He still had Alphen's, but his magic wouldn't light it up.

Their journey through darkness continued around dozens of twists, turns, dips, and inclines, chilly and damp the whole way. Gage hoped that meant they were still in the northern region of the Innaran kingdom, near their army.

They finally reached a cavernous room with stalactites hanging from the ceiling and stalagmites jutting from the floor. Shoddy wooden wall supports held the room together. Dripping noises echoed from every direction.

"We're in a cavern," he told the others.

"We're close, then," Breslin said. "We passed through a bunch of caverns when we first came underground."

Shouts echoed in the tunnels behind them, stopping Gage from replying. The voices were loud. And angry.

"Something tells me we've been found out," Eddly muttered.

"Hurry." Gage led them along the stone path, increasing their pace from a careful walk to a rushed trot.

They hustled through several more tunnels. Gage had barely stepped inside another cavern when a shudder swept through Spark.

Big danger ahead, exclaimed the void dragon.

Gage stopped and searched the area. He saw only puddles and heaps of stone.

"I see light!" Emery pointed toward a pinprick of brightness gleaming across the cavern.

"I see light too, but from the wrong direction," Breslin stated. "The Vaskr!"

Everyone whipped around. Lights bounced and wobbled on the walls of the tunnel behind them. Vaskran shouts erupted down the passageway, the thunder of their footsteps reaching Gage's ears.

Big danger ahead, Spark said, shivering.

Spark, help me stop whatever's ahead of us. We can't go back to the Vaskr. Steeling himself, Gage rushed onward, dragging his chain of companions with him.

They raced toward the light that shone down through a steep tunnel. It had to lead outside. Gage could feel the bitter cold—could taste the fresh air and snow. With freedom in view, the shouts of the Vaskr didn't seem as close or as dangerous anymore.

A rumble swept through the ground, and Gage and the others staggered to a stop. Stillness overtook the cavern, followed by another shake that made the light sway ahead of them. The rocks churned.

"What was that?" Emery squeaked.

One of the large rock piles lifted out of a pit in the floor and rose to three stories tall. A creature unraveled from the stones, sending boulders smashing onto the floor with enormous booms that rattled stalactites from the ceiling. The thing—whatever it was—now stood between them and the tunnel of light.

As more boulders fell away, they revealed black flesh with molten veins of liquid fire running through it. The creature had four legs with hook-like claws that sliced through the rocks. Its long tail curled around the room, and jagged spikes protruded from every inch of its body. Flames licked out of the rocks that clung to its form, and liquid fire dropped into blazing puddles around it, illuminating the cavern with orange and blood-red light.

The beast looked like a fire lizard that had been crushed, ripped apart, and glued back together. Thick black veins ran through its bulging red eyeballs and across its massive body, pulsing and squeezing the life out of it.

"What is that?" Eddly cried.

Big danger! Spark lunged under Gage's cloak, his little body trembling against Gage's chest.

The creature took a step toward them, its massive foot slamming against the floor and sending a cascade of stalactites to the ground. The beast unleashed a scream, flames coiling in its throat, and spewed a wave of liquid fire over them.

61

MONSTER OF THE CAVERNS

Gage summoned a shield of void magic over their heads. The liquid fire slid over the barrier and splashed across the room, devouring rocks and leaving scorched puddles behind.

"What is that thing?" Emery cried.

The creature charged another blast in its throat, but Gage shoved his void barrier at it. The magical shield slammed into the beast and blew it into the opposite wall. Embers exploded around it as it hit the ground with a reverberating shudder and rolled back onto its feet. It unleashed a piercing roar that made the other kids fall back and cover their ears.

Void, screamed a voice inside Gage's head—one that definitely wasn't Spark and definitely wasn't friendly.

Gage held his ground and stared into the creature's lopsided eyes. Had it spoken to him?

"The Vaskr!" Breslin shouted.

Gage spun around. Lights swayed along the tunnel walls, the angry shouts of the Vaskr far closer than before. They were trapped on one side by human monsters and on the other side by a literal monster.

"We can't go back to the Vaskr," Breslin cried.

"What do we do?" Finn asked.

The monster's heavy feet shook the walls as it stomped toward them. Despite the other kids crying out in alarm, its sights remained fixed on Gage. It stalked toward him, its claws puncturing the rocks with each step.

Void, said the hissing voice in Gage's head as the monster breathed out a plume of smoke and embers.

It wanted Gage, not the others. That gave him an idea, and since he was the only one with magic, it made the most sense.

"I'm going to distract it," he called to his companions. "Get out of here and find help!"

He sprinted across the room. Sure enough, the creature scrambled after him. Gage slammed spears of dark magic into its head, shattering several boulders attached to it.

The creature's eyes bulged in its head, and it puked another wave of liquid fire at him, forcing Gage to create a shield and dive behind a pile of rocks. The liquid fire splashed over his shield and rained into puddles at his feet, the rocks behind him melting into a sloppy black heap. Gage flung his shield at the creature, leaped over the puddles, and sprinted to the opposite side of the cavern—away from the exit and toward the Vaskr.

The creature stormed after him, its tree-trunk tail smashing through rocks in the process. As he ran, Gage glimpsed the other kids fleeing through the exit tunnel toward the light. The creature didn't care, wholly focused on spitting blobs of liquid fire at Gage. He dodged and weaved around stalagmites, creating occasional shields to defend himself.

He'd almost made it to the opposite wall when the Vaskr burst into the cavern, Torquil in the lead.

"There he is," raged the Vaskran leader.

The creature coughed up another wave of liquid fire. Gage created a curved magical shield, scooped the liquid fire out of the air, and directed it toward the Vaskr. The men screamed and fled into the tunnel as liquid fire hit the wall and melted the rocks. The tunnel entrance crumbled into a gooey heap. At least that took care of that problem. Gage chucked his dark shield at the creature, who snatched it out of the air and shattered it with its massive fangs.

It inhaled deeply and spewed flames that plumed outward. Sick of running, Gage slid to a stop and threw out his hand, attacking the creature with his magic-destroying magic. To his surprise, the flames dissolved.

He searched for the creature's inner magic and found darkness as black as a cloudy, moonless night. Gage attacked it with his powers, but touching the black magic with his own sent chills through his body and spread bumps across his skin. Despite its flames, the creature's magic felt cold as ice. Its tangled and knotted threads, solid as stone, crumbled like a decayed leaf when his void magic touched it.

Gage tore apart the creature's magic, thread by thread, until beams of light streaked out of the tangled mess.

"What are you?" Gage muttered, flinching.

The monster took slow, pained steps toward him, its knees creaking. It choked and sputtered on embers and smoke, its eyeballs whirling around in its head.

Gage took advantage of the creature's delayed movements and shuffled toward the exit tunnel, still tearing apart its magic. More black threads broke away and revealed white light that glared into Gage's eyes and made his sore head throb significantly worse. Black threads slithered around the light, pinching and contorting it into a smaller and smaller ball. Unlike Gage's magical threads, which shimmered with a purple glow, these were solid, and they devoured every flicker of light around them.

Despite Gage's efforts, he couldn't fully destroy the creature's magic. His energy flagged and he staggered, sweat streaking his face and soaking his clothes.

Tired, Master, Spark croaked.

Gage fought anyway as he moved toward the exit. Soon, he would run. The creature could spit fire at him, but it couldn't chase him through the narrow tunnel. The beast dragged its clawed feet after him and unleashed a gasping scream.

Void! it shrieked, so loud that Gage's eyes blurred. Then the beast whispered, *Save me.*

Gage stopped. The words echoed in his mind, haunting and familiar. The girl dragon in his nightmare, she'd said—

A blast rattled his thoughts. The Vaskr and their beetles blew through the melted wall, drawing the gnarled monster's attention. Gage used the distraction and bolted into the exit tunnel toward the gray light above. Sounds echoed behind him, so he spun around and dropped spears of darkness into the rocks, blowing apart the corridor to cover his escape. Then he ran outside into ankle-deep snow on a dreary plain. Tiny snowflakes fluttered down on him.

Ahead, a ball of fire shot into the air and burst into a massive flower of flames. A second and third followed, each leaving behind clouds of smoke and embers. Gage blinked in confusion at the bizarre display.

A rumble swept under his feet, and then the tunnel exploded behind him, sending him flying. He crashed into the snow and rolled several feet. The jolt to his head sent another wave of nausea through him, forcing him to swallow the contents of his stomach. His vision blurred. Flinching, he propped himself up on his elbows.

Beetles erupted out of the ground in fountains of soil and stone, flooding the plain. Two dozen Vaskran men, axes in hand, joined them. One of the men—a familiar one—landed only a few feet from Gage.

Torquil heaved his axe onto his shoulder and grinned down at Gage with menacing glee. "Hello, worm."

62

KING'S RETRIBUTION

"Why's it always you getting into my business?" Torquil strolled toward Gage, who crawled backward on his elbows, his feet kicking up snow. "I oughta torture you at this point, but you're way too much trouble."

The big man swung his axe at Gage, but a light arrow dropped out of the sky and slammed into the blade, knocking the weapon straight out of his hand. Torquil staggered backward and blocked a second arrow with a stone shield. Alphen dropped into the space between him and Gage.

"Alphen!" Gage exclaimed in joy and relief.

Alphen had landed in a crouch, and he rose slowly, drawing one of his silver swords. Rhemi and an entire unit of allies came after him. Elemental arrows rained over the plain, tearing through the Vaskran fighters and their beetles. Nihsa and Mishu joined the fight, as did many other elementals and their riders.

Torquil glared at Gage, his huge fists trembling at his sides. An axe made of stone formed in his clenched fingers. "When I get my hands on you, worm, I'm going to rip off your limbs, one by one, like the miserable insect you are."

Alphen straightened. "Over my dead body."

"Deal!" Torquil charged, swinging his newly formed axe.

Another massive explosion sent them stumbling. Dirt and stone rained over them as the nasty creature from the cavern clawed its way out of the ground, thrashing its body to break free. It screeched such a terrible sound.

Within the monster's horrible wails, Gage heard the cries of a man.

The beast gnashed its fangs and hurled balls of liquid fire over the entire field. The blobs splattered and burned everything they touched to ash, forcing friend and foe alike to flee behind magical shields. Battle cries turned into terrified shouts.

"What did you do to that thing?" Torquil snarled at Gage, but he didn't wait for a reply. Turning on his heel, he shouted, "Retreat! Fall back!"

He fetched his fallen axe and smashed the ground with his fist, turning the earth over. The ground swallowed him in a single gulp right as a blob of liquid fire splashed over the area. The Vaskr and beetles fled while the Innarans and their allies scattered away from the fire raining out of the sky. Everything blurred behind a haze of smoke.

A mighty light dragon swooped over the field, a familiar man riding upon its back. Even after many months, Gage recognized the extravagant armor and magnificent robes. They must have been closer to the capital than Gage realized, because King Fraylon himself rode across the sky. He held a bow and arrow of light in his hands, one that grew in size and glared with blinding intensity.

"Not now, you fool!" Alphen shouted. "What are you—"

King Fraylon launched a massive arrow at the half-buried creature. Alphen shouted something over the hum of the arrow's energy and threw himself in front of Gage, who still hadn't managed to get out of the snow. Alphen summoned his magic, and barriers of white light flashed across the field, surrounding everyone in the area.

The arrow struck. Blinding light spread over the land, tearing apart everything it touched. Wind, rocks, dirt, and snow swirled into a vortex. Debris smattered against Alphen's barriers.

Alphen flinched against the assault on his magic, his body shaking and sweat pouring down his face. His complexion had turned strangely pale, his lips nearly blue.

Finally, the wind and lights ceased, and the debris thudded to the ground. Gage glimpsed the nasty creature burrowing back into the earth, leaving a heap of molten rock behind that solidified into black stone.

King Fraylon and his dragon circled once before departing over the trees.

63

TAKE OFF YOUR CLOTHES!

Alphen muttered a curse, dropped his shields, and surveyed the area. Their allies had survived, thanks to him, and their enemies had fled. Wobbling, he turned to face Gage, his movements lethargic.

"Are you all right?" Gage pushed off the ground, staggering from his still-pounding headache.

"I'm supposed to ask that question," Alphen said, looking Gage over.

"I'm okay. But you—"

"Gage!" Nihsa called from Mishu's back as they bounded over. She leaped down and wrapped Gage in a fierce hug. Laughing, she said, "You're in so much trouble right now. I'm going to kill you when I finish hugging you." Then she gave him a tighter squeeze.

Spark whined from inside Gage's cloak and shoved his way out of hiding, forcing Gage and Nihsa apart.

"Are you okay?" Nihsa asked.

"We're fine," Gage said, but his brow furrowed. "How did you find us?"

"The flares helped."

"Flares?" Gage recalled the fire flowers in the sky.

"Breslin launched them and led us here."

"She didn't have magic," Gage said.

"Why wouldn't she have magic?" Nihsa asked.

Void magic fading, Spark said. *Was returning their magic.*

Gage nodded slowly before asking, "Did you have to travel far to find us?"

"Not at all." She pointed toward a forest on the edge of the field. "The lake is beyond those trees. Our forces have been combing the area ever since you were taken."

"Thanks to Thad," Alphen said with a weary grin. "The king and his guard arrived to help during the fight, and Calvex insisted we continue on to the capital. Thad refused to budge without looking for you first."

"What are you still doing here?" Nihsa snapped at Alphen.

"Rescuing Gage," Alphen said, pointing at Gage.

"My father sent you back to camp." Nihsa's face darkened, and she crossed her arms.

"And I'm disobeying his orders, as usual." Alphen crossed his arms too.

"You didn't even change?"

"My clothes dried fine."

Nihsa grabbed his sleeve despite his attempt to sidestep her. "They didn't dry," she yelled, tearing her hand away and curling it into a fist. "Alphen, they're frozen!"

"Why? What happened?" Gage asked.

Nihsa backhanded Alphen on the arm. "This idiot led most of the Vaskran army onto the lake and broke the ice, sending them all underwater. Himself included."

"Oh." Gage's cheeks burned. "I sort of did the same thing."

"I know. What were you thinking?" Alphen scowled. "You could have been killed."

"You're one to talk," Nihsa said before Gage could defend himself. "You did it too!"

Alphen huffed. "Yes, but I'm older. It's okay when I do it."

"No, it's not!"

"It's really not," Gage murmured, shaking his head. That earned a glare from both of them.

"Stop being a bad example," Nihsa snapped at Alphen and then turned her hostility toward Gage. "And don't you dare do that again. You put yourself and the other kids in danger."

"We were already in danger. The Vaskr would have killed everyone if we hadn't done something. How do you know what happened, anyway?"

"The kids who escaped saw what you did and ratted you out." Nihsa's eyes narrowed.

"Oh." Gage coughed into his fist and kicked a clump of snow.

People headed toward the forest, some walking, others riding their elementals. Nihsa watched them go before aiming another hostile glare at Alphen—one that actually made him jump.

"Let's head back to camp. You're going to do as my father said and go straight to bed," she said.

"I'm fine," he muttered, not sounding fine at all.

Nihsa's eye twitched. "Gage, go with him. Rhemi can take you back to camp. Your tent should already be set up. I'm going to fetch my dad and meet you there."

"I'm fine," Alphen said with some heat.

Nihsa stuck the heels of her hands together and clapped at him. Twice, for good measure. Then she rejoined Mishu, and the pair vaulted over the trees, vanishing from sight. Alphen rolled his eyes but went to Rhemi. His motions lagged as he climbed onto her, and he flinched with every movement. Gage hurried behind him—in case he fell—and hopped onto Rhemi's back.

Rhemi flew slower than usual, probably to keep Alphen from jostling around. They passed over the forest to an open expanse of snow where they found their army building tents, making meals, sharpening weapons, and training for battle. Rhemi spiraled toward the tent Gage and Alphen shared.

Once they dismounted, Rhemi shifted into her first form and flew to a wooden tent post. Alphen trudged to the opening of the tent, leaning the whole way like he was about to fall over.

"What are you still doing out here?" Nihsa called.

Mishu soared over their heads and landed by the tent, shrinking immediately after Nihsa dropped to her feet. They must have found Thad easily, because Gage didn't think Rhemi had been flying *that* slowly—or maybe she had and Gage was too worried about Alphen to notice. Nihsa stomped toward Alphen, her cheeks red. Mishu pranced behind her, keeping to the prints Nihsa left in the snow.

"We just got here," Alphen muttered.

"Yet here you dawdle." Nihsa pointed to the tent. "Go inside and get undressed."

"Nihsa!" Alphen feigned shock and horror, lifting his voice for all to hear. "Stop trying to make me take off my clothes!"

Several heads turned in their direction. Eyebrows went up. Gage chewed back a smile.

Nihsa's red cheeks brightened. "You incorrigible, rot-brained—"

The flutter of wings distracted her. Gromlin settled on the ground nearby, and Thad slid from his back and crunched toward them with his signature limp.

"Good timing," Nihsa said, setting her hands on her hips. "Alphen needs your help getting undressed."

Thad only had time to lift a single eyebrow before Alphen flung aside the tent flaps and disappeared inside.

"Oh, fine," Alphen muttered. "I'm going."

Rhemi chittered and dove in after him, the flaps fluttering shut behind her. Gage and Nihsa exchanged smiles as Thad approached, a change of woolen clothes in hand.

"He's in bad shape," Nihsa told him.

"I'm fine," Alphen said from inside the tent. His words were followed by clothes rustling and Rhemi squawking.

"He's not fine," Gage stated.

Thad nodded at Nihsa. "I want you to fetch some fire users. We'll build a few fires to warm up the area." To Gage, he said, "I intend to discipline you for disobeying my orders, but for right now, I need your help. Grab some spare blankets from the supply cart and warm some liquids over a fire."

Gage turned on his heel, but the motion sent a stabbing pain through his head, followed by another wave of nausea.

He flinched and turned back to Thad. "Can you please heal me first?"

"Are you injured?" Thad looked him over.

"Just a bump on the head, but it's getting annoying." Gage rubbed the sore spot, finding a knot under his hair.

Thad glanced around. "I'll need an Innaran."

"I can restrain some of my magic now," Gage said.

"Doesn't matter. Your magic will destroy everything I put into you."

Alphen poked his head and shoulders out of the tent. His hair was disheveled and the outer layers of his clothing removed.

"I can help," he said, sticking out his arm.

Thad clasped his wrist and immediately frowned, looking Alphen over in concern. Then he returned his attention to Gage. "Where are you hurt?"

"Here."

Thad brushed his fingers over the area Gage indicated, and his eyebrows sank further, darkening his eyes. "That's quite the bump."

Gage blushed. He hadn't thought it was that bad. Then again, he *was* suffering symptoms of a concussion.

Green light radiated around Thad's hand, sending warmth and healing into him. Most of the pain and exhaustion faded. When Thad finished, not a trace of injury remained.

"Thanks." Gage grinned and spun around. "I'll go get—"

A thump halted his steps. He turned to find Alphen collapsed in the doorway of the tent.

"Alphen!" Gage and Nihsa cried, and Gage scrambled over to help him.

Thad beat him to it. "Oh, blast it, boy!" As he knelt beside Alphen, he flicked a hand toward Gage and Nihsa. "I'll deal with him. You two have your orders. Go!"

He grabbed Alphen under the arms and pulled him into the tent. Gage and Nihsa exchanged worried looks and rushed in opposite directions to accomplish their tasks.

64

COLD AIR, HOT COCOA

The following day, the army gathered on one of several rolling hills to listen to a message from King Fraylon. The king had yet to arrive, but his retinue had cleared away the snow in preparation for his arrival. A line of dragons kept watch over the crowd. The Innarans gathered near the top of the hill while the remainder of the army gathered in the dip between hills. People sat on crates, logs, or sheepskin blankets that shielded them from the snow.

Gage and Alphen shared a sheepskin blanket and leaned against Rhemi's warm belly. She lay in her second form, dozing in the sunlight, oblivious to the cold. Spark sprawled on her head with his belly facing up, cooing as he napped. Gage was plenty warm, but he constantly peeked at Alphen to ensure he was okay. Thad had ordered him to bring two blankets, and Gage had brought him a third, but the prince still shivered underneath them. Alphen had slept all of yesterday, all night, and late into the morning. He claimed to be fine, but he still moved slowly. At least a little color had returned to his face.

Gage's punishment for disobeying Thad had been to keep watch over Alphen through the night. After his ordeal in the Vaskran dungeon, Gage had no qualms about being stuck in a warm tent with his friend. Thad probably thought sacrificing oneself to save the army, getting captured, and almost dying against a lizard monster was punishment enough.

Gage's thoughts drifted to the mysterious creature he'd faced in the cavern. The king had reacted violently to it. Gage couldn't help but think it was the same monster that had stolen the capital from the Innarans, meaning it had killed King Fraylon's father and brother.

"Here you are." Nihsa waltzed around Rhemi and sat on the blanket beside Gage, allowing Mishu to curl up in her lap. Scowling at Alphen, she added, "Why are you out of bed?"

"Thad gave me permission to be here." Alphen harrumphed and stuck up his nose.

"I still don't understand why," Gage muttered. "You should be resting."

"I'll tell you why, Gage." Thad rounded Rhemi, three mugs clasped in his hands. "Take note. If you give Alphen permission with strict guidelines, there's a decent chance he'll obey. But if you refuse him permission, he'll do it anyway—without the strict guidelines. I chose the lesser of two evils."

Alphen scowled while Gage and Nihsa smirked.

Thad offered Alphen a steaming mug. "Drink this."

"I'm fine," Alphen muttered. "I don't need it."

"What made you think that was a request?" Thad didn't budge.

Alphen took the mug and glared at its contents. Gage assumed the green-tinged liquid was a medicinal tea.

"I don't need it," Alphen grumbled, blowing on the steaming drink before sipping it, all while maintaining the expression of a sulky toddler.

"And I don't need you passing out again," Thad said. "You're not a little kid anymore. I can't throw you over my shoulder like I used to."

"I bet you still could." Nihsa shrugged when Alphen glared at her. "What? You're still smaller than him."

Thad handed the final two mugs to Gage and Nihsa. "For you."

Gage accepted his drink with a smile. Delicious cocoa and cream scents swirled up his nose, warming him to his toes. The rich brown liquid had frothy white foam on top. He took a sip and practically melted.

Alphen watched him drink and then glared bitterly at his own mug. "Why do they get hot cocoa?"

"Because they aren't in recovery," Thad said.

"But I'm not sick. I'm cold." Alphen gestured toward Gage's mug. "And hot is in the name of their drink."

Thad ignored him, folding his arms over his chest and viewing the amassing crowd. Gage wriggled into a more comfortable position against Rhemi's side and took several more sips. Spark flew at him out of nowhere, latched onto the front of his jacket, shoved his face into the mug for a monstrous gulp, and then lunged back up Rhemi's side. He whacked the mug with his tail as he went, splashing cocoa onto Gage's pants.

"You don't have to steal it, Spark!" Gage yelled. Nuisance dragons! Spark hissed from behind Rhemi.

Alphen chose that moment to lean closer and whisper, "Can I try a sip?"

"Do as the healer ordered and drink your tea." Gage turned away from Alphen, hiding his mug.

Alphen growled—and then leaned across Gage, eyeing Nihsa's mug. "Psst. Nihsa. Can I have some of yours?"

Nihsa took a long sip and then licked her lips. "Oh, sorry, Alphen. Did you say something? I couldn't hear you over the sound of me slurping down this absolutely delicious hot cocoa." Fluttering her eyelashes, she took another swig.

"Stingy jerks." Alphen slumped and drank his tea.

Gage enjoyed his drink and waited with his friends as more people gathered for the speech. At long last, King Fraylon arrived on his dragon, both wearing extravagant armor. Most of the people stood in respect, others bowed, and many cheered and clapped. Alphen simply looked over the rim of his mug and took another sip.

"Thank you for coming, friends." King Fraylon clasped his hands behind his back and waited for everyone to be seated. Then he said in a booming voice, "Tomorrow night, we will reach the capital. The morning after, we attack. I have positioned armies on all sides of the city. Your generals have already been told when and where to engage. We will strike with the intention of breaking through the city walls. Once inside, we will infiltrate the castle and retrieve the crystal at any cost. I will then use its magic to eradicate the remaining Vaskr—both inside and outside the capital. But for this to succeed, friends, I need everything in you. I know you are weary, but do not give up hope. Not here. Not now. Not when we are so close to victory. For the sake of your fathers and mothers, your brothers and sisters—for the sake of the children the Vaskr seek to claim—rise up, my friends, and fight! We will be victorious!"

A battle cry arose from the people, and everyone cheered as the king mounted his dragon and departed with his honor guard. The crowd began to disperse, but Gage and his companions lingered.

"What are our orders?" Gage asked Thad.

"I'll be positioned behind the frontlines to heal our strongest forces," Thad said. "Nihsa and Alphen will be with me, along with the most powerful knights in our unit."

"And me?" Gage pressed.

"You kids will be near the back, away from the fighting."

Heat erupted inside Gage. He sat up. "You have to take me to the front."

"Why?"

"Because I have void magic. I could be useful."

"You aren't a fighter, Gage," Alphen cut in, swirling the last of his tea around in his mug.

"Yes, I am," Gage snapped.

Alphen's expression and voice softened. "That's not what I meant. You're an excellent fighter, but not in a situation like this. Not against an army of trained warriors. If you're singled out by the Vaskr, you're dead."

Gage slouched against Rhemi and chugged the rest of his cocoa, which had started to cool. Anger bubbled up inside him, but he quenched it. Even though the words irritated him, he knew Alphen was right.

"Fine," he said. "Let me go with you and Rhemi. I can use my magic against the Vaskr from Rhemi's back. It's worked before."

No one answered, and the frowns told him everything he needed to know about what they thought of his idea.

He locked eyes with Thad. "I need to fight. King Fraylon thought I'd help end this war."

Thad folded his arms. His jaw shifted as quiet conflict raged in his eyes. "I'll think about it."

Gage nodded. Good enough—for now.

65

NOT A DREAM

A storm of dust swirled around Gage in the nightmare wasteland where he found himself once again. He hadn't had as many nightmares while traveling with the army. Training with Alphen had made him too tired to dream. But now that they prepared to face their final battle outside the capital, now that he needed to sleep, that's when he dreamt of this miserable place.

"Spark? Are you here?" Gage called. When his voice echoed, he shuddered. Monsters had tried to kill him last time, so he probably shouldn't be yelling. *Spark? Are you there?* he shouted in his mind.

No one answered, so he walked through the wasteland and awaited the usual destruction. His mind wandered to his previous nightmare, when Spark had joined him and claimed it was real. But Gage was definitely sleeping in a tent outside Sarsier right now. Spark might not understand the difference between dreams and reality. That made sense for a baby dragon.

A loud crunch echoed through the dust, halting Gage in his tracks. Another crunch followed, and then another. He moved toward the sound. A form appeared out of the murk. First, he discovered a tail with familiar starburst feathers, then a scraggly body with white feathers peeking through gnarled black spikes. The dragon was bigger than he recalled, but he recognized her.

"Orelia?" He tiptoed closer. She'd saved him last time, so he doubted he needed to fear her.

Moving into full view of the dragon, Gage stopped. Orelia clutched a massive rib bone under her front feet and gnawed on it. Gage took another step toward her and crushed a pebble in the dust. Orelia froze. She turned her head in his direction, and he took an involuntary step back. Her golden eyes now bulged out of her head and throbbed with thick black veins. Black stones clung to her body—stones that hadn't been there before. Orelia had changed since the last nightmare, now appearing uncomfortably similar to the lizard in the Vaskran tunnels.

"What happened to you?" Gage stepped backward, his heart stuttering.

Orelia roared. She definitely hadn't sounded like that before. Wings thump-thumped above him, and Gage glimpsed several dragons circling in the dusty clouds. Orelia stomped toward him, reclaiming his attention.

"Stop!" He extended his hand and sent out a pulse of magic.

Orelia froze, a growl rumbling in her throat. He searched her magic and found tangled black knots identical to what he'd seen in the Vaskran monster, except slivers of light still peeked through hers.

"What is this?" Gage muttered.

Three more gnarled, spike-laden dragons crashed onto the dusty ground behind him. Gage held out his other hand and shoved his magic at them, tearing at their knotted threads. The dragons halted but growled and bared their fangs. All four dragged themselves toward him, scraping their claws along the rocks under the dust.

Gage shredded through their black threads until pinpricks of light exploded outward. The dragons screamed in agony and thrashed on the ground. Gage gritted his teeth and turned his focus toward Orelia. Some of the black shell had already fallen off her body, and she had the most visible light. As he tore at her darkness, she screamed like a wild animal until a second voice broke through, transforming into the scream of a regular girl. Orelia.

Her desperate cries startled Gage. Was he hurting her? The lapse in his focus allowed the other dragons to move. All three lunged at him. Orelia snarled and dove over Gage's head, tackling the other three with her bigger bulk.

Gage, run! she cried, her voice now clearly her own. Familiar, but exhausted. *Please!* She fought the other dragons, tearing at their flesh with her claws.

Gage couldn't leave her—not when he'd hurt her and possibly weakened her by destroying her magic. Instead, he ripped apart the black threads inside the other three dragons, making them stagger. Orelia slammed them to the ground, one after the other, and knocked them unconscious.

A shadow rolled over them as the usual giant shape blotted out the sun. Explosive booms followed—distant, but they still shook the ground. Something formed out of the haze above Gage. Something small, but it grew larger and larger. Something falling at a rapid pace right over his head.

Gage's heart skipped a beat as he turned and ran, but Orelia caught him in her claws and swooped away with him. They slipped out from beneath a shining piece of glass that fell and shattered against the ground, dissolving into glittering sparks. It wasn't glass at all, but a shield like those Alphen created with his light magic. A second piece dropped to their right, and then another to their left.

"What are those?" Gage exclaimed, clinging to the claws around his torso. They flew so close to the ground that he had to bend his legs to keep them from dragging.

The barrier is failing, Orelia told him. She dodged sideways as another chunk of shining magic shattered nearby. *You must not be here now. Gage, you must leap back to your world!*

"Leap back to my *what*?" Gage flinched as another barrier dropped ahead of them.

Orelia tore sideways. Her body scraped along the ground as she turned, ripping off some of her black spikes. She bounded off the rocks with her back legs and darted another direction. The looming shadow followed. As did the barriers raining from the sky.

Leap back to your world, Orelia urged him. Desperation tinged her words. *You must not be here!*

"This is a dream," Gage yelled.

You are not dreaming, Gage. You leaped here. And he will do everything to stop you while you are here.

A million questions ricocheted through Gage's mind. This wasn't a dream? How could one leap here? What was going on? Who was she? Instead of asking any of those questions, he settled on one that seemed far more significant.

"He, who?" For some reason, his eyes were drawn to the ominous shadow swallowing the sun.

The worldeater!

A massive chunk of magic dropped over them and clipped Orelia's wing, sending her into a tumble. She hit the ground and rolled through the dust. At first she kept Gage safely tucked under her body, but she slammed against a rock so hard her claws opened. Gage flew out of her grasp and rolled several feet. Another shadow darkened over them.

Orelia pushed off the ground with her forelegs. *He will kill you, Gage! Run!*

Gage staggered to his feet. Confusion and terror muddled his mind. "Kill me? Why?"

Orelia scrambled toward him, but her wings and hind legs dragged. She was too far and the collapsing sky too close. *Because you are the only one who can stop him,* she cried. *Now leap!*

Gage turned and ran, because he didn't know what else to do. The magical ceiling came down, impossible to escape. He ducked his head and dove for safety he knew he couldn't reach. The glaring white barrier struck his head and shoved him toward the ground.

Instead of being crushed, he jolted upright on his bedroll. He was back in his tent in the Innaran war camp. Sweat soaked his bedding and clothes, and it took everything in him to breathe.

Spark crawled over to him. *Master no take with. Is okay?*

Gage chose to breathe instead of answering, because he doubted he could speak. Spark's words only further confused him. How could he have taken Spark with him? That place and those things couldn't be real.

You didn't see that? Gage finally asked.

No take with. Spark's head sank. *Master go alone.*

A shiver swept through Gage, and bumps spread across his arms. Reality crashed over him—a reality he could no longer deny. "It's not a dream, is it?" he asked. "It's real?"

Spark's eyes sharpened. Quietly, but with a strange fierceness, he said, *Is real.*

66

THE THREE STARS

Gage sat on his bedroll for a long time, trying to regulate his breathing. It took even longer for the vivid images of the not-dream world to fade from his mind. It wasn't possible, was it? He desperately needed answers, but he sensed Spark's confusion on the matter. His dragon knew the place was real, but nothing more.

Then he recalled the dragon sculpture.

Gage glanced at Alphen's bedroll, only to find it empty. "Where is Alphen?"

Went out. Spark crawled into Gage's lap.

Darkness and eerie silence shrouded the tent. It had to be the middle of the night.

Same smell, Spark murmured.

"What?"

Master, Alphen. Is same smell, Spark elaborated, as if that helped.

Gage stared dully at the dragon. Apparently, sharing a small tent with someone had awkward consequences.

"Gross," was all Gage could think to say.

Yawning, he stretched and rubbed sleep out of his eyes. He tossed aside his bedcovers—flinging Spark aside in the process—and grabbed his clothes.

Where going? Spark asked as he untangled from the blanket.

"To find Alphen."

Gage wasn't sure what he'd ask when he found him, but he needed to talk to someone. Especially since Alphen had seen those terrible dragons before. He finished dressing and pulled on his boots. The more he thought about it, the more ridiculous everything seemed. Alphen couldn't have seen the same things as him. The sculpture's similarities had to be a coincidence. Still, he wouldn't be able to sleep now, so he ducked out of the tent and glanced around.

Go here, Spark said, scurrying down a trampled path of snow.

"How do you know?"

Spark flashed a toothy grin. *Because I is good hunt. Good smelling.*

Gage tried not to laugh. He followed Spark through the camp, staying as quiet as possible. Everyone needed their rest. Tomorrow would decide everything.

Spark made it to the edge of camp and climbed onto a post, reaching Gage's eye level. *Is here,* he said, eyeing a trampled path up a hill overlooking the capital city.

Rhemi, in her second form, lay at the hill's summit, her wings folded at her sides and her head settled on her front feet. Moonlight glinted off her white feathers. Gage let Spark leap onto his shoulder before heading up the path. Rhemi eyed them as they approached. Gage stepped around her and found Alphen sitting on a sheepskin blanket, leaning against Rhemi's side, warm in her fluff and feathers.

He looked at Gage in surprise and mild concern. "What are you doing up this late?"

"I could ask you the same thing," Gage said.

"That's not really an answer." The corners of Alphen's lips twitched into a smile.

"I know."

Gage looked out at the capital and had the breath ripped from his lungs. The royal city sat in a mountain range made entirely of gleaming crystal, framed by glittering snow below and twinkling stars above. A river of blue and purple weaved through the night sky.

The city had been built into the crystal mountains, with small buildings at its base and more intricate buildings near the top. A massive stone spire loomed at the city's highest peak, ugly compared to the surrounding buildings with their white stone walls and gold or iridescent roofs. Waterfalls poured behind walkways and bridges throughout the capital, eventually dumping into lakes and rivers in and around the city. Crystal lights in an array of colors shone throughout Sarsier, giving it an ethereal appearance. An enormous wall made of harsh stone blocked off the western, eastern, and southern sides of the city—a Vaskran addition, no doubt. The mountains barred entrance from the north.

Gage flapped his hands at Alphen, gesturing him aside. When the prince scooted over, Gage joined him on the blanket. Spark leaped onto Rhemi and scurried to her head. She huffed in annoyance as he burrowed into her feathers.

"Can't sleep?" Alphen asked.

Gage shook his head.

"Worried about tomorrow?"

"I had a nightmare," Gage admitted.

"Oh." Alphen furrowed his brow.

"I have them all the time."

"I'm sorry," Alphen said, sounding genuinely troubled. He folded his arms and leaned closer. "Want to talk about it?"

Something hard and frozen melted inside Gage. No one had ever asked him that before. Emotion choked his throat, and he had to look away.

"I dream of a place with lots of dust," he admitted, wringing the front of his tunic. "Everything is ruined, and the only living things are creepy dragons trying to kill me. Sometimes there's a big shadow in the sky. I can't see it, but it feels ominous." He swallowed hard as the most recent nightmare returned to his mind. "Tonight, I dreamt the sky was falling down around me."

"I'm so sorry." Alphen's voice cracked with grief.

Gage shrugged and plucked at the sheepskin beneath him. He glanced at Alphen from the corner of his eye. "How did you deal with the nightmares?"

Alphen jolted. It was hard to tell in the moonlight, but it looked like some of the color drained from his face.

"Thad told me you used to have them," Gage said. He refrained from mentioning the dragon sculpture for now.

Alphen looked out at the city and sank against Rhemi. He plucked at the blanket too. "My mom used to tell me something whenever I had nightmares. It helped me get through them."

Gage nodded, biting back unrelated questions. Alphen had never talked about his mom before.

"Have you heard the story of the three stars?" Alphen asked. When Gage shook his head, he continued, "Doesn't surprise me. It's an old story." He lifted his face skyward. "Once upon a time, there were three worlds. Innara, Caladon, and our world, Lycadia. While standing on one of the worlds, you could look up and see the other two as stars in the sky." He pointed toward one of the brightest stars. "See that star? That's the world of Caladon."

"That's a world?" Gage asked, bewildered.

Alphen nodded.

Gage scanned the sky for similarly bright stars. "Which one is Innara?"

"Innara was destroyed by a great calamity," Alphen said. "The star of Innara blinked out, and the Innarans fled their world to Caladon and Lycadia."

"The Innarans came from a star?" Gage raised an eyebrow.

"Not a star. A world. Or so the stories go," Alphen said. "My mom said the calamity traveled from Innara to Caladon, but Caladon fought back. They resisted the calamity and stopped it there, keeping it from reaching us. Even now, they fight and shield us from harm."

"What calamity are they protecting us from?" Gage asked quietly, his stomach churning as he recalled the giant *thing* in his nightmares.

"No one knows for sure." Alphen gazed at the stars. "But whenever things are difficult, I look up and find Caladon. As long as it's still shining, I know there's still hope. Nightmares, wars . . . they come and go, but we can keep moving forward."

Gage looked at the brilliant star of Caladon. It couldn't be a coincidence, could it? The legends and his dreams? He'd always thought it a myth that Innarans had come from other worlds, but now he wasn't so sure. Maybe other worlds did exist. Maybe they were stars shining in the sky. And maybe they were being devoured by a world-eating calamity, one after another.

Maybe he was dreaming about them—or even leaping to them—every single night.

Gage's gaze crept back to Alphen, whose focus remained on Caladon. Pain shone through Alphen's eyes, something Gage only noticed in moments like this. His concern about his own nightmares suddenly seemed unimportant. At least for now.

"You had a nightmare tonight, didn't you?" Gage asked quietly. "That's why you're sitting out here."

Alphen met Gage's eyes and then looked out at Sarsier. "That, and I wanted to check out the city. See if there's anything we missed. Any way to break in and end the fighting sooner. If I could somehow reach that stone spire in the middle . . ."

"What is that thing?"

"It's covering the castle. The Vaskr must realize we want the crystal and are protecting it with their strongest magic. If we could sneak in and steal the power of the crystal, we could end the fighting."

"If it were that easy, I'm guessing your father and siblings would have figured it out by now." Gage leaned back and yawned. "They've been planning this for months, haven't they?"

Alphen yanked on a frayed piece of fluff on the blanket. "There's always a chance they missed something."

"You don't trust your family, do you?"

Alphen plucked at a thread.

"Why not?" Gage pressed. "They seem so kind."

"Yeah, they seem that way, don't they?" Bitterness edged Alphen's voice as he ripped a strip off his blanket. "But people aren't always what they seem."

Now that was an odd comment, but Gage resisted his curiosity. Alphen clearly didn't want to talk about it.

"You're right, you know," Gage said. "People aren't always what they seem. You act like an idiot, but you're actually really smart and kind."

Alphen snorted.

"Why do you do it? You're only pushing people away."

Alphen flicked some torn fluff into the snow. "Sometimes it's easier to protect people that way." When Gage opened his mouth to question further, Alphen added hastily, "You didn't answer my question. Are you worried about tomorrow?"

Gage chose to ignore the obvious deflection and instead considered his role in the upcoming battle. Thad had informed him that he'd ride along with Alphen. He'd be in danger, but Alphen and Rhemi would protect him.

"Yes and no," he admitted. "I'm worried about the people who'll get hurt. But I'm glad we're doing something about the Vaskr. They need to be stopped."

Alphen looked at Gage thoughtfully—almost remorsefully. "Stay safe tomorrow, Gage," he said quietly. "Stay with Rhemi. She'll protect you. And so will I. I won't let anything happen to you."

The intensity of that promise—filled with so much warmth and concern—startled Gage. He struggled over a proper response, but Alphen saved him the trouble. The prince rose and offered Gage a hand.

"We should get some sleep," he said, his trademark smile sweeping away his unguarded emotions. "Tomorrow will be a long day."

Gage accepted the help up and then tightened his grip on Alphen's hand. "You stay safe too, Alphen." He'd never had a friend like Alphen, and he refused to lose him in a stupid fight with the stupid Vaskr. "Okay?"

Alphen squeezed his hand and patted his shoulder. With a genuine smile, he broke contact and headed down the hillside. Rhemi nudged Gage with her snout, reverted to her first form, and flew to Alphen's shoulder. Spark fell from her head into the snow, vanishing under a layer of white powder. When he popped back into view with a pile of snow on his head, he blinked.

Gage watched the two depart before looking up at Caladon. The star radiated light, meaning no calamity would reach them. For now.

67

BATTLE AT DAWN

Dawn broke over the horizon in a dazzling display of pink and gold. The view would have taken Gage's breath away had he not already been breathless. Their army stood at the ready, and he sat with Alphen on Rhemi and awaited orders to move. Today, they would either seize the capital or lose the kingdom forever.

Silence held the army captive. Maybe everyone had lost their breaths—and with it, their voices. Gage had barely managed to squeak out a few words all morning. Spark perched on his shoulder with his head held high, but Gage felt the dragon's anxiety fluttering in his belly.

"Hold onto me today," Alphen said. "We're going to do some crazy maneuvers."

Gage gripped Alphen like his life depended on it. His heart raced, and sweat slicked his palms.

The sun cleared the horizon and unveiled their army surrounding the city.

"Light has dawned," King Fraylon shouted from the frontlines. Others echoed his words so all could hear. "Let this be the day we reclaim our kingdom and our people from the grip of the Vaskr once and for all." He hefted his sword into the air. It pierced the lingering darkness with a beam of light. "Give them no quarter, my friends! To battle!"

King Fraylon took to the sky on his dragon. The first line of dragons and elementals charged with him toward the city walls. Everyone moved with fluid coordination, like many parts of one body. Nothing happened as they reached the wall. No attacks from the city, no Vaskr coming out to meet them.

Gage frowned. "Why aren't the Vaskr—"

Rocks erupted from the city until the entire capital looked like a prickly burr. The stone spines shot outward and forced the attacking elementals to dodge or block with barriers. The Innaran army lashed at the city with their magic, but any rocks they destroyed were immediately replaced by more. The first wave of attackers fell back. As quickly as the rocks appeared, they vanished in flashes of yellow. Sarsier shimmered in the daylight as though nothing had happened.

"We didn't even get close to breaching the city," Gage muttered.

"The Vaskr are battle masters," Alphen said. "Experts at offense and defense. This isn't going to be easy."

A second line of allied elementals formed around the city walls, but now they maintained their distance and launched their magical attacks from afar. Sarsier's stone barrier hurled enormous boulders and high-speed daggers in retaliation. The Innaran army destroyed what they could, but the debris overwhelmed them and forced most of them back. The few knights who approached the wall were again met by knives of stone erupting from the walls.

The main forces of the Innaran army moved in, shattering the spikes and projectiles with an onslaught of water, wind, fire, and earth. Yet as they drew closer to the walls, the ground tore open and swallowed them into yawning chasms. The collapse of the ground troops left the aerial troops vulnerable, and more projectiles struck down dragons and avians.

"The entire area is a trap." Gage's heart sank in despair as their allies fell back once again.

"We're certainly not brute forcing our way inside," Alphen said. He clenched his jaw, scrutinizing Sarsier before meeting Gage's eyes. "How do you feel about bashing through them with void magic?"

Gage gulped. If the strongest knights couldn't breach the Vaskran defenses, how could he? But he shook those thoughts from his head. Fear couldn't control him, not when he might be able to help.

"I'll try anything," he said.

Alphen patted Rhemi, and she took off at once, heading straight for Thad. Their general sat on Gromlin at the head of their unit, awaiting the call to either fight or heal.

"Permission to fight freely, sir?" Alphen called. "We're going to try punching through their defenses with void magic."

Thad glowered. He still hadn't forgiven Alphen for his earlier disobedience. Then he watched as another wave of their forces fell back without gaining ground.

"If we can break through the wall, we can hit the Vaskr and stop their magic," Alphen said. "But we're not winning this fight if we never get past their defenses."

"Fine," Thad grumbled. "But don't you dare let my apprentice get killed."

"I'll protect him with my life," Alphen promised.

Rhemi swooped toward the city, avoiding another onslaught of rocky projectiles from the enormous walls.

"Strike their magic, Gage," Alphen said, forming a bow and arrow of light. "I'll follow you."

Gage focused on the magic swirling around the capital in thousands of dazzling threads. The ample magic throughout the city blurred together before his eyes, forcing him to rip apart the magic everywhere around the wall. As he shredded the threads, Alphen struck with a shining arrow, blowing the wall to dust and revealing the Vaskran men hiding behind it on the city streets.

Shouts of surprise arose from the Vaskr, followed by cheers from the Innaran army—until yellow light flared across the wall and restored the broken rocks. Significantly more magical threads flooded the area as the Vaskr strengthened their defenses.

"It worked, but it looks like we'll have to hit harder if we want it to stick," Alphen said.

He veered Rhemi toward their unit—which had finally joined the fray—and flew alongside Thad and Gromlin.

"You hit them," Thad said.

"Thanks to Gage," Alphen replied. "But we need to strike harder if we want to keep the wall down. Permission to take troops?"

"Granted."

Alphen leaned forward, and Rhemi dove toward the ground troops. They targeted Nihsa, Mishu, and the knights with them.

"Gage is going to soften the wall," Alphen called. "We need to strike hard and take it down with one blow. Follow our lead!"

Without question, Nihsa and the others fell in line behind Rhemi and charged the city. Gage ripped apart the lights along the front wall while his allies launched a deluge of elemental attacks at the places he'd hit. Another huge section came down, revealing Vaskran warriors scrambling for their weapons on the other side. A violent barrage of rock projectiles from within the city forced Nihsa and the others to retreat.

Alphen guided Rhemi to the western side of the city, where he recruited additional knights. Gage weakened that wall, allowing his allies to break through, and then repeated the tactic on the eastern wall. When they circled back to the southern side of the capital, yellow lights flashed across the snowy field. More walls formed, more boulders and spikes blasted outward, and more chasms devoured their allies. Screams filled the air over the constant roar of stone.

To Gage's dismay, all three walls reformed, blocking the approach of the Innaran army. He scrubbed sweat off his forehead and groaned while Spark slumped over his shoulder.

"They're too strong," he muttered. "How do they have so much magic?" Again he looked at the glaring brightness of the Vaskran magic within the city.

"They have the crystal," Alphen said. "They have limitless magic at their disposal. We'll wear out long before they do." He guided Rhemi around Sarsier, circling higher to dodge an onslaught of stone spears hissing through the air. "We need to get inside the walls and deal with whoever is launching these attacks—"

Roars drowned out the rest of his words. An earth beetle climbed over the wall, followed by dozens more.

"There are hundreds of them!" Gage exclaimed.

He shook away his initial horror and focused on attacking the beetles with void magic. Alphen unleashed a light arrow upon every elemental Gage struck, blasting the beetles back into their first forms. Again and again, Gage attacked and Alphen followed, but no matter how many they destroyed, countless more replaced them. Gage's vision blurred as the sunlight glared angry red through a haze of smoke. His head throbbed with a dull ache.

They needed to reach the source of their problems—the Vaskr behind the walls.

Gage refocused his gaze on the magic within the city, seeking the Vaskran warriors rather than their beetles. Bright lights glared from every direction, but he forced himself to push through the pulsing threads until he found one connected directly to the rock wall. Gage followed it to a giant, blazing ball within the wall itself—and then he stabbed it with his void magic. The light died, and the stone barrier crumbled without reforming.

"The Vaskr are inside the walls," Gage said. "If I attack them directly—"

Void! screamed a piercing voice that stunned dragons and avians straight out of the air.

A burst of magical energy erupted from the city and across the battlefield, blowing away friend and foe alike. Rather than resisting, Rhemi rode the energy like a leaf on a wave, turning back toward the city once the blast had faded.

Massive claws curled over the rock walls, and a familiar monster drew itself upright within the city. Gage would recognize its lizard shape anywhere—along with its molten skin, jagged spikes, and pulsing black veins.

The creature from the caverns. It was ugly before, but now it had nearly doubled in size.

"What happened to that thing?" he asked.

Void user! the creature screamed.

It turned its nasty, decayed eyes toward Gage and lunged off the wall—straight at him.

68

BLACK THREADS

The mangled beast soared over the army and slashed at Rhemi with its claws. She dodged the swipe while Alphen struck the lizard in the face with a light arrow. The creature slammed to the ground and slid through the snow, only to leap again and spew curls of flames at them. Rhemi deftly dodged.

"He's after me," Gage said.

"Well, he can't have you," Alphen stated.

VOID!!!!!! The creature screamed in Gage's mind.

Another pulse of energy swept out of it, blasting everyone. Rhemi tried to ride it like the first, but it hit too hard and fast. She toppled in the air and spiraled downward, flailing her wings in a desperate attempt to right herself. The violent motion tore Gage's grip from Alphen. With a startled cry, he flew backward into open air.

Alphen leaped off Rhemi and caught Gage in midair, shielding their landing with a surge, but the monster emitted a second pulse that blew Alphen and Gage apart. Gage clung to Spark as he flew sideways and hit the ground rolling.

Both armies unsteadily rose to their feet. Gage couldn't see Alphen and Rhemi anywhere, and his heart stuttered as the molten beast stomped toward him, liquid fire dripping between its fangs. It spewed fireballs at him, and he tossed Spark onto his shoulder before extending his hand and shredding through the beast's magic with his own. Pain lanced through him from the effort, and Spark whined from exhaustion, but Gage kept attacking. The fiery creature unleashed a bloodcurdling scream as it dragged its feet to reach him.

Enemy beetles surrounded them, and Gage tore at their magic until his vision swam and he couldn't breathe. When ripping apart their threads didn't stop them, he hit them with dark arrows and blasted them back into their first forms. Yet no matter how many he defeated, others took their place.

VOID USERSSSSSSSSS, screamed the creature with a high-pitched hiss, but now the squealing voice mixed with a man's deep tone.

Rhemi swooped over the monster as it towered over Gage. Alphen leaped off her back with a sword of light in both hands, stabbing downward into the beast's back. They landed so hard the ground cracked. While Alphen pinned the molten lizard, Rhemi swooped alongside Gage, allowing him to grab her feathers and yank himself onto her back.

She carried him above the battlefield, where he saw Alphen still piercing the creature with his shining sword. Blinding beams of light radiated out of the knotted black mess of the lizard's magic.

Cut magic, Spark said. *Is heart. Cut is destroy.*

"Got it."

Gage tore the remaining black threads, and the monster exploded into a ball of flames until nothing remained except a tiny first-form lizard. Energy blasted out from it, but Rhemi darted upward to avoid being caught in another deadly roll. She rose higher until the energy ceased, and then she flew parallel with the ground. Ash and embers rained down around them.

They were losing the battle. The enemy army had increased in size while the Innaran forces fell back. If they didn't stop the Vaskr controlling the defenses, they would never win. Someone had to get inside the walls and defeat the men pulling all the strings.

Gage turned his focus to the lights inside the walls. They blurred together with every other light inside Sarsier. He couldn't see clearly enough to break down the defenses from afar. He'd never be able to destroy the magic of every Vaskr in the city, and how many allies would he accidentally strike if his magic went astray? He had to get closer.

Clenching his jaw, Gage threw his legs over Rhemi's side. "Rhemi, find Alphen. Keep him alive, okay?"

Summoning darkness over the land, Gage snuffed out the light of the sun, flames, and magic. Then he leaped from Rhemi's back. She screamed at him, but she couldn't see him to give chase. Gage's stomach flew into his throat as he plummeted.

Master! Spark clung to him and flapped his wings to no effect.

Gage focused his magic on the bottoms of his boots and pushed out a surge—the same way he'd seen Alphen do it dozens of times. His magic gushed out of him and sucked the air from his lungs, but darkness erupted beneath him and launched him across the sky.

Master good! Spark shouted gleefully, gliding alongside him.

The surge drained Gage, but he performed several smaller ones and leaped toward the city. Every use of magic sucked more air from his lungs, until he found it impossible to catch his breath. Spark settled on his shoulder once he landed on a corner of the defensive wall.

From there, he saw every light in the wall in a clear line. Gage pushed out his void magic and smothered the light of their foes. The rocky barrier exploded under his feet and forced him to surge to the next wall, which he destroyed in a similar manner. Leaping to the third and final wall, Gage staggered from dizziness and gasped for breath.

"Someone's inside," a Vaskran man yelled from the street below.

"Activate the defenses," shouted another.

Spikes sprouted from the remaining wall, but Gage surged above it and tore it down, leaving Sarsier open to the Innaran army.

He managed one last surge before his magic gave out. He crashed onto the flagstone street and slammed against a house. Brilliant sunlight tore through the night he'd created—he couldn't maintain the darkness any longer. His vision blurred. He barely noticed the Innaran army bearing down on the city now that the defenses had fallen. Barely noticed them striking hard and fast to keep the Vaskr from restoring their barriers.

He was too busy noticing the Vaskran men charging toward him.

"Intruder!" one man shouted.

"Grab him!"

Gage ran for the open field—toward his allies—but stones erupted around him, forming a cage. Then the rocks broke apart and tumbled down around him, burying him alive.

69

VASKRAN DUEL

"Got him," someone shouted.

Gage ached from head to toe, and the weight of the rocks crushed the air from his lungs. The stones shifted, and strong hands grabbed him and yanked him into the light. Over ten Vaskran men stood around him.

"Got his little pet too," said a man who plucked Spark out of the rocks.

The dragon draped over the man's arm without moving, but he whimpered, assuring Gage he was still alive. At least until the man drew a knife from his belt.

"No!" Gage yanked against the hands restraining him. "Leave him alone!"

"Then stop fighting." The man held the blade to Spark's side.

Gage froze, his heart stuttering. Heavy footsteps thumped toward them, and several men shuffled out of the way.

"Well, well," said Torquil, who approached with murderous rage in his eyes. "Look what landed right at my doorstep."

He grabbed the front of Gage's shirt and slammed him against a nearby house. Gage cried out from the flash of fiery pain that tore through his body, and then again when Torquil swung a dagger at his side. The Vaskran man stopped an inch from striking. He stared at Gage with a cold, calculating look before his face twisted into a feral grin.

"Boys, I think I found a way to end the war," he called. He leaned closer, his sour breath curling over Gage. "You just handed me the kingdom, kid." Torquil flung Gage into the hands of another man. "Hold him and shut him up. Call for parley! It's time for a Vaskran duel!"

"Parley," echoed dozens of men throughout the city.

Their shouts turned into cheers as they rang bells and waved white flags at the edge of the city. Gage vaguely remembered something about Vaskran duels—something about a betrayal that had cost the king his life. He berated himself for not studying his enemy's tactics in more detail.

His captors dragged him through the city. The surrounding buildings had been boarded up, showing no signs of life. Gage knew the royalty had been murdered when the Vaskr took the city, but had they killed the civilians as well? His stomach clenched at the thought.

They reached the city plaza, where colored stones formed flowery patterns around a barren section of rocks in the center. A fountain may once have sat there. Countless Vaskran men gathered around the area like spectators in an arena. Gage and Spark were held in the shadows.

Torquil marched into the center with the bulk of his warriors behind him while King Fraylon and his honor guard swooped in on their dragons. Dozens of elementals came after them. The king slipped off his dragon, his boots hitting the colored stones with an audible crunch. Only then did his honor guard dismount and join him. Torquil leaned casually on his big axe, his beetle dangling from his fur pelt.

"What do you want?" King Fraylon asked, stopping within arm's reach of Torquil.

"The same thing as you, Highness," Torquil said, drawing out the final word with a hissing drawl. "I want this war to end as soon as possible."

"So you surrender?"

Torquil grinned. "No, but I propose a Vaskran duel."

Muttering erupted throughout both armies. King Fraylon stiffened.

"Know what that is, Highness?" Torquil asked.

"I do," King Fraylon said, his voice as tight as his posture.

Torquil circled the king while addressing the Innaran army behind him. "We Vaskr have perfected the art of war. But we love a good duel. A Vaskran duel is fought between the champion of the defenders"—he tapped his own chest—"and the champion of the invading kingdom in a winner-take-all fight to the death." He came alongside the king, a sneer sharpening his face. "By our laws, your champion is whoever first set foot within our walls."

Gage's stomach dropped, and the air went out of him. He stared for what felt like an eternity, and then he leaped and yelled for King Fraylon to reject the offer. The hands gripping him held fast, and another powerful hand slapped over his mouth and nose, smothering him. He kicked and bit and screamed, but someone shoved a wad of fabric that tasted like a dirty sock into his mouth.

"Why would I agree to these terms when I have the city thoroughly surrounded?" King Fraylon gestured to his army behind him. "I need only defeat you, and the city is mine."

"Because you want to save as many lives as possible." Torquil stood face-to-face with the king. "And I have dungeons beneath this city. One strong earthquake will kill every prisoner down there." He licked his front teeth. "If I go down, I take everyone with me."

King Fraylon didn't react, but his warriors shifted uncomfortably.

"You realize I was the first to set foot in the city," the king said. "You will face me."

Torquil said nothing, keeping an apathetic expression. Tears prickled Gage's eyes.

"If I win, you surrender—along with your generals and every warrior within this city," King Fraylon said. "The city and everything in it are mine."

"And if I win, I take the heads of you, your children, and your generals," Torquil said. "The rest of your people will swear fealty to me. Your kingdom is mine."

Muttering resumed throughout the Innaran army. Gage pulled at the hands holding him and screamed into his stupid rag, but that earned him another hand over his mouth and nose. The heat in his eyes intensified, and his vision blurred with tears.

King Fraylon met the eyes of his magnificent dragon, perhaps discussing whether to accept or not, and then sized Torquil up. In a fair fight, the king would win. Only, this wasn't a fair fight.

"I accept your duel," King Fraylon said, offering his hand.

Torquil took it, gave a fierce shake, and drew himself closer. "Oh yeah. I forgot to mention. You weren't the first person to breach our walls, Highness." Shoving away from King Fraylon, Torquil waved his arm in Gage's direction. "He was!"

The Vaskr shoved Gage into the light. All at once, the Vaskr broke out in celebration, stomping their feet and hollering like they'd already won the duel. The Innaran army responded as well as Gage expected—their eyes widened in horror and their jaws went slack.

"No," Alphen yelled, shoving through the crowd. "Gage, no!"

Lord Calvex caught Alphen and kept him from running to Gage, but that didn't stop him from shouting, "No!"

repeatedly while trying to pull free. A few knights helped restrain him.

"The duel is decided," Torquil called to his army, and their riotous cheers shook the city.

"Treachery," King Fraylon said with a snarl. "You deceitful lout of a man! Have you no honor?"

"In war? Never." Torquil sneered. "That's why the capital is mine. Take your honor to the grave with you, Highness." He lifted his axe. "Prepare the grounds. Make room!" While his men cleared the area, Torquil passed Gage a thoughtful—and evil—glance. "Unless the champion wants to surrender. I'll even let him escape with his life. Of course, he'll swear fealty to me like everyone else." His eyes flicked toward the king. "After I behead you, of course."

The Vaskran men shoved Gage forward. He spit out the rag and wiped his mouth, glaring first at his captors and then at the man holding Spark. He glowered at Torquil, who wielded an axe larger than Gage's body. He would never win this fight, especially not now that he'd wasted so much magic.

"No," Alphen yelled, still restrained by his brother. He shook his head at Gage.

King Fraylon's face contorted. Lady Halayna stood behind him, covering her mouth with both hands. When Gage met her eyes, she immediately looked away. Everyone was going to die because of him. Because he didn't know about some stupid tradition. Because he wasn't strong enough.

"Well, boy? What say you? Are you too scared?" Torquil barked out a laugh and marched around the plaza, holding up a fist to incite more jeers from the crowd. Meanwhile, he looked at Gage like an animal ready to rip apart its prey. "Too frightened to fight against a real enemy? One that can actually see you and strike back? Not so tough when you're not skulking in the shadows like a rat, are you? You and your ugly excuse for a dragon."

Laughter arose from the surrounding Vaskr. Gage saw the disdain in their eyes for him and for Spark. For their magic that wasn't normal, for their bodies that weren't big and strong. Their jeers should have further shriveled Gage up inside. Instead, they lit a fire in him. A little spark of defiance that ignited into a flame.

"Look at him quiver with his tail between his legs," Torquil continued, still marching in a circle.

Every step he took and every word he spoke fanned the flame inside Gage. The laughter and disdain reminded him of years spent in Talid with spiteful adults and mocking children. Of people who hated him without knowing anything about him.

"Looks like victory is mine," Torquil shouted, "because the champion of the Innaran kingdom is no champion at all!"

Mocking laughter followed. But Gage moved. He raced into the center of the plaza and slammed his boot down to command the attention of Torquil and his ugly, laughing friends.

"I accept your challenge," he shouted.

70

BOY VS. WARRIOR

"He accepts," Torquil cheered. He laughed with the rest of the Vaskr, their voices ringing across the plaza. "The fight is on! Prepare for a quick show, boys!"

Alphen finally elbowed Lord Calvex in the chin and broke free. He dashed across the plaza and grabbed Gage's shoulders, giving him a firm shake.

"Don't do this," he said with a ferocity Gage had never heard before. "Gage, you can't win this fight."

"I have to try."

"You won't win." Alphen gave him another shake. "He's powerful, and you . . ." His voice broke, and he choked out his next words. "Gage, he'll kill you."

"I'd rather die than stand by and let him kill my friends," Gage stated.

Alphen hesitated before setting his jaw and squeezing Gage's shoulders. "Stay alive," he said fiercely—and desperately. "Please stay alive until I come back." At that, he released Gage and ran into the city.

"Where are you going?" Gage called.

Alphen vanished into the crowd without answering. Torquil's shouts and cheers drew Gage's attention.

"Ready to join the worms, boy?" Torquil taunted.

"Can I at least have my dragon?" Gage asked. "Or are you too scared to let me fight with my elemental?"

Torquil's smile faltered. He gestured to the man holding Spark, who then flung the dragon into a nearby water barrel. Spark thrashed and flailed, scrambling onto the barrel's rim. He blinked wildly, wide awake. Gage snatched him into his arms while Spark hissed at their captors and flicked his tail in annoyance.

"I can use any weapon I want?" Gage asked as he placed Spark on his shoulder.

"Anything." The big man finally stopped his ridiculous pacing.

Gage glanced at the steel sword on his belt. It wouldn't do much good against this monster of a man and his monstrous beetle. He removed the weapon and flung it toward the crowd. The Vaskran people burst into laughter, but some of the jeers died when he summoned a sword of dark magic into his hands. Purple embers sparked around the blade.

His vision blurred from the effort, but he ignored the sensation. He'd collapse from overusing magic long before he'd ever surrender to Torquil.

Torquil grinned and summoned stone armor around his body, complete with rock spikes that would make it impossible for Gage to get close. Rocks erupted from his axe as well, transforming it into a spiked club.

Ready, Spark? Gage asked, surprised to feel only the slightest flutter of anxiety in his belly. Like he was taking a test at the academy rather than battling to the death.

Ready! We is win! Spark snapped his fangs and wagged his tail, moving his entire backside in the process.

Torquil spun his axe around him like a tornado and launched an endless stream of stone daggers. Still spinning, he took slow steps toward Gage, spreading a circle of destruction around him. Gage created a wall of darkness to shield himself and pushed toward his assailant. Their magic collided with the sound of cracking thunder.

Gage gave his barrier a fierce shove, and it tore through Torquil's magic and crashed into the raider. Torquil staggered briefly before smashing his axe into the ground, sending waves of stone across the plaza. Gage dodged some of the rocks and broke others with his magic, skirting around his foe. He lunged from behind to strike, but the big man pivoted and punched with a rock-encrusted fist. Gage sidestepped the blow and planted a surge-infused kick into the man's rock-covered abdomen.

Torquil staggered but swung his axe anyway. Gage dove under the careless swing, spun around Torquil, and thrust his dark sword at his back. When the raider lunged forward to evade, Gage launched the sword from his hand like a javelin, striking and shattering the man's rock armor with a single touch.

The Vaskran leader leaped away from Gage. His grin was gone, replaced by hard lines. Sweat poured off him.

"What are you?" he growled.

"A void user," Gage replied.

Torquil's beetle dropped to the ground and ignited with yellow light. It transformed into its second form directly underneath Torquil, lifting him onto its back. Torquil stood and clung to one of its many spikes.

Gage was heartened by the fact that Torquil now saw him as an opponent worthy of his beetle's time—and terrified that his newest opponent was bigger than a house.

The beetle sent out an explosion of rock spikes that stabbed upward, sank back underground, and stabbed again. The entire area filled with jabbing rocks. Gage retreated to the edge of the plaza and tore apart the rocks closest to him, but his energy flagged.

Inspecting the beetle, Gage flinched against the glaring light of its magic. It had to be the most powerful beetle he'd ever seen. Still, he tore at its threads.

The beetle screamed at his efforts and leaped at him with legs splayed wide. Gage formed a shell of void magic to shield himself and ran through the upheaving plaza. The elemental crashed down behind him, overturning everything around it and sending out wave after wave of enormous stabbing spears.

Gage jumped over the first wave and surrendered to the second, allowing his void barrier to shatter the onslaught of stones before they reached him. The shell around him flickered and cracked with every stone that struck it. His enemies intended to wear him down, and if Gage didn't figure something out quick, they'd succeed. Time to use his size and speed to his advantage.

He ran along the edge of the ring and jumped onto the oncoming wave of rocks. He leaped from wave to wave, gradually moving inward toward Torquil and the beetle. The waves were larger near his foes, forcing him to surge with each jump. Sweat slicked his skin and drenched his clothes. His muscles burned and his lungs strained. Still he ran and jumped toward the center.

Gage rode the final wave to its highest point and then surged into the air, ignoring the agony that seized his muscles. As he leaped, Spark flew into the air beside him. Together, they dove at the beetle—and toward Torquil's exposed back.

Torquil turned and made eye contact, but his beetle hadn't noticed them.

"You—" Torquil yelled.

Gage leaned into his freefall, gripping his dark sword with both hands and letting out a defiant shout. Spark plummeted alongside him, dark mist and purple sparks swirling around them. Torquil summoned a stone spear, but Gage surged magic through his sword so it shot out like a lance. His intentions for the blade were firm in his mind: it wouldn't kill, but it would destroy every trace of magic in Torquil the same way Gage had destroyed the plants and magic in Talid.

The darkness sliced through Torquil's weapon and pierced the man in one smooth stroke, expelling a burst of purple sparks. Every rock in the plaza dissolved into dust and flitted away as yellow glitter. The magic within the beetle imploded into a tiny ball, and the monstrous creature reverted into its first form right out from underneath Torquil.

Spark clung to Gage and flapped his wings to slow his drop, but Gage had to use a lopsided surge to land safely. He staggered, Spark still clinging to his jacket.

Behind them, Torquil slammed to the ground on his back, letting out a pathetic groan. His beetle plopped down beside him, its six legs flailing in the air.

Gage gasped to catch his breath and stood straight. Spark settled on his shoulder. And then cheers from the Innaran army ignited around them, filling the city with exuberant sound.

71

FLIGHT

It took Gage a moment to realize that Torquil had been defeated and that the cheers were for him and Spark. They'd WON.

A flash of dark energy swept over the rock spire surrounding the castle, quieting the celebration. The entire structure crumbled to dust, revealing an elegant castle with white walls and gold spires at the height of the city. A flash of light erupted from its tallest tower.

Torquil sat up on his elbows and stared at the castle. All color drained from his face, and he turned toward Gage with murder in his eyes.

"Let them out!" he yelled.

Cheers turned into screams as buildings exploded, shooting stones and glass through the air. The ground tore open, and felines, beetles, lizards, and avians clawed out of the chasms. Black, pulsing veins and massive spikes consumed their forms, their bodies gnarled and decayed like creatures unearthed from their graves. They unleashed roars and squeals in a cacophony of terrible sounds, moving in a wave toward Gage and the Innaran army behind him.

The Vaskr used the sudden chaos to flee, including Torquil and his beetle. The Innaran army retreated, attacking the creatures that came after them, but to no avail. Nothing hurt them.

Nothing except Gage's magic. He held out his hand and tore apart their black threads, finding streaks of light underneath. His efforts restrained the creatures so the Innaran army could escape, but his magic waned, and his grip on them faltered.

Master must flee, Spark cried. *Is danger!*

Gage pushed against the creatures anyway. People's lives depended on it.

Master!

The first wave of creatures smashed into the plaza, spewing fire, water, wind, and rock in a torrent of brilliant colors.

Gage summoned one last desperate shield of dark magic against the onslaught—and then magic ignited inside him, unfurling in massive dark ribbons with gleaming purple edges. Purple sparks filled the air. The darkness spread across the entire plaza and vaporized any magic it touched. Even the monsters returned to their first forms, the black spikes and veins around them demolished.

Another line of mangled creatures descended upon the plaza, but they hesitated. First, they looked at their shrunken allies, then at Gage and the purple shadows swirling around him, and then beyond him. Gage whirled around at a thunderous roar, his heart stuttering in his chest before leaping into his throat.

Darkness stood behind him in the form of a dragon. Dark scales gleamed like night across its lithe but powerful body—now the size of a small house. Familiar midnight colors painted its leathery wings, and the fluff across the creature's head and spine were unmistakable, as were the glowing purple eyes. The dragon showed its fangs, but it no longer looked like a dorky smile. No—it was downright menacing.

Gage hadn't even felt Spark leave his shoulder.

Do not touch my master, Spark snarled in a deep, masculine tenor. He curled his stark-white claws into the ground, shredding through stone like paper.

He unleashed a bone-shattering roar. Waves of darkness ignited around him, battering the mangled elementals and stripping them of their power. Still more enemies came. Gage added his strength to the attack, but his legs trembled, his arms ached, and his vision blurred. Spark had released a surge of new magic from inside him, but they faced an army with near-limitless magic.

What were these creatures? And how were they so much stronger than regular elementals?

Do not give up, Master, Spark said. *Help is come.*

A flash of light in the air punctuated his statement. A ball of light flew toward them, white at its center and framed by a halo of colors. It descended from the castle like a shooting star, and as it drew closer, its feathery body and wings became clear.

"Rhemi?" Gage choked.

Then he saw Rhemi's rider. Alphen held a bow of light and drew back an arrow radiating hundreds of colors.

"Alphen!" Gage exclaimed.

Alphen loosed his arrow, and it fractured into dozens of arrows that rained down on their foes. Gage and Spark had already weakened them, so they exploded on contact, transforming into their first forms and falling helplessly to the ground. Gage and Spark attacked the next wave, and Alphen answered with another volley of arrows. Again and again they repeated the process until the monstrous army fell apart.

Silence and peace prevailed. Sunlight glittered over the ruins of Sarsier.

"Take the city," King Fraylon yelled from behind. "Take any remaining Vaskr and elementals hostage. Go!"

The knights scattered and went to work in a blur of activity.

Rhemi landed at the edge of the plaza, and Alphen rushed to Gage, relief flooding his eyes. Spark scurried past them, taking his bulky new body after Rhemi.

Alphen glanced at Spark as he passed. "Something's different about you, Sparky. Eat a big lunch?"

Spark ignored him and lunged at Rhemi. She snapped her jaws around his head, body-slammed him to the ground, and pinned him beneath her. Spark whimpered and cowered despite his larger size. Gage smiled before turning his attention to Alphen. His friend offered a hand, and he clasped it briefly until Alphen gripped his forearm instead.

"You stayed alive," Alphen said.

"I won." Gage grinned.

Alphen smiled, too, and pulled Gage into a firm hug, giving him a squeeze and a pat on the back before letting go.

"How did you have enough magic to attack like that?" Gage asked.

"The crystal."

"You reached it?"

Alphen nodded. "I absorbed some of its power." His smile shifted into a scowl. "I was going to come save you, but whatever, I guess."

Another grin stretched across Gage's face.

"You did it, lad!" shouted a familiar voice.

Thad hobbled over and nearly sent Gage flying with a solid slap to the back. He drew Gage into a bear hug, immediately following it with another back slap.

"By the light of Innara, you took back the city," Thad exclaimed. He whirled around and smacked Spark on the rump—the dragon still stuck under Rhemi's front feet.

"And you kept the lad alive, you brilliant dragon!" He offered Rhemi a quick nod before his eyes found Alphen and his expression dulled. "And you're here too." His lip twitched as he patted Alphen on the back.

"Gage!" Nihsa rushed over and nearly tackled Gage with a hug before pushing him back and gripping his shoulders. "I can't believe you did it!"

"Wow, you all really had faith in me, huh?" Gage put on a sulky pout.

"You know what I mean." She rolled her eyes and hugged him again.

"I helped too." Alphen stretched out his arms. "Do I get a hug?"

Nihsa flicked a splash of water at his face but turned away as she chewed down a smile. She returned her attention to Gage. "How did you have enough magic left to destroy the spire around the castle?"

"I didn't destroy it," Gage said, shrugging.

"Really? It looked like void magic."

Gage could only shrug again. It had looked like void magic, but he hadn't touched it. Spark hadn't evolved yet when the spire fell, so neither had the strength to accomplish the task. Another set of footsteps distracted him from those thoughts.

"I owe you a debt of gratitude, Gage Black," King Fraylon said, smiling warmly. "Congratulations on your win. It seems you are a true champion after all."

Gage blushed and offered the slightest nod.

"I will have words with you later, after the city is secured. Until then, rest." The king bowed his head before rejoining his honor guard to sweep the city.

"Rest?" Thad folded his arms. "Bah. Even heroes have to earn their keep." He jutted a thumb toward the entrance of the city. "There are a lot of injured people out there. I need my apprentice to help clean up this mess." Turning a scowl on Nihsa and Alphen, he added, "You two, help secure the city."

"Sir," they all said.

Nihsa and Alphen went one way, Gage and Thad another. Spark returned to his first form and flew to Gage's shoulder. He *flew*. Gage's heart leaped at the realization.

They'd have fun with that later. But for now, they had work to do.

Gage spent the rest of the day helping Thad with recovery efforts. Thad didn't dismiss him until sunset, when he finally told him to grab dinner and get some rest.

In search of food, Gage wandered through the vast camp the army had set up outside the city. The capital had taken heavy damage during the battle, so no one could safely pitch tents inside Sarsier's crumbling walls. Only the castle had been spared.

Despite having to sleep on the frozen ground for yet another night, laughter echoed through the camp. Gage smiled at the lighthearted sounds as he savored a warm bowl of soup. He wasn't even annoyed when Spark practically climbed into the bowl and spilled a bunch of soup onto his pants. Everyone's joy was infectious.

After finishing his meal, Gage made his way toward the city to check on things—and to see if there was anything more he could do to help. On his way, he spotted Alphen strolling out of the city, his hands in his pockets and a grin on his face.

"All finished for the day?" the prince asked.

"For now," Gage said.

Alphen's eyes twinkled. "Want to fly?"

Spark trembled on Gage's shoulder, his wings quivering with anticipation.

Butterflies stirred in Gage's stomach, and he had to fight to keep his excitement in check. "I dunno," he said, forcing a look of apathy. "I'm pretty tired—"

Spark yowled and chewed on Gage's ear, making him laugh. The little dragon was wriggling so much Gage half expected him to launch off his shoulder and take flight without him.

"We're still new at this," Gage reminded Alphen.

"Then let's practice."

Rhemi flew off Alphen's shoulder, shifted into her second form, and circled over their heads. Spark mimicked her, taking flight and transforming. Rhemi swooped past Alphen, and he caught her feathers and swung onto her back as she zoomed by. With the lightest beat of her wings, she went skyward.

Spark attempted the same maneuver. Gage had climbed on Rhemi like this before, but Spark didn't have any experience doing this. Thad could heal them if they got hurt, but Gage didn't want to look like an idiot while everyone was celebrating him as champion of their army. Then again, they had to learn. And sometimes people had to crash if they wanted to learn how to fly.

As Spark swooped low, he turned his back toward Gage. Gage managed to catch a tuft of fluff and hoist himself up, gripping one of Spark's white spikes for stability. He leaned forward as Spark beat his leathery wings, ascending toward the sky.

"And now, we soar," Alphen called.

Rhemi rose high and then dipped downward, spreading her wings and settling into a slow, descending glide. Spark copied her.

Gage's heart sang. Spark's did likewise.

Ahead of them stretched a horizon of snowy forests and the setting sun. The sky and strings of clouds blazed brilliant pink and orange before fading into purples and blues speckled with starlight. The surreal beauty took Gage's breath away.

Their flight brought them over the capital city with all its white stones and gold roofs now colored in sunset pinks and oranges. Even in ruin, it glowed.

Elated by the flight and their victory, Gage couldn't help but feel this was the best day of his life.

72

CHAMPION OF INNARA

Gage lifted his chin, allowing Thad to adjust the collar of his shirt and the ties of his cloak. The outfit was way too fancy, so he'd been forced to rely on the older man to help him with the ensemble. At long last, Thad finished his ministrations and gave Gage a critical once-over. Then he set his hands on Gage's shoulders and smiled warmly.

"You look like a hero," he said.

Gage smiled, but his cheeks warmed. Never had he imagined he'd hear those words from anyone. Thad patted his shoulder and stepped aside to finish his own preparations. He grabbed his clothes and vanished behind a dressing partition.

They'd been provided a small room in Sarsier Castle to make themselves presentable. The castle reminded Gage of Runadel Academy: marble tiles, enormous windows, dragon sculptures everywhere, and furniture made of dark wood with silver and gold accents. This particular room had a dressing area, a table with several high-backed chairs, and a blue couch that matched a rug by the door.

Gage turned toward a big mirror and inspected his dark, elegant outfit, complete with lots of blue and purple accents. The cape had midnight-colored feathers along one side and twinkling fabric underneath. He wore several silver accent pieces, including belts, bracers, and a circlet around his head. It was all a bit much, but one needed to look the part when getting knighted by the royal family.

Knighthood was King Fraylon's answer to Gage's heroism. Gage would continue at the academy as a student, but he'd possess all the honor and privilege of a full-fledged knight. Gage wasn't sure what that meant yet, but it was pretty neat for a kid who'd been considered cursed his entire life. Even if he had to wear a ridiculous outfit during the knighting ceremony.

We match, Spark commented from atop a nearby dresser. He wore his dorky toothy grin and wagged his tail.

The outfit had been designed with Spark in mind—but the colors and feathers definitely looked better on a dragon.

A knock sounded on the door.

"It's open," Gage called.

"Is my dad still—" Nihsa stepped in and froze when she saw Gage. Her face melted into a warm, doting expression. "Oh, Gage, you look so—"

"I'm not cute," he snapped.

She clamped her mouth shut. And scrunched her face tighter and tighter until she looked ready to implode.

"Don't say I'm cute," he warned.

She made a long, grinding sound and then burst out, "But you look so cute!"

Gage sighed and rolled his eyes.

"Are you nervous?" Nihsa asked, smiling.

"Yes and no." He shrugged.

"It's okay if you are. A lot of people are attending. And to stand before King Fraylon and be knighted by him personally . . ." Her eyes twinkled.

"Actually, I asked King Fraylon if Alphen could do the ceremony. He agreed."

Nihsa broke into a fit of laughter.

Gage scrunched his face. "King Fraylon laughed too."

"So did I," Thad said from behind the partition.

"What's so funny about it?" Gage huffed.

"The noble presiding over the ceremony has to be in full royal regalia. Crown and all," Nihsa said. "You know Alphen will hate that."

"I don't care. He can deal with it for one day." Gage stormily returned to the mirror and shifted his hair in the same manner Alphen had in the past. He rather liked the style.

"I have no problem with it." Nihsa leaned on the edge of the table. "Anything that makes Alphen miserable is a win for me."

Thad emerged from behind the screen, still adjusting the buttons of his shirt. Like Nihsa, he donned his knight uniform minus the armor.

"Do you have the report I asked for?" Thad asked Nihsa as he rolled up his sleeves, making himself look a little less impeccable.

"Our knights have explored most of the tunnels below the city," she said. "We found the dungeons and released the captives. There were hundreds of people down there."

"All the captured kids?" Gage asked.

A crease worked its way between Nihsa's eyebrows. "That's the confusing part. There weren't any children. We asked the prisoners, and they said the kids were never down there. No one knows what happened to them."

Gage frowned, wondering what the Vaskr even wanted with children. Torquil had let it slip that they were doing some kind of experiments, but what did that mean?

"Hey, don't make that face." Nihsa put a hand on his shoulder. "We freed a lot of prisoners. And we've sent our people throughout the tunnels. We'll root out and defeat the Vaskr in no time, and it's all thanks to you."

"Yeah, I guess."

A bell rang through the castle.

"That's our cue," Thad said, patting Gage's back.

Gage glanced in the mirror one last time before offering his arm to Spark. The dragon leaped to his shoulder, and they followed Thad and Nihsa down the hall to the throne room doors made of dark wood with gold accents. Two Innaran knights guarded the entrance.

"We'll head in through the side doors and see you at the front," Thad said.

"Congratulations, Gage." Nihsa gave him another hug.

"I just go in when the doors open?" he asked. His mouth felt full of cotton.

"That's right." Thad patted his back and walked down the hall, Nihsa at his side.

Gage stood in front of the massive doors, his heart racing. He wiped his sweaty hands on his tunic and then clasped the fabric to keep his palms dry. Alphen had walked him through the process, but the live ceremony felt different than a practiced event. People would be watching. If he tripped and fell on his face, he'd never live it down.

A second bell rang, and the doors opened. Gage stepped to the threshold.

Crystal dragon statues filled the upper half of the cavernous room, shimmering in the sunlight that poured through the vast windows. Smaller tinted windows let in streaks of color. Marble pillars and more dragon statues lined the room, and wide balconies overlooked everything from above.

Nearly a hundred people gathered inside, and as soon as Gage appeared, all eyes landed on him. No one spoke—at least not with their words. Mouths smiled and eyes twinkled. His fellow students stood in the back. Among them, Eddly,

Emery, Finn, and Breslin grinned from ear to ear. Gage proceeded down the aisle and found knights and recruits, including those from Thad's unit, all smiling. Older knights and Innarans gathered near the front, full of good cheer. Thad and Nihsa stood ahead of them all, and they watched him with pride and affection in their eyes.

At the front of the room, a dazzling crystal dragon stretched its wings over a pair of crystal thrones. White, translucent drapes fluttered along the sides of the throne platform.

King Fraylon, Lord Calvex, and Lady Halayna stood on a carpeted area before the thrones, each dressed in thick royal robes with ample gold and silver jewelry. They wore their hair in elaborate braids around their magnificent crowns. All three stood with their hands folded in front of them, their faces unreadable.

Alphen stood closest to the steps leading down the aisle. He'd replaced his usual clothes with heavier robes, but not quite as extravagant as his family's. While they wore white, he chose white and black with gold and silver accents. A simple gold crown gleamed from his brow. He held a sword of white metal in his hand, the tip of the blade pointed to the floor, his hands folded over its pommel.

Gage reached the end of the shimmering golden carpet and stopped at the steps below Alphen.

"Gage Black and Nightspark," Alphen said, keeping his voice formal and level, "my family and this kingdom owe you a debt of gratitude. Thanks to your bravery, we have reclaimed this city and our hope for the kingdom. But more than that, we have reclaimed freedom for many of our people."

Despite his stiff language, warmth shone through Alphen's eyes. Gage was glad he'd asked for Alphen to do the ceremony—and glad his friend had agreed to wear a crown for his sake. The words of gratitude would have been nice from the king, but they meant infinitely more coming from the man who'd trained him.

"You risked your life for us," Alphen continued, "despite the odds being against you. Your heart and courage are commendable, and so I offer you a position of knighthood within the Innaran kingdom. With the title comes great responsibility. You will dedicate your time and talents to fighting for the sake of this kingdom. Nay—for the sake of this kingdom and beyond, because humans and elementals will rise and fall together. It will be challenging and discouraging at times, but it will be the greatest honor of your life. What say you, Gage Black and Nightspark? Do you accept?"

"I accept," Gage said without hesitation. Spark chirped in agreement.

"Then kneel."

Gage knelt before the steps and bowed his head. Spark leaped onto the first step and bowed as well. Alphen stood over them and placed the blade on Gage's left shoulder.

"By my authority as prince of the Innaran kingdom, I bestow upon you knighthood of the realm. May your courage, strength, and honor increase as you grow into your role." He moved the blade to Gage's right shoulder. "You are now rider and dragon in service of the kingdom. Rise and face your people."

Gage allowed Spark to leap onto his shoulder before standing and turning toward the crowd.

"I now present to you Sir Gage Black, the newest dragon knight of the Innaran kingdom, and his void dragon, Nightspark," Alphen declared.

Everyone in the audience bowed. Every. Single. One. Even Eddly. Gage resisted the urge to bow back. He felt silly standing before them.

"Gage," Alphen said, and Gage faced him. The prince wore a genuine smile, much less stiff and formal than his still-grumpy family. Warmth flowed into his words as he said, "Thank you for everything. Well done."

Alphen bowed, as did his family behind him. Gage exhaled sharply and hastily returned the bow, deeper than theirs. The royal family wasn't supposed to bow to a knight. He was so anxious and moved so fast he almost butted heads with Alphen—which would have hurt considering the pointy crown on Alphen's head.

"It's your fault I'm wearing these stupid clothes right now," Alphen whispered.

"They look good," Gage whispered back.

"Whatever. I'm going to kill you later."

Gage resisted a laugh as he and the others straightened.

"Now then," Alphen said, taking a deep breath as he addressed the crowd. The severe look on his face faltered, and he hoisted the sword to his shoulder and grinned. "How about a feast?"

Cheers erupted throughout the room. They'd apparently reached the end of the formal ceremony. People hooted and hollered, and chanting erupted from the back, led by a familiar voice.

"Voidy! Voidy! Voidy!" Eddly chanted, pumping his fist in the air.

The other kids chimed in, echoing his words and motions until every student chanted, "Voidy! Voidy!"

Gage stared in stunned silence. None used mocking tones. None wore malice on their faces. They sounded like friends cheering on one of their own. Like people who were happy to know him and glad to see him succeed. Like people who were happy he existed.

A smile spread across Gage's face. Starting today, the stories about void users would change. No longer would they speak of death, destruction, or darkness. Instead, they'd tell of the cursed boy and his void dragon—the champions who'd saved the kingdom.

73

THE CRYSTAL

ALPHEN

Alphen slipped into the tower chamber and quietly closed the door behind him. The knights outside wouldn't hear him, but caution was in his nature. The circular room hadn't changed since he'd first broken into the tower. Massive windows splashed sunlight across the tiled floor.

Nothing existed here except the crystal, which sat in the center of the room. It loomed over Alphen, nearly a foot taller than him, and gleamed with a rainbow of colors. Light radiated from it, but Alphen couldn't see through it to find the light's source.

Rhemi flew off his shoulder and changed into her second form. *How long will your magic cover this room?*

Alphen's illusion was powerful. No one could see or hear him now, nor would they see the results of what he did. Even if he stole the crystal, they would see and feel an illusion of

497

the crystal for as long as his magic remained. They wouldn't notice anything out of the ordinary unless they tried to absorb the crystal's magic. Mind illusions were powerful but also the hardest to maintain.

"One day," he muttered. "Two days if we're lucky."

Are you certain you want to do this?

"I have no choice, Rhem. You know that."

Fraylon will not forgive this trespass.

"I know," Alphen said quietly.

He will hunt you down and destroy you.

"I know."

Rhemi hesitated and then asked in a softer voice, *Will you take Gage with you?*

The question sent a familiar ache through Alphen, something he hadn't felt these past several months with Gage by his side. He'd almost forgotten the loneliness and agony he'd lived with for the past ten years. He tried to push away the encroaching misery and reminded himself that Rhemi would be at his side, but he still knew something would be missing.

"No," he said. "He's safer here."

Fraylon may abuse Gage's magic, as he has done to you, Rhemi reminded him.

"Maybe. But I don't think he'll try that yet," Alphen said. "Gage is still too inexperienced with his magic to do what Fraylon wants. And he isn't as young as I was when all this started. I don't think he'll cower and let Fraylon do whatever he wants." He hoped, at least. To assure himself as much as Rhemi, he added, "If Fraylon tries anything, Gage will either fight back or go to Thad and Nihsa. They'll protect him."

Rhemi lowered her head. The dragon's pain twisted in his chest.

And who protects you? she asked in a broken voice.

Alphen flinched. He hated worrying her, but he couldn't do anything about it. Not yet, at least. Story of his life. Not yet, not yet, not yet.

"You protect me, Rhem," he said, offering her the faintest smile. He gripped her face and put his forehead to hers.

Naturally, she said. *I will always protect you, Alphen. To the ends of this world—and to the worlds beyond. But still, I worry for you. You are one human, and you have done enough.*

Alphen wrapped his arms around her and held her. Her warmth spread over him and through him. For a brief moment, he felt peace.

"Thanks, Rhem. I don't deserve you."

I know, but I tolerate you nonetheless. She pulled away so she could meet his eyes. *I go where you go.*

A dagger cut through Alphen's heart. Gage had said those words to him too. He wished they could be true—wished things didn't have to be this way.

Nodding at Rhemi, he stepped toward the crystal and reached into the depths of his magic, tugging on a small, shadowy thread until a dark sword formed in his hand.

Purple embers glinted around the blade. Simply holding the sword drained his energy, but it would destroy the crystal.

His Innaran magic couldn't do that. Only void magic could.

"There's no going back now," he said.

Holding his breath, he thrust the sword into the crystal. The blade sliced through it as if through air. Energy gushed out of the stone in a rush of wind until cracks spread through its surface. Light leaked out and permeated the entire room, forcing Alphen to step back, cease his void magic, and shield his eyes with his arm. The crystal shattered.

The lights coalesced into a feathered being that unraveled four dazzling wings. Despite the creature's small size, it possessed the lithe body and majestic features of a light dragon in its second form. Crystals twinkled like scales across its body, mingling with its feathers, and it glittered with iridescent colors. The elegant dragon opened her piercing eyes and looked straight at Alphen.

"Are you Noor?" he asked. She should be, based on everything he knew.

She didn't answer but simply stared, floating without flapping her wings.

"Can you understand me?"

She certainly can, Rhemi said, shuddering. Awe passed from her to Alphen. *She is timeless. Ancient. I can feel her wisdom and strength. We are in the presence of something very powerful, Alphen.*

Good. That's why he was here.

"We need your help," Alphen said to Noor. "Caladon is in danger. The barrier is failing, and they're running out of time." He took an urgent step toward the majestic dragon. "The worldeater is going to destroy them."

Noor didn't respond. She simply floated, stared, and radiated light.

Alphen tried to breathe. They'd come too far and sacrificed too much to not receive her aid. "Please. Do you know how to stop him?"

Void magic, she said, her voice full and resonant in his mind, clear as a ringing bell. Like a harmony of singing voices with a gentle female voice rising above them all. Or like a bubbling brook in a forest full of chirping birds, buzzing insects, and whispering wind.

Despite the beauty of her voice, her words broke him.

"I know," he admitted. "But there aren't many of us left."

Yours is too weak, she said.

Alphen grimaced at the truth in her words. He'd failed with void magic. That was the problem. He wasn't good enough.

"There is another," he admitted cautiously, forcing the words out of his mouth. "But he's too young. Isn't there some way I can stop the worldeater without laying this burden on his shoulders?"

Together, you will succeed, she said, and the light brightened around her. *Or perish.*

Noor dove, gliding around him without flapping her wings.

He turned after her in haste. "Please wait!"

Rather than leaving, the ancient dragon circled the room, again and again, weaving a web of light magic around him. Like a darting sparrow, she swooped and slammed into Alphen's chest. White flashed over his vision, and he hit the ground on his back and slid across the floor. Warmth and magic poured through him, stronger than anything he'd felt before.

The lights faded, as did the stars flashing over his eyes. Noor zipped away and flew straight through the ceiling. She vanished in a flash, taking the brilliant, ethereal lights with her—along with all of Alphen's hope.

"Don't go!" He scrambled to his feet and staggered to the nearest wall when his legs wobbled beneath him. "Please don't go! You're the only hope we have left!"

Silence answered him. He leaned his back to the wall and slammed his fist against it, harder and harder, until jolts of pain ran through his body and eventually numbed his arm.

"Please don't go," he said, but it came out as a pathetic whimper. He slid to the floor and bowed his head. "You were our only hope."

He'd failed. Again. Story of his life.

Rhemi joined him, snorting a warm breath over him. *She gave you much of her magic.*

Alphen didn't care. Light magic couldn't help them. People for hundreds of years had been attempting to use light magic to solve this problem, only to fail miserably. More of the same was worthless to him, and the stronger his light magic, the weaker his void magic became. Now he was in a worse situation than before.

Why do you not ask for help? Rhemi whispered.

It wasn't a question. It was a plea. The same one she'd brought to him countless times. Alphen didn't know why she bothered asking. She knew why.

"Fraylon will go after anyone wrapped up in this." He refused to say the other part out loud: Fraylon would go after anyone associated with Alphen. Just like his mom and Darian Black. Alphen wouldn't let Nihsa, Thad, or Gage meet the same fate.

He sat in miserable silence for a long while. The sunbeams slanted through the room as the day grew late. His mind whirred, seeking answers, but none came. He was out of ideas and out of time.

No. Not yet. The star of Caladon still shone in the sky. His mother's face arose in his mind, though it had faded into distant memory. Beautiful, smiling, and kind. A void user with dark hair, dark eyes, and warm brown skin, yet she radiated light wherever she went. He remembered her warmth, her love, her stories. She hoped for a brighter future and strived toward it until Fraylon ended her life.

What now? Rhemi finally asked, prodding him with her snout.

Alphen inhaled deeply and exhaled slowly. As long as the light of Caladon was still shining, he couldn't give up.

"We keep searching until we find another way." Alphen slid up the wall, using it to support his weight as he stood.

Rhemi looked at him with grief in her eyes. He felt her hopelessness as if it were his own. But it wasn't over yet. Not while that star was still shining. They couldn't quit until after the light snuffed out—and even then, they had to keep moving forward. Too many lives were counting on him to make this work.

"I won't give up on them, Rhem. Not on Caladon, or Orelia and her people," he told her, standing straight. He pulled his shoulders back. If he stood tall and pretended to be confident, his heart and mind would eventually catch up. "And I won't let Fraylon have his way. I'll stop him—at any cost."

Because if Fraylon did what he wanted, Gage would suffer the consequences, and Alphen wouldn't let that happen. He set his jaw and clenched his fists. No, Fraylon wouldn't lay a hand on Gage. Alphen would protect his little brother with his life.

THANKS

Writing, editing, and publishing books is hard work, and it wouldn't be possible without the help of MANY fantastic people.

Sending much, much, much gratitude to the incredible peeps who've helped me along the way! First, to the awesome cover designers over at Damonza (damonza.com) for making this gorgeous cover that absolutely pops. Second, to my fantastic editor Denica McCall (denicamccall.com) for helping me tighten up and prettify the prose. Third, to the amazing team of early readers who gave feedback to improve the book and offered encouragement when I needed it most: Nicole, Emery, and Finn Nelson; Amy Bryant; and Rachael, Karl, and Onna—thank you all SO MUCH for taking the time to read early copies and give honest feedback!

To EVERYONE who reads my books: thank you for spending your time in my crazy fantasy worlds! I love every adventure we get to go on together. Here's to many more!

ABOUT THE AUTHOR

Britt lives in the frigid wasteland known as Minnesota. While she hates the cold and snow, she appreciates the nice summers, the lack of lethal creepy crawlies, and the pretty forests and lakes. Outside of writing, she loves reading, high-speed walking, and high-speed walking while reading. Yes, that's a thing, and no, she hasn't accidentally walked off a cliff (yet).

ALSO BY BRITT ASHER

GAGE BLACK

Gage Black and the Void Dragon
Gage Black and the Dying Lands
Gage Black and the Worldeater

KING OF REALMS

King of Realms
The Wind Sage
The Land of Hallowed Dark
The Keys to Feldavar
The Revenge of the Ethari King